RIVERSIDE COMMUNITY COLLEGE
1916

P9-AFZ-550

A World of Hurt

A WORLD OF HURT

A NOVEL BY

Bo Hathaway

Taplinger Publishing Company
• New York •

For Nancy Berman

First printing

Published in the United States in 1981 by
TAPLINGER PUBLISHING CO., INC.
New York, New York

Printed in the United States of America

Library of Congress Cataloging in Publication Data

Hathaway, Bo.
A world of hurt.

1. Vietnamese Conflict, 1961-1975—Fiction. I. Title.
PZ4.H3638Wo 1981 [PS3558.A738] 813′.54 80-18147
ISBN 0-8008-8586-4

There never was a war that was
  not inward; I must
fight till I have conquered in myself what
causes war

MARIANNE MOORE

Sleep sounds. Night creaks. Thirty shrouded humps of sleeping men stacked in double-deck bunks along both sides of the barracks bay. Sighs, snorts, a moan, the rhythm of many snores. Each man deep in his dreams and dreading the morning. At the far end of the barracks, a fire light shone above the door, sending a weak red glow through a web of rafter planks and ceiling struts. Near the front, white light flared out from the latrine onto rows of bunks, men, and footlockers. Night came in crisp and still through open windows.

The barracks door banged open, and a fatigue-clad figure with a sergeant's armband pinned over his Pfc. stripe stamped inside. He stood silhouetted in the light from the latrine—face white, sleep-swollen, angry with the injustice of the hour. His legs were spread wide. One hand was knotted in a fist at his side; the other held a whistle to his mouth. He blew the whistle, shrill and loud, then yelled, "All right, you dick-heads, on your feet. If you're not out of those racks when I get to the end of this bay, I'll start kickin' ass."

The sudden flash of bare bright overhead light bulbs pierced the men's startled eyes. The CQ blew his whistle again and started down the row of bunks, kicking each one and shouting, "Get up. Get up. Reveille!"

Each man, freshly yanked from his dreams, had the same thoughts: It's here again. I just went to sleep and already I've got to face it all over again. I've only been here two weeks and I hate it so much I could cry and I've got months and years of it ahead of me.

Some of the men grumbled as they and their beds rattled under the awakening boot. One of them, jarred from too sweet a sleep, shouted back, "OK, OK, we're awake. There's no need to kick our goddamn bunks."

The CQ stopped, aghast. "What did you say?" He kicked the bunk double hard. "Get out of that fart sack, troop, and stand at attention."

What have I got myself into now? the offending soldier thought as his feet hit the cold floor.

"You punk. Talk back to an acting sergeant, will you? What's your name?"

"Madsen," he replied.

"Madsen, huh? OK, you've had it. If this was the old army—if things were the way they should be—I'd beat the shit out of you."

Madsen looked at him and thought, If things were the way they should be, I'd like to see you try. But Madsen kept his mouth shut and forced down his urge to slam his fist up into the man's face.

The CQ sneered at him. "Now I'll have to settle for making your life miserable. We'll take care of you later, smart guy."

By this time everyone was out of bed and hopping into his clothes. The CQ turned and stormed upstairs, where the men were already up and scrambling.

Madsen rubbed his hand over the stubble that had once been curly brown hair and wondered about his punishment. What a way to start the day.

His squad leader was pissed. That's the second time that

guy's mouthed off to one of the sergeants. He's gonna give the squad a bad name. I'd better not say anything to him about it now, though. "OK, second squad, you get to use the latrine first today, but hurry up. We've got to fall out in ten minutes. And do a good job on the bay. I want it looking good so they'll keep off our asses."

The platoon stood shivering in the paling night while squad leaders bustled through the ranks making sure everyone was present and standing in a straight line. "You, third from the end, move it up a little," said a squad leader, stooping and sighting down the line of men, then hopping up in fear as the company first sergeant, followed at a respectful distance by the four platoon sergeants, left the orderly room and walked down toward the formation. The trainee platoon guide at the head of the group came to attention and said, "All right, you guys, come to attention. Platoon, attention." He about-faced, saluted the platoon sergeant, did another about-face, and walked, by straight lines and right angles, to his place in the first squad.

"Platoon, ten-hut," shouted the platoon sergeant. "Squad leader, report."

"First squad all present and accounted for, sergeant. Second squad all present and accounted for, sergeant. Third squad all present and accounted for, sergeant. Fourth squad all present and accounted for, sergeant," chimed the squad leaders. The commands and replies of the four platoons overlapped like a nursery school round.

"All right, you men, I wasn't able to get down there and roust your asses before formation this morning, and I heard there was some trouble. CQ said there was some trouble." The platoon sergeant inflated his voice with menace. "If you men, if you shitbirds, don't think you better jump when that CQ says jump and squat when he says squat . . . That CQ this morning may be just a Pfc., but he's the company clerk, and he's permanent party, and to you goddamn recruits that man carries all the weight and authority of an NCO and you better treat him as such or I'll have the whole platoon doing deep knee bends at two o'clock in the morning, and don't none of you want that. From now on I'm going to be down there personally . . ."

"Company, ten-hut. Report." The company first sergeant's command interrupted the ass-chewing each platoon was getting. The platoon sergeants came to attention, about-faced, saluted, and barked in order, "First platoon all present and accounted for. Second platoon all present and accounted for. Third platoon all present and accounted for. Fourth platoon all present and accounted for."

Madsen's mind drifted back to the Mexico City American Express office. He saw himself standing there reading his induction notice. Now, as he reviewed all the ways he could have beaten the draft, it seemed that, in some cowardly corner of himself, he must have welcomed the summons as an escape from being broke in another country. He had been traveling in Mexico for seven months, sleeping on beaches and floors, eating tortillas and beans, and part of him was weary. He bought a bus ticket to Brownsville and spent his last twenty dollars in a border whorehouse: The girl on his lap, her tongue in his ear, his hand down along her belly, the raw taste of the Mexican rum, Ritchie Valens screaming "La Bamba." Later, in a room with a cardboard closet, a crucifix above the bed, and sheets like damp cheesecloth, her voice was quiet: "Don't be so rough this time. Fuck me slow."

"Parade, rest," shouted the first sergeant.

Last time you make it always seems the best, Madsen thought.

Two hundred left feet jabbed the dirt eighteen inches away from their partners and four hundred hands jerked together behind each pair of buttocks.

And I left all those soft thighs and came to this.

"Two things. First, the latrines still look like shit. I want those urinals clean. And when I say clean I mean you should be able to stick a straw down through the holes, take a drink, and not get no yellow stains on your teeth. That's what I'm going to have the whole company doing, squad leaders and all, if you don't shape up. Second, some people are still talking in the chow line. You will stand at parade rest with your mouths shut or I'll have every swinging dick doing PT for the whole chow time. We don't have to feed you men. We don't have to feed you shit. We can give all that chow to the war on poverty. So if you want to eat, you better cut out the grab-ass and act like soldiers. Company, ten-hut. Platoon sergeants, take charge.

"All right, third squad, you got the latrine. I'm going to inspect it personally after chow. It better be looking good. I want each squad leader to give me the name of any man talks in the chow line. If I catch somebody talking and I don't have his name, I'm going to burn the squad leader's ass. Fall out."

The men trudged back to the barracks to finish cleaning. Madsen expected the platoon sergeant to call him aside and chew him out for being disrespectful to the CQ, but nothing happened. His squad leader, however, glared at him and said, "It's guys like you make it tough for all of us."

"Whaddaya mean? If he hadn't been pissed off about that, it would've been something else. They just gotta yell."

"Well, why do you have to give 'em something to yell about?"

Madsen looked at him wearily and shook his head. "Oh, fuck it."

"Well, after you clean your area, you help the third squad with the latrine."

Madsen stood on the barracks steps watching the first platoon line up for chow. The platoon sergeant and trainee platoon guide were checking the men to make sure they had the proper thirty-inch interval between them and were standing at parade rest with their mouths shut and their eyes straight ahead. The sun slipped up behind some pine trees in the east, tinting the night's dew to a net of blue and yellow. The stars faded into a pastel wash of sky. Beautiful time for a walk, Madsen thought as he went in to clean the latrine.

While he polished the urinals, he imagined the first sergeant inspecting them—bending stiffly at the waist to avoid wrinkling his starched fatigues, briskly extracting a straw, and drinking through the porcelain pee-holes with a detached air of scientific inquiry and a slight slurp. At least the first sergeant has a sense of humor.

After breakfast the company, each man with a pound of cold pancakes and unmelted butter in his stomach, formed for PT. A murmur of dread ran through the formation when the company commander walked out of the orderly room wearing a T-shirt. "Oh, Christ, that bastard's going to give us PT again." It had happened only twice before in the two weeks they had been in basic training, and both times the lieutenant had run them until half the company had given up, dropped out to lie vomiting beside the road.

The company commander was a small, compressed man with sharp features and a widow's peak of bristly dark hair that made his quick black eyes seem all the more threatening. He was twenty-three years old. As he spoke he bugged out his eyes, and his words took on such a cast of exaggerated loathing that the men would have laughed had they not been aware of the pain he was about to inflict on them. "I hope you men are in better physical condition than you were the last time we met. I hope for your sakes you have improved. Because, gentlemen, you ain't seen nothin' yet. I'm going to make you weaklings physically fit if I have to run you till you die. Any man who drops out of the run today will find himself on double KP this weekend. Any man caught fucking off on the exercises will find himself on fireguard every night this week. My NCOs will be everywhere taking names. Is that perfectly understood?"

"Yes, sir."

"I can't hear you."

"Yes, sir!"

"You sound like a bunch of pussies."

"YES, SIR!"

Each took off his fatigue shirt, folded it so that the name tag faced up, and placed it on the ground with his cap and dog tags on top of the pocket. Two platoon sergeants moved down the rows to see that the shirts were properly aligned. "First exercise, the high jumper. Starting position. Ho!" The men hopped to a squat with their arms spread out behind them. "Ready, exercise. One-two-three-*one*, one-two-three-*two* . . ." They jumped up and down to the count, arms swinging and heads bobbing like rows of oil pumps.

This is my life going by, Madsen thought as he hopped. Just this for two years. You're not even getting in shape. If they really gave you a workout it wouldn't be so bad. A lot of these guys must be weak, though. They can't do push-ups, and they drop out of the run, puking on the road after half a mile.

"Next exercise. Trunk twister. Starting position. Ho! Ready, exercise."

That guy's getting his rocks off seeing us act like fools for him, Madsen thought as he swiveled around like a lawn sprinkler. But it's your fault. You let them take you. But I thought it was going to be hard. I didn't know it was just going to be stupid.

"Exercise number six. What is exercise number six of the army daily dozen?" the lieutenant yelled.

"The push-up, sir," the men roared back reluctantly.

"That's right, the push-up. And since you men have not been showing the proper enthusiasm, since you have been cheating, since you have been acting like a bunch of pussies, we're going to elaborate on exercise number six of the army daily dozen. You will stay in the push-up position until I give the command to recover. My NCOs will be moving through the formation. If they see any man with his back sagging or with his knees on the ground, that man has had it. We have a little treat in store for him. Company, ten-hut. Starting position. Ha! Ready, exercise. One-two-three . . ." The men bobbed up and down to his count, and when he stopped at six they froze, each man supporting his body weight on his locked arms. "Now stay that way awhile. I want to see you sweat." He held them there for fifteen seconds before barking, "Seven," and bringing them to their feet. With each repetition, they stayed longer in the braced position, until their arms ached and their backs were strung like quaking hammocks from their shoulders to their heels. Limbs shook, eyes bulged with pain, and some of the men cried out. Soon the sound grew to a low involuntary moan that rose from the formation. "You holler just like a whore in bed," the lieutenant yelled. "I'm keeping you pansies there till you shut up."

"Shut up, goddammit," the men started hissing to one another.

"Get those backs straight. Get those knees off the ground. I'm not going to give the command to recover until every man is in the correct position."

Wherever a man was slumped in exhaustion, one of his neighbors was snarling, "Get up, you son of a bitch, get up."

The sergeants started running through the formation, picking out the worst offenders, kicking them on the heels, saying, "You, you, on your feet." They stood up, relieved to be out of their pain but afraid of what was to come. The rest of the men stayed in position, tears rolling down faces that quivered and squealed.

"I want you men to take a look at those cowards who have caused you to stay in this strain. You may think those men are your buddies, but they're cheaters and fuck-offs, and they're putting you in a world of hurt. All those pussies who weren't man enough to cut it, fall out of the formation. You don't belong with a group of men. Company, ten-hut."

They staggered to their feet, not believing it was over. The weaklings were marched to the front of the formation.

"What a fine-looking crew. So you want to be soldiers. You're the kind of cowards get men killed in Vietnam. Since you were fucking off while your buddies were in a strain, they're gonna take a break while you sweat a little. Company, at ease." The men to be punished stood with jaws locked tight, faces veined. "Group, ten-hut. Front leaning rest position. Move!" They dropped back into the agonizing posture, knowing they could not stay there for long, not knowing what would happen when they failed, knowing it would be dreadful. The company looked on, glad to be out of pain, glad for some entertainment, glad it wasn't them.

The lieutenant knew he had made his point and did not press it. When knees began to buckle and eyeballs stand out, he said, "All right, on your feet. Get back in formation." They walked to their places, heads down. The whole company avoided each other's eyes as they marched from the PT field.

"One, tup, threup, fourp; one, tup, threup, fourp. Shine your boots and let 'em know, Mighty Mike is on the go. Am I right or wrong?"

"You're right," the company sang back as its shiny right boots struck the ground. They were marching to a Troop Information and Education class and were happy because for two hours they wouldn't have to participate in anything. They could sit and doze or think about anything they wanted. There might even be a movie.

At the auditorium, they filed in and stood at attention while the sergeant walked back and forth making sure no seats were skipped. A Pfc. was on the stage setting up charts. Their lecturer strode out from behind the curtain briskly, snapping a pointer against his right leg. "Good morning, men," he said.

"Good morning, sergeant. Mighty Mike all the way," the company shouted back.

"What company is this? I can't hear you."

"MIGHTY MIKE ALL THE WAY," they bellowed.

"Take seats."

"RrraAHR," the men roared as they slumped happily into their chairs.

"On your feet!"

Oh, no, he's going to play this game, Madsen thought as they jumped back up.

"Gentlemen, that was the sloppiest performance I have seen yet. What company is this? Is this Mike Company? It sure don't sound like it. You men better sound off like you got a pair of balls. You gotta show me you're proud. Take seats."

"AAAHRRRR!" they yelled in their most ferocious voices and dropped back into their chairs, hoping he had toyed with them to his satisfaction and would now let them sleep.

"That's better. Now you sound like Mike Company. Gentlemen, the topic for this block of instruction is military history. Our objective during this block of instruction will be to give you a basic working knowledge of our military heritage and its role in preserving freedom for the world. Gentlemen, if it was not for the United States Army, we here in this country would still be saluting the Union Jack or worse yet, the Hammer and Sickle."

Each man slid deliciously into his own thoughts while the sergeant chronicled the country's wars. Madsen dreamed about home, northern Wyoming, where the land and the weather occupied whole rooms of his mind. The land there is always above, built on a slant so you feel you're leaning and looking at it on an angle from below. It begins to rise in the Dakotas, tilts and buckles across the Thunder Basin Grasslands, and erupts into the Big Horns and Tetons farther west. The swelling force breaks the prairie into ridges and basins, cliff crests and green swales where streams start. Hills glaciered off, sheared and scraped into mesas. Gullies cut out by vanished rivers. Buttes with their dirt blown away by epochs of wind, leaving knobs of pocked rock.

Winter storms roll off the mountains in a blitzkrieg of wind-lashed, stinging snow pellets. The sky seems to press two feet above your head. Figures flatten to dark smudges against the swirling gray matte.

Afterward, mounded and iced with drifts, the world has no

corners. Unawed birds hop through new snow. Antelope nudge through it nervously. Then comes man, busy with shovels and automobiles.

The snow is soon gone, soon to return, sucked up by chinook winds that bowl off the plains of Canada and sluice over Montana and Wyoming in great dry roars. The wind uncovers again the pale winter-pounded yellow grasses that ciliate the hillsides.

Winter dies slowly, then breaks like river ice—sudden blue holes in the gray, cumulus floes blown by spring winds, and the storms grow tired. The land wakes up timidly, knowing the first foolhardy flowers and green sprouts are a sacrifice to spring snow. The people are the last to thaw.

In a burst of clouds and rain the season turns. Melting snow courses off the mountains in runoff rivulets that swell streams to brown, roily rivers. Bears and badgers and gophers and rattlesnakes all feel the change and crawl out, hungry.

Spring blows. Old fences lean. Cattle cluster leeward of billboards. The land, a pelt, is curried by the wind. Huge cloud shadows slide across snow fields and rob the earth of the sun's thin warmth. Warmer plains suck clouds from cold far hills and stack them above the prairie in purple shelves. They mass together and break in gashes of lightning and spills of hail. Storm fingers reach down, swirled webs of frozen froth blown to drifting veils and floating trains of rain. One side of the sky still clear—the schizophrenia of spring.

Emptied clouds float free and light. They pile off the mountains and scud across the high, arced sky like galleons. Fat, gray, swelling fluff clumps cut off flat and blue-black at the bottom. Combs of frilly cirrus. Sun-struck, white-billowed cauliflower domes. May clouds.

Summer happens under a sky so wide it stretches the land taut across horizons like curing buckskin. Space grows, time slows. Wind hurries over the land, polishing pliant grasses. It steals water and chaps the earth, turns horse turds dry as puffballs. Spear-tufted yucca crowns hold hard in the flinty dirt, but the wind rips up shallow-rooted bushes and turns them into tumbleweeds, bowling across the prairie like demons till they snag into fences and build shelters for others to grow.

The sun burns above like a shiny, malevolent dime. Streams go underground. Mud flats crack and curl. White alkali beaches rim shrinking water holes. In the dry light, colors drain, sagebrush pales dust green, wheat straw blanches yellow. Ridges are gray-backed sleeping dinosaurs. Rangeland is brown and gullied out. Creamy summer hills are sparse-topped by wind-winnowed buffalo grass. The land charges on, hard and raw as weathered leather. . . .

"The United States, gentlemen, has been in many wars and never lost a one. We don't aim to lose the one we're getting into now. That's why you men are receiving the training you are getting. ON YOUR FEET!"

The words cut through the reverie and Madsen stood up, resentful.

When they marched up to the company area, the lieutenant was waiting for them. "You men are in your sixth week of basic training, and you're not fit to be called soldiers. I've seen Boy Scouts who could march better than you. I've seen Wacs who could do PT better than you do. And I've seen field hands with more pride than you got. Final qualifying tests are coming up in less than two weeks. If you shitbirds think you're going to bolo that test and give Mike Company a bad name, well, you just think again. I'm going to make soldiers out of you bunch of riffraff if I have to work you till you drop. And go ahead and write your congressmen. I think you'll find those congressmen are on our side. They don't want a bunch of crybabies doing their fighting for them.

"Most of you know by now there was one coward in the company who couldn't take it anymore. He decided he didn't have an obligation to defend his country. All he wanted was to get out of the army and go back to his mommy. Last night this man put a couple of scratches on his wrist so we'd have to take pity on him and send him to the hospital. And let me tell you something, he's going to get his wish. He's getting out of the army, all right—with a dishonorable discharge that will follow him the rest of his life.

"I don't know if this fairy infected any of the rest of you, but if any of you punks out there don't want to become soldiers and men, just let me know, and we'll slap a dishonorable discharge on you, and you can run home, too. But just you try to get a job. The first thing any employer wants to see is your military discharge papers. And when he sees that big red dishonorable stamped on them, well, you'll be lucky if he doesn't have the cops there before you get out the door. And for you college types, if you think any college is going to take you with a dishonorable discharge, you better think again. But if you want out that bad, you raise your little hand and we'll fix you right up. How about it? Any takers for a dishonorable discharge?

"OK then, since you all want to be soldiers, you better listen and listen hard. First thing it takes to be a soldier is spirit. And you men ain't got the spirit God gave a worm. Henceforth and from here on out, whenever you move in this company area you will move at a double-time. And whenever your left foot strikes the ground you will sound off with the name of the company. We're going to instill some pride of unit in you men. Any man caught not double-timing or not sounding off with a good loud Mike every time his left foot hits the ground will answer to me personally.

"Second thing we're gonna do is instill some personal pride in you. You men are living like pigs in those barracks, and that's coming to a stop right now. There will be a full field gear and complete personal inspection to include General Orders and Code of Conduct tomorrow morning. Any man who gets gigged spends the weekend on guard duty or KP. Company, ten-hut! Fall out!"

The formation broke into two hundred running men, each one shouting, "Mike, Mike, Mike," as his left foot hit the ground, each one charging back to the barracks to polish his gear for the big inspection.

That evening the platoon sergeant marched them to the barbershop for their weekly shearing. "You got fifteen minutes after ya get your haircut to go to the PX, get what ya need for the inspection, and fall back in formation. And I better not see no beer drinkin', especially back in the barracks."

Madsen sat silently in the chair while the barber zipped off what little hair had managed to grow during the week. I'm beginning to recognize myself with no hair, he thought. That's the scary part.

In the PX he bought six cans of half-chilled Budweiser and began drinking them as he sat down with Rodriguez, a young New Yorker and one of the few men in his squad that Madsen talked with. Rodriguez was busy ripping the contents of a Benzedrex inhaler into little pieces and popping them into his mouth between gulps of beer. "You ever try this, man?" he asked.

"No, I never did that one," Madsen replied.

"You ought to. Get you high like a motherfucker."

"Doesn't it taste like hell?"

"Yeah, but you wash it down with beer, you can't tell. You want one? I got another one here," Rodriguez offered.

"Ah, thanks, but if I got high I'd just go AWOL. Wouldn't be able to stand the place at all then."

"No shit, man. This is the dumbest motherfucker I ever been in. We haven't learned a thing yet that's gonna teach us how to fight better. We oughta be practicin' ambushes and karate, stuff we'll need. They got us actin' like a bunch of skirts, always scrubbin' the floor and worryin' whether we look neat. And I'll tell you something else, I don't know where they get these guys to make up the army, but my little brother knows more than they do and he's twelve years old. These cats are so lame, man, if they ever came to New York they wouldn't last ten minutes. Where do they dig all these dudes up?"

"I don't know, but you'll probably get stationed there."

"No. Fuck no. I'm going to Vietnam. But first I'm gonna get high." He broke open the other Benzedrex. "You know another thing you can get off on is that spray spit-shine stuff. That's some fine shit."

"OK, Mike Company, outside," the sergeant shouted.

Back in the barracks, Madsen drank the rest of the beers with a paper sack wrapped around each while he arranged the clothes in his wall locker for the inspection. Sleeves folded just so, all buttons buttoned, little button on inner pocket of overcoat buttoned, flies all nice and zipped, necktie folded in thirds, chin strap snapped. He rolled his underwear around soda pop cans in the specified manner. With Brasso and an old T-shirt, he polished his belt buckle and the brass discs that stuck on the lapels of his snazzy green uniform. It was a Class A inspection, so all the men would wear Class A uniforms. Bus driver Jeff Madsen at your service, sir. He polished the brass emblem that shone above the bill of his flying saucer hat. He scraped all the rust off his canteen cup, chipped the white flakes off the little chain that held the cap on the canteen, rubbed away the circular stain made by the lip of the canteen pressing against the cork insert of the canteen cap, made sure no dirt remained inside the snaps on the canteen cover. The old man was a real stickler for clean canteens, the platoon sergeant had said. So Madsen figured maybe he wouldn't check anything else.

The trainee platoon guide walked up and down the aisle saying, "OK, hurry up with your personal gear so we can get to work on the floor and the latrine. We're going to have a pre-inspection at ten o'clock, and I want the barracks standing tall. I better not find any beer cans around either. You all know that's a major gig. I know none of you guys want to be on detail this weekend."

Some of the men were drilling one another on General Orders and Code of Conduct: "To walk my post in a military manner, keeping always on the alert. . . . I am an American fighting man. I serve in the forces that keep my country free. . . . To speak to no one except in the line of duty. . . ."

Madsen thought that sometime before he left the army he would have to discard another chunk of dignity and memorize those lofty military maxims. But it wasn't going to be this time. He'd take the ass-chewing or even the KP. Mainly he hoped he would be asked to recite the two he had absorbed in spite of himself. He cleaned his rifle, a job he never minded, and went to bed.

In the morning they made their bunks extra tight, placed their field gear on them, and mopped the floor for the third time.

The squad leaders sighted down the bunks to make sure each display was not only internally correct but properly aligned with those on the other bunks. All the mess kits, all the tent pegs, everything was to be in line. The men were climbing into their uniforms, helping one another tie their ties, patting the lint off each other's blouses, buffing their black low-quarter shoes for that last-minute gloss, lifting their pant legs when they walked so as not to scuff the shine. The trainee platoon guide checked the butt cans to see that each contained the required two inches of water while the platoon sergeant checked the tops of wall lockers and rafters for dust. The man who'd been posted as lookout yelled in, "Hey, he's comin'. He just left the first platoon, and he looks mad."

The men stood at attention beside their displays, the toes of their shoes in line with the leading edges of their footlockers. The company commander, trailed at deferential intervals by the first sergeant and platoon sergeant, stopped beside each bunk and disdainfully picked through the field equipment. He would look at a piece, tick off a few faults to the first sergeant, and toss it back on the bunk. Look what he's doing.

He's messing them up, the men's eyes said. He's not putting them back where they belong!

The lieutenant launched into Rodriguez's display. "Dirty spoon, tent poles not parallel, you got rust in your trigger housing, troop. Crooked chin strap, rusty entrenching tool, this canteen cup is filthy. See this pistol belt, troop? See that white stuff in the eyelets? Do you know what that is, troop? It's corrosion, that's what it is. You're letting your equipment, the equipment the army loaned you on trust, the equipment you need to save your life, you're letting that equipment rot. So you're gonna be on guard duty this weekend, troop, while your buddies are going to the movies. Maybe then you'll take proper care of your army issue."

When he passed, Rodriguez gave him the finger.

The lieutenant's hand darted into wall lockers to discover buttons left carelessly unbuttoned, flies left obscenely unzipped. Footlocker trays whose contents were not properly arranged got dumped on the floor. Underpants were stripped from their cans in search of a Hamm's or a Coors.

He ran his eyes over the men, examining their faces for whiskers and their clothes for wrinkles, made them open their coats to see that their belt buckles were shined and in line with their shirt seams and that no belt loops had been skipped, held a metal gauge to their brass insignia to make sure they were the prescribed five-eighths of an inch from the edges of their lapels, checked their profiles to see if their chins were up, chests out, shoulders back, stomachs in, eyes looking straight ahead, mouths closed, heels together, hands cupped along the seams of their trousers.

"Shoes unshined, marksman badge off center, lacquer on brass, nameplate crooked." He stood beside each man and asked questions hard into his face. "What's your fourth Code of Conduct, soldier?" And when the man's eyes involuntarily moved in the direction of the questioner, the lieutenant snapped, "What are you looking at, soldier? You think I'm pretty? Eyes front. You're at the position of attention."

He moved down the row, getting closer and closer to Madsen with his rusty tent pegs, fungous shelter half, wrinkled uniform, and treasonous ignorance of the Code of Conduct. But when the lieutenant was two men away, he stopped, turned around, and walked upstairs. The men started whispering. "I guess he's through with us."

"Ain't that a bitch. You guys don't get inspected at all and he tore my stuff all to hell, and I probably got detail."

"It ain't fair. He should've inspected all of us. We got shafted."

Madsen just smiled. Since I won't have detail, I can sneak into Leesville and do it proper. Get drunk and find me some fine little Cajun whore and, oh, my, won't it be sweet. Been so long.

They could hear the sound of footlockers being dumped upstairs. "Those guys must be catchin' hell."

"Serves 'em right, the bastards."

"Hey'd you see that gadget he had for measurin' the brass? I'm gonna get me one of them. You'd always know you're right, then. Wouldn't never have to worry about gettin' gigged."

Madsen's name was on the KP roster that afternoon.

"Man, how can they do that?" he cried to Rodriguez. "They didn't go by the inspection gigs at all."

"What did you expect, man? You don't think they'd play by their own rules, do you? He got me for everything. I didn't have nothin' right. But I ain't on the list. I'm going downtown and fuck me half a dozen foxes. I'll tell you about it when I get back."

"Damn you. I hope the MPs snatch your ass."

"Hey, ain't enough of them bald-headed motherfuckers to catch me. Have a good time in the mess hall. Don't wash too many pots."

After eight weeks, the men could do a column of files to the right, throw a hand grenade and run the obstacle course. They knew their chain of command from their squad leader to

Lyndon Johnson, had fired their live rounds and knew their battlesight zero, could do the rifle salute and the night walk. They knew they were American fighting men serving in the forces that kept their country free.

While most were shipped off to learn useful trades like welding and typing, Madsen was sent to advanced infantry training. When he was drafted, he'd had visions of jumping out of airplanes over jungles, swimming rivers with a knife in his teeth, blowing up bridges at the stroke of midnight. So he volunteered for Special Forces under their new policy of accepting two-year men. He was to report Sunday night to a company on the other side of the post for eight more weeks of preparation.

After the men cleaned the barracks one last time, the battalion commander, a heavyset major, gave a brief graduation speech. "You are now soldiers," he said. "You can go to your next duty station proud of your training, proud to be on the army team."

Madsen got a room in Leesville, put on the jeans and Mexican shirt that had been thrown in a box and locked in the company supply room at the start of basic, and looked at himself in the mirror. Almost bald, a little fatter in the face. He wondered if the subtle intimidation—a tinge of cringe—showed in his eyes.

The town was a string of bars, pawnshops, penny arcades, hot dog stands. Madsen walked around, glad to be alone. Everyone he saw, except the shopkeepers and cab drivers, was a GI. Most were in wrinkled civilian clothes but many wore their green bus driver suits. How can they do that? Madsen wondered. He found a bar that wasn't too clogged with drunken eighteen-year-olds and ordered a double bourbon.

"Just setups here," the bartender said. "Ya buy a bottle and pour your own. You can take it with you when ya go."

"OK, fair enough. Gimme a pint of Old Crow." Haven't had

any whiskey in a long time, he thought, and tried to get into the mood of the place. Haven't had a woman either. C'mere, baby, and sit on my face. Ooh, it ain't good for a man to get so horny. Wonder where they keep the whoors.

Country music played in his head. The Hamm's sign flickered the land of sky blue waters. Bourbon burned sweet. The bartender stood in a sleeveless undershirt and suspenders beside a big jar of pickled pigs' feet. Madsen drank some more and began to like the place. He drank half the bottle, and his bayou love fantasies pulled him out of the bar and into the street. Where are all the women? Got to use my prick like a witchin' stick. Go dowsin' for dollies. Louisiana again. Too much. Find me some slow-talkin' black-haired girl and do it Cajun style—French technique, Spanish passion, and a dash of southern decadence. Hoooee. Got to get between some thighs.

He stopped in his hotel room to pick up a jacket, sat down on the bed, and woke at eleven the next morning with a banging hangover and the maid asking him when he was going to check out. Oh, man, I don't believe I did that. I have to go back to the army tonight, and I didn't get laid or even properly drunk, and who knows when I'll have another chance? Jesus, this never happened to me before. Pass out on half a pint and have a head like a baked watermelon the next day. Must be the army. Killed my spirit. Oh, God, no. Gimme a replay.

The room was dim gray. The bedspread smelled of mildew. Church carillons played loud through the window. Maybe it's not too late. I don't have to be back until tonight. Have to get away from this place, though. Those bells.

The town was bright winter-light gray. Church music played all over. All the bars were closed. The curbs were strewn with broken bottles. I gotta get outa here. Madsen caught a cab and slumped in the rear seat. People were coming out of churches. They do have civilians here.

"Say . . . uh, do you know where I can get a piece of ass this time of day?" he asked the cab driver.

"You must be from up north," the driver said, giving him a hard look in the mirror. "People down here take religion serious. All the cathouses are closed on Sundays."

So Madsen went back to base. He had a few beers at the PX, saw an Elvis Presley movie, and checked into his new company that evening.

Fences had not yet tied the land when Madsen's grandfather came to Wyoming in 1899. He was eighteen years old and a veteran of the fighting in Cuba and the open range was the grandest thing he'd ever seen. He worked as a ranch hand, then as a foreman, and eventually saved enough to buy a spread of his own near Jackson. Along the way he fell victim to religious beliefs that kept him from getting rich in the increasingly rapacious land grabs. Soon the men who terrorized the squatters into leaving began forcing the smaller ranchers to sell. After they burned his barn and took a shot at his wife, he sold at a loss and moved to Sheridan to get away from the consolidators.

His youngest son, Jeff's father, took a rueful attitude toward religion, especially when he was bucking bales on land that had once belonged to the family. But the grandfather would calmly tell how most of the thieves lived to see the land stolen from them by the Rockefellers, and divine retribution may be slow but it is inevitable.

When he was twenty-eight, Madsen's father married a young teacher from Philadelphia who was vacationing at the guest ranch where he was working. She won the argument over whether they would stay in the West or go back East, and started teaching school in Sheridan. He drove twenty miles each day to the ranch where he continued tending the horses.

The second world war came as a relief to him. No more shoveling horse turds, he thought as he waited in line at the army enlistment center.

Their first son was born while he was working in a supply depot at Camp Polk, Louisiana. Jeff, their second, was born while his father was garrisoned at a base in England, waiting for D day.

A month after the invasion he was dead in France, trapped in a burning tank.

Jeff grew up on stories of his father. He examined the yellowed letters and pictures of a man with round cheeks, a lopsided grin, and eyes hidden in shadow. He tried to imagine what he had been like. His mother told and retold the stories of his father in the war and made them up when Jeff demanded more. She read him tales from the Greek myths while he drew pictures of heroes. His mind spun with blitzes, short swords, foxholes, bunkers, bucklers, gas masks, phalanxes, the Battle of Marathon, and the Battle of the Bulge.

His mother never met anyone in Sheridan she cared to marry. "It's enough trouble raising two boys without having to take care of a husband, too," she would say.

Jeff spent his kid years running the hills, chasing rabbits, playing Indian brave, mountain man, wolf child. He was usually too bored to do well in school, especially if the classroom had a window. But he devoured books like *The Desert Fox, Thirty Seconds over Tokyo,* and *Guadalcanal Diary.* At home he built a sand table where he battled with toy tanks and infantrymen. Above them, models of B-17s, Messerschmitts, Zeros, Spitfires, and Flying Tigers fought for control of the air. From his favorite power-diving fighter hung his father's dog tags.

On high school summers he followed the wheat harvest through Nebraska, the Dakotas, and Montana, patched trails in the Tetons, ran chain on a survey crew. He resented the jobs because they ate up his time, cutting into his fishing and hiking. But the work put a solid build on his lanky adolescent frame and made him look a year or so older than he was. He had a broad face with large brown eyes set deep under ginger brows on a forehead with a slight basal ridge. A chipped front tooth tattered his smile. His legs were a little short for the rest of his body, and he walked leading with his shoulders.

Madsen enjoyed running, and although he wasn't fast he had good endurance. He loved the empty feeling after a race, the purity of effort and pain during it.

In the fall of his senior year, he quit the cross-country team in a quarrel with the coach over supervision during out-of-town meets. The coach said he would not tolerate moral turpitude in his young athletes. A real champion had to be clean of mind and body. Madsen told him to get fucked. The coach said Madsen was showing off his weak character. Madsen walked out. When the team lost the next two meets, the whole school blamed Jeff. He became openly contemptuous of everyone, idled through his classes, and drank cheap blended whiskey with the Mexicans and Indians and wasted ranch hands down near the cattle pens.

He believed in the honesty of knots; the objectivity of pitons; grommets and rivets through thick stitched canvas; the wisdom of brown trout; old boots; the slow, heavy slide of a rifle bolt; the wellspring of solace and refreshment between a woman's legs.

A couple of athletes who resented his attitude picked fights with him. He won quickly and savagely and earned a reputation as a dirty fighter, a thing almost as vile as a queer by the standards of high school jocks. He stayed long enough to finish exams and was vaguely ashamed of himself for not having quit school. On the night of graduation, he was rattling across Wyoming on a freight train bound for Denver.

The next year, his eighteenth, was spent wandering. He worked when he had to, got laid when he could, and tried to keep moving. He read Kerouac in diners over coffee and pie, and spent a lot of time dreaming in the grass by railyards. Life seemed only a flux of nostalgia and anticipation.

With the intention of shipping out on a freighter, he hitched to New Orleans, but found there was a two-year waiting list to get seaman's papers. Disappointed, he stayed in the French Quarter awhile, then left because he couldn't stand Bourbon Street—its hustlers with wavy black hair, patent leather shoes, and plump necks bulging over the collars of their ruffled white shirts, barkers who tried to herd him into bars full of tired hookers and dollar beers.

To earn money to go to Florida and learn to skindive, he got a job at a car wash in Biloxi, Mississippi, for sixty cents an hour. He started hanging out with the other guys there, who were black. One night two carloads of whites pulled up in front of the restaurant where they were eating and took turns throwing bricks through the windows. His friends told him they couldn't hang out with him after work anymore. He left.

The idea of going to Florida lost its appeal. October would bring snow to the Rockies. He went to Aspen and spent the winter skiing and busing tables. In the spring, when rocks came through the snow, he decided he was tired of playing. After applying to the University of Colorado at Boulder, he moved there, got a job stuffing goose down into sleeping bags, and started school that summer.

When the Dean of Men's office informed him he had to live in a dormitory his first year, he almost withdrew. But a friend at work said that by claiming to be married he could continue to live off campus. Lying to the school improved his mood.

He was fascinated with the idea that people have not changed, that under the tweed we are still Stone Age men. He decided to take a combined major in history and anthropology.

As part of his field work, he spent the next summer at an Indian dig on the Uncompahgre Plateau in southwest Colorado. There he met a girl, a girl with a loud laugh and strong long legs. Her name was Sal. In the evenings they would wash off the day's sweaty dirt in icy showers, put their clothes back on long enough to run over the hill, and then make love while the earth still held the sun's warmth. At night they sat on a ridge and pretended to be Indians, old shamans come to steal some star magic.

They saw each other a lot the next year, studying together, wrestling in piles of leaves, talking about who they used to be. One cold night in the mountains they slept together inside his single sleeping bag, and when they awoke still friendly, tightly wrapped in each other, they decided that the patience and accommodation the night had required were a good test of their feelings. If they could share a sleeping bag, an apartment shouldn't be too difficult.

She put up with his slovenliness, and he put up with her morning crabbiness. They began to learn about each other. Madsen had never had prolonged conversations with a woman before, and it was an awkward, painful unfolding. The words came slowly, at her prompting, for his silences were like a cloak thrown over her. They caught themselves looking at one another with eyes saying, What's next? Each was happiest with the other when they were entwined in activity—painting the kitchen, making love, rolling in the snow.

On the first anniversary of their night in the sleeping bag, they celebrated by staying at a lodge in the mountains. After dinner, lying near the fireplace drinking brandy, she suggested that if they could live together for a year, marriage shouldn't be too difficult. Madsen's chest tightened as if the air had been drawn from the room. He managed to stammer something vague, then lapsed into a moody silence, his mind clogged. That night in the soft double bed was far less comfortable than its predecessor in the cramped sleeping bag had been. She asked him to forget she had said anything, but hurt and a hint of bitterness showed in her eyes. They tried to make love, but for the first time Madsen was impotent. They said good night and rolled over, pretending to sleep.

During the next month, a pall covered them. He remained limp. She chattered nervously. He avoided her eyes. Each unsuccessful attempt at sex increased his panic.

It began to seem as if he'd been in Boulder a long time. In search of a world more exciting than college, he started hanging around the wire room at the school paper, reading the news as it came over the teletype. He would sit by the machine for hours, hoping something would happen.

He became unable to pay attention to what the professors said in class. One morning, in the middle of not hearing a lecture on how Eli Whitney's rifle factory paved the way for industrial mass production, he left. Back at the apartment, he tried to write a note explaining it to her. But again, nothing would come out. Finally he scrawled "Had to go. Love, Jeff" on the back of an envelope and split.

Hitchhiking down through Arizona, the pressure eased. It was good to have nothing but his rucksack, a worn pair of shoes, very little money, and no definite destination. Free again, he tried to tell himself. He relaxed more as he entered Mexico and sank into the tropics. Around the ocean he felt a warm, unzipping release. The sun and water curled him open, peeled back the armor, showed him all pulpy and bare. His brain turned creamy, and his eyelids crinkled when he blinked. The world distilled to four pure, intense elements: water, sun, blue, white. And he was only a dot squinting in the middle of it.

He wandered through the sun-flattened, two-dimensional fishing villages of the Pacific Coast for several months, sleeping on beaches and finally learning to skindive. He crashed around Guadalajara and Mexico City, stayed a long time in Yucatan for the clear water and, when summer came on, went up into the mountains of Oaxaca. His draft notice caught up with him in November in Mexico City. His first reaction was, "Let them try and get me," but he began thinking about his father, feeling his father's shadowy eyes watching him and, although he pushed it from his mind, he suddenly knew he had to go in.

He spent his last night of freedom in a brothel, drinking and shouting and carrying the girls around on his shoulders. The next morning he was broke, hung over, pleasantly thigh-strained, resigned to his fate, and ready to give the army a try. If there's going to be a war, he told himself, I want to be in it.

"How we supposed to be soldiers doing this stuff all the time?" Madsen complained. He and David Sloane, a man in his squad, were raking lines in the gravel outside the orderly room during the first week of advanced infantry training. "Hell, they're just trying to turn the world . . . the whole world into a big footlocker display."

"You bet. Make the gravel stand at attention," Sloane said, raking wavery parallel lines in the pebbles.

"Reminds me of when I used to work on a survey crew," Madsen said. "Whenever we did a road, the guy in charge wanted each guardrail post—each fucking post—measured out exactly with a transit. Cost thousands of dollars just so he could go to sleep at night knowing those posts were within a sixteenth of an inch of where the chart said they should be."

"Hey, maybe that's how we can get out of it," Sloane said, doing a right shoulder arms and a rifle salute with his rake. "Tell them the only way we can be sure it's straight is to have the engineers survey each line. Look at these rakes. How do we know the teeth are exactly the same distance apart? And the same thickness? This one looks a little skinny. Throw off the whole formation. It's enough to make your asshole itch.

And the ground. Look, it's not uniform to begin with. All those little dips. Look at them. They make it all uneven. It's treason, I tell you."

"Yeah, how can they expect just a couple of trainees, sorry trainees, how can they expect us to handle such an important job? Puttin' down a mutiny out here. All these gravels rebelling like this. We need the MPs . . . whip 'em back into shape," Madsen said.

"We need cement."

"Should be some way we could sabotage it," Madsen said. "Like raking it into a big FTA."

"It would bother them even more if we raked it into curves and swirls . . . like a Japanese garden. That would really get to them," Sloane said.

"Now that we got it plowed, you want to get the seeds?" Madsen asked, dragging his rake.

"Yeah. Uh, what will we plant?"

"Poppies, I guess. Every infantry company should have its own Flanders Field," Madsen said.

"Or its own opium patch," Sloane said.

"We can turn 'em into boutonnieres and sell 'em to the VFW. Buy us a night in town."

The sergeant's voice interrupted them. "You men are gonna be here all day if you don't do it right. I said I wanted it raked underneath the building, too. And look what you're doing—you're steppin' on the lines you already raked. Buncha dumb-ass privates."

Sloane gave the sergeant his best Sad Sack look and continued raking.

Having Sloane to talk with had made the past week more bearable for Madsen. But he couldn't figure out how Sloane had ended up in the army. All the people he had known like Sloane had been classified 1-Y—psychologically unfit for military service except in time of grave national peril. And physically he was also an unlikely military prospect. About six feet tall, he had posture like a fork and an uncoordinated, gangling walk. He was thin, bony, and awkward, with large hands and a head that angled out from his shoulders. His quick, infrequent smiles pulled his lips flat across his teeth.

Madsen was glad to have a friend.

The company was in bayonet training, spread across a field with each man standing in front of two stacked bales of hay, while a sergeant in a tower issued commands through a crackling PA system. "At the count of one, grasp your weapon well up on the piece with your right hand. Ready, one. At the count of two, shove the *V* of your left hand into the wooden portion of the stock directly above the butt plate. Ready, two. On the command 'Horizontal butt stroke,' thrust your left arm forward, thus projecting the butt plate of your weapon into the chest or groin area of your simulated opponent. And if you dickheads don't growl loud enough to make the Wacs wet their pants, you're all gonna be doin' push-ups. Horizontal butt stroke, hahr!"

Stroke my horizontal butt, Sloane thought as he lunged and growled at the sergeant's command. I thrust my piece into the groin of my hayseed lover. Climax cries fill the air. And this is all foreplay. They haven't taught us how to use our long shiny bayonets yet.

The men shifted to the on-guard position with rifles jutting out at a forty-five degree angle to their bellies. On command, they growled and whirled to meet an attack from their rear. They learned how to parry left and parry right. But most of all they learned the spirit of the bayonet.

"If this was an actual bayonet duel, all you men would have been dead a long time ago. Why? Because you don't have no spirit! Gentlemen, life is a fight and it takes spirit to win it. Now, all you got between you and that guy who's comin' to get ya, is that big mean bayonet on the end of your weapon. So you gotta have the spirit of that bayonet. And what is the spirit of the bayonet?"

"To kill!"

"If you ain't got no more spirit than that, that enemy done had you by now. He done scarfed you up and been on to the next man. What is the spirit of the bayonet?"

"TO KILL!"

"That's better. You got a fightin' chance now."

Several rows down from Sloane, Madsen was resisting the ritual. He was proud he'd kept his mouth shut while the others were yelling and growling. Sergeants from the bayonet committee, each wearing a chrome-plated bayonet on his belt, walked through the formation to make sure everyone was sounding off. If your mouth was open but they thought you were pretending to yell, you spent the next break policing the area. If your mouth was shut, you were considered a rebel and your name went back to the company for punishment. Madsen could feel his hatred of them begin to crystallize inside him.

Sloane, however, reveled in the insanity of it, rolling his eyes back in a parody of fierceness and yodeling, "To kill, to kill."

Finally they learned the cross slash and the long thrust and were allowed to stab and rip at the bales of hay. "That man is trying to kill you. Get him," the voice from the tower told the growling men.

The next class was called extraction drill. "Once you got your man, you must know how to remove your bayonet quickly and efficiently so as to be ready for the next attacker. If you get stuck, if you can't get it out, you will be without a weapon and left defenseless in the face of the enemy. To withdraw the bayonet, follow the same procedure as for inserting it, but in reverse order. Use a quick, jerking, downward motion of the wrist and arms, and don't twist it 'cause if you get it jammed up in a rib, you're gonna have to stand on the guy's chest and pry it out. And while you're doing that, one of his buddies is going to get you from behind. Ready! On guard! Parry right, long thrust, and hold! That's it. Drive it home. And sound off like you're killers or I'll have the whole company on police call. Recover! On guard! High port! Rear guard!"

Afterward, they turned in their bayonets and picked the loose pieces of straw from the drill field.

Sloane lay on his bunk wondering whether he could take it any longer. He mulled the types of discharges he could get. Unadaptable to military life. Undesirable. Dishonorable. Medical. If you tell 'em you're gay but haven't made it with any guys since you joined the army, they give you a medical. If you tell 'em you've been having midnight trysts in the shower with your bunkmate, you get an undesirable. If you go crazy on the rifle range, you get an unadaptable. But what would I do if I got out? Go back to the Lower East Side, shoot up meth and phenobarb for a month, then O.D. Go out flashing . . . like Carl. No. Can't go back to New York. Can't stand to go home either. Not even for a little while. Parents would be mortified. Whole town gleefully gossiping. A Sloane hadn't been able to take it. Not man enough. Maybe go to San Francisco and see Chris. No, I'll have to stay. Have to stick it out. I'd hate myself even worse than I do now if I gave up. Have to stop quitting sometime.

It wasn't too bad today with the bayonets. When they're that sick, that obviously unhinged, you can feel aloof and healthy. . . . Goof on their beastliness. . . . To kill. Could you kill? The long shaft slides in. The man beneath receives it with a cry. His body twists around the intruder. The man above withdraws and inserts it again, pumping it into flesh. Blood spurts up and both men moan.

The kid on the next bunk was lying on his back, his legs spread wide, holding a cigarette lighter near the seat of his pants. "Hey, watch this, you guys." He farted and a yellow tongue of flame licked out from his crotch. The men who hadn't seen it before were astounded. "Hey, I didn't know you could do that." "What if your balls catch on fire?" Soon half the squad were lying on their bunks lighting farts.

Jesus, Sloane thought, how can I survive two years of this?

Advanced infantry training was climaxed by an overnight bivouac and field problem. They rolled their blankets and shelter halves into World War II horseshoe packs, strapped on the rest of their field gear, and trudged twelve miles to the maneuver area. That afternoon the men chose tentmates and began to set up camp. Unexpectedly, they were allowed to pick their own partners and pitch their tents where they wanted within their squad area. The tents didn't even have to be in a straight line. Around the edge of camp they dug foxholes. Although they were too shallow to stand in, each one had a firing step for better aim and a grenade sump to kick incoming hand grenades into.

They had to eat their C-rations cold because they were observing light and noise discipline and could not build fires. After dinner they sat in their foxholes awaiting the enemy attack. It was one of those rare occasions when they were left alone. Trees and bushes stood flat and black against the night sky. The men leaned on their rifles and thought about the leave they would get next week: going home with no hair, sleeping late in the morning, living among women, coming back to the army. They had received their orders for their new duty stations the day before. About half had an air of nervous bravado. They were being sent to an infantry division in Texas that was rumored to be preparing for Vietnam. The rest were going to Germany, Korea, or to MP school, and a few to jump school. Wherever they were being sent, they all hoped it would be different from Fort Polk.

Be glad to get out of this dump, Madsen thought. Bet my old man hated it too. But maybe there was less bullshit then.

Maybe things were more real. It was Camp Polk then. He might've even been out in this field. My father right here. We might've had the same barracks. The whole place got deactivated, everything shut down after the war. Ghost base. All the barracks standing in silent line, waiting twenty years for another war. He was here.

Suddenly there was shouting and little sparks of fire and the popping sound of blanks. It was the enemy attack! The men grabbed their rifles and started firing back, yelling and watching the flame jump with each shot, cursing the lucky aggressor platoon who hadn't had to dig foxholes. They shot up all their blanks and stumbled back to their tents.

As they lay in the dark with the army shut out, Sloane asked Madsen, "Where will you go on leave? Back to Wyoming?"

"Yeah. But I don't know what I'll do. Be too late to ski and too early to fish."

"Maybe if we get some leave this summer we could go to the Cape," Sloane said. "Oh, wait, I forgot. Hell, I'm going to die next month when my parachute doesn't open. I don't know how I let you talk me into this."

"I didn't talk you into it. I just said I was going."

"I wonder if you come right before you hit the ground?" Sloane said. "Jumping is supposed to be a real sex flash."

"I sure hope so. I'm horny as a young dog," Madsen said. "That's the main thing I'm gonna do over leave. Get me some lovin'. Ummm. There's nothing like it. Even the army wouldn't be so bad if you could get laid every night."

"I don't know," Sloane said. "Probably if we had that we'd all go AWOL."

"Yeah, hell, maybe you're right," Madsen said. "Nobody who's fucking would live like this. I'll tell you, if it doesn't change after jump school, I'm leaving."

Sloane watched the brooding outline of Madsen's body moving in the dark as he breathed. "Sounds good," he said. "I was screwed up enough before I came in the army. Don't need their hang-ups. If it doesn't get better, maybe we can escape together. Go to South America or someplace."

"It may come to that," Madsen said. "Let's see what jump school and Special Forces are like first, though. I never jumped out of an airplane before."

"Most sane people haven't. But that shouldn't stop us."

After the bivouac, the men of the company were free, with two weeks' leave before reporting to their next post. Two weeks with no reveille, no saluting, no uniforms. Two weeks to reclaim themselves, to discover what was left of the person each had been before. They stood around the company area wondering how to get to the bus station.

Most of them followed their instincts and headed for home. David Timothy Sloane went back to Massachusetts, back to the house behind the six-foot wrought-iron fence. He slept in the room he hadn't used since a long-ago college Christmas. He walked on the childhood rabbit-race trails that ran through the hills of the family holdings. He drove through town and hoped no one recognized him in his GI haircut. At last I look butch, he thought. Thick arms, no more jawline, fat cheeks, even my eyebrows are fat. Look like a peasant.

The Sloane family had emigrated to Massachusetts from England two hundred and fifty years before. At the turn of the century most of them retreated to the Berkshires to avoid the Irish hordes befouling Boston. His mother made sure David was well tutored in the Sloane genealogy. A formal oil portrait of the grandfather who had been a congressman hung in the front hall.

The Sloanes dominated their small town by controlling the only industry. The various branches of the family had their houses on a large, stoutly fenced estate. The land had once been well beyond the village but now you could see a road, several houses, and a gas station from David's living room window, although most of the outside was blocked by tall spruce trees.

Acres of woods and fallow farmland surrounded the house. The woods were thick. Ferns and mossy, rotting logs hid in dark caves beneath the trees. Mushrooms lurked in the shadows of fallen logs. Stray from the trail and you walked on pine needles. Shallow streams were crossed by stepping-stones. In the winter you found hollows in the snow where rabbits hid, saw their tracks and the hunting tracks of the fox. Paths on the hills became long toboggan runs. David's cousins played the games of summer and fall with one eye scanning the trees, looking for a perfect pine to cut for Christmas.

But the woods were not for Sloane. When he was little he would go wandering around looking for insects, especially beetles and armadillo bugs. He loved to see them walking and rolling on his white mittens. But he was afraid of the way mushrooms popped when you stepped on them. The ground stank, and the trees scratched. He would sometimes find what a fox had left of a rabbit and would look at the chewed and gutted thing for long minutes, forcing himself to turn it over in an ecstasy of repulsion. Watching the worms writhe; the mud and blood-matted hair; the eyes still open, staring, indifferent; the flat stiff bunny body, its mouth clotted with final blood.

He remembered his father an hour home from work, standing in creased gray slacks and slippers, the sleeves of his French-cuffed shirt rolled up, with no tie, eyes numb and sagging with tiredness as he glugged Scotch into a large glass full of ice and eased into a big chair in front of the fireplace, Mozart coming from the record player, his feet on a hassock, the bottle of Ambassador and the ice bucket on the table beside him, his head sunken toward his chest, staring into the flames. He thought of his father as a gray, tender shadow always on the verge of telling him of the melancholy secret ruin that David knew all men held inside them. But he never spoke, only smiled wistfully into the fire or at David or at the melting ice, sparing his son the dark thoughts that pushed his head farther into his chest.

David's mother's head never sank into her ample chest, and she limited herself to two martinis. "I'm a doer, not a dreamer," she would say. He remembered her always late for a meeting, clacking around the hardwood floor in high heels, pushing a few more pins into her hair to keep it firmly in place, the scratch of fully filled-out nylons against a tightly skirted slip.

They had a house on the Cape, but his mother hated to go there. "All the people who entertain are terribly nouveau riche, and the ones from good families are old and stuffy. And their children! I'm not going to raise my child among a bunch of teenage degenerates. David doesn't want that sort of life." But above all she hated to venture out of her social citadel in the Berkshires to do battle with the equally advantaged women on the Cape.

His father loved it there. He could sail, play cards, and drink with his friends. He disliked being the richest and most powerful man in a small town, where all his acquaintances were subordinates. His summer friends on the Cape were from New York and Boston, and many of them had more money and influence than he. He thrived on their company, listening with longing and regret to their tales of the really big leagues in the cities. They envied him his less competitive country squire existence.

David grew up alone. He had no brothers or sisters and though his cousins lived nearby he rarely joined in their games.

Whole weekends he would spend in his room with the door shut, curtains drawn cool and dark, one shaded lamp glowing by the bed where he lay in pajamas reading fantasy stories and playing with himself. When his mother complained about his inactivity he said he was feeling sick. He built plastic models of people from kits. He had a knight, Robin Hood, Cinderella, a gladiator, Davy Crockett, a marine, a man from Mars. He got his mother to make costumes for them all. They came with clothes already molded on, but David left them unpainted, shiny blue-gray plastic with the glue showing in the seams. He would spend afternoons switching costumes—Robin Hood as a marine, Davy Crockett as Cinderella.

In his second year at prep school, David wrote a parody of Tennyson that attracted his English teacher's attention. The teacher lent him some books and began having him over occasionally after classes to the apartment he shared with another instructor. They talked for hours about how awful the school was, how doomed the world was.

David understood why Gordon hardly spoke to him at school and had him telephone before coming over in the evening. One teacher had been unceremoniously dismissed during the previous term in a swirl of rumors concerning a boy who also left school. Gordon discussed his own homosexuality only indirectly and never made advances. David used to think, What'll I do if he touches me, glides his hand along my leg? But it never happened.

"When I'm forty, I'll probably bitterly regret not having seduced the child, but I can't bring myself to do it," Gordon told his roommate.

"You'd rather have some wax-fingered, toothless old man groping him in a public urinal?"

"Shut up. Shut up. When he goes to college maybe some sweet motherly coed will snatch him up. Or a faculty wife on the prowl."

"A little tea and sympathy?"

"I can give him that."

One evening the three of them were playing Scrabble when a car pulled up outside. The roommate rushed to the window. "Oh, lord, it's Marcus."

"David, we'll have to hide you in the closet until he leaves. We'll try to hustle him out. He'd throw a fit if he saw you here."

David sat down in the dark among Gordon's shoes. He hadn't known that teachers, too, called the assistant headmaster by his first name behind his back. Old Marcus with his worried bustling and auntish enthusiasm, the facade of aloofness, propriety, and erudition he presented to parents . . . David scarcely recognized the voice from the living room.

"Sorry to stop by unannounced, boys. I hope I wasn't interrupting anything. I just had to let you in on the latest scandal. Guess what's been happening in Cooper Hall. Yes, they discovered a whole ring of the little sodomites. A regular daisy chain. And right under our noses. It's enough to drive one mad with frustration. Anyway, I have to speak to each one of the darlings tomorrow and give him a virile, fatherly lecture on saving it for some gash. I'll have to sit behind a desk the whole time."

Later, Gordon and David discussed the importance of discretion, the need for secrecy. For a long time, David imagined that people he came in contact with, especially if they were extraordinary or had elaborate public personalities, were concealing skeins of inner corruption and intrigue.

His long talks with Gordon drained off some of his bitterness, and he began to develop a sardonic detachment. This, coupled with the help Gordon gave him in articulating and focusing his nihilism, allowed him to do well academically.

At the end of David's junior year, Gordon's roommate was discovered in an indelicate situation with one of his students. Both the roommate and Gordon were dismissed in the convulsion of horror that shook the administration. Marcus swung the ax. Gordon was philosophical about it. "You have to learn to accept such things as a natural risk. It can happen in government and the entertainment industry too, you know. Look at Frank Kameny and Johnny Ray."

David was outraged. He openly, loudly, and proudly allied himself with Gordon and his roommate and insinuated that Marcus had been motivated by jealousy and spite, that the boy with whom the roommate had been discovered had formerly been Marcus's lover.

Gordon went back to school to work toward a Ph.D. "Always did hate teaching literature to rich, insensitive, uninterested adolescents."

The roommate went to New York to try the theater again. "I'm sure the whole thing is a blessing in disguise. I can't wait to get back among civilized people."

David withdrew. He cut classes, never studied, rarely read, and spent hours playing bridge with people he didn't like. His grades fell, and Marcus gave him a poor recommendation for college. At first he wasn't going at all, but letters from Gordon convinced him things would be better there. His erratic grades kept him out of the schools he thought he might want; his father got him into Brown.

That summer David grew tall, and his features developed. His face was compact but there was slightly too much space above the upper lip. His nose was long and straight, and straight blond hair fell across his forehead. His eyes wavered between blue and green. The sharp line of his jaw angled to a chin that was a trifle short.

His freshman year was a round of psychology workbooks, explications of "My Last Duchess," and English themes on last year's current events. He was too dejected by it even to rebel. Once a month there was a social mixer with the girls from Pembroke. The boys would stand around the punch bowl, and the girls would admire each other's hairstyles. The band played on, and a few people even danced.

During his second year David started hanging around the Rhode Island School of Design, going to their films and sitting in on a few classes. He felt more of a kinship with the students there, although it was still slight. He was quick to pick them apart in search of flaws, but he discovered that many of the traits he disliked in them he also disliked in himself: dilettantism, affectedness, sensitivity to the point of inertia. The few people he knew who were deeply involved in painting filled him with respect.

Standing in line for a movie one night, he met a girl with long dark hair, dark eyes, wearing a suede skirt. "Why is it I always see you at the depressing movies?" she asked with a wry smile. "You never come to the happy ones."

"The happy ones depress me even more," he said with a laugh. "I saw *The Red Balloon* last week and cried for two days." He looked at her, and she was looking at him and did not look away. Sudden sweat beaded the backs of his knees.

They went to a coffee house afterward and talked. She was twenty-five and working as a teaching assistant in oils while she finished her master's. When he bid her an awkward good night at her door, she wrote down her phone number for him.

He pinned it to the bulletin board above his desk and thought of her throughout the next week, of what it would be like to get to know her and the different things they could do together. After several rehearsals, he decided on what he would say when he called, and, as a precaution, what he would say if someone else answered. But when he finally dialed the number a week later, no one answered, though he counted twenty rings. He intended to call the next day, but didn't, and the number stayed pinned to his board for a month, becoming more and more of a reproach to him. Finally, admitting defeat, he took it down and crumpled it into the wastebasket.

A month later he saw her on the street, but turned and walked off before she noticed him.

As spring came on, he grew increasingly despondent. He had never had a love affair and was beginning to think he never would. His inability to reach out to women was isolating him, walling him deep inside himself. Hopelessly, he quit school, renounced his parents, and moved to New York, into a roachy apartment on the Lower East Side. Once there, living on a street that smelled like the inside of a garbage can and with concrete the color of a junkie's arm, he felt better. His emotional and sexual life improved not the least, but he stayed high so much of the time that he didn't care. When his draft notice arrived in November, he was too strung out to do anything but submit.

Guns might be interesting, he told himself. Push it to the limit. After all, one psychosis is as good as another. Dive in.

Now, after having had the army to hate and struggle against for four months, he lolled around the house reading back issues of *Vogue* and *Town and Country*, drinking lemonade laced with Cherry Heering instead of sugar, and wearing his Thai silk bathrobe. After all the khaki and combat boots, it was like donning a spring breeze, clinging and sensuous. I shall lounge upon divans eating overripe pears, he thought. I shall languidly sip my lemonade while appraising Veruschka's eyelash, her toss of hair and thrust of leg. And all that close-cropped, tight-knotted, fanny-swatted butch insanity will fall away. And in two weeks I'll be back in it, walking 120 steps a minute, turning sharply and squarely, each angle neat and preplanned, the army's own little mechanical man.

His father believed that the army would probably do David good. May snap him out of the bog he seems to be stuck in, he thought. Get him into contact with other kinds of people. Always was a moody child. Maybe the service will bring him back to reality.

His mother was worried. Life in those barracks must be

awful. Thrown in with all the riffraff. The gutter conversation. Coarse manners. Barroom fights and B-girls out to take him for all he's worth. It breaks a mother's heart to think of her son going to women like that. And there aren't any decent girls around those army posts. Camp followers and tramps. I suppose I should be grateful if he just doesn't get a disease. And if that Vietnam mess gets any bigger, they may send him over there. Why did he have to get into something like this? He never was a daredevil as a child.

Sloane had to leave. He packed a few books and a sketch pad and drove out to the Cape. A spring storm blew slanted rain, bent the long grasses, spun birds upside down, melted the dunes, and whipped frothy splashes on the wave tops. David sat in the dark and shuttered house feeling the weather batter the roof and walls. What it must be like to sail in a squall like this, he thought. Ravished by a maelstrom. When the rain stopped and the wind quit, he walked on the beach in stumbling, gape-mouthed awe of the post-coital hush that stilled the wind and water. The sand was rolled flat and dark and smooth. The ocean was slick and slow and heavy as oil. The air was new.

He pulled off his shoes and ran down the beach, feeling the slap of wet sand against his bare feet, air streaming over his limbs, watching the beach come back to life after the storm. He was surprised at his sudden burst of eagerness. He usually just imagined himself doing things like this, or, more often, imagined himself as someone else doing them. This'll get me in shape for jump school. What hell that's going to be. Running for miles. I wonder what Madsen's doing now? Probably making it with some sex-crazed Wyoming cowgirl. Be good to see him again.

Jeff Madsen spent the first few days of his leave at home slumped in a big chair in a dark room, drinking beer and watching television in a buzzing blur. Stowed yourself away for two years, that's what you did. But you thought you'd be getting into something. Paddling rubber boats down steamy jungle rivers. Garroting sentries beneath the moon. Find out why we've been killing one another for the last million years. But nothing's happening. Dullest thing you've ever done. Things are supposed to happen.

He was too depressed to want to see anyone he knew, so he left Sheridan and started hitching south. Back on the road, a sense of freedom returned, and he felt better, even with a bald head and the knowledge that no matter what he might want to do, he had to be in Fort Benning, Georgia, in nine days.

He cashed in his return-trip plane ticket in Denver and headed for the down side of downtown to gulp bourbon and beer in the bars where the alky ranch hands and crop followers spent the winters—a shot and a snort for half a buck. Most of the bars had loud jukeboxes full of mournful country songs. Some had dancing—Mexican and Indian women clumping and chugging around with a bottle of beer in one hand and a cigarette in the other. He found a bar with a stripper—a bored, limp-breasted woman in her thirties, gyrating to the thump of a drummer with a string tie and moustache.

It's been four months, he thought. Four months. It ain't natural. Warps a man to go so long without a woman. He watched the caesarean scar wiggle over the folds of white abdominal flesh, watched the sequined and tassled nipples swinging in pendulous arcs, the pubic stubble peeping out from under the G-string, the doughy flesh below the buttocks rippling to the sensual rhythms of the dance. And she looks good to me. I'd eat her out right on stage. When something like that looks good, you been gone too long. Madsen saw the other men in the place: mouths open, eyes staring, one hand underneath the table. *Ah, si, la gente,* he thought. *Y yo también. Estamos todos lo mismo.* Know how these old guys feel. Most of 'em haven't had a woman in years. Who can afford ten bucks for something that doesn't even make you drunk? They can't even get up a good fantasy to jerk off to. Have to go to the peep shows and strip joints. Man, if I don't get back in the saddle right soon, I'll end up just like them.

He went uptown to the businessmen's bars and found a pretty hooker who looked like a high school prom queen after a bad marriage: her mouth getting hard, makeup too thick, a forced laugh, nervous eyes. Brittle hair bleached and sprayed into a rigid bouffant. Sitting in a red vinyl booth at a round table drinking sloe gin and Seven-up, talking while lighting a cigarette. "For twenty-five dollars I can only spend an hour with you. For fifty dollars you can have me all night." Her fingers along his thigh.

"Don't mess my hair," she said later, arching her back and raising her hips.

Oooo, sweetness, thought Madsen, slipping into the first burst of warmth. Home at last.

He was on the road the next morning, hitching across the great bland middle of America. Come on, gimme a ride, he told the snarl of passing semis. I gotta go jump out of an airplane.

The men were running in a lurching, gasping pack, each one trying not to step on another's bootheels. The cold morning air cut into their lungs, and their leave-softened sides cramped. The training sergeant ran easily beside them, assailing them with rhythmic curses: "You'll never be Airborne. You'll always be a leg. You're a sorry buncha rat-heeled legs. Never ran a mile, did a day's work in your randy-ass life. Your father was a leg, your mother was a leg, you're a leg. You'll always be a leg."

As they ran they could see the jump school class a week ahead of them on the other side of the huge field. They watched the crane of the 250-foot tower hoisting canopies and small specks of soldiers slowly into the air and—pop—snapping them loose to drift over Georgia like an amusement park ride. The running men expected each chute to collapse, to see kicking figures fall to earth.

Madsen and Sloane had been assigned to separate platoons, so their only interchange was an occasional exhausted nod of recognition as they ran to different training areas. Madsen's platoon was first to jump from the thirty-four foot tower. The top was silver like the fuselage of an airplane and had four flights of open stairs leading to it. Men were running up the stairs chanting, "Airborne! Airborne!" with each step. They disappeared into the structure and emerged, hands pressed against the outside of the door, riser straps over their shoulders, eyes looking straight ahead, faces pale. They shouted their numbers and jumped. The cables broke their fall halfway down and sent them bouncing and clattering off to the recovery mound like sacks of clothespins or sides of beef.

Thirty-four feet is pretty damned high, Madsen thought as he looked up at a small figure braced in the door. Oh, well, it can't be any worse than standing at the top of a ski jump and pushing off. Of course you said you'd never do that again, either.

His group struggled into their harnesses. The harnesses were tight, and they bent the men's shoulders down toward their crotches so that they ran stooped over and bowlegged. They reminded Madsen of the rigs mothers put on babies to leash their backs. As the straps were cinched into the groin, each man had the same fear: I'm gonna jump outa that tower, and those straps are gonna catch me and crush my nuts.

After doing ten squat jumps for having a button unbuttoned, Madsen ran up the four flights of stairs like a gnome, shouting with each step, and started toward the door. The sergeant clanged him on the helmet with a metal snap fastener for not moving with the proper flat-footed shuffle, then hooked him to the risers. I'm trusting this guy with my life, Madsen thought.

"Stand in the door," the sergeant yelled.

Madsen shuffled to the opening, shouted his roster number, and looked at the toy soldiers below. The scene made him feel he was jumping into his childhood World War II military sand table, where the general was always his father. The tower sergeant swatted him on the rear and hollered, "Go!" Madsen thought, this is crazy, and leaped into space. He fell just long enough to know he was going to die, and then the risers jerked him back up by the shoulders, popping his vertebrae and sending a shock down to his toes. He saw the ground race jiggedly by, felt his stomach somersault into his throat, and forgot all about counting and proper body position.

"Sloppy jump, 212," the scorer told him. "Your feet were apart and your elbows were flappin' like a chicken."

"Clear, sergeant."

"We don't play here, 212. We all quit school 'cause they made us take recess. If you don't want to land head first, you better stop playing, too. Now get ten."

"Clear, sergeant."

The men ran everywhere they went and spent hours a day doing PT. They did pull-ups, chin-ups, push-ups, rope climbs, and parallel bars till their blisters bled. On every set of exercises they did one extra, "One for Airborne."

A cadre sergeant caught Sloane doing an improper PLF—Parachute Landing Fall—and shouted, "You, 167. Drop! Drop! Get ten." Sloane flung himself to the ground and started pushing it away, his twelfth set of punishment push-ups that morning. His muscles felt stiff and lifeless as beef jerky. Unfortunately the nerves still functioned, sending constant screaming messages of pained overload. When he finished and hopped back to his feet with a good loud "Airborne," the sergeant scowled at him and said, "You look tired, 167. You look like you need a rest. Well, we'll give you one. Get back down in the front leaning rest." Sloane dived for earth again, thinking it was impossible to do any more. "Hold that leg ass of yours straight. You look like a monkey fucking a football. I think we'll make a quitter out of you, 167. You look like a quitter to me. Just tell me you quit and I'll let you up. Come on, 167, we haven't had a quitter all morning. We gotta meet our quota. How about it, huh? Those arms must be gettin' awful tired. You gonna quit so you don't pass out?"

Sloane spoke through clenched teeth: "No, sergeant."

"Well then, you must want to be doing this, don't you, 167?"

"Yes, sergeant."

"Nobody's forcing you to be here, are they?"

"No, sergeant."

"You know you can stop any time you want?"

"Yes, sergeant."

"You don't never learn, do you, 167? 'No, sergeant' is an incorrect response. Get ten more. Only thing a trainee is permitted to answer to a cadre is 'Clear, sergeant' or 'Unclear, sergeant.' Is that clear?"

"Clear, sergeant."

"Now are you gonna quit and give those arms a break?"

"Unclear, sergeant."

"Well, give me ten more on top of those for being so goddamn stubborn."

Sloane, bug-eyed with strain, twisted and curled his way through the push-ups.

"Now recover and get back to your group."

"Clear, sergeant. Airborne," he croaked and ran to the line for the swing landing trainer. He was floating with pain, and the world was in slow motion. Voices and figures were far off and wavery. I could have done ten more, he thought, as blood tingled back into his knotted muscles. They won't get me.

The men stood hunchbacked and bowlegged on the runway, trussed up with parachutes and reserves, checking one another's equipment. The jump sergeant, in an almost friendly tone, spoke through a bullhorn. "Now there's two ways your T-10 parachute can malfunction." The last word sent a shiver along Madsen's back. "You can get a Mae West, or you can get a streamer. You'll know if you got a Mae West when you look up to check your canopy. If your chute's pinched down the middle, bulgin' out like two big tits, then you got one. Don't fuck around with it. Just shake out that reserve. If you got a streamer, it'll let you know right away. You'll go zippin' by your buddies with your chute flappin' like a used rubber. Pop that reserve, gentlemen, and you'll be OK. But if you haven't checked your release pins and that handle jams . . . well, you'll be pullin' on that reserve for the rest of your life—all two and a half seconds of it.

"So test those release pins. If they work here on the ground, they're going to work up there. You got my word on it. If you checked your equipment and you do like we been tellin' you for the past three weeks, all of you are gonna be OK. And you're all gonna want to do it again. All right, men, the aircraft are ready to board. IS EVERYBODY GONNA JUMP?"

"YES, SERGEANT!" the men roared, so loud it startled them.

"What are you?"

"AIRBORNE!"—louder still.

Madsen's group double-timed up the rear ramp of a waiting C-130 and sat down on four long rows of webbed seats. Inside, the fuselage was lined with quilted silver insulation. The ceiling ran with wires and tubing, all looking critical and exposed. "There're no windows in this damn plane," Madsen said nervously as he fumbled with the seat belt. He felt the aircraft rumble as the engines started, and the noise built to a howl until the rear door, closing like a box turtle, muted it. Sealed in, Madsen felt even more claustrophobic. He wriggled around trying to get comfortable, but was too laden with harnesses and equipment. The jump cadre, tolerant, amused, even paternal now, joked with the troops to allay last minute panic. Some of the men were moving their lips in prayer; some, including Madsen, feigned nonchalance; others just let the fear show, gripping their hands and breathing in quiet gasps. The plane was swaying, but they couldn't tell if it was taxiing or just idling. Then the decibels doubled, the fuselage shook, and their bodies leaned sideways as they roared down the runway and into the air. The men looked at one another: No turning back now.

They flew around for forty-five minutes so that the pilot and crew could log flight pay. Then the jumpmaster said to one of the cadre, "Time to let in the hawk." By now most of Madsen's fear had been replaced by discomfort, and he just wanted to get it over with. But when the jumpmaster slid the side door open and let in the roaring shriek of wind and engines, Madsen felt dread clench his chest.

"Stand up," the jumpmaster shouted. Madsen and the others rose automatically.

"Hook up." It's actually going to happen, Madsen thought as he performed the actions he had practiced so many times: snapping the static line to the anchor cable, inserting and bending the safety wire, checking equipment, stamping his foot, and shouting, "OK."

"Stand in the door." The wind slamming through the door rippled the jumpmaster's face like a rubber mask. We're all gonna jump out of this airplane, Madsen thought.

"Go!" Jump out of a perfectly good airplane. He was moving forward, pressed tightly in line, carried along by the momentum of the group. His fear gave way to a manic excitement. The man ahead of him disappeared. Madsen was in the door, surging with adrenaline. Twelve hundred feet below him was a sudden view of trees, a silver snake of river. The man who had been in front of him was now falling and spinning in the prop wash. Another man's chute was being pulled out in a long tube by its static line. And a third man's chute burst into a tight green hemisphere. On down, away and smaller, dozens of drifting canopies dotted the sky.

Madsen leaped. A torrent of wind, engine scream, and hot exhaust snapped him around, shook him like a rag doll, blasted all thoughts, then threw him away, rolling and tumbling. There was a tug at his shoulders and the roar was shut off and the world was blue and quiet and he was swinging in the middle of it and there was a parachute above his head.

Around him were other floating chutes and dangling men. Above and far away was the plane, still spilling paratroopers into the air. Below was a wide field surrounded by a flowing lawn of forest that built to green wavy hills and distant valleys spreading like troughs of blue haze.

The field was erased by a chute drifting close under Madsen. He pulled and strained on his risers to slip his parachute to the side, but was descending too rapidly. His boots sank into the taut nylon canopy beneath him and he found himself standing in the air, his own chute beginning to pancake out and collapse. Madsen bounded across the bulbous nylon, as if trying to run off a giant feather bed, and dived into free air. He fell for a swooping moment, then was again suspended by his shoulders.

He could see men on the field below, closer now. He seemed to be falling into a bowl, the horizon folding above him, ground coming up fast. As he was trying to remember the proper landing position, his body assumed it automatically, and when the sand rose to meet his boots, he rolled down and over and up onto his feet and was again earthbound.

He looked at the field and the tree line, ordinary now except for the paratroopers floating toward it, and resented gravity for forcing him back into this cramped surface perspective. The land appeared stunted and foreshortened, less eloquent. You can't see enough from down here. It's good to know this isn't all there is. I want to go back up. While he coiled yards of nylon into the stow bag, he relived in his mind the precious few seconds in the blast before the chute opened. It's over too soon, he thought. I'd like to be always falling.

At the end of the week, after five jumps, Madsen and Sloane got their wings. Mixed with their dislike of the army there was now a whisper of pride. Now they were Airborne. They had done something most people could not do.

Fifteen men out of the jump school class volunteered for Special Forces and passed the qualifying tests. They rode together in a bus to Fort Bragg, North Carolina. Each of them was worried about being able to take the months of physical and mental torture he knew must lie ahead. "They say Special Forces training makes jump school look like a picnic. They make you run five miles before breakfast and climb a fifty-foot rope to get into the mess hall. Don't even let you sleep in a barracks. You gotta earn a black belt in karate and be able to make bombs just outa stuff you buy in a drug store. At the end they drop you into the mountains at night with just a knife and a canteen, and if you make it out, then you get your beret."

Madsen and Sloane were both relieved and disappointed to discover that most of the training took place in classrooms, PT was given only irregularly, hand-to-hand combat rarely, and not only did they live in barracks, but they had to wax and buff the floors every day as well. The schedule included many weeks of doing odd jobs like painting jeeps while waiting for different training cycles to start, and they found they had little choice as to what training they would receive.

Madsen was assigned to be a radio operator and was angry about it because he had wanted to be a weapons man, but that school was reserved for NCOs. Reluctantly, he started spending eight hours a day learning Morse code, sitting with earphones on, listening to the bleeps and blats and trying to copy them down before a voice told him the answer. After several weeks of this he was hearing Morse in his sleep and seeing all letters as dots and dashes. Later he worked half the day with radios, studying procedure, codes, and antennas. It was depressingly routine, not like what he had thought guerrilla training would be, but he was told he would have to wait for that until branch class, after commo school.

Sloane was assigned to engineer training and at first was pleased. The idea of being a demo man appealed to him. Always did want to blow things up, he thought. To his dismay, however, he found that demolitions was only a small part of the training. Most of it was learning construction skills, which held no interest for him. The class was taught to build simple bridges, landing strips, barracks, fortifications, and bunkers; to make adobe, mix concrete, and dig a foundation; to tie knots and purify water. Finally, at the end of the course, they learned to select and place the proper explosives for different structures, to set and deactivate mines and booby traps, to adjust fuses and improvise detonators, to lay a demo ambush.

During Madsen's instruction in land-line communications, his class went to the demo range to practice laying wire and installing field phones. Sloane's group was there studying incendiary devices. Sergeant Brannon, head of the demolitions committee, called a break when the commo men drove up, and the two groups talked while a few of the men unloaded equipment from the truck.

"So you're putting phones in the bunkers," Sloane said to Madsen as they sat in the shade.

"Yeah," Madsen replied. "Keep you guys from blowing yourselves up."

"We spent all yesterday digging trenches for the wires. Hope you appreciate that."

"I'm glad you're learning a useful skill."

"We're learning how to make Molotov cocktails today."

"You guys get to do interesting stuff. All we fuckin' do is turn dials and send practice messages."

"Don't believe it. Engineers is dull as hell. We spent the past week in road-building class. Didn't learn a thing. Oh, yeah, you're supposed to build it higher in the middle so that water runs off. It's bullshit. Awful."

"Hey, sarge," one of the men called to Brannon, "is it true we gotta get government driver's licenses next week so we can drive for ration breakdown and ash and trash?"

"That's the word."

"Shit, I ain't gonna get no driver's license," another man said. "I ain't seen an army test yet I couldn't flunk if I wanted to."

"If you don't get a driver's license, you gotta do the unloading. You're screwed either way."

"This damn place. Why'd you stay in the army, sarge?"

"I'm not in the army. I'm in the Forces. There's a big difference." Brannon put his foot up on the hub of the truck tire. "Wait till you get out of training and get assigned to a regular group. It's a good life. A lot of missions coming down now. Look at Hooper. Just came back from Turkey. Bought himself a new Corvette. Most of you guys'll reenlist."

"I didn't know there were guerrillas in Turkey," Madsen said.

"He wasn't fighting guerrillas," Brannon said. "He was over there teaching heavy equipment maintenance. Almost all the missions—fucked up way things are now—just train them how to do stuff. Army's turning us into a souped-up version of the Peace Corps. Best way to get a mission is to go to well-drilling school."

"But Sergeant Reilly told us about in Guatemala . . ."

"Yeah, there's still some spook work. I could tell you stories about the Congo. They're good jobs. But damned hard to get anymore."

"What about this rumor our whole class is getting sent to Vietnam?" Sloane asked.

"I ain't heard nothin' about it. But more and more of you are goin' over there, that's for sure. They levied fifty guys out of Seventh last month. It ain't bad duty. . . . OK, commo, let's get those phones in. We got a class to teach here."

The field phones they were installing were small and rubber-coated, and instead of ringing—which might betray your position to the enemy at night—they clicked like crickets. This was called sound camouflage. Madsen helped install one in the forward bunker near the throwing wall and waited there while the lines were being tested. The engineers came up one at a time and threw their Molotov cocktails. Each burst of flame made Madsen wish he was in demo training.

Over in the assembly pit, Sloane sat with a pile of empty whiskey bottles on one side, a bundle of old sheets on the other, and a ten-gallon can of gasoline in front of him. Which makes a better firebomb, Scotch or bourbon? he wondered. He saw an Ambassador bottle, his father's brand, stuck the funnel in it, poured it full of gasoline, then ripped off a piece of old stained sheet and stuffed it in the hole. Army doesn't waste a thing, he thought. Hope those stains are from wet dreams. Make it burn better.

Walking out to the wall, he waved to Madsen. "Hey, Jeff, check out my Hungarian-freedom-fighter imitation."

Madsen flipped him the finger.

Sloane turned the bottle upside down and held it in the air, striking a pose. "This one here's the Statue of Liberty." He looked to make sure Madsen was watching, oblivious of the gasoline seeping down his arm. "Now for the main event." Sloane snapped the flint igniter and—with a whoof—his arm, the rag, and the bottle were all swathed in fire. He stared at the flames, frozen with fear and disbelief. Madsen jumped up. Sergeant Brannon leaped over the back revetment and ran toward Sloane, bellowing, "Throw the goddamn thing." Sloane finally pushed it away, and it spun flaming end over end, then burst into a blazing yellow ball.

He stood stunned, looking at his arm. The gasoline had burned away, leaving the skin pink and hairless. He waited for the arm to fall off or turn to ash, but instead it felt cool and tingly.

"You OK?" Madsen asked, reaching him.

"I guess so. Yeah."

Brannon grabbed him. "You fucking idiot. Damned doofus

trainee. You better not be hurt. I'm not gonna answer to that colonel about how some dumb-ass Pfc. killed himself on my range, troop. We can't have daydreamers handling explosives. You can forget about Special Forces. We're gonna terminate you right now. An absentminded demo man can wipe out his whole team."

Madsen saw the panic in Sloane's eyes. "It was my fault, sergeant," Madsen lied. "The phone rang, and I told him to hold it. I thought it was the range officer."

"The phone rang? And you let gasoline run all down this man's arm while you answered the phone?"

"I thought it was the range officer, thought he had some instructions for him."

"Well, who was it?"

"It wasn't anybody. Must've shorted out."

"What? You nearly killed that man. You better get your head out of your ass, Pfc. Both of ya, get out of here. You fuck up again like that, either of you, you'll be on your way to the 82nd."

As they walked abashed back toward the truck, one of his classmates razzed Sloane: "Hey, Blaze, you just about did it that time. Lucky it didn't get down as far as your T-shirt. You'd be a Buddhist monk."

Sloane shivered.

After months of training and months of odd jobs, they began branch class. Here they were supposed to learn the skills of guerrilla warfare and counterinsurgency operations. The topics to be covered stirred their imaginations: how to infiltrate an area, organize a guerrilla band, set up intelligence networks and clandestine drop zones, use "black" propaganda to win the people to your side, establish safe houses and equipment caches, detect and interrogate enemy agents within the guerrilla unit, conduct raids and ambushes, and sabotage vulnerable points of the oppressor regime. In the counterinsurgency section they were to study the law of land warfare, population and resource control, civic action, penetrating the guerrilla infrastructure, patrolling the insurgent area by hammer and anvil, search and block, search and clear, and search and destroy.

But the material was covered in a cursory, theoretical way, mostly in lectures, and did not give Madsen and Sloane the excitement and release they needed. They were still caught in an unremarkable round of reveilles, fatigue details, dull classes, oblivion drinking, Saturday inspections; they were plodding through a slow desert of days, their minds a jumble of commands, curses, and military jargon.

Madsen and Sloane spent a lot of time together, and there was an easy friendship between them, but they talked mostly of events at hand, avoiding the personal. If they felt an intimacy, it was only in the silences.

"How about a beer?" Madsen asked Sloane one evening.

"Don't have any money," Sloane said, looking up from his book.

"That's OK," Madsen said. "I still got some chits."

They left the barracks and walked across a wooded area toward the EM club. The night was clear and cold. Madsen crushed some pine needles in his hand and smelled the fresh resin. Not quite the same as being in the mountains, he thought. "It's over a year now, we been in," he said.

"I lost count."

"You know, if we want to go, we're going to have to extend."

Sloane stopped walking. "Oh, fuck. That's right. You have to have a full year left, don't you? What would it be?"

"Three months. We'd have to give 'em three more months."

"No. No way I could stand that," Sloane said.

"It's either that or spend the rest of our time here. Just painting jeeps for eleven months. Have it all be for nothing."

"Oh, fuck. I couldn't stand that either."

"Look, it'll be better over there," Madsen said. "We'll get to really do something."

"Maybe it'll be a drag, too."

"It's worth a try. It's our only chance."

"But to extend for three months?"

"Yeah, I know. It's a bitch either way."

"I want to go. I really do," Sloane said. "Something about it. I just hate to give them any more time."

"Ah, it's not so long. Think of the poor fuckers who are in for three years."

"Hell, there isn't any choice," Sloane said, swinging his foot against a bush. "I have to go. It's the only goddamned action there is. I can't stand the rest."

"Good. Best thing for us. Blow it out. I'm tired of waiting."

Sloane gave a tight, close-mouthed smile. "OK. Then let's do it."

Their orders for Vietnam came through a week before graduation from Special Forces training. They were relieved, for they had feared that, since the army knew they wanted to be sent, it would spitefully deny their requests. With the orders they were given passes to town, which pleased them almost as much. They changed into civilian clothes and walked out by the NCO family housing to hitch a ride. Overturned tricycles and tumbling children covered the worn-out lawns of the two-story frame apartment buildings. Madsen and Sloane felt uncomfortable and out of place there, as if they were being watched from windows like potential child molesters.

"Maybe we'll get picked up by some lonely little wife whose old man's over in Nam," Madsen offered.

"Dream on," Sloane said.

They got a ride with a cook whose back seat was full of eggs and milk and pork sausage from the mess hall. He dropped them downtown, near the train station. On the loading dock sat a scuffed olive drab coffin. Its solitary reproach pulled them to it, and on a side handle they found a freight tag—Point of Embarkation: Bien Hoa, RVN. Shipping Agent: HHC 5th SFG, APO SF 94140. Contents: SSGT James Aldridge,

RA 19812283. Receiving Agent: Mrs. J. Aldridge, Fairhaven Trailer Court, Fayetteville, N.C.

"Christ. They treat 'em just like . . . just like a refrigerator or something," Madsen said. "It's a wonder they don't ship em COD. Hell, I'd rather be buried over there."

"Wonder if his wife knows he's lying here on the freight dock. Man . . . man," Sloane mumbled numbly. "You remember all those women we saw up by the church the other day?"

"Yeah?"

"I found out why they were there. New war widows. Every week they meet for group therapy with the post psychiatrist and a chaplain."

They walked through the lower downtown, past the pawnshops, cafés, and novelty stores, peering dully into windows full of paintings on black velvet of paratroopers leaping out of airplanes, luminous canopies drifting across night skies; displays of fatigue uniforms for children, complete with sergeant stripes and jump wings; sweatshirts printed with "Ft. Bragg, N.C.—Home of the 82nd Airborne Division" and "All-American U.S. Paratrooper—Born to Raise Hell;" hundreds of knives, from machetes to tiny stilettos; little trophies for the "World's Greatest Drinker" and "World's Greatest Mom;" bronzed baby jump boots; plastic ice cubes with flies in them; fuzzy dice for rearview mirrors; dashboard hula dancers; flocked plaster cocker spaniels; trick shot glasses; a toy bartender who mixed drinks while his red nose flashed on and off; satin pillows printed in bright off-register colors with a picture of a southern mansion and the words "Fayetteville, North Carolina—Where the Old South Lives On;" shrunken heads with Day-Glo Dynel hair; plastic dolls naked except for lace panties—pinch their bottoms and their nipples light up.

They ate a huge dinner in an Italian restaurant—lasagna, ravioli, manicotti, and two bottles of Chianti. "I love this stuff," Madsen said. "Brings your taste buds back to life. I'd forgot food was supposed to taste good."

"Shall we sample another one of the local bars?" Sloane asked as they left the restaurant.

"Sure. Sure," Madsen said. "Let's see. We been to the Streamer Bar and the Turf Club before. You ready for the Mae West?"

"Lead on."

Inside, the bar was big and dark and booming with voices and a loud jukebox. Above the bar was a mural of a huge, naked blonde with enormous breasts that formed the parachute canopy for a small, kicking paratrooper dangling beneath them. From the floor rose an aroma of stale spilt beer spiced with vomit.

They found a table among the banging, shouting groups of teenagers from the 82nd Airborne, about half of whom were wearing their spit-shined jump boots and Class A uniforms with marksmanship badges pinned to their chests. "Those guys must get a real charge out of wearing their war suits to town," Madsen said with a snort. "Makes you glad to be in Special Forces. You ever notice how the only people who wear berets to town are the cooks and clerks?"

"Yeah," Sloane said. "And they all transferred over from the 82nd. I'd go nuts down there."

The waitress came over with a pitcher of beer. She had a can opener tied to her wrist and a tiny pair of jump wings tattooed on her arm.

Sloane gaped. "Is that a real tattoo?"

"That's right, bub. Just as real as this here can opener. So don't make no smart remarks. That's a dollar and a half."

"Do you believe that?" Sloane asked after she had left.

"You know, I only heard of one guy who ever fucked a Fayetteville barmaid," Madsen said.

"You mean he lived to tell about it?"

They drank and Madsen played all the Junior Walker

records on the jukebox over and over and drank stein after stein of beer. "Never drank so much in my life till I came in the fuckin' army. Gotta wash that Morse code out of my brain."

"You two guys Airborne?"

Madsen and Sloane looked up at the voice. Two kids from the 82nd stood by the table, staring down at them accusingly. "You two guys Airborne?"

"What difference does it make?"

"Well, you see," explained the short one with mock patience, "this here's an Airborne bar. We don't like legs here. So why don't you just get up and go on down the street. The legs all drink at the Four Leaf Clover."

Madsen stood up and stared at the kid. He wore a tailored uniform with infantry braid and polished jump wings. His jump boots were double soled to make him look taller. He was still two inches shorter than Madsen and couldn't have been older than nineteen.

Little fucker must be a mean son of a bitch to talk that way, Madsen thought. Either that or those Brasso'd jump wings make him think he's Superman.

"That's it," the other one said. "You boys just go on down the street, and maybe when you grow up you can go to jump school, too." He was big and knobby and kept grinning down at Sloane. "Lucky you ain't wearing jump boots, you four-eyed leg, or we'd cut 'em off and shove 'em up your ass like we did to those two we caught last week."

Sloane jiggled his foot nervously but could think of nothing to say.

"Look, man," Madsen said, forcing himself to be calm, "if you want to start a fight, why don't you just say so?"

"I don't start fights, leg. I end 'em," said the little one who had chosen Madsen. "See this boot? I got a steel plate in the toe of that boot got a blasting cap in front of it. Fuck with me and I'll blow your balls off. Mess you up for life. But I forgot.

You legs don't have balls, do you? Well, we'll just make your pussy a little bigger, that's all." He laughed loud and prodded his partner.

I hope to hell this guy's bullshitting about that blasting cap, thought Madsen as he smashed his beer stein into the wide laughing mouth. He grabbed the kid by the collar and belt and rammed him into the sharp edge of the booth. It caught him in the kidneys, and he cried out through broken teeth.

His stunned friend started for Madsen, but Sloane jumped in front of him, dancing and waving his arms as if trying to scare away a horse. The man swung at him, but Sloane ducked and the looping punch glanced off his shoulder. He came up jabbing his long fingers into the groin, which brought the man's arms shooting up in panic. Sloane hit him three times in the face while he was seized up, then stepped back, hoping he would fall over. Instead, the guy grabbed him and started pounding his head against the table, shouting, "You queer. You fucking queer."

Madsen was grappling on the floor. He pushed himself loose and jumped up. The kid lay there holding a handful of broken fingers and crying. Madsen raised his foot and drove the wedge of his heel into his coccyx. "OK, Blasting Cap."

Sloane's head was still bouncing off the table. He tried to break away, but the other man was stronger. "Hey, let me up. Let me up," he yelled.

To his surprise the guy did. Sloane clutched him around the head and tried to pull him down. The guy's face was all over him, grunting—whiskers rasped his cheek, hot boozy breath clogged his nostrils. What'll I do with him now? Sloane wondered. There was an ear. He bit, grinding it between his molars, tasting the blood. The man screamed.

There were shouts all around. The bartender was rushing over with a club. The barmaid charged in swinging her can opener like a claw. Madsen pounded on Sloane's back. "Hey! Hey! Let him go."

They ran from the place with the other GIs chasing them and yelling, "You goddamn legs. We'll kill you."

Around the corner they flagged a cab and hopped in.

"Where to?" the driver asked.

"To? Oh, uh, away. Yeah. Get us away from here. Go down that street."

"Cops ain't after you guys, are they?"

Madsen looked around nervously. "No, uh, not yet. No. We just been in a fight."

Sloane looked at Madsen and forced a laugh. "How the hell did that happen?"

"I don't know, but I'm glad it's over."

They found a quiet tavern and tried to drink away their jitters. "Bastard broke your glasses. Hey, you're still shaking," Madsen noticed.

"Yeah. I haven't been in a fight since I was eleven," Sloane said.

"What'd you think of it?"

"It wasn't so bad. There was . . . there was something about it I liked. That we won, I guess. I always thought it must hurt like hell, you know, getting your head bashed. But it's not all that bad."

"You did a great job on the big son of a bitch."

"Ah, thanks. I knew he was stronger than I was . . . only thing I could do was to freak him out. He must have been terrible stupid to let me up that way."

They drank at the bar with a Special Forces weapons sergeant who told them about fighting in Laos with the Meo tribesmen against the Pathet Lao. "Got so we could look across the valley and see the Russian cargo planes dropping supplies to the Pathets. We got resupplied every two weeks, and they got resupplied once a month. Used to think it'd be a lot more efficient if they could get together. You know, use one big plane and drop to both of us at the same time. Divvy up the cost."

"But if you knew where their drop zone was, why didn't you ambush 'em?" Madsen asked.

"Ambush 'em? Shit. We were worried about them ambushing us. Too many. We were just barely hanging on. Drew some fat per diem, though. Course that was back when the Agency was still running the show. Before MACV and all that bullshit."

The fight had sobered them, so they drank fast until their heads were again awash.

"Godda go back, David. Time to go back," Madsen said.

"Dowanna go back."

"Godda go back."

Sloane rose.

"You have a good tour over there, now," the sergeant said.

It was late. They felt fine, walking down to the bus station, passing a quart of beer between them.

Madsen stopped, choked, spitting beer, pointing at their feet, saying, "No. No. Look what we're doing. Walking in step. Ever since we left the bar we been fucking marching."

Sloane skipped to break the pace. "Can't have that. Can't have none of that." The two of them walked the rest of the way studiously out of step.

As they sat in the station waiting for the bus, Madsen said, "Army's not quite as bad as it used to be. Easin' up a little, doesn't it seem?" He looked at Sloane. "Man, are you still shaking?"

"Yeah, uh, I guess so," Sloane said. "Can't get that fight out of my head. What was your guy like?"

"A pushover. All bluff. Listen, you gotta relax."

"Weren't you bothered 'cause he was littler than you?"

"Fuck, no," Madsen said. "I was glad he was littler than me. Listen, man, I just fight to win . . . 'cause I don't like it, you know, and I want to get it over with as quick as I can. But the thing is, you gotta be relaxed, too. If you're tense, the other guy's got you. Look. First thing you do when you see you're gonna have to punch somebody out—you calm yourself. Calm yourself way down and then fight cold . . . stone cold. See, you watch the guy all the time, the way he moves. And when you see your chance, you jump in there and hurt him as bad as you can."

"No matter what you have to do to him?"

"Goddamn right," Madsen said, finishing the beer. "Listen, there's no such thing as a clean fight. All that shit about honorable fighting is just bullshit. That fuckin' Marquis of Queensberry would get his ass kicked in Fayetteville. The only reason you fight is to win. Remember what Blalock said about the Forces: 'We don't always fight fair . . . but we don't always lose, either.' "

They rode back to Fort Bragg on the last bus, the Vomit Comet, full of kids from the 82nd puking and singing jump songs. Sloane looked through his cracked glasses and the bus window at the shut-up streets of Fayetteville and thought about the man he had fought. Wonder what he's doing now? Nursing his wounds? Sleeping? Thinking about me?

It was two o'clock by the time they got to the barracks. Reveille and a clanging hangover were three and a half hours away. They climbed into their bunks, and Madsen said, "Tonight was bullshit, David. Next month it'll be the real thing."

Sloane whispered as they lay in the dark, "Ever notice how they never play taps? It'd be nice if they played taps. Make you feel like you were in a movie or something. Make you feel cozy."

"Squad meeting, right now. Hop to it," Sergeant Hein, Madsen's squad leader called down the bay the next evening.

The men stopped talking or writing letters or sleeping, and reluctantly gathered in the center of the barracks.

"Now listen up. We got word the colonel's making a surprise inspection tomorrow. And we're all gonna be ready for him when he gets here. I want the squad area spotless. Zero defects. And all your personal gear has got to be STRAC. I'm not going to stand up in front of that colonel and have to tell him why my men weren't battle ready. If we all cooperate, we can get this work done in a couple of hours. So let's get the mops out, and Simons, you're assistant squad leader. You be in charge of the buffer."

Madsen sat on his bunk, brushing the dirt off his boots and rubbing on Glo-Coat to make them look like they had been polished. How come I have the only stupid squad leader in the platoon? Madsen wondered. He stuffed his books and old hitchhiking maps and dirty tennis shoes into his laundry bag where he hoped they wouldn't be discovered, then straightened his footlocker display and buttoned the buttons on his extra uniforms. Zero defects! Hope they send him back to the 101st. He mopped his part of the shiny brown floor and crawled around on his hands and knees spreading yet another coat of paste wax over it. Must be two inches of wax on this damn floor already. All of this so that pompous old fart of a colonel can walk through and find some dust and tell us to shape up, we're gettin' soft. In the colonel's office, where he had pulled cleaning detail many evenings, a model airplane collection had to be dusted every night. A carefully drafted diagram on blueprint paper showed how the planes were to be arranged. Each propeller and helicopter rotor had to be dust-free and at a specific angle. It was the first thing the colonel checked every morning. If it wasn't exact, the whole staff caught hell.

Lunatic, Madsen thought, as he rolled his underwear around an empty soda pop can. He stopped. Look at me, I'm the one who must be nuts.

"Madsen, you got the worst boots in the squad. Look like you used a Hershey bar on 'em," Sergeant Hein said, sitting down beside him on the bunk. "Colonel sees those and he'll have both our asses in a bind. Here, let me show you how to do it right. Guy been in the army as long as you and he still don't know how to spit-shine boots. First you get an old T-shirt. Some guys say cotton balls, but a T-shirt's better. This is how we learned it at the Third Army NCO Academy. You take a T-shirt and you gotta find the softest side. Yeah. They ain't both the same. One side is always softer. You put your base coast on with melted polish. Just get a candle and melt some polish in the lid. Pour it over the boot good and thick and let it dry. Then buff it out." He held up a boot and gestured with his hands. "Then take your T-shirt with just a little bit of water—most guys use way too much—and don't use spit, it's unsanitary and don't work as good, just a little bit of water, cold is best. Take up a tiny dab of polish and rub it around and round. When you get up a good gloss, you finish it off with lighter fluid. Seals the shine. Just spread some on and light it. It'll burn about ten seconds. Melt that wax down and put a shine on those boots you could shave in 'em."

Madsen looked at Hein. He had a round head with low cheekbones and a heavy jaw. His eyes were large, soft brown, and bloodshot. Lord, he thought, I've got to sit here and listen to this and be polite.

"And hey, Madsen, you got a hole in your pants. Your ass is hangin' out. Colonel sees that, he'll have a fit. Get some new ones tomorrow."

"I'm broke, sarge. Couldn't I just dye my underwear green so the hole won't show?"

"Stop shittin' around. This is serious. You're gonna have to shape up, Madsen. You're not in Vietnam yet. You get some fatigues and some jump boots, too. It's a disgrace, you walking around an Airborne post with leg boots on."

"Fuck a bunch of jump boots. I wouldn't have a pair of the damn things. You expect me to spend thirty dollars for jump boots? I can stay all night with a whore in Fayetteville for that. Jump boots, my ass."

"Dammit, you got no pride, Madsen. You're what drags the army down. But as long as you're in my squad, you're gonna straighten up. You better listen, if you want to stay in Special Forces. First you get those boots spit-shined. Then you get rid of those fatigues. Then, for mouthing off, you're gonna dust all the windowsills and wall lockers. And the rafters. Don't forget the rafters."

"Dust the rafters? We just dusted them two days ago," Madsen said, starting to lose his temper.

"I don't care if you dusted them two minutes ago. You're gonna dust them now, and you're gonna dust them 'cause I tell you to. And they better be perfect. That colonel's been known to check for dust with white gloves on."

"Well, fuck him and fuck you!" Madsen stood up and threw the soda pop cans across the bay. "I've had it with dusting rafters. That's all we goddamn do. Polish our boots, wax the floor. . . . I didn't join the army to be a janitor. Fuck it. You can get yourself another monkey."

"Hold it, Pfc. You don't talk to me that way. I'll burn you in a flash. You shut your mouth and get to work, before I put you on report."

Madsen kicked over his footlocker and shouted, "Get off my back, dammit. You dust the fucking rafters, you care so much about them."

Hein stood up, angry. "OK, Madsen, that's it for you. I'm putting you in for termination. You're not going to Vietnam. You're going right down the street to the 82nd Airborne. They'll take care of you right quick. You're not Special Forces material, that's all there is to it." Hein stomped into his room, and Madsen sat back down on his bunk, fuming. Sloane had come upstairs when he heard his friend shouting and caught the last of the exchange. "Bastards," Madsen said, trembling. "I can't do it. They just keep pushin' me. I'm not going to be their goddamn dust mop anymore."

Sloane sat down beside him and put his hand on Madsen's shoulder. "Just hold on, Jeff. Just a week. Just a week more and we'll be gone. We'll be in the fucking war . . . and we can fuck the world. They can all go to hell. If they make you stay here, then they've got you. Just hold on a little longer and we're out of it."

"Hold on. Hold on. That's all there is," Madsen said, shaking his head. "I been holdin' on for thirteen months."

"But damn, Jeff, you think this is bad . . . if they send you to the 82nd, you'll crack up. Go talk to Lindsey about what it's like there. This is summer camp compared to that place. All they do is pull detail and clean the barracks. They make you buy tailored fatigues and they make you buy jump boots . . . and you'll be spit-shining the damn things every night. They don't even let you wear them in the barracks. You have to take them off outside and tiptoe around the edge of the floor so it stays shiny."

"Chickenshit fuckers," Madsen said.

"Dig it," said Morris, one of the men in Madsen's squad. "They send you to the animal farm, 'specially the way you're feelin' now, you'll be in the middle of deeper shit than you know what to do with. They'd have you in the stockade in two weeks. Here, you don't play along and they give you a hard time. Over there they jail your ass."

"He's right, Jeff," Sloane said.

"Yeah," Madsen said, kicking through the mess from his overturned footlocker. "Yeah, I've done it now. That dumb fucker Hein . . . send me to the 82nd . . . I'll miss my chance to go to Nam . . . my only damn chance to do something real. . . . Man, I've really blown it this time. The bastards always know what you want most."

"Hein's not that hard to get along with," Morris said. "Go talk to him."

"Eat crow, you mean. Beg. Show him I respect him. God, I wouldn't mind doing it for somebody I *could* respect. It'd be great to have somebody you could look up to, who'd really done something. I haven't met one of these damn guys worth looking up to."

"We got to go to Nam, Jeff."

"Yeah, I know. Fuck it, I'll go do a shuffle." Madsen walked over and knocked on the squad leader's door.

"What do you want now?" Hein said when he opened it.

"Sergeant, I just wanted to say . . . to say I'm sorry I blew up like that. I been under a lot of strain lately. I just . . . I just lost my temper . . . and it was stupid. You're right about the inspection and my gear and all."

"Strain? I'm gonna put you in a strain."

"If you give me another chance, sarge, I promise you I'll shape up."

"Another chance, huh? What makes you think you can run around disobeying orders?" Hein asked, softening a bit. "You undermine the whole army when you do that. Did you ever think what would've happened . . . what would've happened when it really counted . . . say, back during World War II? Suppose people just decided to do whatever they wanted? Do you think they could've beaten Hitler? Suppose when they were trying to get off the beaches on D day . . . what would've happened?"

A shudder ran through Madsen and his face lost color. He said slowly, "They would've all died right there at Normandy. I know. I know you're right."

"And it's no different today," Hein said. "The army runs on discipline."

"They never would've gotten off the beaches . . . all of them killed right there." Madsen stopped, then spoke gravely and sincerely. "It's true . . . you have to have obedience."

"Well, then, why do you act like such a rebel?" Hein asked, looking at him levelly.

Madsen couldn't think why. "I don't know. I lose my head sometimes."

"Well, Special Forces can't have men who keep losing their heads."

"I won't keep doing it. If you give me a break, just this once, I'll show you. Just let me stand the inspection. There won't be a gig on any of my stuff."

"There better not be, Madsen. And you better be damn glad I'm not a hard-ass. Talk to most NCOs that way and you'd lose a stripe and a month's pay."

"You're right, sarge. And I appreciate that."

"OK. I'll give you another chance. But you better get with the program."

"Thanks, sergeant. Thanks a lot," Madsen said with an exhalation of relief.

"Oh, and Madsen. In addition to the other things . . . you have to Brasso the fire extinguisher."

Madsen walked back to his bunk, and Sloane asked, "How did it go?"

"I'm back in."

"Good. I'm sure glad. Had me worried there. Thought I might have to go fight the war by myself. What did he say? Was he a son of a bitch about it?"

"Leave me alone, hey."

Sloane shrugged and went downstairs. Madsen grimly reassembled his footlocker display, retrieved the soda pop cans, and wrapped his underwear around them, stuffing the overlap into the open ends to give a neat cylindrical appearance. He carefully dusted the windowsills, the wall lockers, and the rafters, polished the fire extinguisher, and laid out a freshly starched pair of fatigues for the morning. Then he thought, I have to spit-shine these boots, too. How the hell did he say to do it?

As he was trying to determine which side of the T-shirt was softer, a man walked up to his bunk and asked, "Are you Madsen?"

"That's me," he said, annoyed.

"They told me downstairs I could find you here." The man

was thin with dark hair and dark eyes and a prominent Adam's apple. "You got orders for Vietnam, right?"

"Yeah."

"I know 'cause I work in personnel." The man gave a nervous laugh. "Look, I got a business proposition for you . . . a way to make you a lot of money."

"Yeah?"

"You got a leave coming up before you go overseas, right?"

"Sure do."

"How'd you like to have an extra hundred bucks to spend on it?"

"What do you want?"

"Well, it's a business deal. Everybody going to Nam gets a ten thousand dollar government life insurance policy, you know?"

"Go on."

"The deal is . . . I give you a hundred bucks, cash. Spend it any way you want. You name me as the beneficiary on the policy. Signing the papers is easy as can be. Just takes five minutes at personnel. We can do it tomorrow, and I'll give you your hundred on the spot. No strings."

"What do you mean? Sign over the policy so if I get zapped you get the money?"

"Well, it's not going to make any difference to you who gets it. I'm offering you hard cash. I got three guys want to do it already."

"Get out of here. Get out of here, you scum," Madsen stammered. "I'll collect *your* goddamn insurance."

"No need to get all pissed off. It's just a business proposition."

Madsen sprang up, his fists white. The clerk saw the look in his eyes and bolted for the stairs, calling back, "Stay poor, then. See if I care. Be damned."

At the end of the week, after a gigless inspection, Madsen went home to Wyoming, wearing his uniform so he could travel for half fare, feeling self-conscious to be among civilians again. In the Denver airport a few of them whispered as he passed, and—after making sure his fly was zipped—he realized they were noticing him because to them he was a Green Beret, a "fighting soldier from the sky." A middle-aged couple approached him diffidently and said they would like to congratulate him, that they were proud to have young men like him defend the country. He answered in a polite mumble.

Once home, he found he had to leave. His mother kept breaking into tears, and Madsen knew no way to respond. When Sloane wrote inviting him to California, he made up a story to his mother about having to report in early for port call, said good-bye to his father's picture, and flew to San Francisco.

Sloane was staying with a friend from New York who now lived in Marin County. Madsen hitched to Marin from the airport, got lost five times, finally found the town, and called Sloane, who came loping down the hill a few minutes later with bare feet, cutoff blue jeans, and a sunburn.

"Hey, didn't take you long to get loose, did it?" Madsen said.

"It's all camouflage," Sloane said. "Good to see you."

They carried his duffel bag up the hill through the village to a small house hidden, except for its moss-grown wood-shingled roof, behind tall hedges. As they walked into the yard, a tanned and lanky man with a droopy moustache and shoulder-length auburn hair saluted from the lawn chair where he was sitting and said, "Come on in. You must be Jeff Madsen. I was hoping you'd have your uniform on so the neighbors'd think we'd been invaded."

"I changed at the airport," Madsen said. "Don't much care to wear it."

"Well, make yourself at home. My name's Chris." He turned to Sloane and said, "You show him around, OK, Timothy? I want to catch some rays."

"Timothy?" Madsen said.

"That's me," Sloane said.

"Oh?"

"What is this?" Chris asked. "That's not your name anymore? The army changed your name?"

"I use my first name now," Sloane said. "I see the whole sordid mess is going to come out."

"You mean the army decided D. Timothy Sloane was no fit name for a Green Beret?" Chris asked.

"No. I decided it. I thought if I was going to change my personality, I should use a different name. A whole new me."

"There're easier ways to change your personality, you know, without joining the army," Chris said. "Since acid came along, you can change personalities like changing your socks. But, OK . . . David it is. But why'd you stop there? Why don't you call yourself something like Rock? Or Ripper?"

"How uncouth," Sloane said, turning away.

The house was built on a hillside. There were three rooms above and a separate room below reached by steps that ran past a small untended rock-lined pond half-filled with standing water, thick and green as jade. They dropped Madsen's duffel bag in the lower room he would be sharing with Sloane and went upstairs. The living room was paneled with raw wood and strewn with amplifiers, cords, two guitars, and several small drums. A picture window opened out onto a cluster of rooftops down the hill, a long swath of beach, and what looked like half the Pacific Ocean.

"Pretty nice barracks, isn't it?" Sloane said. "You want to hit the beach while there's still some sun?"

"Let's go."

The sand bounced back against their thrusting bare feet as they ran by the water. Gulls awked and cawed above them, and tiny crabs dived for their holes.

"Sure can run a lot faster without combat boots on," Jeff said between puffs. "I don't believe I'm here."

The ocean was green and blue and yellow and gray, and broke in white curves that pushed up the beach. Clumpy green hills tumbled into it, holding back their groves of gnarled oak and jagged fir. The sky was light at the horizon and a dark ink blue overhead, with a gull, a gliding scoop of white, against it. In front of them was the beach, a slash of khaki stretching for two miles.

"Ready to go in?" Jeff asked.

"Are you kidding? That water's so cold, it'll shrivel your scrotum. Man, you'll look like a peanut."

Jeff ran kicking through the small waves for a minute with the water splashing sharp against his thighs, then dived through a breaker and came up on the other side, gasping and shouting at the shock of it, flailing his arms for warmth. Finally he relaxed and the cold left and he swam among the shadow eyes that winked between the wave swells. I'm alive, he thought. I'm free. I'll never have to go back to Fort Bragg.

David slowed to a walk as he watched Jeff stroking beyond the breakers. He found a periwinkle shell and put it in his pocket, half expecting someone to blow a whistle at him. Ahead, crabs were eating a bird corpse. Foundered in trawler oil, tossed up on the beach, feathers tarred—every day a different dead bird on the beach.

Jeff got out shivering, and the two of them walked back toward the house. "You look a little blue around the edges, but I guess you'll thaw," David said.

"Yeah, it's great once you get used to it," Jeff said.

"What were you yelling about?"

"I don't know. I was swearing at Neptune for not making me a porpoise. What I'd really like to do is fuck one. Can you imagine, rolling around in the water with some sexy little cow porpoise? That fantastic body action they've got? All you could do would be to hold on."

"If the women hear that, they'll feel left out," David said.

"They do grow some pretty ones here, don't they?" Jeff said, dashing his tongue over his chipped front tooth. "I hope you have them all catalogued as to, ah . . . duration of orgasm and preferred method of stimulation."

"I haven't had much luck."

"Well, we got two weeks."

Chris was trying out a new amp for his guitar the next day while Jeff and David listened to the feedback and stared bored out the window at the rain.

"How about some dope?" Chris asked. "Ever smoke any weed, Jeff?"

"Couple of times in Mexico."

"You like it?"

"Sure."

"I got some boss stuff here. M & M's . . . Michoacán soaked in mescaline. David'll tell you what it does to your head."

"Twists it totally," David said. "I never smoked anything that strong back in New York."

"Scene was just starting then. You've been missing out. Whole bunch of stuff's happened since you been gone," Chris said, then added, "Who knows where things'll be at by the time you get back from your silly war trip."

"Well, let's get high," David said.

Chris brought out a sandalwood box of marijuana, and they smoked and smoked some more and sat staring out the window again, no longer bored by the rain.

"Why don't you blast Jeff with the Beethoven like you did me?" David said.

"Yeah, good day for it." Chris turned on the record player, put earphones on Jeff, gave him binoculars, and told him to look at the ocean.

Sound crashed through his ears and sea through his eyes, and they danced together in his head. Birds swooped and spun; fog sifted through rain. The music orchestrated the waves, took him away. A pain rose and grabbed him. Look what I've been missing. I could have had this every day. Swimming in beauty. What have I done with my life? An army. A soldier. So much time, lost. Gone.

Jeff took off the earphones and wandered around muttering.

"He looks done," Chris said.

"I don't know what I'm gonna do," Jeff grumbled.

"You want another toke?" David asked, offering a joint.

"What this place needs," Jeff said, "is some females."

"We should be able to arrange something like that," Chris replied.

"How about Cathy's friend, the dark-haired one—Sharon?" David said. "And don't forget to ask Cathy, too."

"Sure, I'll call them. Maybe a couple of other folks to round it out. Play a little music . . . "

"Sounds good," Jeff said.

"Want another toke?" David rasped, holding his breath.

"No."

The rain had stopped by the time people drifted in, bringing food and instruments. They sat in the living room talking softly and brushing the hair out of their eyes. David smiled at a girl across the room and said to Jeff, "I really like her—

Cathy, the blonde one over there. Maybe you could get it on with Sharon?" His voice held a slight note of pleading.

"She looks nice. You been gettin' anywhere?" Jeff asked.

"Not yet. We just talked some a few days ago. She plays the flute."

"Well, maybe tonight's the night."

Jeff moved across the room to ask Sharon if there were porpoises this far north and what was the name of those birds that dive into the water and would she like to go outside. He took her hand and they walked out into the still wet garden with its profusion of nasturtiums and trellises of wild-rose bushes, none yet blossoming. They found a Frisbee near the pond and tossed it back and forth. In the gathering twilight it whirled between them like a bat.

David watched them play from the window, then went over and sat beside Cathy. "Hi. What have you been doing lately?" he asked.

"Oh, this and that. Not much."

"I saw you carrying something. Did you bring some exotic delicacies?"

"Just some millet-buckwheat bread I baked."

"Sounds delicious. You going to give me a piece?"

"It's macrobiotic. People who eat meat don't like it."

"I bet I would. What's in it? Tell me about it."

"I can't now. I want to practice my flute some before the music tonight."

When she had gone, two guys sat on either side of David and began talking across him. "Hey, I met this chick last week turned me on to catnip," one said.

"Catnip? What? You can't get high on catnip," said the other.

"You wanna bet? It's like a two-dimensional pot high. Very hard to recognize. You gotta slip into it sideways."

"Really? Did I tell you about the first time Brian smoked hash? Yeah, he walked around the house for two hours with his hands in his pockets croaking like a frog. 'Stoner . . .

stoner . . . stoner . . . stoner,' over and over, just like a frog. Whenever anybody asked him anything, he'd bulge out his eyes and croak, 'Stoner.' It blew everybody's mind."

"OK, Mark," Chris said to him. "Mellow out now . . . or we'll turn you in and collect your runaway reward."

"Would you listen to that?" said an older blond and tanned man. "What we could turn you in for, Chris, is something else again."

People served themselves food from a long table and ate and sang and smoked. "I brought a treat for dessert," one of them said. "Five big ones laced with DMT."

"Solid," said Chris. "Let's get ripped . . . play some music. If we get David and Jeff stoned enough, maybe their hair'll grow."

"More likely it'll fall out," Jeff said.

People tuned guitars, and several began a reverberating rhythm with congas, dumbeks, and water-bottomed brass bowls. The beat stumbled whenever a joint had to be passed. They sang and played harmonicas. Jeff and David sat on the floor, not really feeling a part of the scene, but glad to be there. The sounds of Chris's electric guitar floated and bounced in the air, then burst into quick black silences. Cathy's flute fluttered, and Chris started singing:

When the blue light hangs in cellophane shrouds
and your eyes are underwater
and your ears are in the clouds,
then it's time to get together
get it out and get it on,
time to trip together, strip together
never be alone. . . .

He ended with a stream of platinum notes that hovered in clusters. Candlelight fell on frozen faces. No one moved for fear they would shatter the bubbles into glittering shards.

"I like the way you played the flute," David finally whispered to Cathy. "Why don't we take a walk? Down by the beach. It must be really beautiful down there."

She looked at him, put a silent finger to her lips, and turned away.

Across the room, a pipe of hashish made the rounds. What's happening to the party? Jeff wondered. Everybody's starting to nod out. He crawled over to Sharon, and their eyes smiled in the dark. Gliding one hand over the back of her neck and another onto her arm, he helped her up.

Outside was fresh, air cool and damp, fog close. The moon came through like ivory. They walked to the rock pond, leaving dark foot-holes in the dew. The black surface of the water held a quivering opal.

"Say, it catches the moon," he said.

"It's in Cancer tonight. It's at home. . . . Do you want a Life Saver?"

"A what? Oh, yeah, sure."

"Did you know they make sparks when you crunch them?"

"What do you mean?"

"Watch."

He looked at her lean, angular face framed by straight dark hair parted in the middle. Her cheekbones were high and her nostrils narrow. She put three candies into her mouth and bit down. Blue sparks jumped between her full lips.

"I'll be damned. Does each flavor give a different color spark?"

"I don't know. Maybe we can experiment and find out."

He reached a hand behind her, pulled her close, and kissed her.

"I didn't mean that," she said.

He kissed her again, running his hand over her bottom.

She kissed him back lightly and said, "We should go back in."

"Right." He led her through the door into his room.

"Not here," she said. "I meant back upstairs to the party."

"There's nothing happening up there," Jeff said as he brought their bodies together and kissed down her neck.

"But I don't even know you."

"Sure you do. I'm the guy you played Frisbee with this afternoon."

"You know what I mean."

He covered her mouth with his and kissed her deeply. Her tongue glided with his, but when his hand went under the back of her short dress and pressed the soft skin at the top of her legs, she broke the kiss and tried to twist away. Her movements only worked his hand deeper between her legs.

"Don't," she said softly.

He stroked the back of her neck with his free hand until she was a little calmer, then slid it around her shoulder, picked her up, and carried her to the bed.

"Jeff? We shouldn't do this."

"Sure we should. Just blame it on the moon."

He eased her onto the mattress and lay down with one leg between hers, one hand petting her eyes and the side of her face, the other caressing her breasts. He kissed her, and she kissed back, and their bodies picked up a rhythm. Driven by an urgent erection, he pressed and kneaded her small covered hillock until her breath came in short gasps and wetness seeped through the nylon. He stopped long enough to slip off her dress and kiss her moist eyes. Then he rolled her over onto her stomach and pulled her panties down. He buried his face in her round white ass and spread it with his tongue while he stripped off his clothes. Under his probing, she raised herself, and he moved up over her back and massaged her wet folds with his hand.

She undulated and sighed, and he lifted her hips and positioned himself and pushed until he was full inside her with his belly pressing against her rump. She writhed to his slow pumping, pushed back and moaned while he held her in front so the bulge of her clitoris throbbed between his fingers.

He kissed her ear wetly, then bit the rear of her neck below her tumbled hair, bit it until she curled it back, murmured deep in her throat, and jutted her tongue with each of his thrusts. He tried to build slowly, but he avalanched and was stroking her fast and wild, flattening her on the bed under his rushing spurts.

He kissed her as they rolled to face one another. Left too soon, she was furiously naked, her eyes wet fire, arms flailing, mouth opening and closing breathlessly.

Jeff went down her long body with his tongue, pausing at her breasts and belly, then working through her mossy wetness into the tart pink folds. He held the yearning bud between his lips and slowly loved it with his tongue. He tasted what he had just given her while her bottom swiveled in a slow small circle. One of his hands rubbed a nipple while the other pressed the flesh of her lower tummy. She sighed and moved faster and pressed against his face. He sucked it and trilled it and stroked two fingers inside, bringing her breath in rapid pants; then she stiffened and broke and cried out, her body clutching and giving in bursting spasms. She pulled him back on top of her and held him while she shook with waves.

They lay a long time rocking.

"But I wasn't going to," she said in a small voice.

He smoothed her hair and her forehead and pressed her into him. "Sleep with me, Sharon."

"No . . . I didn't want to . . . my boyfriend would die if he knew."

"Where's your boyfriend?"

"Jail."

"That's too bad," Jeff said, and thought, That's fine.

"Now I want to go home."

He helped her dress, and they walked into the garden and kissed with the air wet all around them.

"Go back," she said. "You're naked."

"You fucker," David said. "You won't even tell us about it."

"What's there to tell?" Jeff said, lying on the grass watching the windblown sprinkler spray rainbows in the sunny air. "We sat out here and watched the mushrooms grow, that's all."

"Come on."

"We just did it. It was . . . OK. I was too horny."

"*You're* too horny? What about me?"

"What about Cathy?"

"Couldn't get anything going with her at all. I think your music hypnotized her, Chris."

"I thought it might loosen her up," Chris said, rising to his elbow and shielding his eyes from the sun. "Maybe you ought to try someone else."

"But she's the one I really like. Could you call her? If you could get her over here I could ask her if she'd come with us tonight."

"She's a Libra, David. Never chase a Libra. You have to make them come to you."

"I only have three days."

"I'll call her."

A half hour later Cathy arrived with her flute, and she and

Chris played while David listened attentively and tapped inaudibly on a conga drum. After a few songs, Chris said he had to go do his asanas. Cathy got up to leave and David said, "Oh, but stay here and play. I like to hear you."

"I have to go. I was in the middle of making bread."

"I'll walk you home, then."

She was a thin girl with an upturned nose, almost blonde hair, blue eyes behind long lashes, and an open-mouthed way of smiling that showed small, even teeth. The trees along the road were fragrant with early spring blossoms. They walked through mottled patches of sunshine and, to David, her long hair shone like pounded gold. Almost as pretty as a cigarette commercial, he thought, then rebuked himself. Stay here. Stay in close. Drawing up all his self-assertiveness, he reached out and took her hand.

"Look, I was thinking, well, we—I mean Chris and Jeff and I—we're going into San Francisco tonight. And I was wondering if you wanted to come. It'll be a good time and we could . . . I don't know, do something fun."

"But . . . my dog is sick," she said, looking away. "I, uh . . . don't go out."

"Don't be that way. Give me a chance. Just let's get to know one another."

She took her hand away. "I'm really not into seeing people. I've got a lot of planets progressed into the twelfth house. That's why I came out here. To get my head together." She tried to smile at him.

"Come on," he said, "I'm not asking you to fall in love with me or go to bed with me or any of that stuff. I just want you to like me. Just to spend the evening with me. I like you so much. I get shivers whenever I'm around you."

"But I do like you. You're sweet. Look, I'll tell you something I wouldn't ordinarily say to a guy. You have to learn to come on to girls in a more subtle way. Your type of approach turns girls off. It robs the thing of all its glamour. That's all I can say."

David stared at her, then bitterly stammered, "Glamour? People are dying and you're talking about fucking glamour. Don't you see? It's all murder. The only way to quit . . . How can you shut yourself off behind all those . . . those mating games? There's just you and me, and we're both just here. We have to try."

"People aren't that way," she said. "They have to have —" David's choked cry cut her off. He ran from her with his fists knotted in his pockets.

What got into him? Cathy wondered. All he could do was talk about it. Pathetic. I seem to be attracting a lot of freak-outs lately. What's wrong with me now?

"What do you want to see in San Francisco?" Chris asked.

"Everything," Jeff said. "What's on?"

"There's a Godard film. Do you like Godard?"

"I dunno," Jeff said. "I never been able to sit through one of his movies long enough to find out. But let's not go to a movie. I'd rather run around."

"There's a good group at the Fillmore, if you wanna rock'n' roll."

"Sounds great."

"Solid. We'll fix a snack and rumble on into the city."

"Are we gonna kill the fatted calf?" Jeff asked. "Or the fatted turnip?"

"You gross carnivores. Actually we're gonna have some head food. I made a dozen marijuana muffins. Special blend."

They ate them dripping with butter and honey, then climbed into Chris's panel truck and drove the winding road over Mount Tamalpais. The hemp came on so strong they had to pull over and get out. As they walked across a padding of pine needles, it seemed someone had waved a wand and spread a hush in the air. The space between redwoods washed with the echoes of eons of stillness. Jeff expected to see elves dancing in grave silence, or naked nymphs hiding among ferns. Then he saw the hillside as a potential ambush site, thinking of where to deploy his troops, likely avenues of approach into the enfilade, best locations for machine gun emplacements, the length and depth of the killing zone.

David stood off to the side, watching two ladybugs mount on a dead leaf. "I never knew there were boy ladybugs," he said with a short laugh.

The sound of his voice broke the spell, and they returned to the truck and drove on. Chris talked about his theory that the earth's wobbling in its orbit between Mars and Venus is what spins us between war and love. David stared at his reflection in the window and nervously tapped his foot.

San Francisco rose ahead of them, white and hilly, with Alcatraz nestled in the bay looking like one of the muffins they had just eaten. The cerulean water winked and danced. Sailboats floated by—thin, wind-driven crescents. Bounding motorboats slashed white wakes. Gulls winged by, waving.

Once across the bridge, they were shocked by the jumble of concrete and noise. David took out his camera and began shooting pictures, pretending the viewfinder was a rifle sight.

They ate a long dinner in a Japanese restaurant, and when they came out it was evening. Chris lit a joint as they walked to the Fillmore.

"Don't you worry about getting busted, smoking on the street?" Jeff asked.

"Nah, no way. They can only bust you if you think they can. They don't have any power over us. We got psychic immunity. Besides," Chris laughed, "there's always a breeze in San Francisco."

They smoked and walked and watched the trolley wires flash in the plum-colored fog.

Inside the auditorium, drums pounded like the heartbeat of a wounded animal, guitars ripped like bear claws, and a mad voice wailed above it all. The musicians lurched around the stage, glutted with power.

All anyone could do was dance. Hundreds of girls shook inside cocoons of sound. So this is where they keep the women, David thought as he hopped up and down.

The light show splashed colors throughout the room. It melded bodies and walls, washed out face features and the yearning lost looks of might-have-been lovers.

David bopped over to a girl and hollered, "Hey, do you want to dance?"

"I am dancing," she said and writhed off.

He tried talking to girls between songs. "What group is this?"

"The Dead."

"They're really good. Would you like to dance to the next one? Or maybe go out for a drink?"

"I don't date straights."

Why can't one of them? It wouldn't matter what she looked like. From two inches away, everybody's beautiful. But it won't happen. I'm going to crack up, and it won't even matter. He saw himself facing the world with a twisted leer and an M-16 rifle. Next stop, Vietnam. War is the only door unslammed.

David stood on the dance floor, lost in a barrage of noise and flashing lights.

Music was flooding onto the sidewalk as they left.

"Have a good time?" Chris asked Jeff.

"OK time, but it was too loud."

"It's second chakra music. Like, shock rock . . . cock rock. Supposed to jolt you all the way from your frontal lobes to your scrotum."

"It tried."

They climbed into the truck and headed for North Beach.

"Want to smoke some more dope?" Chris asked.

"Not me," Jeff said. "I've had it."

David shook his head silently.

The place they stopped at for coffee was brightly lit and shiny with mirrors. Drinking cappuccino, David was again mesmerized by his reflection. He longed to dissolve, to be but a ricochet of light on the glass, too quick to be caught.

Jeff sat beside him, looking at a poster above the counter. FLAPPING YOUR ARMS CAN BE FLYING, it read, in frosted Day-Glo colors. Jeff snorted and said, "Glad the Wright brothers didn't believe that." He turned to David. "Well, so much for civilianville. Nothing really happening here either."

"No. It doesn't make it," David said. "Not for us, at least."

Cautiously, Chris said, "You're actually going to go, huh? Run over there and dance with Kali? I was hoping you'd change your minds. Thought you might decide you had better things to do."

"No. There's nothing to do," David muttered.

"Well, OK . . . it's your karma."

They pushed out the door and walked past the dark locked shops with bag-wrapped wine bottles on the steps, past empty salami crates from Genoa, shoyu barrels from Tokyo, down a side street to the truck, and then drove out of the city across the Golden Gate and over the breathing mountain to Stinson Beach.

Jeff took a late walk along the shore. The water was smooth, the air still, and waves fell with hollow crashes. A gauze of cloud hid the stars, but the moon shone through. Taking off his shoes, Jeff walked down the beach with his eyes closed, enjoying the uncertainty of blind footsteps. He stubbed his toe on a log and faltered into several sandy depressions, but kept on, wandering sometimes into the water, sometimes into the prickly dune grass, hands braced for a fall. He felt he was stepping through empty space, inventing the universe under his feet.

David sat in the garden watching the moon's reflection waver through the floating algae of the pond. No fish, he thought. Just moss and frogs and water like crankcase oil. And me. Tossed up on the far shore like a duck drowned in an oil slick. The coin has been flipped, and the other side is murder. Let's go.

Saigon steamed under photogray skies. Miles of fetid air filtered the everywhere sun. Stepping off the plane, the men felt the city first in their noses and lungs. It was like walking into the bottom of a compost heap of fermenting odors. Motor exhaust, decaying plants, rotting bug bodies, wood and tobacco smoke, spoiled food, food already digested and deposited, incense, and flowers, all heated and stirred with water vapor to keep it from exploding. The men breathed the fumes deeply to absorb what little oxygen was left.

Madsen and Sloane rode to the Special Forces compound through noise and dust and a streaming menagerie of vehicles: three-wheeled autos and front-driven motorbikes, aged Citroens and Renaults, Vespa scooters, bicycles, bull-snouted armored cars, cyclo pedicabs, army deuce-and-a-halfs, staff cars, and jeeps. Dainty young women rode sidesaddle on the backs of zipping Hondas. Dogs trotted through the dust of rumbling trucks.

Madsen saw men with guns and buildings with wire mesh grenade screens. It's for real over here, he thought, sweating inside his heavy uniform. Finally where the action is. The women excited him, too. "Look at that," he said to Sloane. "Can't wait to get into one of those sexy Vietnamese vixens."

"Maybe we can go to town tonight," Sloane said.

But the new group commander had put Saigon off limits to all Special Forces personnel, due to a shortage of penicillin. They drank beer in the NCO club and eavesdropped on the conversations of men who were going home. The stories challenged them, and made them feel callow.

The next morning the operations sergeant told Madsen he had to be on a plane at noon to fly to group headquarters at Nha Trang. "Radio operators are in short supply over here," he said. Madsen hoped that wasn't because they had short life expectancies.

Sloane sat down dumbly when Madsen told him he was leaving in an hour. "That's rotten," he said finally. "That's not fair. We just got here. Fucking army . . . We might not see each other."

He went to the operations sergeant and tried to get on the same plane, but the sergeant said he had to stay two more days. "Sorry about that. You got the wrong MOS. Demo men are a dime a dozen."

That night Sloane put on civilian clothes and took a cyclo into town, ignoring the ban. This is what Jeff would've done. I'll go around and carouse and get laid and have a rip of a time. What can they do if they catch me? Send me to Vietnam?

Downtown there were trees and wide streets and buildings with curved corners. Sloane walked around, pleased to be in a foreign city. The people were pliant and graceful, attractive in a chaste way. Their language was fast and soft and sounded like kittens crying. Although it didn't seem at all Indo-European, it was written in Western characters. Sloane wished it had been all squiggles and slashes, as it sounded.

While he was walking the sky darkened and the wind stopped; as the street grew quiet, rain began to fall. With the first few drops, umbrellas appeared and people walked faster, crowding the awnings. Sloane found a café that wasn't full and watched the storm build.

With the sky pouring water, everyone stayed inside except the children. They bunched up under awnings and balconies, taunting each other to go out. The dares turned to shoves until a kid of about five was dragged into the deluge by two big guys—about seven. All three were instantly drenched, to the laughter of everyone. Since they were sopping, there was nothing for it but to get naked and enjoy all the water. They skinnied out of their pants and shirts, flipped away their sandals, and went skipping, kicking—bare butts wiggling, little dicks bouncing—through the rain.

Within a minute six more naked, shiny wet bodies were squirming and shrieking at one another, wrestling in the puddles that swamped over the curbs. They writhed, hitting, spitting, splashing water, knocking each other down, piling on one another—a Laocoön of little bodies, twisting and rolling. Laughs, screams, and jabber blended with the sound of rain.

Occasional raincoated and umbrellaed adult passersby were greeted with howls of derision and splashed unmercifully. A jeep stopped at the light, the passenger side covered by a bright floral umbrella. Kids swarmed the jeep, jumping on the hood, waving through the windshield in mad giggle glee. They snatched away the umbrella, revealing a startled Vietnamese courtesan, dressed luxe and European, and her red-faced American officer escort.

Delighted, the kids danced around the jeep, kicking water in through the sides, spouting it from their mouths on the major and his mistress. Several tried to crawl inside but were beaten off with petulant and furious slaps. The girls did coquettish, mocking dances for the officer. The boys waved their dicks at the courtesan. She sat stiffly, her face white and expressionless. He revved the engine threateningly but was afraid to run the light. Finally it changed. He slammed the jeep into gear and roared off. The children returned to their games.

To play naked in warm rain, Sloane thought. Never played naked with other kids. These kids must do it all the time.

The rain stopped almost as quickly as it had begun. Sloane meandered along the tiled sidewalks, looking into the shops, enjoying the washed air and early evening coolness. He found a slow brown river bordered by small parks and floating restaurants. Lovers strolled arm in arm, watching the river flow, wincing at the occasional distant sounds of artillery.

Sloane had dinner on the water. A girl with a keening voice sang songs he did not understand. The haze turned to night, and with the night came more rain. He drank wine and watched lightning break the sky. With each flash he caught a different scene: a sudden baffled bird flying sideways in the wind; a woman in a canoe, one arm working the oar, the other clutching a child; freighters docked three abreast at the waterfront; a drenched, bareheaded man shouting directions on the prow of a tug; one oblivious floating duck; smoke rising into the rain from huts across the river; clouds stacking to make temples. Rain pocked the river. The river yielded.

Each burst of thunder excited Sloane. Again he promised himself that he would spend the night with a woman.

Hailing a taxi, he went to a club he had heard about at the compound. It was owned by a Parisienne who had been a wealthy call girl before the French were driven from Vietnam. The bar was almost empty. The proprietress sat at one end near the cash register giving instructions in French to the Vietnamese bartender. An oil painting of her lying nude on velvet drapery showed how she'd looked fifteen years ago. She was still attractive and mannered, and Sloane thought the wrinkles around her eyes made her look worldly.

He sat at the other end of the bar near a glass brick window. The people and streetlights and cars outside appeared rippled and green. He drank Scotch and tried to decide whether he was looking into an aquarium at a submerged world or whether he was inside the aquarium peering out at the real world. How could he tell? Through the liquor, it seemed an important question. He drank some more and wished Madsen were here with him.

The lady looked at him awhile, then got up and walked over. "And may I join you?" she asked in a voice drenched in cognac and French. Sloane nodded and tried to smile but could not speak. She had the bartender bring over her padded wicker stool, her brandy snifter, and her bottle of Courvoisier. "It is not many I join. It is a great compliment that I join you."

"Thank you. . . . Nice place you have here," Sloane said in an anxious grab at conversation.

"No . . . no, not now. But years ago . . . you should have seen me years ago." She gestured dramatically at the painting above the bar.

Sloane looked at it but couldn't say anything.

"Oh, another shy one. I had a shy one like you . . . years ago. And he, too, was tall. A tall, fine young man. One springtime we had together. In Hanoi. Before . . . before they ate him up." She was silent, staring into her glass. "So long ago that was. . . . But we should not talk of such things." She sat up and forced a smile. "It is not that time now, and a fine young man like you will want to go upstairs to the young girls."

Sloane was mute.

"Ah, not ready yet. Well, you stay down here as long as you like." She poured cognac halfway up the snifter. "You will have some more whisky?"

Sloane drank, his mind spinning. To make it with her . . . What would it be like?

"There are so many young Americans now . . . and before them so many young Frenchmen. I've seen them all come, chéri, and I've seen them all go. Ah, all the beautiful St.-Cyr cadets. You should have seen them, each new class as they marched through Hanoi. Proud, heads up, those shiny black boots and parachute wings. Essence of French esprit impérial."

She took a long drink. "And then those who came back. They were broken, mon ami. They could not look you in the eye. Convicts, they were. And then the others came. The People's Army. The Victorious People's Army. The ones who had turned all those . . . all those gleaming . . . those fine strong young boys into wrecks, hollow stumbling wrecks. They came to Hanoi. And they were the ugly brown little smelly men. The gibbering monkeys who peddle the cyclos and pack merde into bricks for burning. These were the men. Ah, you cannot call them men. Gobblers, cannibals. . . . They ate up all our fine young boys."

She patted his hand and looked at him with bitterness. "And it will happen to you, chéri. To you and all your camarades. All be eaten by the brown gobblers. It makes me weep to think of it."

She daubed her eyes with a lace handkerchief and patted Sloane's leg. "But I should not talk so. Enough tristesse. Come, drink your whisky. You are still young."

Sloane got up, feeling frozen. He tried to think of something to say. He put some money on the bar.

"Ah . . . you are not ready to stay. Now you are very young. You can come back when you are ready. Bonne chance."

Sloane felt shivers along his back as he walked from the club. Outside, the rain-brought coolness had worn off, and it was again stifling.

Madsen walked around the 5th Special Forces Group headquarters at Nha Trang looking at the sandbagged buildings, mortar pits, displays of captured weapons, Nung mercenaries wearing camouflage fatigues and carrying submachine guns, listened to the talk of last month's rocket attack and the big operation going on near the border, and was impressed. A real war, he thought. I'm in a war. I wonder if this is how my old man felt?

But he soon discovered it was still the army, even in a combat zone. He spent all afternoon sitting in the personnel office while the clerks processed his 201 file. He looked at the rows of drowsy typists, the gray filing cabinets, the meaningless directives on the walls. At least it won't be this way when I get to my team.

Madsen was slipping off into a garrison stupor when a colonel banged through the door. A gloss of sweat shone on the tight bulgy flesh of his bald head, making him look like a freshly peeled hard-boiled egg.

"Ten-hut," the sergeant major yelled.

As soon as everyone had struggled up from his desk, the colonel said, "Keep your seats, men." He strode into an office, and the room settled back down.

No, Madsen thought. Not the same games over here. "Who the hell is he?" he asked a sergeant on his left.

"That sorry fucker is the group commander. He was a leg until a couple of months ago. They brought him in to wreck the Forces. Turn it into just another conventional outfit."

"Why do they want to do that?"

"Why? Shit. We were doin' too good a job. Killin' too many VC. Rest of the army was lookin' bad."

Finally his name was called and a personnel sergeant told him, "Madsen, you're being assigned to Two Corps. They got priority on all commo replacements now. You'll go to the C-team at Pleiku, and they'll send you out from there. Go over to S-4 and draw your gear. Be ready to ship out by noon tomorrow."

The supply people gave him jungle boots, camouflage fatigues, nylon rucksack, collapsible canteen, pistol belt, ammo pouches, compress bandage, and, most important, a rifle. "Here it is," the supply sergeant said. "One each XM-16E1, commonly called the plastic death machine. Give 'em hell."

Madsen examined it carefully. He drew back the bolt and looked inside. He checked the action and the sights. He felt as if he were being introduced to someone who would play a crucial part in his life. He wanted it to like him. He hoped it worked. The chamber was a little dirty, and the stock was scratched. He wondered about the guy who had had it before. Did he make it OK?

Madsen rode to town that evening. In a flooded field near the compound a girl waded, ochre water up to her thighs, transplanting new spring rice. The paddies gave way to row after row of tin and cinder block barracks and warehouses. On the other side of the road was the ocean. He looked at the blue water through the spirals of barbed wire strung along the beach. A huge gray warship rode in the harbor. In its shadow, men in a fishing boat were casting their nets.

The downtown buildings were mostly two or three stories of pastel stucco. They were a blend of tiled roofs, sandbagged entranceways, tree-shaded courtyards, steel shutters, balconies hung with barbed wire and flowers.

Madsen walked around until he found Marie Kim's, the unanimously recommended whorehouse. Inside, the Supremes sang "Where Did Our Love Go." Bodies milled through the dim blue light. Shouted talk and laughter fought with the music. Beneath it was the churning drone of air conditioners recirculating stale air redolent of cigarette smoke, beer, and perfume.

Two girls came up and asked him to buy them drinks. He wanted to see what the others were like so he told them no. Ordering a bourbon at the bar, he looked at the women. So graceful, he thought. Willowy. Don't seem to have much fire, though. Maybe they save it for bed.

He saw the back of one's head, straight black hair in braids, and was jogged back to the first time and an Indian girl who wore her straight black hair in braids and whispered wondrous things in Madsen's ear as he moved on top of her on the floor of a boxcar. Madsen felt his chest tighten and his breath catch in his throat. To have her again. It'll never happen. Even the real girl couldn't live up to the memory. But this little one was nice. She'd be fine for tonight.

He intercepted her on her way back. "Come have a drink with me."

"I no can do now. You wait ten minutes, I come see you."

When she finished her drink at another table, she came and sat beside Madsen. She had a bright face and busy eyes. "You buy me Saigon tea?" she asked.

"What the hell is Saigon tea?"

"You no know Saigon tea? How long you been Vietnam?"

"Two days."

"Ooh. You cherry boy. Saigon tea number one. You drink whikkey; you buy me Saigon tea. Cost two hundred P. Very cheap. Other bar cost three hundred P."

"OK, Saigon tea it is. Why'd you leave your boyfriend over there to come and sit with me?"

"He no my boyfriend. I sit with him one hour, he buy me two Saigon tea. Number ten. I like you. Two days Vietnam, you buy me boocoo Saigon tea."

He tasted it when it came. It was Seven-Up. At least they could put a little crème de menthe in it like they do in Mexico. "What's your name?"

"Mai."

"Pretty name."

"What your name?"

"Jeff."

"I like you, Jeff," she said, patting his crotch. He smiled and she smiled back, showing a front tooth plated with gold except for a heart-shaped cutout where the enamel remained.

They danced close a couple of times, and he could smell her lilac perfume and feel her supple leanness. I want her now, he thought. To hell with that Saigon tea.

"Let's go upstairs."

"No. No can do. We drink first. Beside . . . go upstairs cost boocoo money."

"How much?"

"One thousand P. One half hour."

He thought a moment. That's over eight bucks. More than it costs in Fayetteville. Have to do it, though. Don't know when I'll have another chance.

"OK. A thousand P."

"No. You buy me one more Saigon tea."

"Fuck a bunch of Saigon tea." He pushed a thousand-piaster note into her pocket and led her upstairs.

Inside her gray cubicle she lit a cone of incense. He held her from behind and stripped off her loose nylon pajamas. A few lines around her mouth told him she was older than he, but she was small and thin as that long-ago girl and had the same budding breasts and skinny hips and faint fuzz of hair at her center.

While she stood watching the neon sign flash outside the window, he watched her lithe nakedness and pulled off his clothes. Their bodies touched, and he rose rigid against her. They lay down on the thin mattress. He kissed her and his fingers sought the way into her. Teasing her nipples with his teeth, he thought of that other time, of slipping between a pair of skinny legs into a new world. He stroked her lower lips; they moistened, and her legs spread. But when he touched her clitoris, she giggled and squirmed away.

"No. Number ten."

"You just never been done right, baby . . . that's all. Just relax and let me give you a surprise." Starting at her toes, he flicked his tongue up the inside of her leg into the soft wet folds of her tangy sex. He sucked her slowly, holding her down with one hand.

"No, no . . . no can do," she said, kicking her feet and pulling his hair. "Boocoo tickle. Vietnam girl no like tickle. You fuckee fuckee now. Fifteen minute we fini."

OK, he thought, have it your way. He rose above her and she grabbed his phallus and steered it into her.

Madsen sighed as he slid into the wet warmth. He moved in her slowly, pulling almost all the way out and pushing back in. She lay there staring at the ceiling with her mouth slightly open.

This won't do, thought Madsen after several minutes of no response. He scooped her up in his arms, rolled to the edge of the bed, and stood up.

"What you do? You dinky-dow GI," she said, hitting him on the back with little fists.

He hoisted her by her haunches and rode her up and down on his cock.

"Choi oi!" she said, closing her eyes and wrapping her legs around him.

The next day Madsen flew to Pleiku and spent a week

learning the different commo networks and radios used in Vietnam and the organization of the Special Forces Group—four C-teams, one for each corps area, each with three or four B-teams under it, and finally the A-teams, seven to ten for each B-team.

Madsen was sent to the B-team at Qui Nhon and began working twelve-hour shifts in the radio room. He hated the noisy, numbing dullness of it and the frustration of sitting in a rear area copying messages from people who were doing the fighting. After a week he was pleased when the B-team sergeant major told him he would be leaving the next day for camp Cung Hoa.

He tossed his gear into the small Otter aircraft and climbed in. Finally going to my A-team, he thought. After all this time, I'm finally getting into the thick of it. The plane flew west toward the highlands and after half an hour banked sharply and circled around a camp on top of a hill. Looking through feathered prop blades, Madsen could see the land flickering by like an old-time movie.

A tall black sergeant with a sidelong lope came out to meet the plane on the dirt airstrip. "You're the new commo man?" he asked.

"Yeah."

"My name's Wells. I'm the intel sergeant. How long you been in-country?"

"About two weeks."

"You're doin' great. Only fifty to go. Ha. Makes me feel good every time I meet somebody who's got more time than me." They walked to the jeep. "How's the U.S.A.? Still hangin' in?"

"It's pretty dull."

"But the women, man. Are there still any round-eyed women left in the world?"

"You mean the kind that move?"

"Yeah, that's it. I see you been dippin' your dick into the

indigenous variety. Believe me, even that'll seem good after a couple of months out here."

"You mean there aren't any women?"

"It's hands off. The troops don't like us fucking their sisters. Prejudiced little bastards."

"So whaddaya do?"

"You fuck your fist, that's what ya do."

Wells drove fast, dodging potholes in the dirt road. The Montagnard guard at the camp gate saluted as they roared to the top of the hill. He skidded the jeep in a half circle and stopped near a cluster of flimsy buildings set around an observation tower.

The largest was the U.S. team house. They opened the screen door and entered an office area with two desks, a typewriter, and a briefing room with maps and camp diagrams on the wall.

"Put your stuff down," Wells said. "We'll go find Randall."

They walked past several sleeping rooms, curtained off with parachute cloth, through a kitchen complete with refrigerator, deep freeze, and kerosene stove, into a dining room with a bar in one corner covered with *Playboy* centerfolds. Ammo belts, grenade bandoliers, and M-16s hung on the walls. Coffee perked in an urn on a table. Two kittens played on the concrete floor.

"All the comforts of home," Madsen said.

"All except one," Wells said.

Two men came through the side door, and Wells introduced Madsen to the CO, Captain Langley, and the team sergeant, John Randall.

"Come on, Madsen," the captain said. "I'll show you your burrow."

Outside next to the team house sat a flat dome of concrete with radio antennas sprouting from it. They walked down a dugout stairway. It was dark and cool inside and smelled like an old cellar, concrete long damp and wood beginning to rot.

"Welcome to your new home," the captain said. "This is the

commo bunker. You'll be spending most of your time down here. You can sleep in either of these two bunks. It's the safest place in camp, so if we ever get hit, you'll have lots of company."

In the next room a sergeant sat encoding a message near two banks of buzzing radios. He stood up and Captain Langley said to him, "This is Jeff Madsen, your new partner."

"Hi. Sure am glad you're here. My name's Paul Torrez."

"Hi."

"Haven't had a second radio operator for two months now," Langley said. "Torrez has been working the job alone."

"What happened to the last one?" Madsen asked apprehensively.

"His tour was up. He's back at Bragg now."

"Do I get to go to town now?" Torrez asked.

"You'll have to wait a week to make sure Madsen knows the job. Torrez is the horniest man on the hill. Hasn't been off site in four months. Everybody on the team's afraid to take a shower with him."

"It's a lie," Torrez said.

The CO showed Madsen the rest of the camp. At the center was a cluster of buildings, including the U.S. team house, the LLDB Vietnamese Special Forces team house, a dispensary, a large storeroom, and quarters for the interpreters, mechanics, clerks, and recon platoon. The buildings were low with tin roofs and cement floors. Split bamboo matting served as walls, reinforced waist high with sandbags. Several battered, mud-caked trucks, a disordered clump of fuel drums, a shed housing a pair of 5kw generators, two squat and widely separated bunkers—one for ammunition and another for explosives—one four-deuce mortar pit, two 81mm mortar pits, one 57mm recoilless rifle, one .50-caliber machine gun—all this, plus miscellaneous sheds, washrooms, and outhouses, was enclosed by a shallow, crumbling trench and two spiraling coils of barbed concertina wire.

"This is the inner perimeter here," the captain said. "It's

our last line of defense. The troops live in the outer perimeter. Come on, I'll show you."

They walked through a barbed wire gate. A guard saluted and grinned at them. Taken aback, Madsen returned the salute awkwardly.

"We got about 400 CIDGs in the strike force. CIDG stands for Civilian Irregular Defense Group . . . and believe me, irregular is an understatement. Most of them are guys from the village. About half of them are Vietnamese and half are Montagnards. The Yards fight better and work harder, but they'd all just as soon sit on their asses. That's our biggest problem over here, getting these people off their asses."

The captain was a big man with strong arms, but his face was small and almost delicate. His eyes seemed always to be squinting.

"There're only eight of us here, Madsen, and everything we want to have done, we gotta convince the LLDB it's what they want to do. They're the ones who have to give the orders. So it's damned important we get along with them. You'll be working with the LLDB commo man sometimes. You got to try real hard to keep up good relations with him. But don't let him steal too much. And don't give him too many batteries. They sell the extras down in the village, and the VC get ahold of them. We had one of our troops killed last month from a mine set off by a U.S. battery. So at first, when he comes and asks for supplies, you check with Torrez or Randall."

The outer perimeter held more bunkers and mortar pits and machine gun emplacements. A zigzagged trench shielded by a low wall of sandbags connected the firing positions. The bunkers and gun sites were also sandbagged. The bags were old, and weeds grew from some of them.

Sandbags all over the place, Madsen thought. Must have been a bitch of a job filling them all.

Beyond the wall was a triple stack of concertina wire. The

lower slopes of the hill were covered with claymore mines and barbed wire barrier aprons.

"I don't see how anybody could get through all that," Madsen said.

"It'd take a hell of a lot of men, but if Charlie wanted it bad enough, he could take it. We're pretty isolated here. Closest Americans are at the SF camp at Chu Pong twenty miles up the river." Langley looked across the wire to the forest. Around the camp were waves of hills that rose to mountains far away. They were young and jagged and covered with green nappy rain forest. Below the camp, a mile away, a village straddled a crooked river.

Each day started the same. At 5:30 A.M. with five hours' sleep and a mild smudge of a hangover, Madsen stumbled out to start the generator. He was brought fully, painfully awake by the starter cord snapping his arm and leaving a welt or by gasoline pouring into his mouth from a siphon hose held a moment too long or, on mornings when things went right, by the scream of the generator as it built to cycles.

By 6:30 the team—sleepy-eyed, shaving cream behind their ears—was slumped around the big table in the team house, drinking coffee and waiting for eggs. "Come on, Cookie, grease the troops." The cook was addled and nervous. He had been an unsuccessful blacksmith in the village before the camp came. Now he was trying diligently to learn a new trade. And he was failing.

Mornings were spent sitting in front of the single-sideband radio with Torrez, copying messages from the B-team, encoding the daily sitrep, talking about women, the war, the army. To Madsen's discouragement, hours each day were consumed by paperwork—records and inventories of minutiae. In the afternoons, if he was lucky, there was work to be done outside the commo bunker. The generators needed an oil change, wiring had to be installed in the new CIDG canteen, old batteries had to be dumped down the outhouse to keep the VC from getting them.

The evening brought another load of messages, but it was more relaxed, and often he could drink beer and read and listen to the radios with one ear. Two sets had to be monitored. One was the single-sideband tuned to the B-team frequency, and the other was the Prick-25 turned to the operation in the field. A chaotic background wail of garbled voices, roaring static, and Vietnamese Morse code poured from both of them. The noise and beer and fatigue deadened his mind and abraded his nerves. Each bleep of code was another tiny jabbing needle.

By eleven or twelve he could sleep, but he would be awakened for guard duty once during the night. Guard duty involved sitting in the team house for an hour drinking coffee, monitoring the field radio, and watching bugs whirl around the solitary light bulb.

"Madsen, you've been working too hard," John Randall, the team sergeant, said after several weeks of this routine. "There's a Caribou full of tin coming in. You can help me offload it. Give you a chance to see the village."

They drove down the hill to the airstrip in a deuce-and-a-half truck with a squad of Montagnards. The plane made an awkward, casual landing, and the crew slid two pallets of tin down the rear ramp.

A small group of Vietnamese stood by the edge of the runway. One of them ran to the truck and asked Randall, "Where plane go, sergeant?"

"Nha Trang. You got people want to go there?"

"Yes, sergeant, six people."

"They got papers?"

"Yes, have."

"Wait here." He walked up the ramp and said to the crew chief, "We got six of them over there wanna go to Nha Trang. If you want to take them it's up to you."

"Shit. Well . . . OK, we're empty. Just make sure you check them out."

Randall went back and called to the interpreter. "Tell 'em to come over here, show me their papers." He turned to Madsen. "You look through their bags. A VC left a bomb on a plane in Three Corps couple months ago."

Madsen felt foolish looking through the flimsy tin suitcases full of clothes and food. What if I find a bomb? he thought. What do I do then? What if it's the kind that goes off when you open it up? Wish I was a demo man.

No bombs were found, and the plane took off with its six passengers. Madsen and Randall helped the Yards load the tin onto the truck. "Been waiting months for this tin," Randall said. "This time every damn bit of it goes to the refugee village. We want to get 'em some decent roofs before the monsoon. Twenty of them died of pneumonia last wet season."

Randall was from West Virginia, and his looks had a streak of sinewy Celtic meanness. His body was thin and hard, with veins standing out above the muscles. His face was narrow with high knobby cheekbones, a taut jawline, and eyebrows that grew together so that he appeared to be glaring continuously.

In the hot, somnambulant village, people sat in doorways or moved slowly through the heavy air—stepping, gliding on bicycles. They watched the large, clattering truck lumber through the small streets. A girl carrying her baby brother on her hip called out to one of the CIDG, and he answered.

They stopped in front of the only two-story building. "This is the ARVN detachment," Randall said. "We have to pick up the district chief. He's gotta go along to make it official. And we gotta go along to make sure he doesn't charge them for it."

The district chief wore tapered starched fatigues and freshly polished boots. Madsen wondered where he managed to find starch in Cung Hoa. From the way his pants bloused over his boot tops, Madsen knew he had tin cans inside to give a crisp military appearance. "Good afternoon, Sergeant Randall," he said formally.

"Good afternoon, Dai-uy Nhien," Randall replied. "This is Spec Four Madsen, the new man on the team."

The district chief nodded at Madsen.

In the main village the houses were stucco or thatch, depending on the wealth of the owner. But in the Montagnard refugee settlement they were made of sticks and built on stilts. The builds of the refugees were different, also. While the Vietnamese appeared slight, thin-boned, and fragile, the Yards were solid and strong, with hard, compressed bodies. Their skin was reddish brown, the color of rubbed wood, and smiles spread across their faces, showing gapped teeth. Their speech was like pony hooves over stones.

The district chief passed out the tin—two sheets to a family—while Randall and Madsen stood to the side. Afterward, the Montagnard headman asked them into his house. They left their boots outside and climbed up a notched ramp into a long room. As they entered, his wife covered her breasts with a sash and began fanning a charcoal fire, never looking at them. Mats of woven palm covered the stick floor. Against the walls were baskets, oil lamps, bedrolls, a loom with a half-finished breechcloth, fishing nets, a crossbow, a brass gong, two machetes, and a home-forged adz with handle worn to glowing smoothness. Pinned to the walls were pictures from advertisements in American magazines.

The headman brought out bottles of Vietnamese beer, and they sat crosslegged and drank the warm beer and complimented one another. The district chief was uncomfortable and anxious to leave. He kept making signals to Randall, but Randall ignored them and kept drinking toasts with the headman in a mixture of French, Rhadé, Vietnamese, and English. When the district chief stood up to leave, however, Randall and Madsen followed him out.

"Get your shit together, Madsen. You and me are going out on operation tomorrow," Randall told him.

Madsen was surprised and excited. "Where we going?"

"South of the river. Wells's got some intel about a VC company down there. He was supposed to go, but his leg's still bum. So it's you and me."

At last, Madsen thought, as he cleaned his M-16. At last something real is going to happen. Get to see what the war's all about. He realized that whether or not he came back depended to some extent on what he took out with him. The most important thing, he figured, was plenty of ammunition. He loaded fifteen twenty-round magazines. Then he thought, Jesus, what if I run out? No way to get more out there. So to be on the safe side he loaded five extras. Then he filled two canteens with water and taped a little bottle of iodine tablets to one. He went to the supply room and chose ten C-ration meals. Being able to open the cases and pick which meals he wanted gave him a new sense of power. Before, on field problems in the States, the cases were opened upside down so the labels wouldn't show, and everyone had to choose at random. It cheered him to think he would never again have to eat ham and lima beans.

Wells gave him the maps for the sectors they would be operating in, and Madsen covered them with contact acetate to protect them from water. He taped two hand grenades to his pistol belt harness. The grenades, pin rings exposed, hung on his chest. He imagined himself crawling over rough ground. A ring snags on a branch. The pin pulls out. He claws frantically at the tape—four and a half seconds to live.

Madsen very carefully fastened down the rings. Into his rucksack, on top of the food and ammunition, he put a compass, flashlight, binoculars, signal mirror, first aid kit, several changes of socks, one extra pair of underwear, hammock, poncho, suspension line, and poncho liner. He had to rearrange it all several times to get it to fit. He put the rucksack on and walked around camp with it. It was damned heavy, but he figured better too much than not enough. After all, Rogers's Rangers first rule of patrolling was "Don't forget nothin'." This isn't like a hike back in the States, he told himself. Here it really counts.

It was five o'clock in the morning and dark when they filed out of the camp and down the hill. Before he reached the bottom, Madsen's pack had become a sagging weight. Sweat, smelling of soured beer, rolled down his sides. His muscles were stiff and silted with acids from two months of inactivity. Now the toxins poured into his bloodstream, making him feel groggy.

The sun was just coming up, beautiful and unwelcome. Madsen had already drunk half a canteen. He could see the rest of the column now, a hundred men strung out and plodding. They carried many kinds of weapons: stubby grease guns like mechanics' tools, A-6 machine guns with tapered metal stocks, chunky Thompson submachine guns that Madsen thought were used only in James Cagney movies, M-79 grenade launchers with wide, short barrels that could have shot whiffle balls, small carbines that reminded Madsen of the rifles in carnival shooting galleries. He hoped they were more accurate. Randall held a sleek but scarred Swedish K. The littlest Yard Madsen could see was festooned with belts of machine gun ammunition, and carried an M-1 almost as big as he was. He looked like a twelve-year-old masquerading as a Mexican bandit. But we're all pretty weird, he thought, wearing clothes supposed to look like leaves, carrying all these toy guns. Bunch of kids out for trick or treat.

"If we get hit," said Randall, "you grab hold of that guy packing the radio and don't let him get more than two feet away from you. And don't you get more than two feet away from me."

"Got it."

"First thing you do is call back to camp and tell them to send us a plane. And then you see if you're still in one piece."

"OK."

The mountains to the south grew slowly larger and by late morning Madsen could see the tallest trees standing out above the crumpled green mat of rain forest that hung in loose folds from peak to ridge of the building hills. It had not rained for several weeks and the green was the dusty gray green the navy paints everything, and Madsen felt dry looking at it. He drank the last of his water, hoping to find a stream when they reached the mountains.

The land began to rise and became clotted with vegetation. The trees grew taller until other trees were growing beneath them. The tallest trees seemed to reach as high as a football field was long. Their trunks were smooth and limbless for most of their length. Then they branched into a spacy webbed roof. What a great place to be a monkey, Madsen thought. Chasing around up there. I wonder why we ever came down.

On the ground it was dark, and only occasional splotches of light splashed on their fatigues. The air was hot and stagnant. It seemed to cling and trail like smoke, in resentment at being stirred. The lower plants were a snarl of bushes, vines, and stunted trees. They and the exotic flowers they bore were the kind of plants Madsen thought grew only in florist shops. Seeing them wild and real supplied the same alarm as skin-diving in Mexico for the first time and discovering that tropical fish come from the ocean.

But the streams were dry here, and soon Madsen began to droop along with the foliage. His eyes felt pinched, his tongue swollen, and the only moisture in his mouth came from the bile that retched up from his stomach. Everyone else seemed to have water, but he'd be damned if he'd ask anyone for some.

The trail became much steeper, and soon it was not a trail at all, but a rocky flume leading straight up the hillside. Just enough water seeped from the ground to make it muddy and tease Madsen's thirst. He had to clamber over the large rocks, pushing with his knees and elbows, and several times he slipped on some mossy mucus and left blood from his knees and elbows on the rocks.

Soon he was stiff with pain and exhaustion. The weight of his pack made him feel a thousand years old. His shoulders were molten and his stomach cut with cramps. Rocks that he normally could have climbed over with ease he now had to sit on and swing his legs over. The other men seemed not to be suffering as much. The strikers exchanged grins at the American's plight. All Randall said was "How's it hangin'?" to which Madsen could only grunt.

He withdrew deep into himself, dropped through oceans of tiredness, twined in a silent rapt struggle with his pain. His breath came in shallow, fast, sobbing gasps. He could not remember where they were going or why. He was no longer sure it would end. He had forgotten why he could not stop and collapse, but knew it was not a possibility open to him. There was only one course: to continue to march. He had no other life beyond this immediate struggle.

They broke out of the ravine into a dazzle of sunlight on the edge of a plateau that ran for miles. The column stopped. Madsen couldn't believe he was sitting down and blinking and rolling out of his pack and it was over. There was even a breeze, and he took off his shirt. I did it, he thought over and over. I didn't give up. I made it to the top.

Randall walked back to where he was sitting. "We'll rest here about ten minutes. I got one platoon out on guard. You look pretty dry."

"Yeah." Thirst screeched in his body.

"How many canteens you bring?"

"Two."

"That's not hardly enough. Guess you found that out."

"Yeah."

"There's supposed to be water about a click from here . . . if it's not all dried up. What you can do in the meantime is take a pebble and keep rolling it around in your mouth. Stirs up the spit."

"Thanks."

The rest was long enough for Madsen's muscles to get stiff, but not long enough for them to recover. Within twenty minutes he was again trudging dumbly in a shell of pain. Now the sun filled everything, bounced off each blade of grass into his squinted eyes. The grass was waist high, and spears sliced his hands.

The strikers began whispering, "Nuoc, nuoc," and Randall said, "They got water up ahead." The words roused Madsen from his stupor. He saw himself splashing nude and cool in a bubbling stream, spouting water from his mouth.

The stream turned out to be a murky pothole three feet wide with water as gray and translucent as a dog's eye. Madsen stared in choking disappointment. Suddenly he was desperately thirsty, and it might be hours before they found drinkable water. Then he watched unbelieving as Randall pushed his canteens through the surface scum down into the pool.

"Don't you want some water?" the sergeant asked, his bald spot glistening in the sun.

Madsen couldn't answer.

"Come on. The strikers won't fill their canteens till we're through. They know how Americans get upset if the water's all stirred up and dirty."

"You mean we can drink it?"

"Drink it? Shit. You can drink anything that pours, long as you put two iodine tablets in it. This is good water. There's a spring down there."

Madsen pushed his canteens into the pool. Instead of being warm and greasy, the water was a cool delight to his hands. He dropped three tablets into each canteen and shook them to make them dissolve faster.

For the rest of the afternoon he rationed his water carefully, taking small sips and swirling them around in his mouth before swallowing them. The pack dragged his steps. He walked on, suspended underneath the sun, swaying toward delirium. When Randall said, "We'll stop here for the night," the words didn't register for about thirty seconds. Then some part of Madsen smiled, and he sat down in a glassy heap.

"Pretty bushed, huh?" Randall said.

"Yeah," he said, looking up. "I guess I'm in worse shape than I thought."

"You'll feel better tomorrow."

Madsen doubted it. It'll probably get worse and worse. Five days. God, can I make it? He ate the contents of the three heaviest cans in his pack, tied his hammock between two trees, and collapsed into it. Weightlessly rocking back and forth, he felt luxurious sleep approaching. His body jerked and twitched as it relaxed. Tomorrow. Damn. I've got to keep going, no matter what. If I crap out now, the whole team will find out. I've got to make it. The others don't seem to be hurting so much. Randall acts like he's just been out for a stroll. I must really be in sad shape. Have to start exercising more. Randall's turned out to be a real hard-ass. Can't let him see how beat I am.

Morning came fast and beautiful. The air was cool and the sky pastel blue. A bird even sang. Madsen had coffee and a can of peaches. He was stiff and sore, but the exertion had cleaned him out and he felt lighter. His shoulders ached as soon as he put on the pack. The land was rolling and grassy and rimmed with mountains. Looks like Africa, Madsen thought. He walked across it pretending he was on safari, hunting eland with a company of native bearers. Then he realized people on safari probably pretend they're on a combat patrol hunting men. Trouble with people is they're never satisfied.

"Do you know where we are?" Randall asked when they stopped for lunch.

"Well . . . we're still on that big plateau. And we're going south."

"No, I mean exactly . . . the map coordinates. What if we got hit now, could you call in air support? Where would you tell the planes to come?"

Madsen took out his map and compass and aligned them. I better be right, he thought tensely. Randall doesn't seem like he'd allow too many mistakes. He looked at the terrain and then at the maze of contour lines on the map. A cluster of narrowing vermiculations stood out from the rest. "This must be that mountain over there. We can shoot off it to get a back azimuth." He sighted at the peak through the compass. "OK . . . that'll put us along this line someplace. Now if we can get another reference point. That little butte over there." He sighted again. "That puts us here. OK, let me check. We're on kind of a knoll . . . and there's that ravine off to the west. Yeah, I'd say we're here."

"You sure? You got the lives of a hundred men depending on your decision. Most important of all, you got my life depending on it. You gotta be sure."

Madsen looked again. "Yeah, this is it. And that must be that ridge line over there."

"Well, I guess you did learn something in branch. But you should get a feel for it so you don't have to shoot azimuths, so you can just look at the land and find yourself on the map. You should get so you can look at a mountain and tell what the other side is going to be like. But you did real good. You'd be surprised how many people they send out to A-teams who can't read a map. Officers especially. I've had to teach West Point captains how to read a goddamn map."

Madsen started checking their position every half hour. He noticed when they changed direction and tried to keep track of how many clicks—kilometers—they had gone. You did real good, he repeated Randall's words to himself.

He gradually slipped back into the aching sack of flesh his body had become. Running sweat stung his eyes. His socks kept wrinkling under his feet, rubbing blisters in new places. His underpants were bunched up in the crack of his ass. He kept having to boost the pack higher on his shoulders to keep it from digging into his kidneys.

Most of the country was still open and climbing toward another range of mountains but occasionally they had to cross steep, stream-worn ravines. They would descend sliding and scraping, their hands slashed by thorns. When blood oozed from the cuts, flies landed to drink it. At the bottom they slopped through the stream, tromping leaves into the water, watching them turn silver as they went under. Then they scrambled up the other side, pulling and clutching and swearing.

They stopped for the night at the top of a small hill. Madsen was glad to rest, but this time he knew he could walk farther if he had to. Instead of eating cold C-rations and collapsing as he had done yesterday, he forced himself to wash his face and hands, cook a meal, and dry his socks.

"That's about the biggest damn pack I've seen over here, Madsen. What'd you do, put your girl friend in it? Special Forces supposed to travel light."

"It all seemed like necessary stuff."

"Let's see that pack. Let's see what you got in here," Randall said. He turned it upside down and dumped everything out. "Goddamn, no wonder your ass is dragging. Look at this shit. You're young and dumb, Madsen. You don't want to bring C-rations out here. Weighs a ton. Why didn't you bring the rice packets, like everybody else?"

"Where do you get those?"

"Down in the supply room. Boxes of them, all different kinds. Fish, chicken, beef, all freeze-dried. Weighs about a third of what C-rations do."

Madsen stood there feeling foolish.

"And another thing, Madsen. How many magazines you got here?"

"Uh, I got twenty, including the one in my rifle."

"Look, I know you're eager as hell to win the war, but that's way too much ammo. You just want about six magazines on your belt, and maybe three or four cartridge boxes in your pack. You know, the paper ones. No point in carrying any more metal around than you have to. That way you can just refill the magazines. Two hundreds rounds is plenty. If we get into such deep shit that you run out, well . . . there'll be plenty of carbines laying around from all the strikers that got shot or ran off. You can shoot a carbine, can't you?"

"Yeah . . . we fired them at Bragg."

"OK, the next thing is these binoculars. Around here Charlie stays in the trees, where these things ain't gonna help. Can't use binoculars in the jungle. And hand grenades . . . you can carry them if you want, but the damn things are heavy and dangerous, and you'll probably never get a chance to use one. The main reason the strikers carry them is to kill fish."

"Oh, OK. I always thought . . ." Madsen trailed off with a shrug.

"And underwear . . . I know you had a proper upbringing and all, but out on operation we don't even wear underwear, let alone bring out a clean pair. Just gets all caught up in the crack of your ass. Makes your balls sweat more. Damn,

Madsen, half the shit you got here you don't need. Considering all the weight you were lugging, it's a wonder you made it."

Madsen looked at all the useless equipment he had carried so many painful miles. He felt a flash of anger at Randall for not telling him beforehand. I did it, though, dammit. I kept on. If I had to, I could do it again. He wished he could throw the extra stuff away. Instead, he burned his underwear and went to bed.

They walked off the hill in the slanting early morning sun. The air was cool, about ninety degrees, and there was a slight breeze over the grass. So this is a search-and-destroy operation, Madsen thought. Walking around with a gun and a mean look. Oh, well. Something'll happen.

As the day wore on, Madsen's awareness again contracted to his immediate situation: the toes of his boots, the back of the man ahead, his own rank odor, and the smoky smell of the Yards, the sound of boots, the taste of vomit, the weight of the pack on his pulpy muscles. Occasionally he would pull himself out of his slogging trance long enough to check the map, so Randall wouldn't think he was unconscious. Then he would slide back.

He was nodding toward oblivion across a small clearing when gunfire splashed like ice water on his senses. Adrenaline surged through him like a piston, driving away pain and fatigue.

"We got contact at the point. Let's go," Randall yelled.

Madsen ran forward, one hand on the radioman's collar, eyes searching ahead, expecting at any moment to be shot. At the head of the column a small group of strikers stood in a circle talking and gesturing excitedly. Must've got a VC. Hope there's some left for us, he thought in exhilaration. We ought to be fanning out looking for the others. They'll get away. He pushed through the circle. In the center lay a large wild pig, dead.

The strikers were exultant. The one who had fired the fatal

shot was parading around with his rifle over his head, grinning and accepting congratulations. One of them pulled Madsen's sleeve: "Chop chop number one!"

"No wonder they're so excited," Randall said. "This is their biggest victory in months."

They dressed the pig and slung it on a pole and hauled the trophy up a small hill. "This is as far as we'll go today," Randall said. "LLDB wants to send out squad patrols from here."

"Can I go?" Madsen asked. He thought he would have a better chance of finding VC with a small group because they wouldn't make as much noise as the whole company clomping through the brush.

"You're all fired up, huh? Well, it's your first operation . . . but as long as you don't do anything stupid. That Yard squad leader knows a hell of a lot more than you do about the VC around here. So you go along with his program. And keep your ass down."

Madsen dropped his pack with a feeling of luxurious relief. To walk without fifty pounds of dead weight on his back was a new experience. He stepped lighter and higher, as though he were bouncing along on the moon.

The patrol moved fast, and they were soon out of sight of the company. Away from Randall, and with only ten men instead of a hundred, Madsen began to feel vulnerable. He checked his map every five minutes and stayed near the striker with the small walkie-talkie squad radio. The men were talking and tramping down bushes, rifles slung forgotten on their shoulders. He was sure any VC within half a mile could hear them. And it would take only a few VC to wipe them out. A couple of hand grenades. A mortar round. One piece of shrapnel in the radio and they'd be cut off from the company and any hope of air support. What if he got shot—zing, an awful sucking chest wound—and the VC came up and stood around him and shot him in the head?

The Yards ignored their peril and Madsen's gestures for them to be quiet. Whenever they came across anything edible, they burst into excited chatter and began filling their empty packs. A grove of wild banana trees caused them to call back to the company on the loud, squawking radio. The squad leader marked the place on his map for future reference while the men hacked away at the youngest trees. One gave Madsen a tender stalk and motioned him to chew it. The spongy fibers released a flow of cool, sweet water into his mouth. The mature trees bore large buds that would grow into banana bunches. These, too, went into the packs.

They were following a stream, and Madsen remembered his lessons about never walking along a stream bed because it's an ideal setup for an ambush. He looked at the slopes on both sides and realized that if they got hit they would be trapped in a perfect enfilade. His eyes searched for rustling bushes or protruding rifle barrels. The strikers were scanning the trees for fruit. They discovered a clump of sugarcane and set to with their machetes while Madsen stood guard. When they had as much as they could carry, they struggled back toward the company like farmers returning from the harvest.

At the bivouac, most of the men lay sleeping in hammocks. The rest were tossing armloads of wood onto a huge fire blazing in the afternoon heat. Randall was sitting near a smaller fire, heating water. He looked up as Madsen trekked in. "Welcome to Pork Chop Hill. How many VC you get?"

"Hell, it's a wonder they didn't get us. These guys . . . damn. Made as much noise as they could . . . and careless. More like a scavenger hunt than a patrol."

"That's why the guys on the team don't go out with squads. The recon platoon's the only one I'll go out with. They're not so bad. The leader used to be a VC . . . until they shot his brother. You want some coffee?"

"Hot as it is? I don't see how you could drink coffee."

"Cools you off. Best thing when it's hot. Warms up your insides so it don't seem so hot outside. Try it."

"OK, sure. What are they trying to do with that fire?"

"Fixing dinner. We're gonna have roast pig. They're building up a bed of coals. A big victory celebration."

Instead of impaling the pig on a spit and turning it above the fire, they simply tossed it onto the coals with a great cheer. The pig hissed and popped and swelled up. The odor of burning hair wafted away. In old ammo cans they cooked a mixture of pig's blood, limes, peppers, and bottled fish sauce. They boiled banana blossoms in water that they then poured into their bags of instant rice. The pig was turned to ensure that it would be done on both sides. They dragged it from the fire, chopped it into chunks, and knocked off the burnt outer crust. It was astoundingly good.

Lo-ee, the Montagnard interpreter, showed Madsen the protocol for dipping meat in the sauce, scooping some rice up, and munching it all together. They broke open the banana blossoms and ate the green sprouts inside.

"These things get you drunk, you eat enough of them," Randall said.

"Sounds good. I think we should open a franchise on the whole deal."

They had sugarcane for dessert. Madsen lay in his hammock chewing it, remembering as a kid sucking the sweetness from young cornstalks. Must be related to sugarcane. All those jointed segments . . . hollow inside. Bamboo, too. I wonder if bamboo is sweet? Today was a real picnic. That damn fire, though. All the smoke. Any VC'll have us pinpointed for sure. They'll hit us tonight, if they're any good. We should have moved to a new position after we ate. We should never have shot the pig.

The next day they began looping back toward the camp. The high, grassy plateau sloped down into brushland. Shrubs and trees slowed their progress. Soon the flanks had to be called in, and the whole company was snaking along single file through the tangled foliage. The trail narrowed more as it dropped into a ravine. Trees covered the sky, sealing them in a descending tunnel of humid vegetation. Although it hadn't rained in weeks, the plants dripped water. The ground was slick as a wet belly.

If we got hit in here, we couldn't get out, Madsen thought. They could seal off either end and chop us up. And what a place for booby traps. His eyes strained for trip wires. I'd hate to be that poor bastard on point.

The troops were quiet for the first time since the operation had begun, but despite Randall's motioning them to spread out, they walked close together, almost touching. "Christ," Randall swore under his breath, "the way they're bunched up in here, one claymore would wipe out half a platoon. You can tell they're scared when they shut up and stick to each other."

Madsen couldn't reply.

Relief flowed through the men as they broke into the light. Madsen was exhausted from the tension. When he recovered he asked Randall, "Why didn't they ambush us back there? Or at least put in a few booby traps? They must know where we are."

Randall looked at him. "You sound disappointed. Charlie gets lazy too, you know. Sometimes he's not much better than the CIDG. Don't forget, he's got to use these trails himself. He doesn't want them booby-trapped."

"They why don't we mine it with claymores . . . then come back in a month and take out the ones that aren't exploded?"

"A bunch of reasons. First, you'd end up killing some civilians, and Charlie loves us to do that more than anything."

"I thought the civilians from out here all lived in the refugee village now."

"They're supposed to, but they're mostly Yards, and they don't get along too good with the Vietnamese. So they get pissed off and split back out here. And think about the troops who'd be taking them out. You've seen these guys. They're worse than Boy Scouts. They'd either blow themselves up or just leave them in and hope it wasn't them that got it. And look, another thing about this is . . . you don't get a body count with a booby trap. A VC blows himself up, his buddies drag him off, and you never know. The way it works now, if it ain't gonna boost the body count, it ain't policy."

They walked on under the sun, and Madsen stopped thinking about booby traps and ambushes and just watched the trees hobble by. At noon they rested in an abandoned village. The people had left only a few years ago, but already the place was preparing itself for the archaeologists: shards of broken pots scattered in corners, grass growing through floors, walls crumbling, dirt climbing up steps. There was just enough thatch left on the roofs to shield the men from the pounding sun.

Madsen asked Lo-ee where the people had gone.

"They live Cung Hoa now."

"Why did they go?"

"Why they go? VC come, take rice, take men go fight. CIDG come, say, 'Everybody go Cung Hoa!' So they go. No can say no."

"Don't they come back?"

"Come back? Why come back? Maybe helicopt see . . . shoot."

"Maybe come back at night."

"Come back at night, maybe VC take . . . go fight."

Madsen watched ants carrying away a dead beetle. I'll bet if we patrolled more at night we'd get some action. There have to be VC around here someplace. Been out four days and nothing's happened. Where are the bastards?

They saw no VC that day or the next, and when the camp came into view, Madsen felt let down. "Don't you think we're doing something wrong, to be out for five days and not find any of them?" he asked Randall as they trudged the last hill.

"We're doing lots of things wrong . . . but it probably just means Charlie wasn't in the mood for a fight. You seem to be the only one in the mood for a fight around here. I'm just in the mood for a beer."

Madsen slipped out of his pack and stripped off his stinking clothes. A cool shower flushed away the sweat, grease, and dirt that had been blending on his skin like gravy for five days. A cold beer rinsed some of the heat and fatigue from his mind. He sat with Randall, and they felt tired and clean and self-satisfied.

"You did OK, Madsen. Thought we were gonna have to medevac you for a while there, but you gritted down and did just fine."

"Next time I'll know how to pack."

Wells came in rolling up some maps. He had a wide face, a medium dark complexion, and a closely trimmed moustache. "Look at our two heroes. My, aren't they spiffy . . . clean as a desert bone. What's this I hear about you putting each other in for the Silver Star? Holding off the charge of a VC pig. Tell me about it, Top. Was he going for Madsen's jugular vein when you drilled him through the head? I know what really happened. Madsen buggered the poor thing to death."

"Would you listen to that," Randall said. "You don't have to cheer us up, Wells. Just give me the bad news . . . everything that fell apart while I was gone. I know I can't be away from this place five days without things getting totally screwed up."

"Well, as a matter of fact . . ."

"I knew it."

"Seems our friend the district chief decided the Yards didn't deserve to stay dry. Went around and tried to charge them a hundred P. for each sheet of tin we gave them. When they couldn't pay, he took it back. Right off their roofs."

"That son of a bitch. Fuckin' sorry sack of shit. He makes the LLDB look honest. I knew by the way he looked at that tin he was going to try to get it. Where does he have it? Has he sold it yet?"

"No, it's stacked up in the compound. Guess he's waiting till the rainy season starts so he can get more for it."

"OK, tell the LLDB we're going to have to kick ass downtown. Madsen, you round up two squads of the meanest looking Yards you can find . . . from the recon platoon. They'll scare the shit out of that district chief and his Ruff-Puffs."

Soon they were roaring down the hill in a deuce-and-a-half. They skidded to a stop in front of the gate at district headquarters. "OK, champ," Randall hollered down to the Vietnamese guard, "get your boss out here. Yeah, you know who I mean."

The baffled guard called nervously over his shoulder. After a minute, the district chief emerged from the building buttoning his shirt.

"Tell him we've come to get our tin," Randall said to Lo-ee. "Tell him if he steals from the Montagnards again, the CIDG will burn his compound."

The district chief avoided Randall's eyes, but glared at Lo-ee and spoke to him contemptuously.

"He say he no steal tin," the translation came back. "Montagnard no can pay tax. He buy tin from them for pay tax. He say CIDG come on compound, he report you to province chief."

"Tell him refugees don't pay taxes, and if I hear of him trying to collect any, we'll arrest him. Tell him go ahead and call the province chief. Tell him he can call Ho Chi Minh for all I care."

The district chief replied in a high voice.

"He say CIDG come on compound, CIDG same-same VC. RF-PF shoot," Lo-ee translated.

"The RF-PF couldn't shoot their own toe." Randall shouted a few words of Rhadé, and all the strikers on the truck chambered shells into their rifles. Randall swung down from the truck and walked toward the barbed wire gate. The district chief thought he was after him and scurried to the other side of the truck. The guard at the gate stepped away before he was walked on. Randall grabbed the gate and dragged it open, and Wells drove the truck into the compound.

The RF-PF stood by nervously while the Montagnards jumped off the truck and started loading the tin. After a while the RF-PF went inside. Restraining his fury at being humiliated in front of his men, the district chief walked back and forth, staring at the ground.

When they were done, Randall spoke to the interpreter. "Tell him once more that if he steals from the Montagnards again, the CIDG will burn his compound."

"He say he go now to report you to province chief and American colonel."

"If he gets me mad enough, we'll burn the province chief's compound too."

The Montagnards gathered around the truck as it pulled into the refugee settlement, but drew back when they saw the tin.

"Lo-ee, tell them we brought it back for them," Randall said. "Tell them Rhadé soldiers won't let them get cheated."

After Lo-ee explained what had happened, they came back, talking and laughing with the soldiers and touching the tin. Randall had the CIDG pass it out this time. Afterward, the headman spoke to Randall.

"Sergeant, he say thank you. Rains come next week."

As they drove back up the hill, Randall said to Wells, "We'll have to watch our friend Nhien. He'll have to try and get back at us somehow. Especially we'll have to be sure he doesn't gyp them on their rice ration. Have your intel net keep a check on what happens down there. Madsen, if anyone asks you about it, I never threatened to burn him out."

"Sure, Top. . . . I thought it was great."

"We may have some chickenshit colonel down on our ass. But if we work these reports right, we'll get rid of that thievin' son of a bitch."

"Yeah, and they'll send us another one just as bad," Wells said.

"At least it'll take him a couple of months to learn the ropes. And listen, Madsen, don't get any ideas about our being the Peace Corps over here. Those Yards are the only good troops we got . . . and most of them are related to the refugees. So if you wanna keep the troop morale up, you gotta see their families don't get fucked over. The way it works is this: The higher their morale, the more VC they kill."

Torrez went to Pleiku to get laid, so Madsen was working sixteen hours a day. One night between messages, he and some operators from different A-teams were sending FTAs to one another. FTA stands for Fuck The Army and has a nice rhythm in Morse code. The B-team commo chief, Sergeant First Class Mundt, broke in on voice. "Cut that stuff out right now. Just 'cause you're out there on A-teams don't mean you're exempt from military discipline. If I hear any more unauthorized transmissions, I'm gonna put you in a hurt. And don't think I can't tell who's sending. I ain't been a commo chief for twelve years for nothin'."

Madsen laughed at the distant threat, and he and one other sent FTAs in reply.

"Regal Snuff, this is Bent Smoke, over."

Oh, shit, he thought. How did he know it was me? Maybe he doesn't. Maybe he just took a stab. Madsen waited ten seconds to make it seem as if he had been across the room. "This is Regal Snuff, over."

"Snuff this is Smoke. There's a new member of your team wants to talk to you. Over."

"Roger, go ahead."

Sloane's voice crackled over the radio. "Hello there, Regal Snuff, I'm coming to relieve your besieged garrison tomorrow."

"David! Hey, damn, that's great . . . outrageous. How did you swing it?"

"Just a little grease. Had to bribe a couple of personnel sergeants. Cost me a hundred bucks."

"Wow . . . it's really good to hear your voice. . . . Be great to have you on the team."

"What's it like out there?"

"Oh, it's OK. No worse than anyplace else, I guess. It's a good team."

"Are there a lot of VC? Do you make much contact?"

"Uh, not yet. I guess they're hiding till you get here."

"That's OK. The two of us together are bound to find them. Look, so I'll be in tomorrow. Can't wait to see you again."

"Right. I'm really glad you're coming. See you tomorrow." He hung up the mike. Old Sloane. A hundred bucks. I wouldn't have done it.

Madsen was reading the monthly bulletin from group headquarters at breakfast the next morning. One sheet, the one everybody read first, was made up of ten or so paragraphs, each one identical except for the name and serial number. Madsen stopped at one and reread it slowly with his breath catching: "Any personnel having claims against the estate of SSGT Ronald (NMI) Hein, RA 14873281, are hereby directed to notify S-1, SFOB, within 30 days of above date."

Madsen had never liked Hein, but now felt the loss as if he

had been a close friend. He dropped the paper and stared at his food, which was suddenly repulsive.
"What's the matter?" Randall asked.
"A guy I knew in training group . . . got killed."
"Who was it?"
"Hein."
"First time you've had to find out that way about a friend getting it?"
"Yeah."
"It's tough. It's a bitch. . . . I'm afraid it gets easier. Why don't you get outside for a while? Take a couple of hours off."

Sloane's chopper came in that afternoon. Madsen watched his friend's long body jump out and run awkwardly toward him, baggy fatigues flapping in the rotor wash. They laughed and grabbed each other's arms.
"So you bribed your way to Cung Hoa. That took some nerve."
"Hell, I wasn't going to let a little thing like army bureaucracy break up a friendship."
"Did you hear about Hein?"
"That son of a bitch. Is he over here?"
"He got killed. I just read about it."
"Well . . . then at least we don't have to worry about being on the same team with him."
"It seems really sad he died, though."
"Yeah, but hell . . . you didn't like him, did you? I mean, he was awful. All he did was hard-ass you."
"Yeah . . . but somehow it really made me feel bad. They don't even say where he was or how he got it. Just list his name."
"Hey, come on, show me around your fortress here. Have you been hit yet?"

Captain Langley explained to Sloane what he would be

doing. "You're stepping into an E-7 slot, you know, and I hope you can handle it. It's a damn big job. You've got the trenches, the claymores, and all the wire to keep up. Plus you have to supervise all the building that goes on in camp. And if you have any time left over, you'll be helping the people down in the village with their projects. First thing for you to get started on is the fougasse. We need at least a dozen barrels of it."

"Do you want them detonated from the mortar pits or from the bunkers?"

"All the demo is fired from the commo bunker. There's a board with the claymores already wired to it. You're going to have to check all the claymores, too. Sometimes the strikers take the C-4 out of them to cook their rice with. Oh, and another thing, there's a stump you'll have to blow. It's blocking our field of fire."

Blowing the stump appealed most to Sloane, so he decided to do it first. He got a detail of CIDG and began digging with them around the base. His hands became crusted with dirt and he had to stop and wash them. He prepared the blasting equipment while the strikers finished digging. When there was room under the roots, he inserted two blocks of C-4, then thought what the hell and tossed in another. He plugged the blasting caps into the plastic sockets with the CIDG looking over his shoulders, whispering. He ran the wire twenty meters back to a trench. Be close enough to feel it this way.

The strikers were talking and pointing excitedly. One tried to explain to him that this was too close, that he should be farther up the hill in a bunker. Sloane smiled and waved him off. He watched as they all ran back to the bunker and peeped out of the firing slit. They think I'm crazy.

He lay on his back in the trench so he could watch the sky fill with fire. "Fire in her hole," he yelled and spun the detonator and the ground punched him and the air was gone and it came back in a slapping crash of sound that shot white pain between his eyes and left him ringing and laughing. Dirt and splintered wood fell out of the sky and covered him. What a rush. What a rush. I'll have to write Chris about this. It's better than amyl nitrate.

He peered over the edge of the trench and saw a huge crater where the stump had been. Damn, I guess I used too much C-4. The blast had shredded one of the barbed wire barrier aprons and almost buried a mortar position. I gotta get this cleaned up before the captain sees it.

The CIDG were patting him on the back, saying, "Number One . . . Number One."

"Hurry, hurry," he said. "Put the dirt back."

As they were trying to scrape up enough dirt to fill the hole, Sloane saw Captain Langley walking out of the inner perimeter toward them. He tossed down his shovel, grabbed the demo gear, and ran up to intercept him.

"Everything all right down here?" the CO asked.

"Oh, yessir, yes. Took care of it just fine."

"You made a big enough bang doing it. Knocked my maps and Wells's nudes right off the wall. Madsen thought we were getting shelled."

"I guess I should've let everybody know before I set it off."

"Let's have a look."

"Oh, sir, it's fine down there. Just a big hole. I was wondering if you could show me where the barbed wire is stored. I thought where the stump was would be a good place to put in a new apron."

"Well . . . OK, come on, I'll show you. We can always use more defenses." Sloane should be all right, the captain thought. He seems to care about the place.

Sloane's next job was installing barrels of fougasse around the camp. While the strikers dug more holes, he sat off by himself preparing the thermite charges. He wired them to the bottoms of empty fifty-five gallons oil drums and eased them down into the holes so that they stuck out at a forty-five degree angle. He pumped the drums full of jellied gasoline and capped them tightly. Very nice, he thought. Barrels jutting out like stubby cocks ready to spurt. Hope the camp gets hit so I can shoot them off.

He went down into the commo bunker to attach the wires to the demo control board and saw Madsen where he always seemed to be, sitting in front of the radios scribbling a message.

"Heard you got startled," Sloane said. "Hope I didn't make you change your underpants."

"Hell, I was disappointed it wasn't the real thing. So fucking boring down here."

"I'll see what I can arrange."

"You get to do all the interesting stuff."

"Yeah, but if you were a demo man too, we couldn't be on the same team."

"Well . . . unfair. I'll give you a hand soon as I finish decoding this."

At the top of the board was a diagram of the camp with all the claymores numbered on it. At the bottom were rows of knife switches, each with the number of a claymore above it. Tempting, Sloane thought, touching his fingers together. He picked up one of the new knife switches he was working with and pushed the prong down into the two open contact posts. Spread 'em.

Madsen came up as Sloane finished wiring the switches. "What can I do?"

"Come on, I want to show them to you."

They walked out to the first of the drums protruding from the hillside.

"And the thermite's supposed to blow the napalm over the VC . . . in a big spout, hm?" Madsen asked.

"Yeah. Deep fries 'em."

"Do you really think that'll work? Sounds like something out of a comic strip to me."

"You don't think it'll work? I bet you won't sit on it to see if it'll work."

"I don't want to get near the damn things. After that earthquake you caused, I'm waiting for the whole hill to explode."

"That'll be my masterpiece. The CO said when I finished you could take me down to the village and give me the guided tour."

"Good, I'll go tell Randall. You get a jeep."

As they drove out they saw the CIDG unloading the weekly parachute drop of rations. The crate containing the hogs had landed wrong and one of them had broken its hind legs. The strikers were laughing at its attempts to stand. Two of them grabbed the twisted legs and started dragging the animal away. Its screams cut the air like the wails of tormented saxophones. Bleating and pleading in total pain, the hog floundered on its belly and pawed with its front legs. It howled in lost helplessness as a bone tore through the flesh and stuck out jagged and white amid the blood.

The strikers laughed louder and pointed and poked at each other.

"Those sons of bitches," Madsen said.

Sloane felt the screams in his eyes. "Stop. Stop!" He leaped out while the jeep was still moving and ran at the strikers, picking one up and pushing him into the other, kicking at them both as they scrambled away. Then he stopped and looked down at the pig heaving in spasms on the ground, its nostrils flaring, its lips bubbling foam. He walked clenched and trembling back to the jeep, got his M-16, and returned to the crying animal. While one eye looked up at him, he put the barrel behind its twitching ear, pulled the trigger, and walked away with blood splattered on his boots.

Madsen drove silently down to the village with Sloane slumped in the seat, looking old.

The village was cooled a little by the shade of overhanging

palm trees. Birds and dragonflies lived in the air. Real people, not just soldiers, walked through the narrow dirt streets. The bald hilltop seemed hot, glaring, and barren by comparison.

They stopped at the only café and sat on the porch drinking warm Vietnamese beer. It was rare to see Americans in the village, and people walked past them staring. A gaggle of kids formed, ogling with wide dark eyes, pointing at them and whispering among themselves. Most were dressed in pajamas or shorts with straw hats or pith helmets. The youngest wore only cotton shirts and bare bottoms. Their faces showed a blend of curiosity, fear, delight, hostility, shy embarrassment, and blank indifference. Several were fascinated by the hair on the Americans' arms. After much goading, the bravest walked up with a big smile, pulled a blond tuft from Sloane's arm, and ran back to the group. They all gave their opinions of this strange growth, and when they saw that Sloane and Madsen were laughing, they crowded around, pulling out more hair and touching their clothes.

Madsen was first to get annoyed and shoo them away.

"You still haven't told me about the operation you were on," Sloane said.

"It was . . . kind of a letdown. Just trampin' around the bush. Didn't see one VC the whole fucking time. I kept expecting something would happen, you know . . . but it never did. Didn't even get sniped at. Might as well have been on a field problem back at Bragg. What was it like in Nha Trang?"

"Terrible. It's a lot better out here. All we did was pull detail. At least out here things make some sense. I'd a whole lot rather play with fougasse than unload trucks."

"But out here we can't even get laid," Madsen said. "At least in Nha Trang you could get laid."

"Yeah . . . I suppose."

"I guess what I mean is, we been in the army all this time, just doing nothing. Finally we get over here . . . and there's still nothing happening. All we do is get ready for it . . . but it never comes off."

"I know. I wish we'd get into it, too," Sloane said, draining the dark green bottle. "But it's still better over here. I've felt a lot better since I got to Nam. Things are more out in the open. Not all covered up with smiles. And hell, we know the real stuff is over here. We just haven't found it yet."

"Yeah," Madsen said wryly, "there must be a war going on someplace."

"Sloane, the air force wants us to do a bomb damage assessment for them," Captain Langley said. "They got it in their heads they caught some VC up north of here. Want us to check it out. Gotta get that body count, you know."

Sloane was excited when he told Madsen about it. "Was that where you went, up north?"

"No, we went south. But Randall could tell you about it. He knows the whole area."

"What should I take?"

Madsen laughed. "There I can advise ya. Don't take anything you're not sure you're gonna need. Nothing extra."

"You think I should take out a .45?"

"A pistol? Fuck, no. They weigh four pounds. I tell you, every ounce you carry is pain."

"Where can I get a bayonet?"

"You don't want a bayonet. There's no use for it."

"You mean you don't take bayonets out? You mean I'm not going to get to bayonet anybody?"

"Yeah, all that good training's gonna go to waste. Come on, we'll get you some food."

That night Sloane broke down his M-16 and laid it piece by piece on a new towel. He cleaned each part and rubbed a thin coat of oil over all except the bolt. Have to keep this little part bone dry. Don't want it to jam up on me. He reassembled it, rubbed a little oil over the outside (though he knew it was supposed to be dull finished to reduce visibility), and propped the shiny black shaft beside his bed. Then he showered, set out his favorite pair of jungle boots, and laid a clean set of camouflage fatigues over a chair next to his pack. Just like getting ready for a big date, he thought. Hand grenades instead of falsies.

Early the next morning with the sky still dark, he tiptoed into the commo bunker with his rifle in his hand and his rucksack on his back. He watched Madsen breathing in sleep. "Good-bye, old Jeff," he whispered, and left.

They followed an old road, now unused and overgrown, for the first few hours. It ran through an abandoned village. The remains of a large stucco house stood with a palm tree growing inside its roofless walls. The hull of a truck rusted in a field near several half-decomposed outbuildings. Behind them were heaps of thatch and bamboo that had once been huts. The place still held a watching presence.

"A French planter used to live in that big house," Langley said. "His workers lived in the huts. Used to haul sugarcane out of here, all the way to Pleiku. You couldn't drive that road now in a tank."

"Do you know what happened to him?"

"I don't know. They probably shot him. Viet Minh wiped out a whole French battalion not too far from here."

Several kilometers past the crumbling plantation hung the skeleton of a bridge blown up long ago. Its twisted iron girders drooped gracefully into the stream bed like roller-coaster tracks. Massive wooden beams lay strewn in casual piles. The river slowed to a tawny pool around the fallen span. A plate on the abutment read, "Pellier Fils—Saigon."

That's the nicest piece of metal sculpture I've seen in years, Sloane thought. Those Viet Minh demo men really know their stuff.

They followed the river until they could ford it, then trudged north across a dry savanna. The sun turned the sky into a griddle above their heads. There was no breeze, and they seemed to be breathing the same air they had just exhaled. Sloane's clothes felt like tight rubber.

But late in the afternoon clouds massed across the sky, and soon the sun was gone and a breeze came over the plain. They stopped for the night at the edge of the hills. Sloane dropped his pack with a groan of relief and went off to the bushes. Never thought I would so enjoy a simple leak. Wind caressing my stagnant balls. Wish I was naked.

Sloane awoke during the night to the sound of rain thwocking against his poncho shelter. He smiled to be dry so close to the rain. The sound lulled him back to sleep. In the morning, however, he was soggy and cold. Water had seeped down the nylon cords into his hammock.

Langley showed him how to tie drip-strings to divert the trickles. "The monsoon got us," he said. "It'll rain for months now." Sloane pictured the patrol stepping along with umbrellas and yellow galoshes, whistling.

With the hills began the forest. It was a tall snarl of plants, each fighting for the little light that filtered through. Every leaf was dripping and breathing. Sloane could sense them growing, reaching for him. He felt he was in a line of fleas burrowing through the fur of a large, wet animal. The still air stank with fertile decay; birth and death were breeding each other on the floor of the rain forest. He could hear birds and monkeys fleeing the clomping men, but could not see them through the shadowed screens of foliage. Puffs of mosquitoes raged around his head. The humidity was like wet cotton blocking his mouth and nose. He was exuding so much dermal ooze that he wasn't sure where his skin stopped and the air began. The column was moving straight uphill, and his breath came in choked whimpers. His clay-clotted boots and the weight of his pack pulled him back half the distance of each step.

Part of Sloane removed itself. He watched his pained, plodding body struggle up the hill. He forced it to continue as though he were flailing an overloaded and exhausted pack animal. The spell was broken by the sight of a leech clinging to his arm like a piece of bruised lip. He jerked and batted at it, shuddering with revulsion.

Rain fell throughout the afternoon. Sloane was reduced to minutely examining the passing vegetation, hoping to find some clue to why he was here. The moving column seemed to pull him along, threading through vines tangled like Pollock paintings, over crushed, sluglike creatures and trampled plants twined in parasitic embrace. His eyes ran over it all with dull curiosity, trying to discover how he had happened to come to this strange planet and to be in such pain.

When they reached a clear space with a stream nearby, Langley said, "We'll stop here for the night. It's close enough to the target area. Should be able to get there first thing in the morning."

All Sloane understood was that he could stop now. He dropped his pack and sat down in the mud.

"The LLDB lieutenant thinks Charlie may hit us tonight to get even for the air strike," Langley said. "He's having the men dig in. That means we have to, too."

"Huh?"

"Dig, champ. You have to dig a foxhole. You know, like they do in a war."

"Oh . . . OK. You mean we don't get to sleep in hammocks?"

"Yeah, you can sleep in a hammock. You just have to dig a hole beside it so you can hop in if we have visitors during the night."

Sloane had recovered his senses by the time one of the Yards lent him an entrenching tool. He started digging, thinking, This makes as much sense as any of the rest of it. Dumb. At least the rain softened up the ground.

The earth came away in hunks with a sucking sound. Night soil, Sloane thought. Dig it. Generations of decomposed worms . . . fermented tiger turds.

He scraped out what he figured was the minimum possible foxhole and stepped back to look at it. Damn thing's already filling with rain. If we get hit I'll probably fall in and drown.

The CIDG were building intricate shelters with ponchos, hammocks, and tree limbs. They slept close together so that extra ponchos could be used as side screens. What goes on in there at night? Sloane wondered.

When the ponchos sagged with rain, they drained the water into empty plastic rice bags and sealed them for later or drank right then, holding the long, narrow bags across their open palms, sucking the water out. "Number one nuoc," they told Sloane, grinning.

When the downpour stopped, many of the strikers stripped off their fatigues and hung them in front of fires to dry. They played, throwing sticks at one another and singing mocking songs, their thorn-scratched adolescent legs stemming out from short red underpants. The jungle is a woman with long fingernails, Sloane wanted to say.

He walked down to the stream. Several strikers were bathing nude. They splashed and laughed and dunked one another. When they saw Sloane, they stopped and giggled self-consciously. One Vietnamese boy stood with water coursing around his thighs. He cupped a hand over his balls with a shy smile. Sloane could see the little bud of his penis, the mushroom tip swelling through the foreskin. The youth disappeared beneath the surface and came up again, water running from his body, wet heavy hair falling across his broad forehead. I should take off my clothes and get in with them. I better not. Might freak them out. Besides, the water . . . probably got leeches in it or something. Look at them. I bet they're not so modest with no Americans around. They probably really carry on.

He filled his canteens. Rain dripping from leaves made rings on the water. "Go ahead and play. Go ahead and play," he urged.

They laughed and turned their backs.

Next morning Langley and the LLDB plotted the course. A steep ridge lay between them and the valley where the air strike had taken place. No trails led over it, so the men broke out their machetes and hacked and clawed their way up the slope through the brush. Rain and wet leaves soaked their clothes and thorn vines tore them. Their hands bled from grabbing the wrong parts of branches to hoist themselves up through the mud. They reached the top, then slid and lurched down the other side, using bushes for brakes.

On the map the valley floor looked fairly level, with a stream running down the middle, but when they got to the bottom, they found it was a boggy washboard of small ridges and hills with dozens of little creeks between them.

"Damn these maps. They could be behind any of these rises. We'll have to fan out into squads and sweep the area. You can see how Charlie can hide," Langley said. "We could walk past a whole battalion and never know it."

They started looking, moving up the valley, splashing and glopping through the mud. What are we doing? Sloane wondered, absentminded with fatigue. Oh . . . looking for bodies. Wandering around looking for bodies. Like Easter eggs hidden in the bushes.

Two hours later, in a clearing on the side of a hill, they found them. The corpses looked as if they had been dropped from planes along with the bombs. They were strewn and tumbled about, frozen in contorted poses: legs stuck in the air, backs humped, some bodies partly buried, others in two parts, one man tossed into a tree. The rain fell with quiet evenness over everyone.

Sloane felt hushed, as if he had entered a church. He walked slowly into the clearing toward the bodies.

"Get back here, Sloane," Langley called with a wire edge to his voice. "You want to get your head blown off?" Then he put his hand on the interpreter's shoulder and spoke wearily and deliberately. "First have the men check everything for booby traps. Then they pick up weapons. Then they check dead men for papers."

"I can take out the booby traps," Sloane said.

"OK, you can help them check . . . but watch yourself."

Sloane wandered among the bodies. Two of them were lying on a heap of churned-up ground like children who had fallen asleep after digging in the sandbox. When he got closer, he saw they had been burned black and naked by the napalm. Their limbs were swollen like huge sausages, and black blood had run from their eyes, ears, nostrils, and mouths. Puddles of yellow shit had collected between their legs. Their faces wore stunned grins. Sloane heard a droning sound and looked to see a swarm of excited horseflies sucking the crusted flesh. Ants marched in file into and out of a mouth.

The trees were broken and burnt and stood like scarecrows. Trees got it too. Poor dumb trees. Sloane drifted on images of what it had been like and reconstructed the scene from the moment the men realize that the planes, like hawks on mice, are diving on them. As they try to decide whether to run or hit the ground, the concussion sprawls them, sucks their breath into the vacuum, leaves them choking on the ground with fire covering them. Screams high and silent as dog whistles. Inside the airless, gobbling conflagration, eyeballs pop, ganglia frazzle, brains boils. Flesh curls back in layered scrolls. Tendril fingers twitch and crisp. Testicles dry to brittle ash.

"Must have killed everybody," Langley said, vacant and

slow. "Or else the weapons and bodies wouldn't still be here. Eight men. Squad. Their unit's probably still trying to figure out what happened to them. Got one over there just died yesterday. Pulled himself over to a tree. Too bad most of them are burnt so bad. We probably won't be able to get any papers . . . tell us what they were up to."

"VC Hanoi, VC Hanoi," the LLDB said excitedly.

"Yeah, they're NVA all right. Probably new troops, to get caught in the open like that. No booby traps, huh?"

"No," Sloane answered.

The strikers took vicarious pride in the kill. Some of them kicked and spat on the bodies. Others posed like mock conquerors, one foot on a singed chest, an arm raised in victory, grins on their faces, handkerchiefs to their noses.

Sloane looked over a pile of weapons and personal belongings: toothbrush, hand-sewn wallet, bags of rice, sandals, an AK-47 assault rifle, new except for the heat-blistered green paint. NVA. Broken dolls. They got them. Why not? Why the fuck not? he thought over the screaming in his mind.

"Let's get out of here," Langley said.

They walked out of the valley with the rain still falling and their muscles refreshed from the rest. Late that afternoon they stopped, and Langley gave Sloane a message to send back to camp on the field radio.

"Hello, Regal Snuff, this is two-seven Alpha. Over."

Madsen's voice answered, "Hello there, two-seven Alpha. This is Regal Snuff. Over."

"I have a message for you. Over."

"Roger, send it."

"Bomb damage assessment completed one three zero zero hours. Eight November Victor Alpha's Kilo Bravo Alpha. All ordnance on target. Negative friendly casualties. How copy? Over."

"Negative copy on Kilo Bravo Alpha. Don't you mean Kilo India Alpha?"

"Wait one, I'll check. . . . Negative, Kilo Bravo Alpha—Killed By Air. Over."

"Oh, roger."

"I thought you were supposed to know all that stuff."

"I am supposed to. How do you like it out there in the boonies?"

"It's OK. We haven't had any action yet, but it's OK. Better than being in the army."

"That's a rog. You going to send me your position for the night?"

"Roger. Bravo Tango, I shackle, Lima Quebec Romeo Charlie Delta Bravo, unshackle. How copy? Over."

"Good copy. You got anything else?"

"Negative further here. Over."

"Say, you really know that radio procedure, don't you? Maybe when you re-up, you can go to commo school."

"I wouldn't re-up for all the radios in the world."

"That's good. Just checking. Well, call me if you get overrun tonight."

"Wouldn't have you miss it for anything."

Sloane crawled into his hammock while the light was fading and listened to the rain. When he closed his eyes, he saw a body dangling from a tree. Dark eyes set in a pale face stared into him. He opened his eyes and looked out at black hills like giant leeches looming in gray fog.

The next morning Sloane was sure they would be ambushed as they plodded through the drizzle. They're bound to know where we are from all the smoke and noise we've been making. They must want to avenge that air strike. Probably hit us while we're still bogged down in the muck. Eyes hiding behind leaves. He walked on tiptoes, squinting through his rain, grease, and sweat-smeared glasses, trying to pierce the tree line of every clearing they crossed. It's better this way, he thought, when you could be ambushed any minute. Makes it not so monotonous. Don't feel so tired either. Anything for a hit of adrenaline.

But the hours passed with no ambush, and Sloane eased back into apathy and fatigue.

"VC, VC," the strikers whispered and pointed in tense excitement.

The magic word brought Sloane back to life. Good . . . we got 'em. We'll get 'em. He saw them pointing at a narrow spire of smoke rising from a hillside three kilometers away. Damn. Too far away. Take us hours to get there. Still he felt a tingle of excitement. So there really are VC, live ones. Right over there. Wonder what they're doing? Wouldn't it be great if they were looking at us right now.

"You know, if this was North Carolina, smoke like that would mean a whiskey still," Langley said. "Here it means Charlie got careless cooking his rice." He checked his map. "Hey, they're just inside four-deuce range. Let's call back to camp and give the troops some practice. I'll figure out the coordinates. You get Randall on the radio. His number is one-eight."

Sloane picked up the mike with a slight tremble. "Regal Snuff, this is two-seven Alpha. Over."

"Regal Snuff, over," Madsen answered. Sloane was glad.

"Hi. Looks like we got some VC out here. We need to talk to one-eight."

"Right. I'll get him."

Sloane took the Prick-25 radio off the back of the little Montagnard who was carrying it and set it on the ground. The Yard pointed at the smoke. "Fini VC," he said, making a noise like artillery, and grinning.

"This is one-eight."

Langley took the mike. "This is zero-two. Looks like we got something. I want you to check these coordinates with the LLDB and the district chief. Coordinates Bravo Tango 824917. See if there might be any friendlies in the area. And have three-zero set up the four-deuce. Over."

"Roger, got it."

They sat down to wait. Afternoon haze was beginning to

pile pale blue in the valley. The smoke was a curling wisp. Beneath it, tired men were talking and laughing, unaware that other tired men were calibrating their destruction.

"This is one-eight. Those coordinates are clear. District chief says no one from the village is up there. And there aren't any recon patrols in the area."

"Roger, good enough. Put three-zero on."

"Right here," said the voice of Joe Kobus, the heavy weapons sergeant. "I got a radio here in the mortar pit. We're all lined up and ready to go."

"Roger. Let's drop in on their picnic."

"Ready whenever you are."

"Do it."

"On the way."

They heard a whirring overhead and saw a sudden white carnation bloom far up the hill from the smoke plume.

"Way off, way off," Langley said as the crump of sound reached them. "Come down three hundred, left fifty."

The campfire smoke began to fade as the second round exploded down the hill.

"Go up fifty and you'll have 'em."

Sloane imagined frantic men kicking dirt on the fire, grabbing packs and rifles, racing the mortar crew.

The smoke was faint by the time the third explosion swallowed it. The CIDG cheered.

Men are dying over there now, Sloane thought.

"Good. Fire for effect. Six rounds," Langley said.

But maybe they got away. Outran it. Maybe they're panting and safe. And a lot more excited than we are.

The shells exploded every four seconds like tolling bells.

"How was that?"

"Fine. Looked good."

"Got any other targets?"

"Not right now. We'll keep looking."

"Roger. Glad to help. Call me anytime."

"Roger. Wilco."

"So," Langley told Sloane as they walked away, "the air force won't get all the glory this operation."

"How many you figure we got?"

"Damned if I know. And we're sure not going to bother to check it out. Be dark by the time we got over there. To hell with the body count."

When they stopped that night, Sloane put up his shelter and watched the strikers make camp. He was amazed how the Yards could build fires so quickly in the rain. Then he wondered if anyone was watching their smoke . . . and adjusting a mortar tube.

The next day they walked across the flat abandoned fields toward camp in the rain. When they could see the hilltop garrison through the mist, the strikers broke into excited conversation. "Nothing like five days in the field to make that damn place look good," Langley said. Sloane was depressed because it meant there would be no firefight this operation. What a waste. I never get to do anything. Just watch. Watch myself watching. Just goes on and on. Be good to see Madsen again, though. Wish we could go out together.

Langley and Sloane dumped their packs in the team house.

"Damn, sir," Randall said as they passed his desk, "I didn't know captains were allowed to smell that bad. You're supposed to set an example for the men."

"Smell? How could I smell? I spent the past four days in a shower," Langley said.

"We scored a major victory while you were gone. You know that engineer outfit near Ba Tre? Wells swapped them two captured carbines and an old VC flag for a case of steaks."

"Steaks! I've been dreaming about steaks. To spend five days in the field and come home to steaks! Wonderful. We have to get Wells promoted." Langley sat down wearily and Sloane followed.

Randall stood up. "You two can lay around looking miserable if you want to, hoping somebody'll take your picture. I got work to do."

"OK, Smoke."

Randall found Madsen in the commo bunker. "Madsen, we're going to let you out of your box for a couple of hours. After you send these messages, you can go listen to Sloane tell his war stories. Then you can help Payton hold sick call down in the village."

"A vacation. Thanks."

Sloane told Madsen about the operation while he was washing. It sounded interesting to Madsen, and Sloane admitted it would have sounded interesting to him, too, but the living of it wasn't. They couldn't decide why.

Then Madsen went to the dispensary to find Sergeant Payton, the team medic. The dispensary was a long building with sandbagged split-bamboo walls and a tin roof with a red cross on it. Payton was changing the dressing on the leg of a camp worker cut by an adz.

"Soon as I finish up here, we can go," he said to Madsen. He had a large-boned gaunt body, and his nose protruded from hollow cheeks.

After loading a jeep with medical supplies, they drove out the gate. Twenty new recruits for the CIDG were standing in ranks trying to learn the Vietnamese national anthem. An LLDB sergeant in front of them vigorously led the feeble singing with his right hand while his left pointed to the words printed on a piece of cardboard.

"I went to the Montagnard village last week. This time we have to see how the Vietnamese are doing." Payton took a silver flask out of the side pocket of his fatigue pants. "Have a hit of Scotch? It's the best—Chivas."

"Uh, no, thanks. Too early for me."

"Don't let a little sunshine stand in your way." He drove fast with one hand and took a long pull from the flask.

"I haven't seen the sun all week," Madsen said.

"All the more reason to take a drink."

Fifty people were waiting for them as they drove up. Payton spoke to them in Vietnamese, and they formed three lines.

"I didn't know you could speak Vietnamese," Madsen said.

"You been here as long as I have, you pick it up."

"How long?"

"Twenty-one months. I got eighty-six days to go, and I'm never coming back. Extending my tour over here was the worst thing I ever did." He took another drink.

"You'll be going back to Bragg?" Madsen asked.

"Fuck no. I'm not going back to the States. I haven't been back there for anything except leave in five years. I'm going to the Eighth, down in Panama. They can take the big PX and stick it. Every time I get back there, the place is worse than it was before. Give me Germany or Okinawa anytime. Even this place is better than the States."

Their first patient was a man drained of color, bent over, holding his abdomen. "Dau. Dau, Bac-si," the man said in an exhausted voice.

Payton examined him. "Appendicitis," he said while he gave him an injection. "This'll hold him for now. Put him on the stretcher and we'll take him back to the dispensary. We may have to medevac this one. I sure as hell don't want to have to take it out."

Next came a child, shaking and sweating, carried by his father. Payton spoke to the boy and sounded his chest. "He's got pneumonia. You can tell the monsoon has hit." He gave him a shot, handed the father a packet of pills, and told him how often the boy should take them.

Most of the people had come because of skin diseases. Oozing pustules pitted their bodies. Payton swabbed the sores with antiseptic and spread cortisone or antibiotic salves over them. Madsen applied adhesive bandages and gave them each a bar of soap. Payton paused frequently to suck on his flask. Madsen realized the pink flush on Payton's skin wasn't a sunburn.

A girl with a swollen jaw and a pained face walked up to the group accompanied by her little brother. "Looks like we're gonna get to play dentist," Payton said. He looked at the tooth and selected a pair of dental pliers. "Madsen, you get the best job of all—you hold her still while I pull it."

Her eyes went wide with fright as the pliers entered her mouth. They shut tight in pain when he touched the tooth. She squeezed Madsen's hand and cried. The tooth came out long and bloody. Payton rinsed her mouth, put cotton in it, and gave her some pain pills. "Thank," she said, trying to smile. Payton offered her the tooth. "No," she said. "Number ten. Boocoo dau."

The little brother held out his hand. Payton dropped the tooth into it. He pretended to jab her with it and she threatened him in rapid-fire Vietnamese, then stopped to hold her jaw. They walked off with the boy carrying the tooth like a torch.

Payton treated several cases of dysentery and gave a penicillin shot to a nervous young man who whispered his ailment in his ear. Then Payton and Madsen packed up and drove back toward camp with the appendicitis victim groaning on the stretcher. "Damn," Madsen said. "I wish I'd gone to medic training. This is really a job. This is really doing something."

"It gets dull like everything else," Payton said, taking a swallow.

An old man walked into the road waving his arms and blocking their way. They bumped to a halt. The patient on the stretcher cried out.

"Damn fool," Payton called. "You want to get run over?"

The old man walked up and bowed and showed a broad, wheedling smile. He pointed at a gangly brown dog skipping across the field and then at the two M-16 rifles in the jeep.

"What does he want?" asked Madsen.

Payton looked at Madsen. "He wants us to shoot the dog."

He shouted a few words in Vietnamese and lurched the jeep forward. The patient cried out again. The old man stood in the dust.

"What did you say?"

"I told him I'd rather shoot him than shoot that dog."

"Hurry up with those steaks, Cookie," Randall called as the team sat around the dinner table in hungry anticipation. "Wells, you're the best horse trader I've seen. You ought to quit the army and sell used cars."

"Those leg engineers believe anything," Wells said. "At first they weren't goin' for the deal, but then I told them we got the flag off a VC whorehouse you captured. Told 'em how you took it down after you personally liberated each whore."

"You're shittin' me."

"I wouldn't shit you, Top. You're my favorite turd."

"You can tell 'em anything you want, Wells, as long as you get the steaks. Dammit, Cookie, we're hungry."

"Ready right now . . . everything ready," the harried Vietnamese cook said. He and his two helpers carried out bowls of coleslaw, string beans, and rice.

"The steaks, Cookie, and they better be rare."

He scurried back to the kitchen and emerged with a steaming pot containing ten thoroughly boiled T-bone steaks.

Wells quivered. Randall jumped to his feet, his jaw hanging open.

"Number one eat," said Cookie.

"You bastard," Randall yelled, shaking his fist. "You . . . butcher."

The cook, baffled by their rage, dropped the pot on the table and ran from the room.

"After all we done for that guy," Kobus said, banging his fist.

"Backscuttle Buttfuck strikes again," Wells muttered.

Langley slumped in his chair. "It's the saddest thing I've ever seen. Only time I felt like crying since I been in this damn country. We've been waiting for months." The team sat in grieved silence. "Well, we're not licked yet, dammit. We just captured a bunch of weapons . . . and we can get Mama-san down in the village to make us some flags."

That night Madsen sat alone in the team house pulling the

first guard shift. He was drinking a beer and looking through a tattered *Playboy* magazine. Randall walked in dressed in the Vietnamese black pajamas most of the team wore at night. "I thought you were asleep," Madsen said.

"Wanted to check the guards on the outer perimeter, make sure they're not cheating . . . posting half shifts."

"Were they?"

"No, they're all there. They were even awake, which really surprised me." He took a beer from the refrigerator. "How did it go today with the medcap?"

"Great," Madsen said. "I sure liked it. Made me wish I was a medic."

"How was Payton?"

"He did a damn good job. Really knows his stuff . . . and the people respect him, too. They all call him doctor."

"Was he drinking?"

"Uh . . . yeah, I think he did have a few."

"Beers?"

"No . . . Scotch. He did his job, though."

"I know he does his job. That's not the point. If he keeps drinking this way, he's gonna do himself in. Payton's a damn good man. . . . We worked together on Okinawa. In the past six months he's gone to pieces."

"What happened to him?"

"What happened?" Randall tossed the question back and stared out at the night. "He did a great thing his first tour. A medevac chopper got shot down in the middle of a VC battalion up near the A Shau. Payton and some Yards broke through and got the crew out. Colonel put him in for the DSC."

Randall paused for a long drink. "But Payton couldn't leave it at that. He extended to go to SOG. Had to go the whole route. They were doing a lot of recon over in Laos then, six-man teams putting in sensors along the Trail, calling in B-52s. They got set down in the wrong place one time . . . crawling with NVA. Two of the Yards got killed right off. The rest made a run for it, trying to get to the pickup point. They were almost there—chopper was on its way—when the other American—Wilson, his name was—got hit in the leg."

Randall looked down at the floor. "Payton left him."

Madsen's throat tightened and he couldn't say anything.

"He's been trying to drink himself to death ever since. I have to send him on patrol to dry him out."

"I didn't know. It's . . ."

"It happens all the time. And you never know who it's gonna happen to. So we gotta try to keep him off the sauce . . . at least till he leaves here."

"OK."

"I'm going to bed."

Madsen had another beer and tried to keep his mind on the fold-out nude.

"Hey, Madsen, you wanna go kill some rats?" Randall's voice boomed through the commo bunker.

"Sure," Madsen said, folding up the message log. "Anything to get out of this place."

"You mean you don't appreciate all this expensive equipment?"

"I hate it. Being a commo man's the worst thing that happened to me. I belong in the field, Top. I been here three months, and I've only gone on one operation."

"Hang tough, Madsen. Radio operators just don't get to go out as often. You know that. We need you here in camp. You're doin' a good job. But we'll try to get you out again in a couple of weeks."

"Thanks."

"Look, if you're so eager for some combat, those rats'll put up a hell of a fight. And if you get bit, Payton'll give you a Purple Heart and a rabies shot."

"Deal. Where do I go?"

"Take a bunch of shovels down to the CIDG kitchen. The

rats've been eating up too much rice. Strikers wanna clear 'em out. You give 'em a hand and make sure we get all the shovels back."

"Sure. You want me to bring back a few fat ones for lunch?"

"As many as you can eat."

Storage bins and earthenware ovens stood outside the smoke-stained mess hall. Inside, the Yards greeted Madsen with eager smiles. "Poteep, trung-si, boocoo poteep," they said, pointing at the wooden floor. They dragged the floor away in sections. The ground underneath was wormed with tunnels and runways. They circled the area and began hollering, jumping up and down, beating the ground. Small furry bodies scurried out in panic. The Yards closed in, swinging shovels and clubs. Rats ran in circles, leaped squirming in the air, died splatted on the ground. More rats tumbled out of tunnels, running a gauntlet of shovels and clubs. They darted over their dead and tried to break through the ring of boots. The strikers kicked them and stomped them. Rat blood stained their boots; small rat bodies stuck in the cleats, heads and tails dangling from the edges.

Beneath the excited laughter and yells of the strikers, Madsen, standing off to the side, could hear the squeals and chirps of dying rats. Good thing Sloane isn't here. He'd be fighting on the side of the rats. Madsen saw a few break through the tightening circle and escape. One ran near him. He raised his boot to step on it, then caught himself and watched it run free. I almost got into it.

They scraped the bodies into a pile outside the mess hall and began digging at the tunnel openings. Pink and hairless blind baby rats stumbled out of nests and groped around mothers who stood on hind legs, spitting in fury at the men.

"Em . . . em poteep," the strikers told Madsen. He nodded weakly as they were crushed.

One rat remained alive in the ring. The men, not wanting to end their sport, let her run frantically over the battlefield.

After a while she stopped among the bodies and looked up, wriggling her whiskers, trying to figure it out.

"Trung-si," the platoon leader called to Madsen and offered him his shovel to dispatch the champion rat. Blood and bits of fur clung to the metal. Madsen shook his head. The platoon leader smiled, swung the shovel, and cut the rat in half. The mothers and their still-squirming infants were shoveled onto the pile.

The platoon leader poured a can of gasoline over the bodies and dribbled the last of it along the ground to make a fuse. He struck a match and it went up with a whoof. Rank smoke wafted from the pyre. The strikers, still jubilant, began wrestling with each other. When the flames died, they scooped the charred remains into a can. Madsen stared at the many crescents of sharp and shiny teeth gleaming white amid fire-blackened flesh.

Back in the supply room, putting the shovels away, Madsen, as always, heard rats rustling through ration boxes. This time it chilled him. A rat ran across the floor in front of him, and he dropped the shovels. The clatter brought the sound of many more rats scurrying in all directions. They know, he thought, sweat trickling down his side. He spun around and was out the door before he could stop.

"The hero returns," Randall said as Madsen walked into the team house. "I hope you got the body count all tallied up. We're a little low this month."

"What an awful job."

"You ready for the commo bunker again?"

"I'm afraid there might be rats down there."

"Well, you're the expert on rodent control . . . officially appointed."

"I say poison them."

"You don't want a bunch of poisoned rats rotting underneath your bunk, do you? It's bad for morale."

"I gotta finish that message log."

"Watch your step."

"Sloane, there's a chopper going to Nha Trang today," Randall said while the team was eating breakfast. "You can go along and fuck off for a couple of days. Wells'll give you a list of stuff to try to scrounge up. Madsen, I know you been here longer and it's your turn, but we can't spare you right now. I'll try to get you to town as soon as we can."

"OK, Top."

"Sloane looks hornier than you anyway," Wells put in.

"Nobody could be hornier than me," Madsen said. "I get horny looking at those stale doughnuts."

"My girl in Germany sent me a cunt hair the other day," Wells said, leaning back in his chair. "You can sniff it if that'd help."

Captain Langley lowered his fork. "A cunt hair? Your girl sent you a cunt hair?"

"Sure. I told her to, 'cause the women here don't have any. A man gets homesick for cunt hair."

"Hey, Wells," Kobus said, "is it true what I heard about you, that you won't fuck a broad without eatin' her first?"

"Damn straight. They don't call me Lickety Split for

nothin'. You think I'd stick my dick in somethin' I ain't tasted?"

"Wells volunteered for Special Forces 'cause he thought being three-qualified meant skydiving, skindiving, and muff diving," Randall said through a mouthful of pancakes.

"I didn't think the girls over here liked it," Madsen said. "Tried to eat one of 'em at Marie Kim's, you know, and she freaked out. She didn't want it at all, scared her to death."

"You're an amateur, Madsen. That's your trouble," Wells said. "When they say no, you swat 'em across the mouth a couple of times. Teach that funky bitch beware. Grab her legs, wrap your arms around 'em so she can't kick, and stick your face right in it. Then you just glom onto that little button down there, that little boy in the boat, and suck it till she hollers. After that, hell, that chick'll do anything for you. She's all yours. Don't ever have to give her money after that."

"Sloane, I want you to try that out on those Nha Trang whores," Randall said. "And bring us back a full report."

"Is that an order?"

Later that morning Madsen drove Sloane out to meet the helicopter. "I feel rotten going to town when it's your turn," Sloane said.

"Hell, I wouldn't feel rotten about it at all," Madsen said. "Have a good time. I can last a little while longer."

"Anything I can bring you back?"

"Yeah, but I don't think you could fit her into your duffel bag."

They waved good-bye, and Sloane ran toward the chopper through the thick wind and noise. The exhaust fumes made the valley below look wrinkled and wavy. I'll be able to get some grass in Nha Trang. Make everything look like that. He saw his face reflected in the cockpit glass, skin puttied and hair whirled by the rotor wash. On the other side of the glass the pilot sat unruffled and impassive, talking into his headset. An M-60 machine gun protruded stiffly from the pod of the chopper. A man straddled it, chewing gum. Sloane sat in the doorway with his legs hanging out. They lifted off with the sun strobing through the rotor blades as wind exploded the puddles. Sloane watched Madsen get little. The land passed beneath him like a rug, and the sun was in every pond.

They stopped at three other camps to exchange passengers, mail, and supplies. Approaching Nha Trang, they flew over a long stretch of tin-roofed hovels, a small business district, and miles of barracks and military warehouses before setting down at the Special Forces headquarters compound.

"Get on some decent-looking fatigues and get some polish on those boots," the sergeant behind the desk where he signed in told him. "We got a USO show coming in tonight with a shitload of VIPs. No civilian clothes till after they're gone."

"I just want to go to town."

"OK, sign the pass book . . . but don't hang around here looking like that."

A poster outside the PX showed a picture of a blonde girl in a bikini, smiling at a microphone: "From Las Vegas, Song Stylist Miss Penny Bell." A picture of four young GIs dressed like VC in black pajamas and conical hats: "The Charles IV, Top Rock 'n' Roll Band of the MACV Support Command. Brought to you free of charge by your USO." An evening to remember, Sloane thought, going inside to buy the team supply of skin magazines.

He walked back out across the compound with its neatly raked gravel lawns enclosed by borders of whitewashed rocks. As he stood outside the gate hitching a ride, he saw the girl in the poster walking, live and in person, on the other side of the fence. A major, two captains, and two middle-aged civilians in sport shirts escorted her. The GIs in the area gaped and a few whistled, but all kept a respectful distance. She walked fast, covered by false eyelashes and smiles, and avoided meeting their stares. "Wait till tonight, boys," the major called back as the group disappeared into the officers' club.

It was still light when Sloane got to downtown Nha Trang, but the neon was on and the sidewalks were crowded with GIs. He hailed a cyclo and climbed into the elevated rear seat. The driver turned to him and asked, "Where you go?"

"Do you know where I can buy some dope?" Sloane asked.

The driver looked at him, puzzled. "No biet," he shrugged. "What you say?"

Sloane tried it in his college French, but the driver only eyed him suspiciously and repeated, "No biet." They stared at each other across a gulf. "You want girl? Number one girl?" the driver offered.

"No, not yet. I want . . ." Sloane pointed at the cigarette in the man's hand and made a gesture of smoking a joint.

The man's face brightened with understanding. "Ah . . . you want number one smoke!"

"Yeah," Sloane said. "Number one smoke."

They rode down back streets to a shuttered house. The driver knocked on the door and spoke to the old woman who opened it. After looking Sloane over, she nodded and motioned him to come in. Inside, two other women sat beside a block of marijuana the size of a hay bale. They were weighing chunks of it and wrapping it in brown paper. More dope than I ever saw in my life, Sloane thought, breathing deeply to absorb the cannabis spores hanging in the air.

"You buy whole lot grass," the old woman said to Sloane, proud of her foreign slang. She motioned toward the pile and said, "You take."

Sloane smiled and crunched across the twiggy floor. He found a section of the block that was laced with pale yellow flowerets and broke off a great double handful.

"One thousand P.," the woman said after weighing it.

Fantastic. Jeff and I can get loaded every night . . . stay ripped for months. "Cam-on, cam-on," he said, thanking them, as he left.

"Cam-on," she said. "Number one high."

He had the driver drop him at a hotel and tipped him 100 piasters. His room had gray walls, musty curtains, and a thin mattress, concave over sagging springs. After a shower he lolled on the bed, nude and dripping. Stoke my head with some good boo. Go out and find somebody who'll fuck me till I feel like a person. He stuffed marijuana blossoms into the bowl of his crooked Montagnard pipe and pumped the smoke into his lungs. Ah, yes, the real stuff, he thought, letting it out with a sigh and a grin. Wish Madsen was here. We could have a time.

He smoked till the walls turned baby blue, then dressed. Civilian clothes . . . haven't worn civilian clothes in months. Won't wear any underwear, either. Delicious. He put on thin cotton pants and a wash-and-wear shirt. Look like a kid in a 1950s college yearbook, crew cut and all. My pupils don't quite fit the picture, though. Now I'll promenade down to the phallus palace and meet my rent-a-bride.

The bar was crowded with soldiers and girls. Johnny Cash sang "Ring of Fire" on the jukebox. An old woman sat hunched over the money drawer, smoothing and sorting the bills. Her face was taut with concentration, her eyes bright. A conical hand-rolled cigarette hung on her lip. It was too spit-wet to stay lit and she continually rekindled it from twists of paper thrust into a candle mounted on a Schlitz can.

Will it be you, Sloane thought, or will it be one of those wind-up dolls looking me over from the bar, or will it be Song Stylist Miss Penelope Pudenda, sent to remind us of the wonders of the round-eye?

One of the girls from the bar walked up to him and took his arm. "We sit down. You buy me Saigon tea. I make you boocoo happy."

"Sounds fair."

He paid for the drinks, and she patted him on the knee and then on the thigh and then between his legs. She looked around the room while stroking him absentmindedly. Sloane tried to look down her tight dress, but couldn't see much. She was thin and muscleless and made him think of dry leaves and the hollow bones of birds. She reminded him of a boy.

"I gotta go," he said, standing up.

"What the matter? You cherry-boy, GI?"

"I just have to go."

"You buy me only one Saigon tea. You number ten GI."

Outside, he leaned against a wall and breathed deeply. Air was terrible in there, he thought. He walked down side streets away from the brightly lit bar area. I'll pretend I'm not in the army. Just a traveler drifting through the Orient. It's another time. . . . There never was a war. I'm just walking along in the evening. I'll feel the air around me, hear people laughing inside their houses, see them eating dinner at the windows. That will make me hungry. I'll drift into a quiet Vietnamese restaurant, have dinner in the evening. I'll be real.

He found a place with no Americans in it and sat down at a low wooden table. The other diners stopped talking and looked at him with curiosity, but then resumed their conversations. When Sloane was unable to decipher the menu, one of them, a middle-aged man who spoke some English, helped him order shrimp with vegetables and rice. The shrimp were tender and spiced with ginger, but the vegetables reeked of nuoc mam, fermented fish sauce. Think I know what that smells like. He ladled some over his rice. Might as well get used to it. Get me ready for tonight. But the flavor proved smothering, and he couldn't finish the meal.

As he walked back toward the main street, a girl stepped in front of him, blocking his way. "Fuckee fuckee all night, boocoo blow job one thousand P.," she said. She was a little rounder than the other, and her breasts were small enough so that she might not be wearing falsies. At least, Sloane thought, she doesn't look like a CIDG in drag.

"You have hotel?" she asked, taking his hand and looking up at him.

"Yes."
"We go."
In the room he paid her, and she stepped out of her dress. Her body was pudgy, and when she uncovered her breasts they melded into her soft formlessness. Sloane took off his clothes and hung them on the chair. She's looking at me. Must be sizing me up. The girl lay down on the bed, raised her hips and pulled off her underpants. There it is. Look how smooth, with a faint froth of hair. Split frontal hemispheres . . . like a dividing ovum, or a second pair of tiny buttocks. She must be at least twenty . . . but I'll pretend she's ten. A prepubescent pudding.

He started toward her, but the superheated stuffiness of the room clogged him and he went to the window to breathe. The mildewed curtains blew against his body and he recoiled.

"What matter, GI . . . you sick?"

"No. I'm all right." He joined her on the doughy mattress, closed his eyes, and began moving his hands over her body. Which one will it be tonight? Maybe doctor. Examine her like all the little girls I never did when I was little. I could peel her open and look inside. Tell her to be careful what she does down there. I could give her a shot, take her temperature. You like that one, don't you? You're starting to get big, aren't you? Make her stick her little rump up in the air. For a special thermometer.

He opened his eyes, saw her looking at him, and closed them again. Stay in close to the scene. Don't break the flow. A little girl behind the barn. We're both about seven. It was her idea. I'm just showing her mine so she'll know what to watch out for if the bad boys try to get her to do anything.

"Can do now fuckee fuckee," she said, taking hold of him and rolling it between her palms like modeling clay.

He kneeled above her and looked down at her body. It's all dark and open. Like a wound. Ripped flesh on the bodies we found. They had vulvas on their arms and all over. Wore them on their sleeves. This is better than doctor. Here we go among them with our guns. A real body. And just a hint of the same smell for seasoning. Go get it, gashman.

He fell across her, and she reached down to put it in.

He was soft.

"Hey, GI, what matter with you? No can do, hey?"

Oh, no. I tried too soon. I'm not going to be able to. I knew it. Maybe if I start over and explore her some more. Get a new fantasy. Look at her from all different angles. Examine her crack. Make her stand on her head. Shit. It's limp as a worm.

He imagined he was sitting on a roof across the street peeping on them and jerking off. That stirred a faint swell of interest. He closed his eyes tightly and tried to make the scene more vivid. I'm holding binoculars in one hand and my cock in the other. And it's hard. I'm watching myself, my airborne thighs, taut buttocks, driving into her. And she's moaning and writhing and begging for more. You want to be ravaged by a savage, don't you, baby? It's working, it's working. A little life in the soft-on.

He quickly tried to push it into her, but it bent and slipped away. He rubbed the shrinking organ against her furrow, hoping the aroma would awaken it.

"You no can do? OK. You go sleep. Tomorrow you see me, we boocoo fuckee fuckee." She was off the bed and into her dress. Sloane watched her, one part of him thinking, Make her stay. You paid for all night. You can try again after a while. Smoke some more grass, you'll have some fresh ideas. The other part of him just wanted her to hurry up and leave so he could be alone.

"You go sleep now," she said as she high-heeled out the door.

Sloane lay on the bed, his mind throbbing with failure. He looked down at his penis lying limply along his leg. I know it's not your fault. You're just following orders.

He smoked another pipeful while leafing through *Playboy*.

The photographs mocked his inadequacy. Girls safely showing off their perfect breasts and buttocks, demanding demigods. The men were posed around them, confident under their H.I.S. slacks. Sloane's mind painted a line of male cheerleaders, tanned and arrogant, wearing white bucks, white ducks, and white mohair sweaters, down on one knee, pistoning their arms, chanting, "Punch 'em. Prong 'em. Poke 'em in the pussy—Y-e-a-a-h, TEAM!"

The centerfold wasn't bad. She was twisted around to display as much of her as possible, and her eyes held a faint invitation. He sucked on the pipe and looked at her and kneaded his sluggish member. Closing his eyes, he pictured the girl cutting his clothes away with long slashes from a straight razor. He saw his cock blooming and the girl holding the blade above it, smiling. She nicked it once, and when it bled she squatted beside him Vietnamese style, her breasts dangling between her knees, and began sucking.

He opened his eyes, saw he was starting to get hard, and closed them right away. It's working. Go back. But the girl was gone, the scene would not return. He sorted through his mental file of fantasies for a fresh one. The one about her undressing you gently and leading you to bed by your sprout? Then she lays you out and straddles it? No, that one's all used up. Jerked off to it too often. A little girl? I just tried that one.

He looked through the magazine to find inspiration. Want one that looks you in the eye. Want big tits with hard nipples . . . some ass showing. Oh, fuck, here's one with her tongue out. That's it, here we go. A tongue shot'll get me every time.

His organ stiffened. He stroked the shaft with one hand and jiggled his balls with the other. Plunk your magic twanger, Froggy. My big long sliding thing. We're gonna do it now, aren't we? Now that we're all alone. He closed his eyes and squeezed it and imagined the girl in the picture enveloping him. Then he began pumping it to the rhythm of the words that pulsed through his mind: look at that split tail, flick her slit, twist her nipple, flash gobble gash, gonna hump her, heave your slug, plumb her sump, gonna shoot, start to spurt, and here it comes.

The white fluid throbbed out of him and stained his lover, who was now sneering at him from the magazine. She hates you, he thought to himself. She's right. You're no more of a person than she is. All you can do is flog your pud. You'll never get out. Give it up. Get used to solitary.

He fell asleep with the magazine beside him. When he awoke in the morning, the girl's provocative smile still mocked him through the wrinkles where his semen had dried on her picture. His penis was chafed and swollen. The smell of dusty drapes filled the room. Guess I'll go home. No reason to hang around here. Go back to Cung Hoa. Go on patrol as soon as I can. You got work to do. Only way out. You knew it all along. That's what you're here for. Get into it. You can't lose. Burn through the fire. Yeah, murder. It's OK. Just love turned inside out.

On the street the sky was hazy gray and the air smelled of wood smoke and airplane exhaust. Heat covered him like a soaking glove. A squealing of unoiled machinery came from a new hotel and bar being built next door. Most of the workers were women. They carried bricks and lumber and buckets of cement. The rhythm of their labor was strong and graceful. Sloane walked toward the residential section. The streets grew quiet and shady. On the porches of the pastel stucco houses, men lay in hammocks, fanning themselves. They turned languidly to watch Sloane pass by. I have to get out of here. He hitched back to group headquarters and signed on for the next flight to Cung Hoa.

Wells met him at the airstrip the next day. "Hell," he said, "we didn't expect you back for a week. Must've got so fucked out in two days, you had to come back to rest up. Bet you went through 'em like a buzz saw, didn't you?"

"I did my best. Where's Randall?"

"He's with the LLDB, planning a new operation."

"Good."

Sloane found Randall and asked him if he could go along.

"It's Madsen's turn," Randall said. "Besides, you're probably too wore out from fucking to hump a rucksack into those hills."

"Can I go on the next one?"

"OK, the next one."

Madsen was in the commo bunker putting fresh batteries in the field radios. "What're you doing back so soon?" he asked when Sloane walked down the steps.

"I got homesick. You're going out tomorrow?"

"Yeah. Up to the northwest. Haven't had any people up there in months. Only way the LLDB agreed to do it was if we sent a whole company, plus the recon platoon and three Americans."

"Damn, there must be something up there. Who are the other Americans?"

"Randall and Kobus. . . . How was town?"

"Terrible. Made me really appreciate this place."

Madsen packed his gear that night. Recalling past agonies, he chose the simple rucksack Randall and the strikers carried because it was lighter than the regular issue. How else can I save weight? Ah, dog tags. Sure don't need those. He took them off and tossed them into the mosquito netting above his bunk. The VC can shoot me as a spy, I don't give a damn. I'm not carrying an ounce more than I have to. He took the refill out of his ball-point pen and left the rest behind. He broke off the handle of his toothbrush.

The next afternoon he wished he had shaved his head and clipped his fingernails to shed a few more milligrams. The men were struggling over a chain of steep, jagged hills. They did not speak, except to grunt as they pulled themselves up the slope, or to curse when they slipped back down, but they felt bound together by their shared pain and the common problem of putting one foot above the other. The Montagnard trails they followed went straight to the top of each hill, down the other side, and straight up the next.

If they're not going to use switchbacks, they should at least put in steps, Madsen thought as he climbed sideways up the hill, his boots twisting and pinching. Too steep to be just hills. Must be new mountains, shooting up out of the ground. I'd like to see it in time-lapse. The Rockies must've been this way back when there were dinosaurs. That's what this land is like. It's the kind of place where dinosaurs would live. Be great if some were left.

The group rested atop one of the crests. Only here was the vegetation thin enough to be seen through. Madsen sprawled on the ground and looked out over an ocean of hills. From above they looked smooth and easy to work. A tufted rug of rain forest, green fading to blue, hid their raw, man-hating hardness. All the gullies and crags and jagged ridges were contoured out and covered by the nappy cloak. An occasional rock face, crumbly and hung with creepers, protruded defiantly from the triple canopy.

"The views . . . make it worth it," Madsen said between pants. "Must be why the trails . . . all go to the top of the hills . . . instead of in between."

"The Rhadé think the gods live on top of the hills," Randall said. "They have to come up and pay their respects to them. It'd be an insult to go around."

"OK. But I don't see why they can't use a few switchbacks to get to the top. Would that be sacrilegious?"

"You're talking like a leg," Randall said, limbering his arms and stretching as he walked around. "It's good training. Hell, when I was your age, I used to run up hills like this."

"Who were you running from?" Madsen asked. "The sheriff?"

"Damn you, Madsen, you're gonna end up carrying the mortar rounds, you keep talking like that. Get up on your feet and jog around a little. We gotta set a good example for the troops. You don't see me layin' down, do you?"

"Look at it this way, Top—you've had about twenty more years to get in shape than I have."

"You're just lucky you're fighting the goddamn sorry-ass VC. You'd been in Korea, those Red Chinese would've scarfed you up a long time ago."

"You mean you wouldn't protect me?"

"You wouldn't have been able to keep up with me."

Joe Kobus, the heavy weapons sergeant, hobbled in with the rear of the column.

"Ready to move out, Kobus?" Randall mocked. "We been waiting on you."

"Fuck you."

"Fell back a little, didn't you? Or were you trying to protect us from a sneak attack from the rear?"

Kobus collapsed on the ground without replying. His skin was drained of color. His eyes and cheeks hung in flat curtains.

"Damn, sergeant, you're out of shape. Setting a bad example for this young spec four here," Randall said.

"Shit."

A half hour later they picked up their resentful bodies and continued. In the valleys, a dripping mist thickened the air. Shadows dissolved into shadows. Vines drooled from the trees. The ground was swampy, bristling with reeds, and smelled of sewers. No wonder the gods live on top of the hills, Madsen thought through his fatigue. His strength had been wrung from him long before, and he was running on will. You said you weren't going to fall back, and by damn you're not going to. If you end up dragging along back there with Kobus, Randall won't have any respect for you at all. Now move.

After an eternity of hills, they stopped to make camp for the night. Madsen was happy and a little delirious. Time works after all. It's over. I made it. Even the army will be over one of these days. I did OK. The first day's the worst, and it's over. His shirt was stuck like a bandage to his back, and he peeled it off to let the late afternoon air dry the sweat.

"About time we stopped," Kobus said, angry with exhaustion.

"We could've stopped three hours ago, Joe. I just been trying to find the hill with the best view," Randall said.

"Fuck a bunch of view," Kobus said, sinking to the ground. "Did you notice that damn LLDB wasn't even carrying a pack? Has a Yard carrying it for him."

"Yeah, he's one of the sorrier ones. That Yard's going to have to cook his chow and put up his hammock, too."

"What is he, anyway?"

"He's a lieutenant. The XO. Don't you know who your counterparts are, Kobus?"

"I don't have nothin' to do with them fuckers. That's your job, bein' political."

"If that colonel in Nha Trang has his way, you'll be saying sir to that Vietnamese officer over there, sergeant."

Kobus squinted up at Randall from where he lay. "Sir, shit! The day I say sir to one a them slope-headed motherfuckers . . . Look, Randall, you're the team sergeant, you be nice to 'em. I wouldn't give a shovelful of shit for the whole lot. The men can't fight, and the women can't fuck. No use to anybody."

"Well, Joe, if you don't hurry up and win this war, we're gonna have to take them all back to the States with us."

"States, shit. I thought we're fighting to keep them out of the States. 'Course the way things are back there now, they'd fit in real good. Go on welfare like all the civilians."

After dinner, Kobus crawled into his hammock and fell asleep. Madsen and Randall talked by the fire. "You kept right up with us today," Randall said. "You been doing wind sprints in the commo bunker or something?"

"I learned how to pack."

"Yeah, that weight makes a big difference. You're doing a good job, Madsen. The troops notice it, too."

Madsen's face brightened. "Good. Thanks."

"We'll be pretty much out of the hills tomorrow, so we're going to split up. You go with Kobus. I want you to take the company on a sweep of the valley. I'm going to work along the ridges with the recon platoon."

"Why can't . . . why can't Kobus take the recon platoon, so you and me could take the company?"

"You know why. He couldn't handle the recon platoon. And neither could you, for that matter."

"OK."

"You're going to have a lot of responsibility out there," Randall continued. "You gotta make sure they stay on course and keep the flanks out. And you want a good squad of Yards on point. But don't you get up front. You don't know enough. If you get any contact, first you call for a spotter plane and then call me."

"OK . . . I'll be able to handle it."

Madsen awoke with the sky still dark. The hills were greenish black haystacks. He felt quiet and happy in the solitude of his hammock. The eastern sky paled from purple to pre-dawn violet. Then the sun was up, fast and implacable. The last wisps of night faded in a few moments. Birds riffed. A white glow spread across the sky. He could see trees and men and rifles. Light grew in everything as bands of pink clouds lined the western sky. He stood up, blinking in the sudden brightness.

"Pretty, ain't it?" Randall said from his hammock.

Madsen turned around startled. "Yeah . . . it sure is."

"Hey, Kobus," Randall called. "You see all that? Ain't it enough to make you want to extend your tour?"

"What? Fuck you. Lemme know when the coffee's ready."

During breakfast the three Americans, Lo-ee the interpreter, the LLDB lieutenant, the CIDG company commander, and the recon platoon leader compared maps and checked the routes they would follow for the next two days.

"OK, let's saddle up and move out," Randall shouted. "Chung ta di. Let's go. Let's go. Cac-a-dau VC."

The CIDG laughed and yelled. A series of Vietnamese and Montagnard commands followed his voice. The men shouldered their packs and carbines.

"Now Kobus, you're gonna have to watch out for Madsen here. Make sure he doesn't try to rape any water buffalo. You know these young spec fours."

"I'll keep him in line. OK, Madsen, it's you and me and the zipperheads. Let's go."

The two groups walked down the hill in different directions. I wish to hell I was going with Randall instead of this guy, Madsen thought.

In the first few hours they went up and down two more hills, then followed a stream that opened out onto a broad valley. In the west, clouds had merged, and half the sky was raining, dark blue-black masses with gray slanting sheets trailing in the air. The storm was pushing toward the men, borne by fresh-washed wind, and the remaining patches of clear sky looked deep blue and far away. The white mounded towers and puffy spires clumped together and turned to murky slabs above their heads. Rain came down all over them. In the dark western caverns of the sky, silent lightning zigzagged to earth. In the east, the sun lasered through clouds to prism the fringes of the rain. Steam rose from the grateful jungle.

The ground slowly turned to spongy mud. It sucked at their boots and stuck like wet cement to their clothes. Smells that had been dehydrated now blossomed into full reek.

"Hey, Lo-ee," Kobus called, "tell that LLDB to slow the men up. They're gonna get lost in this goddamn rain. Shit," he said, turning to Madsen, "that fucking Randall sends me out on another operation, I'm transferring back to the B-team. You young guys, it don't matter, you got lots of resistance. I'm too old to fuck around like this. When I was your age, I could outwalk anybody here."

"How old are you?"

"Thirty-four."

"But Randall's over forty."

"That fucker is crazy."

By the time the men stopped for lunch, the wind had swelled. They shivered underneath flapping ponchos as it chilled their wet clothes. The gusts of rain that blew against them felt warm by comparison. Gradually the wind died down, the rain stopped, and the sun emerged to silver the mud. They continued down the valley, walking in a long file on a trail.

"If we're supposed to be sweeping the valley, shouldn't we be spread out across it so we can find anything that's here?" Madsen asked.

"Fuck it," Kobus replied. "They'd just get lost. Long as we got flanks out in case of an ambush . . ."

Madsen had diarrhea, and when he went into some bushes to leave another puddle behind, he saw scattered bones and a human skull broken on the ground. "Wow," he said, and his voice sounded loud. He thought of leaving, but then he dropped his pants and squatted in front of the staring eyeholes. Hope you're not offended. I'd rather have you looking at me than those strikers. At least you don't giggle at a man with a sore gut. The bones were yellow, edged with black fungus. Several had been gnawed and splintered. The back of the skull was missing. A few shreds of jerkied flesh sagged from the ribs. How long have you been here? Could you have been from the French? Just hanging around all this time, watching the different uniforms go by? Maybe not that long. How long does it take bones to crumble? Maybe only a couple of years, especially since something ate the meat off you. If you're new, you could be . . . what? An NVA caught in an air strike? A CIDG shot from ambush? A prisoner pushed out of a chopper for not talking? What brought you here? Maybe you're an American. From a recon team that got squashed. Anyway, I'm sorry you're still here. The place probably has bad memories for you. Madsen wiped his ass and stood up. Well, good to meet you. Hope you're not bitter.

He caught up with Kobus, but didn't mention his discovery. The sun had dissolved the clouds and seemed to be taking over the entire sky. Harsh light ricocheted off rocks and grass; heat covered the men like gelatin. They stepped slowly, dully, withdrawn. Madsen, like most of the others, unbuttoned his shirt and rolled up the sleeves.

"Cover up, Madsen," Kobus said when he saw him. "You can tell you're an American a mile away. I don't want no snipers being able to zero in on the command group here. We gotta look as much like the slope-heads as we can."

"You want us to walk on our knees?"

"Don't get wise."

"It's not going to matter if my arms show."

"Arms, your belly, you're white as a sheet. I don't want you around me. You stand out too much."

"Well, I'm trying to get a suntan so I'll blend in."

"Suntan, shit. Just button up before you draw fire."

Madsen grudgingly rolled down his sleeves and fastened his shirt. He thought about the bones he had found. Better to be out in the open like that than cooped up in a coffin. What was it that ate him? It sure wasn't just birds. Maybe a tiger. Be something to get ambushed by tigers, a whole pack of them, instead of VC. Put us in our place. It could've been wild dogs, too. Supposed to be a lot of them. Get left behind by the refugees. If it keeps up, there'll be a whole new strain of wolf. That would be fine. Best times back through history were when there were lots of wolves roaming around. That's the trouble with the States. The wolves are losing. But here they're coming up. Maybe we're in for another cycle. Wolves howling down long dark halls.

They camped that night on a small cuesta that looked out over the valley. "We better dig in and sleep on the ground," Kobus said. "I got a feeling Charlie knows where we are. I don't want to be in no hammock if he decides to drop some mortars in on us."

"But Charlie can always tell where we are at night 'cause of the cook fires," Madsen said, displeased at the thought of sleeping on the ground.

"I ain't taking any chances. If the LLDB didn't want to send an operation up here, it must have been for a reason." Kobus started clearing the ground where he planned to sleep. He wrenched a bush up by its roots, and a swarm of bugs poured out of the hole and over his boots. "Motherfuckin' termites," he said, dancing and kicking. "Fuckers'll bite the hell outa ya." He threw the bush away and swore. "We can't sleep on this ground. Won't be nothin' left of us. OK, we'll use hammocks. But we sleep with our boots on, dammit. If we get hit during the night, we gotta be ready to di-di. And keep that radio right beside you. Put up the long antenna so we don't have no trouble calling back to camp. Let's move over there. Termites! That's who runs this fuckin' country."

Madsen decided not to put up a poncho; he'd gamble on it staying clear. He strung his hammock far enough from Kobus so he wouldn't have to talk to him. After dinner, he climbed into it and stretched out in luxury. A breeze swept up the valley, taking with it the heat and fatigue of the day. He rocked contentedly and looked up at the hacking, swaying chunks of evening sky through palm fronds overhead. A lone helicopter flew high above. A river wound out of the hills into the valley. The horizon was dissolving to deep greens and blues. Madsen listened to the thrum of frogs and crickets and the faint boom of artillery marching down another valley far away.

Darkness fell as suddenly as it had fled that morning. Tomorrow night we link up with Randall, he thought as stars came out. Might actually be able to find some VC then. They're out there someplace right now. Hope Randall makes it OK. All this quiet. Hard to think that somebody's in contact out there. Must be at least a dozen firefights going on someplace in the country right now. Where? Two operations and still no combat. Wish it was the second world war and I was out on patrol with my old man. We'd find them together. Maybe it was just as good that Randall wasn't here today. I wouldn't have wanted him to see me slouching along with the dribble-shits.

As the last light disappeared, spots of phosphorus began glowing on the ground around Madsen's hammock. Stars, he thought before he slept, stars everywhere.

He awoke soaked with dew and with his feet swollen and clammy inside his boots. He changed socks and wished he had ignored Kobus's instruction. Should've put up a poncho, too.

As the company continued down the valley in a long line, they began passing land that had been recently cultivated. "Charlie's been in here growin' shit," Kobus said. "Go up and check the point and make sure those fuck-heads are out far enough. We could get hit anytime now. Charlie don't like us messing with his chow."

Madsen stayed with the six Montagnards on point until Kobus called him on the HT-1 squad radio and told him to get his ass back. As he turned to leave, he saw some huts hidden in a stand of palm trees. He touched the squad leader's shoulder and pointed to them. The men crouched down and whispered among themselves. One of them grinned at Madsen. "VC."

Madsen called Kobus and told him what he had found. "Hell. Stay right where you are. . . . Don't move," the sergeant's voice came back. "I'll send a platoon around, and we'll flank 'em."

Madsen and the squad spread out and waited for enemy soldiers to run from the trees. After a half hour he saw movement. He tensed his grip on his rifle and switched off the safety. Then he recognized the familiar uniforms of the CIDG. The point squad stood up, waved, and started walking toward their comrades. Madsen's foot had fallen asleep, so he limped as he walked.

Near the huts, two old women squatted beside a pile of yams, tossing them into pack baskets. They each wore a dark blue skirt with a red stripe. Their naked breasts hung like the tubers they were handling. One of the strikers pinched Madsen and pointed to them. "Boom-boom, trung-si, boom-boom," he said, banging the heels of his hands and giggling. The women squinted at them and went on filling their baskets.

Kobus arrived with the rest of the company. "Stay away from all the hooches," he told Madsen. "They may be booby trapped. I don't like the looks of this. Charlie knows we gotta take them refugees with us. Look at 'em, they're packing already. Lo-ee, you tell them, they no tell where VC go, we cac-a-dau them."

The LLDB began interrogating the women. He stood above them, looking menacing and shouting questions at them. They stared at the ground and gave short replies.

"They say VC come two days ago, take men. Take men go work. Boocoo VC," Lo-ee translated.

"Where did they go? That's what we wanna know," Kobus said.

"Go hill that way."

"Damn buncha lying old hags." He shook his rifle at them. "I bet they left about an hour ago. They're just waitin' out there . . . waitin' for us to come lookin' for 'em."

"Lieutenant say CIDG burn house now."

"No . . . no, not yet. We'll eat here. We got plenty of time." He sat down against a tree and took some rations out of his pack. The strikers got the idea and started confiscating yams for their lunch while the women watched impassively. Two chickens wandered back from the bushes and were promptly killed and plucked and put into the pot. Madsen couldn't eat because of his stomach, so he walked around the perimeter checking security.

"Three months left to go in this motherfucker," Kobus told him between chews when he returned. "Three months and

I'll be back in the land of the big PX, suckin' on that sugar tit. Old Fort Bragg's gonna look mighty good after this shit hole. Just roll around Fayetteville, pull my little detail every day, and head for the NCO club. I even miss my old lady. . . . Never thought that'd happen."

After dozing for an hour, the men hoisted their gear and formed a line. The two women put on their pack baskets. They stared blankly while the CIDG set fire to the thick thatched roofs of their huts.

"Burn, baby, burn," Kobus said. "Don't do no fuckin' good, though. They build them back in a day."

The CIDG cheered the gobbling, popping flames as they filed out of the area. Several disconsolate-looking chickens hung upside down from their packs, flapping feebly. Madsen started sweating when he stepped back under the sun. Too soon, he thought. Still sick. He took four salt tablets and two yellow oxytetracycline pills. His empty stomach knotted at this affront. He was dizzy, and his mouth poured saliva. Each step sent new cramps through his abdomen.

The shock of gunfire pierced Madsen's pain. The shots were incoming, each report in two syllables—thock-POWwww, thock-PeOOww. All ache and dullness fled with the sound. His mind was racing. Where's it coming from? Where the hell's it coming from? He clicked off the safety of his M-16 and strained his eyes into the trees. I gotta get one of the bastards.

Kobus was on the ground yelling, "Call back to camp, goddammit. Get us a fucking plane."

The CIDG opened up in all directions, and the air was clapping with the sound of rifles. It's happening, Madsen thought, listening to the light crack of the carbines, the heavy stutter of the BAR. He grabbed the radioman and crouched down in the grass. "Regal Snuff, Regal Snuff, this is Alpha. Over."

He waited a long moment before he heard Torrez's voice. "This is Regal Snuff. Over."

Kobus scrambled to the radio. "Ya got 'em? Lemme talk to

'em." He grabbed the mike. "We got contact here. Probably a company of VC or NVAs. We're right out in the open, and they got us pinned down. You get us a plane up here."

"Roger, what are your coordinates?"

"You give them to him," Kobus told Madsen.

Madsen read off their position, and Torrez said, "OK, hang tough and we'll get a FAC right away. Do you need a medevac?"

Kobus took the mike. "Not yet, but tell them to stand by."

"Roger."

Madsen was trying to figure out how to go in after them. Probably have some squads crawl up close . . . grenade assault. The firing died down, and most of the CIDG were on their knees peering over the grass toward the trees a hundred meters away. They talked excitedly and refilled their magazines. Why don't they open up on us again? he wondered. Maybe they're bringing in mortars. We shouldn't stay here like this. We should move up on them, fire and maneuver. "Lo-ee," he called, "did anybody see any of them? Do we know where they are?"

"No . . . no see."

The LLDB lieutenant crawled over to Kobus. "Can get airplane?"

"Yeah, we get airplane. Where the mortars? Get them firing at that tree line." The LLDB looked at him uncomprehending. "Lo-ee, tell cock-face here to get some mortar fire into those trees."

"How we going to move up on them?" Madsen asked.

"Move up on them? You try to move up on them, they'll be on you like stink on shit. We're going to hold our position."

"You mean we're just gonna stay here?"

"You fuckin'-A right we're just gonna stay here. We got some cover. This is as good a place as any."

"But they just fired a few shots," Madsen said. "It wasn't even an automatic rifle. There're probably just a few of them . . . trying to slow us down while they get away."

"You don't know what they're doing. That's the old sucker ploy. Fire a couple of shots and get you to chase them and then they hit you with all they got."

"Maybe we could do a pincers," Madsen said. "There couldn't have been more than a squad of them staying in those huts."

"You don't know how many of them there are. Look, Madsen, I'm a short-timer. I ain't risking my ass. Fuck that shit. We'll call in the goddamn air force. That's what they're there for."

Nothing's going to happen, Madsen thought. This fuckin' guy. I'm never going to get into it. He crawled over to Lo-ee. "We're just going to wait here," he said.

The Montagnard nodded. "LLDB speak same. No want fight VC. Bullshit."

The LLDB lieutenant was pushing and cuffing the two women. He yelled at them and pulled back the bolt on his carbine. They spoke in a blur of words.

"What the fuck did they say?" Kobus hollered at Lo-ee.

"Women speak have maybe six VC."

"Lyin' bitches. They probably got a whole company in there just waitin' for us to come in after 'em."

The lieutenant kicked over their pack baskets and walked away. The CIDG started firing mortars into the trees. There was no return fire.

Twenty minutes later they heard the thin drone of a Forward Air Control spotter plane. Madsen called the pilot on the radio and directed him to their position. The inactivity had caused the strikers to grow fearfully silent, but at the sight of the plane they began talking and pointing. One of them tugged at Madsen's sleeve. "My bai cac-a-dau VC," he said happily. The pilot told Kobus he would call for gunships and circle the area looking for signs of the enemy.

Fifteen minutes later a speck appeared on the horizon. It divided and slowly grew into two armored helicopters. "Alpha, this is Shark three-two inbound your location," a voice wavered by rotor noise spoke over the radio. "Understand you're having some trouble down there. Over."

"We're pinned down by about a company of 'em," Kobus said. "I think they're dug in along that tree line."

"Is there any firing going on now?"

"No . . . negative. They're layin' low."

"OK, we've only got three minutes on station, but we can hose down the area for you. I want you to consolidate your friendlies and mark your position with smoke. We'll make our run from the southeast."

"Roger." Kobus took a smoke grenade from the radio pack and popped it into the clearing. Yellow smoke plumed upward.

"This is Shark three-two. Confirm yellow smoke at your position."

"Roger."

The first ship came in low and ponderous, like an overweight locust. With a brapping roar, the six barrels of its mini-gun spewed out fifty rounds each second. The front trees withered like wheat in a hailstorm. The strikers cheered. "That's it," Kobus yelled. "Bring pee on them motherfuckers."

The second ship chugged in and fired two rockets. They shivered the air and erupted into orange and black pumpkins amid the trees. The ship peeled off to the east while its partner came in for a second pass. Involuntarily, Madsen followed them with his eyes like a gunsight. They looked slow and vulnerable. What a thrill to shoot one down.

They made two more passes, alternating between rockets and mini-guns. The lead pilot's voice came back on the radio: "That should keep them off your back for a while. If they get you pinned down again, just give us a call. We'll come back out and even the odds."

"Roger. Thanks a lot." Kobus put down the radio and put on his pack. "OK, Madsen, we're gonna have to go in there and check that area out. It's a rule. When you get an air strike, you gotta check it out and give them a report. Now this time we stick together. None of that shit about you staying up on point. The Americans always gotta stick together. No telling what we're gonna find in there. These fucking slopes will bug out on you in a second. Now, lemme get ahold of that FAC before he leaves." He picked up the radio again and called: "Pirate, Pirate, this is Alpha, Alpha. Over."

"This is Pirate one-five. Over."

"Roger, Pirate. We're going to recon that area now, give you a damage assessment. Can you stay with us in case they're still dug in?"

"All right. I'll fay a little north and see if I can see any movement."

The men were quiet as they entered the woods. Many of the trees were shredded or broken. Some of the rocks were chipped. Where rockets had struck, the vegetation was charred and smoking. They found two dead monkeys and several birds, but no sign of VC.

"Looks like they left," Madsen said.

"Just as long as they went the other way from us, I'm satisfied." They walked in silence for a while. Then Kobus said, "Hell . . . we done our job. Every camp's supposed to keep the VC outa their area. That's our mission here. And that's what we done. Those fuckers won't stop for twenty miles."

They halted while the strikers skinned and cleaned the monkeys and wrapped them in a poncho for the evening meal. One soldier pointed at the skinny carcasses and said, laughing, "VC, VC . . . my bai cac-a-dau VC."

"Cac-a-dau you," Kobus said. "Shit, we're gonna have to give the air force a good damage assessment. The bastards get the ass at us, they won't come out again." He picked up the mike and called, "Pirate, this is Alpha. Over."

"Pirate. Go ahead."

"Roger. Your men did a great job. We got three bunkers and, let's see, five automatic weapons positions destroyed. And . . . they caved in about twenty meters of trench line. Really tore hell out of the place. Over."

"How about body count?"

"Well, they must've dragged them off. We found quite a bit of blood. I'd say they must've had at least six killed. Probably three times that many wounded. Over."

"Anything else?"

"No, no, that's about it. Real fine job. Ah, looks like the rest of them might try to ambush us . . . to get revenge. We gotta push through some pretty rough country to link up with our other unit. Can you stay with us and sorta scout out the area ahead? Over."

"Negative on that. I'm low on fuel. But we can come back out if you get hit again."

"Roger. Negative further here. Out."

The men turned around and walked back out of the tattered woods and continued down the valley. If this was the second world war, we would've gone in after those snipers, Madsen thought. I bet we would've got them, too.

An hour later they heard the crackling of distant gunfire. "Randall . . . Randall's in trouble," Madsen said. The CIDG stopped and looked around anxiously.

"Get down," Kobus said as he dropped to a crouch. "They may hit us, too."

"He's only got a platoon," Madsen said. "We have to get there. We have to help him."

"Randall can take care of himself. This is his third tour over here."

Two grenade explosions, followed by more shots, echoed off the hills.

"Let me take a platoon of Yards and double-time there."

"Forget that. We're keeping the company together. No telling what might happen."

Madsen tried unsuccessfully to raise Randall on the radio.

"He doesn't answer. Maybe he's hurt. There's got to be something we can do."

"Pipe down. He's not hurt. He's too busy to answer the fucking radio. Randall's doing fine. He loves that shit."

But when the gunfire died out and the last shots were not the staccato bursts of Randall's Swedish K, and when both he and Torrez back at camp had again failed to raise him on the radio, Madsen thought he must be wounded or captured and decided to go help him. He checked the map for Randall's probable location. Shouldn't take us too long. Cut across here to their trail. "I'm going up on point to speed up the pace," he told Kobus.

"You stay here. We'll get there soon enough."

"I'm going up on point," he said and ran forward with his pack slapping against his back and Kobus shouting after him to stop.

"Chung ta di. Chung ta di mau len, mau len," Madsen called to the strikers, ordering them to go faster.

After half an hour of jogging across clearings, crashing through thickets, and then running down a trail, Madsen was stopped in his tracks by Randall's angry shout: "Hey, you trying to get greased? Get over here. We just about cut you in two."

He turned to see Randall and several members of the recon platoon emerging from the bushes. "Are you all right?" Madsen called.

"I'm all right. You just about weren't. We thought we had our second batch of trophies. You're still dumb, Madsen."

"You didn't answer the radio. I thought . . ."

"You thought what? Shit. Don't worry about me. It'll take more than those sorry VC to zap my ass."

The dozen Yards who had kept up with Madsen wearily greeted their friends in the recon platoon. Madsen's sides were aching from the forced march, but his relief at seeing Randall unharmed outweighed both his fatigue and his chagrin. He noticed that the vein in Randall's right temple was protruding and pulsing visibly. "What did you do in the firefight?" Madsen asked.

"Same thing we almost did to you. We were down the trail about a quarter mile, heard some noise. Just went back into the bushes and waited till they chogied by. Then we opened up on them. No big deal. Killed two, wounded a couple more. We got one striker wounded."

"Is he hit bad?"

"He'll be OK. The medevac's on its way in now. What happened to you guys? Sounded like D day over there."

"It was nothing. Just a lot of noise. I better let Kobus tell you."

"I already know. Your strikers just told mine about it. Looks like somebody cried wolf. Where is Kobus, anyway?"

"He's coming with the rest of the company."

They walked to the edge of a clearing where a young Montagnard was lying on a stretcher made of ponchos and tree limbs. Madsen had noticed him before, on his first operation, dwarfed beneath an M-1 rifle and belts of machine gun ammunition, and was now sorry to see him grimacing in pain, with one leg naked and bloody and wrapped in a dirty green bandage.

Randall knelt beside him and spoke in Rhadé. He pierced open a morphine Syrette and slid the needle into the swollen leg. The Yard squeezed Randall's arm and tried to smile through the pain.

Two captured enemy soldiers sat against a tree with their arms tied tightly behind them. They were guarded by a short, proud Montagnard. One had a bloody wad of gauze stuffed in his mouth and a blood-soaked bandage wrapped around his head. The bandage was off center and revealed the edge of a wound. Beneath a ragged hole in the man's cheek, Madsen saw shattered teeth and a pulpy tongue.

"He's lucky he just got hit with a carbine," Madsen said. "Anything else would've blown his head off."

Sweat ran down the prisoner's blanched face, stinging his

wound and darkening the gray fatigues. His eyes were closed, and his lips quivered over the gauze in his mouth.

"Should we give him some morphine?" Madsen asked.

"I don't give them morphine. They leave their wounded with us 'cause we take better care of them than they do. Plus they know it slows us down, and they may get a chance to nail a medevac chopper . . . with their own man on it. I don't like them, Madsen. Especially the NVA. I want him to understand what happens . . . what happens when you come down here and raise hell. I want him to tell the boys back home about it."

The other man was naked except for a pair of black shorts. His body was bloated and punctured with dozens of tiny shrapnel wounds. The dried blood made them look like flies.

"Grenade got him," Randall said. "Knocked him about ten feet in the air. He's a local."

The man's eyes were open, but registered nothing.

A helicopter chuffed in the distance, and Randall directed it in to their position. He and the platoon leader carried out the wounded striker and slid him aboard. Madsen helped support the North Vietnamese, who stared frightened at the helicopter but hobbled toward it. An NVA, Madsen thought, feeling the man's thin arm over his shoulder.

Two strikers loaded the third man, carrying him sagging like a hammock, and the chopper took off while Kobus and the rest of the company straggled in. Kobus sat down exhausted and began splashing water on his face. "Your boy here took us on a run," he said to Randall. "He was sure Charlie had your ass."

"He should know better than that. Hell, sounded like you two had all the action. Must've been some heavy contact."

"Nah, it wasn't much," Kobus said. "Got hit out in the open, pinned down. They were dug in, layin' for us. We got some gunships and cleared 'em out. We were pretty lucky, actually. Didn't even get anybody wounded."

"How much did they fire at you?"

"Hard to tell. You know, the strikers opened up. . . ."

"What was it, automatic?"

Kobus looked at Madsen, then said, "No, don't think so. Sounded like a MAS-36."

"Uh huh, that's what most of the boys we ran into had. I guess you were trying to use good tactics, hm? Driving them our way. Blocking force, hammer and anvil, all that good shit." Kobus shrugged, and Randall continued. "From the way the strikers've been telling it . . . well, sounds like you got some sniper fire and froze up. Called in the air force to chase 'em away."

"Sniper fire, shit. No tellin' what they had in there." Kobus glared at Madsen, who was listening with silent satisfaction.

Randall acted genial, clapping Kobus on the shoulder. "You fucked up, Joe. Callin' gunships for a sniper. Should've gone in after him bare-handed. Set an example for the troops."

Kobus took the out. He forced a smile and said, "Yeah, next time I'll just bring a piano wire."

The LLDB lieutenant congratulated Randall on the successful ambush. But when Randall told him they should now pick up the trail of the VC who had escaped, he refused and said they must head back to camp at once. The men were tired and low on ammunition.

Randall said they could rest here and get resupplied with ammunition by helicopter. The LLDB shook his head adamantly and insisted they return.

"Hell," Randall said, walking away from the Vietnamese officer. "Run home a day early with our tail between our legs. Dammit." He smacked his rifle against his side. "OK, folks, you heard what the man said. He's the boss."

The column turned around and started back. The troops moved rapidly, eager to get back to camp, most of them happy the patrol had been cut short.

"What kind of shape your refugees in?" Randall asked Kobus. "They going to be able to keep up?"

"They're OK," Kobus said. "They move right along. Old fart-nose mama-sans. Wish we'd find some young women on these operations. Hey, we ran across a bunch of fields—manioc, sweet potatoes, whole bunch of crud. We can put it on the shelling list for the four-deuce. If Charlie knows there's food growing there, he'll be back."

At dinner that night, the Yards offered the Americans chunks of broiled monkey meat. Madsen thought of the frail, infantlike carcasses and shook his head.

Kobus waved his hands. "Fuck, no," he said. "I don't eat that shit."

When Randall took a big piece and ate it with gusto, the Yards flashed their gold teeth in broad smiles. "You never had monkey?" Randall asked Madsen and Kobus. "It's real good. Even better than dog."

"Three fuckin' months," Kobus said. "Three fuckin' months and I'm goin' back and have me a porterhouse steak."

After dinner, Randall and Madsen walked around checking the perimeter. "Guess you learned quite a bit today," Randall said.

"Yeah . . . I wish I'd been with you."

"That doesn't matter. The main thing you should've learned is how you gotta work to keep the respect of your troops. None of those strikers will do anything for Kobus again."

"They must feel the same way about me, then."

"No, they know who's in charge. You gotta prove yourself, though."

They walked awhile in silence. Then Madsen said, "Oh, been meaning to tell you: I found some old bones out there. Human, a skull and everything."

"Bones, huh? Did you claim it as a body count?"

"Probably should have."

"Sure, we'd put you in for a medal."

The next day they followed another valley, which gradually spread into a plain of low hills. Much of it had been burned off to destroy ground cover that might allow the VC to hide from spotter planes. Breezeless heat clung to the dry, barren land. Ashes stirred by the marching men clogged their nostrils and stung their eyes. The light trails of rabbits, mice, and other small animals crisscrossed the blackened earth. Nothing scampered. Madsen looked hard and saw the green undertone of new grass coming through.

Randall talked to Wells as soon as he returned to camp. "We got a rucksack full of documents from that ambush," he said. "Try to get them from the LLDB as soon as you can. I want to know what they're up to. Looked like a couple of NVA couriers. And some locals for guides. I don't guess Nha Trang sent us any interrogation reports on the prisoners yet?"

"No. Probably take two weeks. I got some intel, though," Wells said. "We're getting heavy movement along that western edge. Had about a dozen sightings from three different agents. Squad-sized units. They're carrying everything from rice to some new kind of rocket . . . and they're all NVA."

"How reliable are your agents?"

"Two of them are the best I got. And the air force has been sending us infrared spottings all along there."

"Hmm . . . OK. I'll see if S-2 at the B-team knows what they're up to. But don't tell the LLDB yet."

"Right."

"Oh, and Wells, one of those KIAs was mine. Dropped him with my first burst. That means I got . . . what? Three more personal kills than you, right?"

"OK . . . OK, but I'll catch up with you, you old fucker. I'll go out and shoot me a half dozen strikers, dress 'em up like VC."

"Wells, no category you can catch up to me in. And that's nothing against you personal. Not a man on this hill can soldier hard as me."

"You're right about one thing, Top. . . . I'll never catch up to you in the bullshit category."

The following evening Madsen and Sloane sat behind the demo bunker and got high. They felt like ancient Montagnards, looking out over the valley from their hilltop, passing the pipeful of marijuana between them. Madsen thought with a mix of euphoria and dejection of sitting with Sal on their ridge in Colorado. "Stone 'em into the bomb age," he said as he exhaled. "Time for dragons again. Maybe a few elves." The sky pressed above like a cool velvet hand. Hills were hazing into dark blue pools. "Fuck a bunch of people."

"It is better over here, isn't it?" Sloane said.

"Yeah . . . yeah, 'fraid so."

"At least here people know what it is they're doing. Everybody back there, they're doing the same stuff. They just don't know it." Sloane got up and sat on the sandbagged .30-caliber machine gun emplacement.

"'Course we haven't done anything," Madsen said.

"We're trying," Sloane said. "It's the effort that counts." He swung the barrel across the sky. "You know, the worst thing about getting zapped would be you'd never get out of the army. You'd be stuck. They even bury you in a uniform."

"Hell of a way to get to be a lifer. What're you going to do when you get out?"

"Who knows?" Sloane said. "I get this picture of going back to New York and making sculpture. But it'd be more like furniture, all these huge stuffed cunts and cocks and tits, all made out of vinyl or something. It could be a big exhibit. And people could sit on them and drink gin and pretend everything was normal. You could lean up against a cock . . . or curl up around a nipple. Wrap yourself up in a twat."

"Those gals in Nha Trang must've really given you a ride."

"What'll you do?"

"I don't know," Madsen said. "Come and visit you. Drink all your gin. New York, huh? I could think up ads there. Do a whole campaign of commercials about the war. Can't you see, like some Medal of Honor winner coming off patrol saying, 'After a tough day of killin' Cong, I like to unwind with a tall glass of Tab. Tab's sugar-free sweetener helps keep me in good fightin' trim.' "

Sloane laughed and said, "Or look at Westmoreland hopping out of his command chopper, kind of prissy, and he says, 'To stay fresh in the field, I use Five Day Deodorant Pads. You too can smell like an officer and a gentleman. Take a tip from Westy: It's no sweat with Five Day.' "

"How about: 'Shell shock? Combat fatigue? Take Anacin and feel better fast.' "

"We ought to go into business together," Sloane said. "We'd take Madison Avenue by storm."

"We oughta smoke some more dope."

A week later a message came from group headquarters listing those who had sufficient time in their present pay grade to be promoted. Madsen and Sloane were made sergeant E-5s, and Wells was made sergeant first class E-7.

"We've gone over to the other side," Madsen said to Sloane as he handed him the message.

"A sergeant, huh? How about that. Remember back in the States when we hated anybody who was a sergeant?" Sloane asked.

"Yeah. And now we is one."

"You two butt-hooks made NCO?" Kobus said when he was

told at lunch. "Shit. They'll promote anything these days. Well, look, you and Wells gotta kick in your first month's raise. We'll have a big party."

"How we gonna have a party out here?" Wells asked.

"What the fuck? We got booze. We'll play a little poker. You three gotta lose your first month's raise. Keep up the old Special Forces custom. Ain't that right, sweetie?" Kobus goosed one of the maids who was stooped over sweeping with her short broom. She yelled and swung the broom at him. Kobus laughed and grabbed at her as she ran from the room. "Yes, sir, play some cards." He clapped his hands together. "I gotta win some money so's I can buy a decent piece of ass."

That night they cleared off a table for the game. "Come on, Sloane," Kobus said. "We'll take your money, too. We ain't prejudice, eh, Wells?"

"I don't know how to play," Sloane said, looking up from his book.

Randall was carrying over a chair. He stopped and looked down at Sloane. "What's the army coming to? An NCO who can't play poker. You're a disgrace, Sloane. No respect for tradition."

"Probably just got good sense," Wells said.

Payton set bottles of Scotch, bourbon, and vodka on the table and opened a new deck of cards. "Hot damn. Let's do it up right." He had just returned from five days of R and R in Thailand. "You guys gotta lose and help me out," he said, shuffling the cards. "Those pretty little whores took all my money."

"Hey, I hear the women there are different from the Vietnamese. They know how to fuck," Wells said.

"You bet they do. What do you think they call it Bangkok for?" Payton said. "Those cunts know so many ways to do it. . . . They got this thing called the bead game, you know, where they shove this string of greased beads up your ass, and then—right when you start to come—they pull the string.

You wouldn't believe how that feels. I tell you, those Thai broads are really something. They even got tits." Payton sat, deck in hand, lost in the memory.

"Deal, Donkey Dick," Wells said.

"I'd give my left nut to go there," Kobus said. "A man gets overworked and underfucked in this damn place."

Madsen started off losing. He gradually worked up to forty dollars ahead, then slipped back to twenty dollars down and stayed there, winning a few dollars, then losing it again.

Wells was winning steadily and taunting the others. "Couple more hands like that, I'll be set for life. Yes, indeed, fame and fortune and hundred-dollar whores. Come on, Randall, gimme another queen."

"Dammit, Wells," Randall said, slapping the card down, "you're not supposed to win. You got no respect for tradition either."

"I respect your money, though. That's something," Wells said, leaning back in his chair.

"How about you, Madsen? You don't seem to be contributing too much to my retirement fund," Randall said.

"Don't want to lose you."

"Well, fuck you guys," Randall said. "Taking money from an old man. I fold. . . . I'm going to bed."

"Want a glass of hot milk, old man?" Wells asked Randall as he left.

I should leave too, Madsen thought. Soon as I break even.

"Sloane, hey, Sloane, you four-eyed fucker," Kobus said, waving his empty glass at him. "If you ain't gonna play with us, if you think you're too good to play with us, well goddammit, the least you can fuckin' do is . . . here, bring me one of them bottles of Jim Beam . . . one of them bottles over there."

Sloane put down his book. "You don't seem to be in any shape to do it yourself, do you? I'd hate to have to see you get sober . . . just because you couldn't walk over and get a new bottle." Sloane went behind the pinup-covered bar and brought out a quart of bourbon.

"As long as you're up, young buck sergeant, you might fetch us a fresh bowl of ice," Payton said.

"You guys are really incapacitated," Sloane said.

"Wise-asses," Kobus said as he splashed his glass full. "Both you and Madsen are wise-asses."

"Better a wise-ass than a fat-ass, Kobus," Madsen said.

"Listen to that shit. Listen to the new sergeant . . . dud sergeant. Madsen, you ain't fit to be a private, let alone an NCO."

"Well, I'll be a civilian in four months. You can stop worrying about it. Four fucking months. Can't wait."

"That's the attitude. Typical fuck-it private attitude. Lemme tell you something, Madsen. You don't belong in the army. You wouldn't even be a good leg. And you sure as hell don't belong in Special Forces."

"It's your bet, Kobus," Payton said.

"Don't belong in Special Forces?" Madsen said. "OK, Gunship, why don't you give us a class on sniper tactics."

"Oh . . . oh, so that's it. Madsen, of all the shifty dip-shits I seen in the army, you're the worst."

Wells put down his cards and said, "What'sa matter with you tonight, Kobus? You got a wild hair up your ass? Ease up."

"Ease up? Listen. This guy's supposed to be a commo man, right? Am I right? Ain't you a commo man, Madsen?"

Madsen, his lips drawn thinly together, watched him without answering.

"Well, you are, whether you know it or not. And I'll tell you something. You don't know shit about them radios. I know more about them radios than you do . . . and I'm a weapons man."

Madsen poured himself some bourbon. "To hell with you, Kobus. I never claimed to be a good radio operator. I hate sitting down there. But I'll tell you one thing—in the field, I'll outsoldier you any day."

"The field . . . the field, he says. Would you listen to that? You don't know shit when it comes to the field. You'd be dead right now, wasn't for me. And I tell you, I ain't goin' out there with you again. You're a fuckin' menace. I ain't gonna get my ass zapped just 'cause you wanna go chargin' off by yourself. No, sir, you ain't got no sense of loyalty. You're the kinda dick-head leave a buddy to the VC."

"Hey, Kobus, what is this?" Payton said.

"What is this? What is this? I'll tell you what it is. This guy here is a bug-out."

"Man, what the hell are you talking about?" Madsen demanded.

"Talking about? That's it. Act like you don't know." Kobus turned to Wells and Payton. "This fuck-head almost gets me killed out there, and now he says what am I talking about."

"OK, Kobus. That's enough of your bullshit," Madsen said, putting his glass down.

Kobus leaned across the table toward Madsen. His eyes were white in his red, pinched face, and he spoke through a twisted smile. "Bullshit? Bullshit, shit! You can't weasel out of it that easy, Madsen."

"Then tell me, dammit. Tell all of us."

"It ain't no concern of the guys here. You wouldn't want it spread around the team. Don't you worry. I'm gonna take it up tomorrow with the team sergeant. Team sergeant, he gotta know about it, 'cause it's his job to run the team. And if my guess is right, when he hears about this, he's gonna run you right off this team."

Madsen stood up, shaking and stuttering with anger. "You . . . you son of a bitch. You're not going to get away with this. You're not gonna mess me up. You goddamn well tell me what this is all about."

"This between me and the team sergeant."

"Look, if you . . . you're not gonna tell him a bunch of lies about me. You're gonna tell me. And we'll settle it right now."

"I ain't tellin' you shit. And it's for your own good. You don't want these guys hearing what you did."

"I don't care about them. I want to hear what you're gonna tell the team sergeant. Now, we'll just go outside and you can tell me in private."

"I ain't tellin' you shit."

Madsen reached across the table, wrenched Kobus up by his shirt and bellowed, "Get up, you son of a bitch."

Sloane stood up, startled by Madsen's fury.

"Pipe down, Madsen," Wells said, tugging on his pant leg. "You're taking his jive too serious."

Kobus stepped backward in a stiff-legged stagger and knocked over his chair. "You don't belong on a team. You got no loyalty. I'm gonna goddamn well kick your ass."

"Sit down, Joe. We'll settle it in the morning," Payton said.

"We'll settle it right now," Madsen said, walking around the table toward Kobus. "We'll go outside and you'll tell me what this is all about. Then we'll forget about it."

"Ain't tellin' you. Tellin' the team sergeant."

"We'll see about that." Madsen pushed him toward the door.

"Fuckin' traitor . . . take care of you once and for all," Kobus said as he backed outside.

Madsen started out the door, and Wells grabbed his arm. "No, Madsen. He's drunk."

Madsen jerked loose. His face was knotted and red. He walked out into the mud and shoved Kobus in the chest. "What'd you say, huh?"

Wells, Payton, and Sloane followed Madsen outside, partly to intervene and partly to watch.

Kobus raised his hands in a drunken imitation of a boxer's guard. "You've had it, Madsen. Lucky we found you out before you got a buddy killed."

"You better tell me now and save yourself a lotta shit," Madsen said.

"I'm tellin' Randall. Gonna go get him right now."

"The hell you are."

Madsen pushed him on the shoulder, and Kobus swung a wild hook. Madsen pressed in on him, shoving him, forcing him back. His mind clicked through depths of rage. I can't actually punch him out. I gotta hurt him, though. I gotta.

"OK, stop it," Payton said. "You two have made big enough fools of yourselves."

Madsen saw the mortar pit behind Kobus. He feinted with his left and shoved him a few quick times to set him up.

"Team sergeant's gotta know," Kobus said. "He'll boot you off the team."

"Watch out!" Madsen yelled. He pretended to grab Kobus's arm to pull him away, but instead he toppled him backward into the five-foot pit.

A pitiful scream leaped from the earth. It cut through Madsen's hatred and left him standing there revealed. The three men stared at him, then ran to the mortar pit. Kobus was crying like a helpless and baffled and very young animal. Payton jumped in and bent over him. "Get my bag, and a flashlight," he called.

Sloane ran back to the team house, glad to get away. He brought the medical bag and held the flashlight while Payton gave Kobus a shot of morphine. "This'll help, Joe. We'll fix you up."

Kobus was lying on the ground, his leg twisted at an impossible angle around the four-deuce tube. He was sobbing, and his face was wet and white.

What did I do? Madsen thought. Nobody deserves that.

Wells looked at Madsen with contempt. "He was drunk, Madsen. I told you he was drunk. And he's way older than you."

"We gotta medevac him," Payton called. "Madsen, get on

that goddamn radio where you belong and get us a chopper here."

Madsen stumbled to the commo bunker thinking, No, it's not happening. I didn't do that.

He called in the medevac request, and the B-team replied, "Roger, Regal Snuff. But I don't know if we can get a chopper to come out so late. Are you under attack?"

"No, it . . . was an accident."

"Stand by."

Madsen paced the room.

"Roger, Snuff. Dustoff says they'll be there in three-zero minutes. Request illumination flares and lights."

"We'll be ready."

Madsen returned to the mortar pit. The whole team was standing around it. To one side stood a group of curious whispering CIDG guards. Kobus's cries had stretched into a protracted moan.

Randall turned and looked at Madsen. Madsen trembled. "Get back to the commo bunker," Randall said. "You've done enough damage for one night. I'll deal with you later."

The words slapped Madsen. He turned and walked back to the bunker with his insides pounding.

The next morning before breakfast, Randall came down to the bunker. Madsen had lain awake most of the night dreading this moment. He was sitting in front of the radios pretending to be busy, but his mind was stewing with doom. Their eyes met, and Randall was looking at him in a new way.

"I've been trying to decide what to do with you," Randall said. "Kobus swears you pushed him. But Sloane says Kobus was stumbling into it, and you tried to pull him back. I don't know. Wells and Payton aren't sure. . . . Either that or they won't say. So . . . it's up to you. Did you push him?"

Madsen felt the question enlarge to fill the room. Finally he looked at Randall and said, "Yes."

Randall's face changed from shock to disappointment to anger. He spoke slowly. "You . . . you pushed him into the mortar pit . . . backwards. You did that?"

Madsen looked back from a great roaring distance.

"I'm not going to ask why," Randall said. "There's no reason good enough to do a thing like that. He was your teammate, and you put him in the hospital. You could've killed him."

Madsen tried to speak but couldn't. He stared at the gray floor.

"I probably should kick you off the team," Randall said, and Madsen's throat tightened. "But . . . I can't do it. I just can't do it." Madsen eased a little. "And that means I can't bust you either. When the B-team sergeant major heard why, you'd be out."

"Thanks . . . thanks for not sending me away."

"I haven't figured out what kind of punishment you should get. But the first thing—you were supposed to go to town, relax for a couple of days. That's canceled. And until we get a replacement for Kobus, you're going to have to stand double guard shifts. We're down to seven men now."

"OK."

"You'll get more, too. Goddammit, Madsen, why did you have to fuck up like this? You were coming along real good. All you would've had to do last night was to come and get me. As soon as the row started, you should've let me know. We could've settled it right then. Everybody knows Kobus is a bullshitter. But now it's all on you. Some of the team won't want to go on patrol with you now."

"Do you feel that way?"

"No . . . no, I don't. But you got a lot of growing up to do."

Madsen continued to look down. "I guess so. Could Payton tell how bad Kobus was?"

"He thinks he'll be all right."

"Thank God. I'm so damn sorry."

"You're going to have to work like hell to get the team to trust you again."

"Thanks for giving me the chance."

Randall walked back to the team house thinking, Maybe I should've come down harder on the kid. If Kobus raises a stink, I could get burnt. Probably I should cover my ass, report it on up through channels. But dammit, it's part my fault, and I can't hang the kid. Should've known better than to call Kobus down in front of Madsen. Can't let him know that, though.

Each succeeding day brought more reports of increasing enemy movement to the southwest. Wells's agents—woodcutters and cattle herders who traveled the area—told of seeing North Vietnamese platoons moving openly down the trails. They carried large mortars and pulled carriage-mounted machine guns. Wells marked each sighting on a large map. Soon they formed a stream of red dots. He and Randall and Captain Langley sat in front of the map in the briefing room drawing up plans for an ambush. The walls were covered with parachute cloth and hung with captured weapons that hadn't yet been traded to rear area supply sergeants for food and beer.

"The only way to really nail them," Randall said, "is to string about six platoons along the trail. Just keep hitting them as they come down. Put 'em about a click apart and have 'em change position every day."

"LLDB would never buy it," Langley said. "We'll have to have at least a reinforced company, all in one place, before we could convince them."

"Depends on how much of this intel they got," Wells said.

"We'll find that out when we try to get them to approve the operation," Randall said.

"We gotta make it look like a sure thing," Langley added. "Plenty of security . . . a FAC."

"I know a place," Randall said. "Remember the last time we were down there, Wells? That place after the bend that's got the rocks all up the slope? Lemme see if I can find it. It oughta work. Yeah, here." He pointed at an area of stacked contour lines. "We got the butt end of a ridge running right down to the trail. Too steep for Charlie to climb. Plus the rocks. We could hide a company in these rocks easy."

"Yeah, but if Charlie gets in them, we'll have a hell of a time prying him out," Wells said.

"We'll set claymores along the bottom. Let him try to get in." Randall stood up and drew on the acetate covering with a grease pencil. "Look, we'll put the main body up on top with the mortars. A platoon on each side for flank security. If we use the mortars right, once we get 'em runnin' we should be able to channel 'em out into this open area where the gunships can scarf 'em up."

"What if they get tipped off and try to hit us from behind?" Wells asked.

"Brush is so damn thick back there," Randall replied, "all we'd need would be a couple of listening posts."

"Sounds good, Top," Langley said.

Randall tossed down the pencil. "'Course with us bunched up like that, we'll be lucky if we make contact at all. Charlie'll probably just go around us."

"I think it's our best bet, though," Langley said. "Let's see if we can sell it."

In the LLDB team house that night, Captain Bao, the camp commander, listened politely to Captain Langley's presentation. "Such an operation is a very good plan," the middle-aged Vietnamese officer said when Langley had finished. "Very good plan. But now we have not enough men to make available for such an operation. All men now must work in camp. Camp defense are very bad. You can for us order much barbed wire? We put more wire, more bunker. Make camp very strong. Then will be time for operation. Think how bad for both of us if Camp Cung Hoa suffers to be overrun."

Langley offered more arguments for the ambush, but when Bao graciously rejected all of them, he scaled down his request: "Perhaps, dai-uy, we could just send out two platoons for reconnaissance. We have not had anyone in this section for many months."

"Highest priority must be to defense, captain. If no camp remains, then can never be operations."

"At least we could spare a squad from the recon platoon," Langley said. "The B-team will expect us to have a patrol out."

"No," said the camp commander in a tone of reluctant annoyance, like a host who has been imposed upon too long and is forced to reprove a tactless guest.

"Very well, dai-uy," Langley said and took his leave with chill civility.

Randall and Wells read the results on his face when he returned to the U.S. team house. "They got the intel," he said. "They're not budging from this hill."

"Looks like my counterpart over there has a better intel net than I thought," Wells said.

"If we don't find out what the NVA are up to, they may damn well overrun us," Randall said. "Maybe the B-team could put some pressure on Bao."

"Yeah. I'll forward the reports . . . see what they can do," Langley said, discouraged. "After all this time trying to find the bastards . . ."

The next morning Madsen received a coded list of night campfire spottings from infrared cameras flown miles above the jungle. Accompanying the list was a demand from the B-team for a series of ambush patrols along the new infiltration route.

Captain Bao again refused to send out any patrols, reminding Captain Langley that the American B-team had no jurisdiction over his camp.

A pall of uselessness and frustration hung over the team that night. After a halfhearted attempt at a game of darts, the men wandered off to their rooms early to drink a beer and go to bed.

Several hours later Sloane was sitting in the team house pulling the one o'clock guard shift. He was reading a copy of *Naked Lunch* that Chris had sent him and wondering if he should smoke another pipeful of marijuana when the air quivered and the floor jerked. The room glowed lambent. He felt a vacuum, and his ears popped; then a sound like Ka-ROP fell on him so loud his teeth ached. As he reached the door he saw fire standing in the air. CIDG were screaming and running. Another concussion smacked him, and he ran back for his M-16 thinking, It's here, it's here at last.

Randall stood in the hall in his black pajamas. "Make sure Madsen's awake and on those radios," he called to Sloane. "Air cover right away. And tell him to stay in the commo bunker."

Sloane ran the short distance from the team house to the bunker feeling thrillingly stripped and vulnerable. Madsen was sitting at the radio calling the B-team. He grinned at Sloane. "It's for real, huh?"

"Yeah, who knows what'll happen?" Sloane said. "We need air cover right away. And Randall says you gotta stay down here on the radios."

"Goddammit."

Sloane ran back out and saw Langley coming from the team house. "Sloane," the captain called to him, "if they get inside the inner perimeter, you gotta blow the demo bunker. Wire it up now and stay by it."

"What about the claymores and fougasse?"

"Madsen'll have to handle those from the commo bunker. We need you out here." The captain ran up the steps of the observation tower to direct the firing.

Sloane ran toward the demo bunker, and another mortar round exploded halfway down the hill. He had an urge to hide. Next one could be here. But he kept on running, waving his rifle. Each step was taken with voluntary madness and made him feel more exultant. Rifles were firing in all directions.

He opened the demo bunker with a key he always wore around his neck. Inside, the stacked cases of explosives looked cool and peaceful. He attached wires to the pre-planted charges, grabbed a detonator, and backed out the door, unspooling wire as he went. While locking the door, he heard the chik-chik-chik of bullets striking the concrete bunker. Motherfucker, he thought as he hit the ground. Getting realer and realer.

He crawled to his alert post, a sandbagged .30-caliber machine gun near the bunker. In the spongy mud of the trench, he lay on his back hooking up the detonator. Bullets were slapping into the sandbags and cracking like bull whips as they passed low over the trench.

A flare lit the hill with silver light. Now, Sloane thought. He lifted his head to see a long gray line of men wavering up the slope. They walked as though underwater, raising their knees high and stepping slowly.

"They're in the wire!" Langley shouted from the tower.

Sloane slapped in a belt of ammunition and pulled back the cocking lever. He wrapped his arms around the weapon and held the cool metal stock close to his cheek. A distant figure stood in the sights. My eyes are on you. Can you feel?

The machine gun jumped, and the tiny man at the end of the barrel pitched forward to the ground. First time. Must've got him in the legs. Randall was saying if you get 'em in the head it knocks 'em backwards, and if you get 'em in the belly they crumple up. Maybe I'm aiming too low. Man that weapon, boy.

Inside the commo bunker Madsen was tormented by the

muffled sound of gunfire and explosions. All this time I been wanting this, and now it's right here, right outside the door, and I can't go out. Fucking radios. While waiting for the plane to call in, he checked the incendiary grenades he was supposed to use to destroy the radios and crypto safe if they had to abandon the camp. He hunted through a musty cabinet and found the small exfiltration radio they were to take with them when they fled. Wish I'd practiced with this damn thing. Don't even know if it works. How will I know down here if we get overrun? Probably find out when Charlie tosses in a couple of grenades. Die like those rats.

Randall and Wells were on top of the commo bunker firing the 57mm recoilless rifle. They saw a wink of light on the opposite hill. "One coming this way," Randall shouted. "I'll teach them to camouflage their goddamn mortars." He swung the big tube toward the spot and sighted in. Fire spewed from both ends of the weapon, stunning them with roar. Through their ringing ears, they heard the enemy mortar round tearing the air. Explosions burst on both hills. Randall saw that his rocket was on target before he fell backward under the concussion, a shock jumping down his arm. He lay in afterstillness, feeling spinny.

Wells bent over him. "Where is it?" he asked anxiously.

"Arm . . . I think. Bastards. Get some more rounds in there . . . before they get away."

Wells started to rip the top of Randall's black pajamas. Randall sat up. "No. It'll wait. Get some more rounds in there. I'll load. We were right on. They're gonna get away."

They fired three more rockets. A large secondary explosion billowed on the hillside. "That takes care of their ammo," Randall said. "Fuckers."

Wells tore open Randall's shirt. Blood was trickling from under a flap of skin at the top of his shoulder. "Don't look too bad," Wells said. "About an inch long. They won't even send you to Nha Trang for something like this."

Randall craned his head and peered at the cut. "Shit. I thought it'd be good for at least a trip to Japan."

"How is he?" Langley called down from the tower.

"It's nothing," Wells said. "This red-neck fucker's too mean to get hurt."

"Nothing, shit," Randall said. "Hurts like hell."

"We're gonna need you, Top," Langley said. "They're hitting us from three sides now."

"That's bad," Randall said, breathing hard. "Better they hit us from all around. Damn strikers'll only fight if they think they're surrounded. Go down there and keep a watch on 'em, Wells. If they try to bug out through that open side, we'll send a company of Yards to guard it. They don't care which Vietnamese they shoot."

"And Wells," Langley hollered, "tell Payton to get up here and check on Randall."

Wells ran toward the dispensary. An eerie sound of bugles broke through the crackling rifles. Oh, shit. More of 'em. Under the harsh, swaying flarelight, he saw the other side turning around and retreating through the holes they had blasted in the barbed wire. "How about that?" he yelled. "We whupped their asses. They're goin' home." He grabbed a startled Montagnard and swung him in the air.

Sloane ran the snout of his machine gun across a fleeing man, clipping him off at the legs. Takes two to carry a wounded.

Soon the VC were out of range of all but the .50-caliber. Randall fired it in short bursts, picking off the stragglers. The tendons in his neck stood out, and his face and hands were white from the pain the recoil sent through his shoulder.

Payton arrived with his medical bag. Randall chased the last man into the trees. "Bastards sure can run," he said as he released the gun and lay back on the cool concrete bunker.

Seeing the shoulder wound was slight, Payton looked him over for other injuries. "Is that it?" he asked.

"You sound disappointed," Randall said.

"You want some morphine?"

"Well, I want it . . . but we gotta make sure they're not just regrouping . . . hit us again."

Beneath Randall in the commo bunker, Madsen rang Captain Langley on the field phone and told him a C-47 dragon ship was on its way in and needed target information.

"He's about too late, but I'll talk to him," Langley said.

"What's happening up there?" Madsen asked.

"Looks like we ran them off . . . for now."

"Is everybody OK?"

"Randall got hit."

The words cut Madsen. "What? What happened to him? How is he?"

"Take it easy. Payton says it's just a nick in the shoulder."

"He's OK?"

"Yeah."

"Let me know when I can come up."

"Hang on down there."

Langley radioed the plane and gave it a list of routes the VC might be taking away from the camp. Five minutes later the twin-engined C-47 banked around the hill. A powerful spotlight shone out of the night sky, like the sun breaking through storm clouds. The light moved along nearby trails. When the men in the plane saw movement below, a second, much thinner stream of light jetted down—the tracers from their cannons.

A line of sparks arced up from the opposite hill toward the plane. Maybe they'll shoot it down, Sloane thought. He imagined it nosing over, the flash of panic among the crew, the final smashing explosion. We could probably hear the VC cheering.

Instead, another finger of light reached down from the plane to snuff the sparks and the enemy gunner who was sending them.

"Too bad Puff didn't get here ten minutes sooner," Payton said to Randall while he was bandaging his shoulder. "Charlie would've been up shit creek."

Randall winced and said, "Charlie's pretty much learned how much time he's got . . . to get in and get out again before the air force comes along . . . and smokes him."

The plane continued circling and dropping flares, but when it could find no more targets, the pilot radioed Langley: "If you're not receiving any more fire, we're going to return to base. I think we stung 'em, at least. We'll be on call all night, if you need us again. Over."

"Roger. Thank you much," Langley said.

The plane churned back toward the coast. Darkness descended upon the hill again. The men felt vulnerable and isolated. An occasional nervous striker fired his carbine. The camp waited.

Several hours later the CIDG heard noises along the outer perimeter and lofted a flare. The pop of light woke Sloane from the sandbags where he had been sleeping, and he looked up to see it blossoming in the air like a droopy chrysanthemum. Down the hill a dozen VC were salvaging weapons and dragging away their dead. They were running by the time Sloane cocked the machine gun. His bullets toppled two of them from behind. Tracers ricocheted into the night like reversed shooting stars. Sloane leaned against the warm gun and gradually slipped back to sleep.

When the sun woke him in the morning, he saw turned-up earth and twisted wire where several mortar rounds had struck. A CIDG guard station was splintered. Some of the sandbags around his machine gun had been torn open by enemy fire. He patted the gun, and a spider scurried down a web it had spun from the barrel to an ammo case. The web fanned out in a sagging net of dew-hung strands. Must've been working on it all night.

He stood up, careful not to tear the web, and looked around for more damage. There was a hole in the side of the CIDG mess hall. One of the radio antennas had been knocked down. Nothing much, he thought. In front of his position lay a puddle from the last rain. Pieces of concertina wire stuck out of it and were reflected crisply on the still surface. A gust of wind rippled the pool and waved the barbs into dancers' arms.

He disconnected the detonator for the demo bunker and walked stiffly and sleepily to the washroom. Madsen was inside brushing his teeth.

"Hey, there you are," Madsen said. "How was it? Tell me what happened."

Sloane splashed water on his face. "It was OK. It only lasted—actual fighting, you know—a couple of minutes. But it was pretty hot. I got about four of them. That little A-6 works real good. Range isn't far enough, though. Next time I'd like to try the .50-cal."

"Hell, all I did was send messages," Madsen said. "I could've been a thousand miles away, for all I got to do."

"Yeah, I was hoping you'd at least get to shoot the fougasse."

The cooks were too frightened to come to work that morning, so Madsen was drafted to make breakfast. "You're the only one who got to sleep in a bed last night," said Torrez. "It's only right you should make us breakfast. I ended up sleeping next to a damn mortar. Used a bunch of those little increment bags for a pillow."

"You have to work the radios next time," Madsen said. "My turn to see some action."

"Let's see some action with those eggs," Randall said.

"How's the shoulder?" Payton asked Randall.

"Stiff . . . it's OK."

"Does it still hurt?"

"Oh, yeah."

"I want to send you back to Qui Nhon for an X-ray. Might've chipped a bone."

"OK, you're the doc. But you guys have had it if they hit you again tonight. I won't be here to run the bastards off."

"We'll get along," Wells said.

"Where're those eggs, Madsen?" Randall demanded.

"Eggs? I thought we'd have something easy, like peanut butter sandwiches."

"I like my eggs over easy and the toast not too dark."

Captain Langley came in looking tired and muddy and much older than twenty-nine. "You get all the casualties medevacked?" he asked Payton.

"Right, sir. Strikers found a couple more wounded VC in the wire, so I stuck them on the chopper, too. That makes six VC wounded and eight KIAs."

"All locals," Wells put in.

"We still just two strikers killed?" Langley asked.

"Yeah, if the guy with the chest wound pulls through," Payton said.

"That's not bad," Langley said, "'specially since Charlie must have dragged off a bunch more. How about that sapper they captured? He's unwounded, right?"

"He's just got a lump on the head. One of the strikers cold-cocked him with a carbine while he was setting a satchel charge," Payton said.

"Give that man a medal," Torrez said.

"Top," Langley said to Randall, "I want you and Wells there when he's interrogated. Make sure they don't kill him. Sloane, first thing you gotta do is put some extra claymores where the wire was blown. All in all, camp's in pretty good shape. One of the mortars knocked a hole in the supply room. Strikers got in and stole a bunch of stuff. Have to get it patched up right away. Also tell the B-team to send us more ammo and wire." He saw Madsen in the kitchen cracking eggs. "Got a new cook. huh?"

"Yeah," Randall said. "He kept talking about how he was cheated 'cause he didn't get to do any firing, so we told him he could man the stove."

Randall, Wells, and Lo-ee walked into the cement-walled interrogation room while the LLDB intel sergeant was wrapping bare commo wire around the prisoner's little toes. The prisoner's face was white and stiff. Behind him stood another LLDB holding a pistol to his head.

The LLDB intel sergeant looked up guiltily and spoke rapidly to Lo-ee, who translated: "Sergeant say they try first be nice. He no talk. He speak number ten. Have to know what VC do. Maybe tonight boocoo VC come, kill CIDG, take camp. Must find out what VC do. No can wait."

Randall nodded formally. "I agree with Sergeant Vinh. We have to know if the VC will attack the camp again. We have to know. Now."

The LLDB intel sergeant smiled at the translation and attached the other end of the wires to a battery-powered field phone. He spoke to the prisoner, who shook his head and stared sullenly at the floor. The LLDB cranked the phone. A pained gasp broke from the prisoner's mouth as his feet, then his legs, jumped and quivered. His arms shot up, clawing for the wires. Another fast jolt froze them, and he fell off the chair.

Sergeant Vinh asked again. The prisoner looked at him with silent hatred. A charge lifted him from the floor in a wave, his legs writhing up and his torso wiggling after them. His midair face was painted with surprise until a quick fit contorted it. He collapsed on the floor in a heap until another shock scooted him across the concrete.

After five minutes the words came out in a rhythmic keen. "He say he live Phu Doc," Lo-ee translated. "NVA come one week . . . tell his platoon, 'Come, you go shoot Cung Hoa.' "

"How many NVA were in the attack?" Randall asked.

"No . . . no have NVA attack. NVA tell VC attack. NVA stay Phu Duc."

"Bastards. Are they going to come back?"

"He speak no. NVA say one time, fifteen minutes, then go Phu Duc."

"Why did they tell them to hit the camp?"

"He no know. NVA no say why. Just say go shoot camp."

"That fits. OK, Lo-ee," Randall said, "tell Sergeant Vinh he did a good job. When he finds out everything the guy knows, you give Sergeant Wells a translation of his report."

The prisoner was rubbing his toes and panting. He glared at the Americans as they walked from the room.

Randall briefed Langley on the interrogation. "That shock therapy really does a job," Langley said.

"Sure does," Randall said. "Sometimes you just have to show them that telephone and they start talking."

"You think he was telling the truth?"

"Yeah. I don't think they'll try it again. They didn't want to take the camp, anyway. They're just trying to scare us. Wasn't a full-scale attack, even . . . more of a probe. Get us to stay in camp, not send out any patrols. Let 'em push all the supplies through they want."

"Looks like it worked, too. Bao said this proves he was right. Now he wants me to ask the Fourth Division to send us an artillery battery."

"Shit. We gotta get an operation out there," Randall said.

"When you're in Qui Nhon, I want you to talk to the major. See if he can shake up the LLDB from his end," Langley said. "Oh, and try to get back tomorrow. We need you."

Randall grinned. "You at least gotta give me time to get laid."

That day and the next everyone worked to repair the damage. Sloane directed the stretching of more coils of concertina wire around the camp. For a break from the radios, Madsen was allowed to supervise a sandbag-filling detail.

Randall returned to Cung Hoa with a piece of imported Chinese shrapnel a doctor had plucked from his shoulder and a promise from the B-team CO that all available leverage would be used to persuade Captain Bao to order ambush patrols along the new infiltration route.

To celebrate the CIDG victory and to boost troop morale

before moving against the NVA, a camp feast was prepared. The strikers quit work early in the afternoon and played volleyball and wrestled and told lies about all the Vietcong they had shot. Captain Bao and Captain Langley made short speeches congratulating them for fighting well and warning them not to get drunk tonight because the VC might come for revenge.

Sloane was showing Randall where he had placed the additional claymores when they saw a circle of strikers bent over talking excitedly. They walked up and peered over their shoulders and saw two huge tarantulas fighting inside a metal pail. The spiders stalked each other, fencing with their hairy legs. Suddenly one pounced on the other and seized it in its jaws. The weaker flailed around until it broke free, leaving one of its legs in the grip of its attacker. The strikers whooped and bets were paid.

Sloane thought he heard little noises coming from the pail. He wanted to thrash the strikers. "We shouldn't let them do it."

"You can't interfere with the customs," Randall said. "The Yards'll beat a dog to death with bamboo sticks before they roast it, so the meat'll be tender. And when they're on the move, they take a cow with them. Just cut off a steak when they get hungry. Sort of a walking refrigerator."

"I can't stand it," Sloane said. "Animals can't fight back."

The LLDB and the Americans dined that evening with elaborate courtesy. Toasts and compliments masked the tension between the teams. The two captains were especially polite, wishing one another every good fortune, while each considered ways to get the other relieved.

The food was concealed in sauces and had a vague odor of old wounds. Sloane chewed the dark, nameless lumps of meat and hoped they weren't dog. To cover the ripe taste, he ladled pepper sauce over everything. Least it ought to kill the germs, he thought.

After dinner and more forced smiles and diplomatic conversation, the Americans walked down to the Montagnard barracks. The small, nut brown men with the wide grins hooted out greetings. They sat down together on sleeping boards or on the floor and talked in a hash of languages.

"Now we can relax," Randall said. "Just folks." Large crocks of rice wine were carried in. "Well, well, a little noum pai. I thought this might happen." He turned to Madsen and Sloane. "You boys never been to a Montagnard initiation, have you?"

"Nope," said Madsen.

"Well, you're about to become members of the tribe." Randall spoke in Rhadé to an old sergeant. The man nodded solemnly and led Madsen and Sloane to chairs in front of the biggest jugs. The Yards laughed at the two puzzled Americans, and someone started playing a slow, insistent rhythm on a monkey-skin drum, and the men began to chant.

The two initiates drank from long reeds protruding from the tops of the jugs. The taste was rank and strong, like Thunderbird wine mixed with Everclear.

"Whew," Madsen said. "Sure is awful. No wonder these Montagnards are so mean."

"Shut up and drink," Payton said. "That stuff's good."

"Oh, yes. Sure is," Madsen said. "Yessiree. Almost as good as that sploe they make in North Carolina."

"You oughta taste the stuff they make in West Virginia," Randall said. "It'll knock your eyeballs out."

"You mean the stuff your uncle makes back there?" Madsen asked. "Say, Top, Wells told me you were thirty years old before you drank any whiskey from a bottle with a label on it."

Randall turned to Wells. "You been tellin' stories about me again?"

"Top, would I tell stories about you?" Wells asked. "You're my fuckin'-A favorite ridge-runner."

"We got a whole roomful of ridge-runners here, so watch your tongue."

As the level of the jugs dropped, they were refilled with

water from a canteen cup. The mixture became easier to drink as it was diluted. The chanting built up, and when Madsen and Sloane had each drunk a quart and their heads and stomachs were spinning, the old man marked their foreheads with red clay and clasped brass bracelets around their wrists. The chant crescendoed to a holler, and the Yards jumped up and pounded the new members of the tribe on the back.

Lo-ee pointed to their bracelets. A smile wrinkled the corners of his oxblood eyes. "You . . . me . . . both Rhadé."

Madsen hugged him. Between the wine and his emotions he could only stammer, "Thank you, Lo-ee, thank you. I'll try to be a good one."

Three helicopters arrived the next day full of colonels and their staffs from the U.S. and Vietnamese Special Forces and the U.S. Fourth Division. After arguing all afternoon, they agreed on an operation plan. A battalion of the Fourth Infantry would sweep through the area, and a company of CIDG would act as a blocking force to keep the NVA from escaping. Captain Bao gave his consent after he was promised that a U.S. infantry company would be sent to reinforce his camp if it was attacked again.

"Well, here it is," Randall said when he gave the plan to Madsen to be encoded and radioed back to the B-team. "It's going to cost about a million dollars . . . and it won't accomplish shit."

"A whole battalion? They should do some good," Madsen said.

"They're just going to walk through it," Randall said, discouraged. "Make so much noise going in, move so slow once they get there, Charlie'll just bug out till after they're gone."

"But we got the blocking force."

"Hell. LLDB's gonna take the strikers out and sit their

butts down on top of the highest hill they can find. That's their idea of a blocking force."

"Who's going?"

"Wells and Sloane. We had three colonels and about eight majors in there, and none of them knew jack shit about small unit tactics. I tried to get them to set up a lot of little ambushes. Only way you're going to shut off an infiltration route like that. Bastards said the logistics were too complicated. You know what that means? That means they can't bring the troops hot food on a chopper every day. Sorry-ass excuse for an infantry."

Madsen was pleased because Randall was again speaking frankly with him. "Looks like being over here hasn't changed that kind," Madsen said. "Hell, all they do back in the States is make sure everything is neat and the forms are filled out right. Inspect latrines. Even when they go to the field, they're more concerned about stuff not getting banged up."

Randall paced the room. "Play it safe and cover your ass, that's all they know. They got no business fighting a war. Dammit, if Yarborough was in charge, you'd start seeing some real patrolling. You can be damn sure we'd find Charlie . . . and we'd lose fewer men in the long run."

"He doesn't fit the mold, though," Madsen said.

"Nope, he doesn't. Neither do we. Fuck it."

Sloane's M-16 had lain in the muddy trench beside him while he fired the .30-caliber machine gun and had then stood uncleaned beside his bunk for two days. When he heard he was going on operation, he cleaned it immediately and apologized to it for the neglect. I hope I get to use you this time, he thought as he carried it to the CIDG range for a test firing. Facing a dirt bank, he flipped the selector switch to full automatic, braced the weapon hard against his hip, and squeezed the trigger. Do it to it. But a small metallic click was the rifle's only response. No. Not this. You're not supposed to do this. He nervously pulled the bolt back to chamber another round. Again it would not fire. Jammed up. Jilted. Are you mad at me for using the A-6 instead of you? That's not fair.

Sloane found Randall in the team house and told him about the malfunction. "You can't trust those M-16s," Randall said. "I wouldn't have one of them."

"Could I get a rifle like you've got?" Sloane asked.

"You mean my Swedish K? There's probably not more than a dozen in the country. I got it working for the Agency in Laos. Best damn weapon there is. And no, you can't borrow it."

"Maybe I could get a Thompson . . . or a grease gun."

"You've been seeing too many movies," Randall said. "A Thompson's too heavy, and a grease gun ain't accurate. Take a carbine. They always work. We got a bunch of new ones in the supply room."

"Do we have the kind with the folding stock?"

"Boy, you really think you're John Wayne going to take a screen test, don't you? I know they look good, Sloane, but you can't aim the damn things. And that's what it's all about."

"OK," Sloane said. "I'll go down and get a carbine."

"Maybe if you're lucky out there, you can capture an AK-47. They're damn-sight better than most of what we got. Just make sure you snatch up enough ammo."

The carbines were stacked in boxes in the supply room. Sloane looked them over, then closed his eyes and ran his fingers over the long cardboard boxes, trying to divine the one meant for him. This one, he thought, and pulled it out. You'll be mine. Unpacking it, he saw it was sheathed in Cosmoline lubricant jelly. Greasy steel. You'll do fine.

The carbine performed satisfactorily on the firing range and, when fitted with a long banana clip, looked sufficiently glamorous for Sloane's taste. He zeroed it and took it to his room, where he packed for the operation.

Fires were being lit inside dark houses as the company filed through the outskirts of the village before dawn. Grumpy chickens ruffled their wings. A woman jogged back from the well, her legs moving in a swinging gait and the top half of her body steady under the weight of two square water cans suspended from a pole over her narrow shoulders. She smiled through the strain and spoke to a soldier she knew.

Several kilometers past the village, the column headed south. Monsoon rains had turned the river fat and dirty. Fearing it was too deep to ford, the LLDB sergeant ordered a squad of Montagnards to test it. They clomped into the river while the others watched to see if they could make it across.

Water rose to their armpits. They held their rifles above their heads. The LLDB turned to Wells and said, "Maybe no can do." But then their trunks began emerging and they sloshed out on the other side and turned around and waved.

The rest of the company followed them. Sloane plunged in, delighted to be in another element. The water was as warm as his body and made him feel naked. It flowed up his legs and swirled around his balls. We're all joined here, below the waist, he thought while looking at a young Vietnamese, tawny as the river. The warm water dissolved tension in his legs. He cradled his rifle in one arm while his free hand unzipped his fly and rubbed his floating penis. A long relaxing stream of urine rose from inside him and flowed out into the river. What luxury. Four years old again.

By afternoon they were shambling down the trail in a long, tired line with flank squads crashing through the brush thirty meters out on each side. A small plane began circling and broadcasting at them through a loudspeaker. The plane was too high for the words to be anything but a windy jumble.

"We're being psyoped," Wells said. "They think we're VC. Fucker's afraid we'll shoot him down if he gets any lower."

"What's he say, Lo-ee?" Sloane asked.

"I no can hear," the interpreter replied. "All over noise."

The plane made another pass and spilled a load of papers into the wind. They fluttered down over the laughing men like butterflies. Wells caught one. It was a red and yellow leaflet urging them to surrender. "I'm sold," Wells said, wiping his forehead. "Hell, I been tryin' to surrender ever since I got over here. Just can't find anybody to give up to."

When they camped that night, Sloane used some doughlike C-4 plastic explosive to heat his meal. It burned with a smokeless, almost invisible flame.

"What'd you bring that shit for?" Wells asked. "Just 'cause you're a demo man don't mean you can't use wood to cook with."

"Well, I figured we might need it to interdict the trail," Sloane said. "Blow a bridge or something. Might have to set up a demo ambush."

"Need more than C-4 for a demo ambush anyway."

"That's why I brought some claymores."

"Claymores? Damn, Sloane, if you want to carry extra weight around, I'll give you some of my stuff. What else you got in there?"

"Oh, some detonators . . . few caps . . . bunch of wire."

"Man, remind me to stay away from you. You're a walkin' motherfuckin' booby trap. Sloane the human bomb. You don't actually think you're gonna get to use any of that stuff, do you?"

"That's what we're here for."

"Around here, Sloane, a blocking force is just another name for a vacation. These guys are going to find someplace safe and lay up for a week. You'd been better off to bring a book."

"Fuck it. That's not what I came in the army for."

"Look, I tried to win the war my first time over here, too," Wells said. "Don't bother. Nobody else gives a fuck. Why should you? Just put in your time and get out."

"What about the Yards?" Sloane asked. "You just going to let them get screwed?"

"They're gonna get screwed soon as we leave. Don't matter who wins."

They pushed on the next day into the hill country, closer to the infiltration route. For the first time the strikers were quiet and alert. By noon they reached the base of Chu Mat, the highest hill in the area. Instead of stopping for lunch and rest, as Sloane had hoped, they began climbing immediately. The incline increased the dragging weight of Sloane's pack. He shifted the straps from one sore spot to another and walked for a while with his thumbs hooked under, holding the load away from his aching shoulders. At least it's something. At least it's intense. His head was buzzing and his skin was creamy with sweat and oil. It smeared his glasses and trickled into his mouth. Greasy as a carbine. Greased and ready to kick ass. Sloane kept having to spit to clear his throat of dislodged wads of phlegm. Women hardly ever spit. What do they do with it? Do they swallow it? Or don't they get it? They don't fart, either. Do they learn not to fart?

Two hours later they struggled to the summit and looked out over the Annamites. For as far as they could see, mountains rose beyond mountains, each one half again faded into mist. The company sprawled out, exhausted. "These bastards can't fight, but they sure can walk," Wells said between breaths. "'Specially when they're trying to get away from Charlie."

The rest of the day was spent digging firing positions along a defensive perimeter and building shelters. In the morning the LLDB sergeant refused Wells's request to set up ambushes along the trail. He assigned a platoon of Montagnards to carry water up from a spring and dig latrines. The rest of the company lounged in their hammocks.

Wells slouched down beside Sloane. "Gonna be a long week," he said. "Should've brought some cards."

"Yeah, we could use our bullets for poker chips," Sloane said. "Not going to have any other use for them. This is awful, just lying around here. Do you get a Purple Heart for dying of boredom?"

"Hell, relax and enjoy it," Wells said, flinging spears of grass through the air like miniature javelins. "You gonna will your pecker to the cock bank?"

"What? What did you say?"

"Ain't you heard of the cock bank?"

"Come on."

"I ain't bullshittin'. They got a thing now where if you get it shot off, they got a store of 'em. All frozen. You just pick the one you want, and they sew it on."

"Get outa here, Wells."

"You think I'm shittin' you? They get 'em off guys dyin' in the hospital. Nice and fresh. Look here, young buck sergeant, the army takes care of you. They don't want morale to get low."

"Sure, sarge. Do you have to get shot to get one? I mean, what if you don't like the one you were issued to begin with? Can you go in and trade? Pick a new prick?"

"Well, you gotta re-up to do that. That's a special benefit."

"Forget it."

That afternoon Wells finally convinced the LLDB sergeant to send out patrols. He argued that since their defensive positions were now built, they needed forward security elements to give warning in case the North Vietnamese tried to take the hill. The LLDB agreed to dispatch two squads to guard the avenues of approach.

Sloane wanted to go as soon as Wells told him about it. "I can set up a demo ambush. Bound to get a bunch of 'em."

"No, you better stay here. Bad idea for the Americans to split up. Besides, you go getting yourself zapped . . . well, the team's shorthanded enough. I don't want to have to pull your guard shift," Wells said.

"Come on," Sloane said, "I'll write a note to Randall. I'll tell him I made you let me go."

"Look, Audie Murphy, the Vietnamese get nervous as hell if there's only one American around. They know if something happened to me, there wouldn't be anybody to call in air strikes or artillery. We gotta stay here with the radios."

Sloane sulked off, one side of his face twitching in nervous frustration. What a dud war, he thought. Never get it out. Fourth Infantry must be chasing lots of VC down those trails. I gotta get me one.

He went back and argued with Wells. "You know nothing's going to happen up here. You said so yourself. Only way this whole operation is going to do any good is if one of us goes along tomorrow to make sure they block those trails. Otherwise, they're just going to hide out at the bottom of the mountain . . . if they go that far. I mean, there is a reason for it all."

"Don't give me that shit, Sloane. I know you're jivin'. Reason, huh? You don't believe that any more than I do. You just got an itch." Wells paused, then continued, trying to conceal a twinge of hurt and anger. "You wanna off yourself that bad, go ahead. Go play hero. But you come back in a body bag, don't blame me."

Sloane was elated. "Thanks. Thanks a lot."

"You know, Sloane, I used to think you just had your head in the clouds. Now I know you got it up your ass."

"You've been here longer than I have. You've seen it already."

"And it's not worth seeing. But go on," Wells said with a weary shrug. "Find out for yourself."

Sloane sorted the demo gear he would need and spent an hour cleaning his carbine. In order to be well rested, he climbed into his hammock after dinner. Thoughts crowded his mind and kept him awake, but after an hour he drifted into swirls of dreams. Snails are undulating over the sunny sides of his eggs, headed for the barbed wire. They turn into dewlapped dogs loping in slow motion, their paws bursting the yolks into splattering fireballs. They keep coming in a line, long gray men. Ashes, ashes . . . all fall down.

He had an early breakfast with the CIDG squad. They looked very young. Three had no hand grenades, so he told them to borrow some from friends. He had two of them trade their carbines for M-79 grenade launchers.

Wells walked over, barefoot and sleepy. "So you're leaving me here, huh? Leaving me here with nothing to do but beat my meat."

"Yeah, I thought you'd be embarrassed if I stuck around."

"Not me. Well, have a ball."

"You too," Sloane said, giving a mock salute and starting down the hill.

"Hey, come back here," Wells yelled after him. "Where's your damn hat?"

"I left it here. It's bound to be shady down there."

"Go get it. And put it on. Charlie sees all that blond hair, you be one dead honky."

Sloane shrugged and walked over to his hammock and pulled on the floppy camouflage hat. "Do I look like a Montagnard now?"

Wells waved him off. "Get gone, numb nuts."

The patrol lurched and skidded down the hill. Above them, packing the sky, clouds hung like ripples of gray fat. Heat sat on the men, spongy and heavy. As they neared the bottom, the rain forest grew thicker until only an occasional slice of sky could be seen through the trees.

Sloane was happy to be out with ten men instead of a company. This is the only way to find any VC. Lurid, flaunting blossoms dangled from the vines, lush and velvet-petalled. Sloane pulled one loose and stuck it through a buttonhole on his fatigues. A corsage for the dance. Mosquitoes batted around his head, and the air was stagnant and thick as fog. Sloane felt he was breathing inside a plastic bag. The ground and the foliage were slippery with moisture. Where are we? Spelunking down into the Earth Mother's lavish cunt. This is far enough.

The strikers were worried because the squad radio wasn't working; they were unable to contact the main company. They walked cautiously along, listening for movement coming their way, looking for a good place to set up an ambush, hoping they wouldn't run into one themselves. Sloane vetoed two locations they wanted. Both were secure defensively but wouldn't allow him to place his demolitions for maximum effectiveness. The men were anxious to stop and grew increasingly sullen as he forced them to continue.

Finally they came to a bend in the trail. There was good visibility both ways and a fairly open killing zone where Sloane could set his claymores. A stream ran nearby. Its sound would help cover their noise. A steep rise to a thick clump of brush would protect the men in case the VC were well-disciplined enough to charge their position.

With relief the CIDG climbed the slope and began preparing their defenses. They posted two men on the trail to warn if anyone approached. Sloane placed the claymores one after the other so he could fire them consecutively as the VC ran through the field. They sat in the grass like tiny curved billboards.

At the rear of the killing zone stood some trees. Sloane figured any VC who survived the claymores would crawl behind them for shelter. He broke off hunks of plastic explosive and molded them around electric blasting caps and laid them next to several trees. They looked like snowballs in the jungle. He connected them to a long double strand of wire, which he gathered together with the claymore wires and extended up to the CIDG position. Where the wires crossed the trail, he buried them in a shallow trench. Then he covered everything with dirt and dead leaves and stood back to survey his work. Immaculate, he thought.

In urgent pidgin, the squad leader insisted to Sloane that if more than six VC came down the trail, his men would not attack. Sloane ignored him and walked back up to their camouflaged defenses. This is what we should be doing every day. What's it going to be like, face to face? What if I have to strangle one of them? Garrote him with a strand of wire. Could I do it? What if he turned around while I was doing it to him, turned around and stared his bulging eyes right into mine?

A light, steady rain began falling. The men ate cold rice and watched the trail. Although they were well hidden in the brush, Sloane forbade them to smoke. This made them more restless and grumbly, and Sloane started to worry that they would decide it was time to go back. He knew someone would come down the trail eventually. He would have to find a way to force the men to stay until their quarry appeared.

While mulling it over, he sat on the soaked, miry ground with his back against a dead tree. Mushrooms grew from rotting wood. In the rain they smelled like semen, and Sloane imagined drifting spores seeking fungal ova. Squish. It's squishy here. He broke off one of the caps, turned it over, and saw a hundred-legged worm crawling in circles over the fluted underbelly. Sloane shuddered and flung it away. The strikers looked at him curiously. He brushed off the back of his shirt and moved away from the mushroom log.

While he was looking for a clean place, a CIDG tapped him on the back. He turned around, expecting to have a worm thrown in his face. Instead, the CIDG pointed through the hatching of palm fronds to a group of men in gray uniforms walking down the trail.

Sloane sucked in air with a swoop. They're here! This is it.

"Boocoo VC . . . VC Hanoi . . . we no can do," the squad leader whispered.

Sloane glared him into silence. They were only five, and he knew he had them. Sudden sweat, more acrid than any he had smelled before, slicked his body.

The CIDG, eyes big with fear, got down into position. Sloane picked up the detonator for the first claymore. His heart had turned into a bird's and he couldn't catch his breath and he wanted to run. He saw the men more closely now, walking absentmindedly down the trail. One carried his rifle upside down by the barrel, resting the stock against his shoulder. Another man wiped rain from his forehead with a sash tied around his neck. Am I going to do it? Kill those men? Have to. It's no crazier than anything else. We're partners. This is the senior prom. And now we do it.

As the men slogged in front of him, Sloane stood up

screaming. Their heads jerked toward the sound, and when all their startled eyes were on him, he squeezed the detonator. With a rending clap, a swarm of fire and steel pellets cut through the men. When the air cleared, Sloane saw three of them running for the trees. The remaining two were still on the trail, one lying in a heap, the other on his knees, swaying back and forth. The CIDG were firing their carbines, but Sloane's head was ringing so loud that he did not hear the reports but only saw spent cartridge cases flipping from rifles.

The NVA were almost to the second claymore. Sloane groped in the mud for the detonator, squeezed it quickly, and saw from the location of the explosion that he had fired the wrong one. It blasted the grass in front of the men but left them untouched and running even faster. Cursing himself, he fired the remaining claymore, but the men were now beyond its lethal fan.

One of the running men spun around, struck by a CIDG bullet. He fell slowly to the ground while the CIDG yelled and the other two reached the cover of trees. Branches snapped above Sloane's head as the men returned fire. The zipping closeness of death gave him a second burst of exhilaration. Now . . . I just hope they picked the right trees. He twisted the large detonator, and the underbrush erupted. Two trees fell over, and a body lofted gently into the air, wrapped in fire.

The strikers cheered and began firing their grenade launchers randomly into the woods. Sloane grabbed his carbine and shouted, "Come on. Let's go." He ran down the slope eagerly, his weapon on full automatic, his mind swimming with murder. On the trail, one of the men still wobbled on his knees, staring incredulously at his intestines as they spilled into his hands. Another man lay beside him, his skin puffy with pellet wounds, one side of his face smudged and crushed.

Sloane ran across the field, expecting to be shot. He passed a man trying with quivering effort to raise his head. Leave him for the strikers. They brought him down. The ground was scorched from the claymores, and the air was full of fine floating dust. A hollow, stunned silence roared in his ears. A fire-blackened man, humped and skewed, was sprawled beside a ripped-up tree. From his body rose a funk-gut, burnt-shit smell. Blood flowed from his nose and ears and frothy blood like strawberry chiffon bubbled out of his mouth.

A dazed bird sat heavily on the branch of a crippled tree. Sloane wandered around aimlessly, fighting to repress a billowing, giddy hysteria. What did I do? All my spent and broke-back lovers lying in the field. The CIDG shot the man in the head who was swaying on his knees, and he fell forward onto what had been his face.

This is how we work it out. Boys and girls don't like each other very much. . . . This is what we do instead. Where's that other little devil? I know there were five of 'em.

Sloane felt his hands, then looked at them. How did they get dirty? Didn't touch any of them. He walked to the stream and hopped down from the bank to the sandy edge of the water. Death, he thought, while washing his hands in a deep lazy pool. I brought them death. He knelt there slightly stunned, not quite knowing where he was, watching raindrops spread rings across the water.

A soft pop was followed by a rustle in the brush. He looked up to see a hand grenade curving through the air. It thunked on the bank above him, bounced once, and sat there. Sloane's mind overloaded with panic. His arms cradled his carbine to his chest, and his legs propelled him froglike into the pool. He started to bob back up, then grabbed a rock on the bottom and pulled himself down to it. The concussive slap wiped out the rain rings and bucked him coughing and pawing to the surface. I don't want to die, I don't want to die, he thought, expecting to be ripped by shrapnel. Instead he was pelted by falling dirt and pebbles. He looked up cautiously. The bank was collapsed and scorched. Rain again dappled the water. The current was nudging him against some rocks. Maybe he's going to throw another one. Maybe he's going to shoot me. Sloane's wet body broke into shivers. He pulled his muddy carbine from the water. You'd better work, dammit. Mud's no excuse.

Raising the rifle in the stream, he heard the crunch of feet treading on foliage. His shivers became trembles. He's coming to get me. I don't want to die. He shouted the words in his mind. I DON'T WANT TO DIE.

Gunshots cleft the air so close he could feel the wind waves. NO! I'm not going to let him! His mind, clear and detached, rode a torrent of energy. More bullets kicked into the water behind him. He vaulted over the bank and into the brush. Go wide and circle him. No noise. The commands came from a place of quiet resolve. From there he watched his quick, deliberate movements, and he watched his simmering fear. Eyes seemed to spread across his face, registering nuances of light and shadow. Ears extended into antennae, sifting the sounds of the rain forest. Toes guided his step toward twigless spots. His mind stretched out, searching for another. Where is he—my man, my other? Searching for me.

Sloane picked his way through the rank, teeming vegetation. Stems and vines and sprouts curled like an orgy of snakes. Their clutching, slippery touch set his fear boiling. His inner observer took hold of him again. You've got to crawl through it. That's the only way he's not going to hear you. You've got to crawl through there on your belly and kill him.

Sloane dropped into the loathed mud and started scrabbling through it with his feet and elbows, his hands holding his rifle in front of him. Wet leaves lapped over his neck. The putrid stench of fertile rot gagged his throat. Sweat mingled with the ooze and slime that covered him. He thrust his way ahead, spitting mud, part of him eerily serene.

Breaking through to a small clearing, he paused, straining

to sense the man's presence. He raised his wet, reeking body to its knees, waited again, and cautiously stood up. Grass in the clearing glistened with rain. Then out of the bushes stepped a slight youth in a gray uniform. His features etched themselves in Sloane's mind with indelible clarity: a small nose, Modigliani mouth, large curved earlobes hiding in sleek black hair. A dark brown mole graced a light sienna cheek. The curving eyebrows looked as if they had been done with a broad pen and India ink. The eyes themselves were a dark pipeline into Sloane. Around his neck was a yellow scarf. His shirt was unbuttoned halfway down his chest. At his waist he held a carbine identical to Sloane's.

He's wonderful, Sloane thought. I've got to take him.

The two minds met. Simultaneously and in slow motion, the men raised their rifles like figures in a mirror. Each looked deep into the other and exploded. In a flash of white they fell, senses swirling.

Sloane was gone a long time. When he finally spun back to his body, he was surrounded by Vietnamese with carbines. Captured. Now they'll cut my nuts off.

The rusty taste of blood filled his mouth. He touched his face, and pain leaped across it. His hand came away dark and wet. Shot in the head, he thought, expecting to die.

One of the Vietnamese knelt beside him. Sloane blinked the blood from his eyes and recognized the CIDG squad leader, who stared at his face and shook his head. The strikers were talking and pointing. One of them held up a small survival mirror. Sloane saw a deep gash on his nose, flecked with pieces of his shattered glasses. Blood was welling out of it, covering his face and dripping off his ears. Maybe it's in my brain. Maybe the bullet's in my brain. No . . . you wouldn't be here. Maybe I'm paralyzed. He slowly and painfully raised himself to a sitting position. No. OK. Must've just clipped you. He checked the rest of his body. It was all there.

Where is he? What happened to him? I remember. We

were on fire. He dimly saw a figure lying on the ground across the clearing. He tried to crawl toward it, but the squad leader stopped him and talked soothingly while he wrapped a bandage over the wound. Sloane pulled it down so he could see and kept crawling. He reached the man with whom he had been joined. The face was instantly and vividly recognizable. It's him, he thought with jarring dismay. The man was lying on his back and his shirt was soaked with blood. Sloane pulled it open and was startled to see blood pulsing gently out of a hole in the lithe, delicate chest. Have to help him. He put his hand over the hole but the blood flowed on, mingling with his own. We'll medevac him. I want to take him back. Don't want him to die.

Sloane patted the limp hand. "I'll take care of you. Don't worry." He looked again into the eyes, seeking the same deep communication they had shared a few minutes before. But the eyes were solidifying to agate. The hand twitched against his, and life sighed out of him like the airspent plunge of a penny balloon.

A cry tore from Sloane, and he collapsed, falling hand in hand with his partner through a dark cavern.

When he came back, the hand he held was cool and still. He's gone, Sloane thought. Something in Sloane crumbled to powder and sifted away.

The CIDG squad leader approached. "You number one. Kill boocoo VC. VC fini," he said and offered him a dried apricot.

Sloane was tying to decide whether he was hungry when he realized he was being presented with a severed ear. If they cut him up, he thought, if they touched him, I'll kill them. He pushed the squad leader away and examined the body. Both ears were intact, and he was unmarked except for the wound Sloane had given him. One of the strikers held out a knife so he could collect his trophy. Sloane lurched to his feet, glared at them all, and said, "He's mine, damn you, and he gets to keep his ears."

They looked at him perplexedly. Sloane saw they had

emptied the man's pack. Scattered on the ground were a small cook pot, a ball of glutinous rice, a poncho and a hammock, a tiny kerosene lamp made from a perfume bottle, and a packet of letters and pictures. Sloane started to pick them up, but decided against it. I couldn't face that. Anyway, I don't want him to have a past. Just our moment. He claimed the man's carbine, though, and laid it next to his own.

As the shock began to wear off, an intense pain took its place. The pain was yellow and crawled behind his eyes. Can't stand it. Have to do some morphine. He recalled and instantly dismissed the prohibition against taking morphine for a head wound. Best reason there is for taking it.

Sloane sent one of the strikers to get his pack and when it arrived he took out his extra pair of glasses and a morphine Syrette. The glasses with their elastic retainer band increased the pain, but he was afraid he wouldn't be able to find a vein without them, and he knew he couldn't wait for an intramuscular injection to take effect. He looked for something to tie off with, then stumbled over to the man he had killed. Kneeling beside him, he unfastened the red-star NVA belt buckle and noticed that he, like Sloane, dressed left. Sloane slipped the belt from around the thin waist, wrapped it tightly around his arm, and pumped his fist to build pressure. When a vein bulged on his forearm, he unscrewed the cap of the Syrette and tried to push the needle into it. But the point was wide and dull, meant for jabbing into a muscle, not for fine probing. Every time he thrust, it pushed the vein to the side and added another jot of pain. Goddammit, no self-respecting junkie would be caught dead using works like this. Finally he pinched up and held the vein while sliding the needle into it. He squeezed the contents of the tube into his bloodstream, loosened the belt, and in less time than it takes a grenade to explode, he was hit from behind by a giant pillow that burst open and filled him with feathers. His jaw sagged, and he melted to a puddle beside the man who had given him his wound. From far off he saw the strikers staring at him. He felt he was turning into a curled worm. Warm fuzz covered him. His pain slept.

Sloane returned from his nod to see a prisoner lying nearby. From the wound in his leg, he knew he must be the one who had been shot by the CIDG while running for the trees. The squad leader stood above Sloane, holding a carbine and saying, "VC no can walk. CIDG no can carry. Cac-a-dau VC." Sloane reached out to stop him, but then realized the impossibility of carrying a stretcher back up the hill and remembered they had seen no clearings large enough for a medevac chopper. Leaving him might betray their direction. He looked at the squad leader and they both shrugged.

The prisoner lay on the ground with his eyes closed, rubbing his tied hands. At the sound of a rifle bolt being pulled back, he opened his eyes to see the carbine pointed at him. The man started to speak, but terror choked the words. With his one good leg, he tried to crawl away, but bullets tore into him, jerking his body. Sloane was so close he could hear what they did to his flesh . . . did to his flesh. One splatted into his back. Another broke away a piece of his head. His body shook with spasms that gradually tapered off.

The CIDG were in a hurry to leave and began gathering up enemy equipment and documents. Sloane, anxious to show them he could walk so they wouldn't shoot him, struggled to his feet and shouldered his pack and the two rifles. He was numb and couldn't tell if he was moving very fast or very slowly. The morphine made him feel he had mud instead of blood in his veins. Men, he thought. It's all just men.

The strikers filed out of the clearing, but Sloane lingered for a moment, looking for the last time at the man he had killed. He felt he had known him since before he was born. The body was now inert and drained of color. The eyes were dry and dull. We were so close.

The trail was easy, but Sloane stumbled on with short,

paddling steps because the morphine and the bleeding had weakened him and the bandage kept him from seeing the ground at his feet. He felt he was floating above his body like a balloon, attached by a thin strand, looking down on himself, bemused. One of the strikers, cocky and scared, taunted him to go faster. "Di-di. Mau len," he said, imitating a tough sergeant. Sloane was oblivious, but the other CIDG told the man to shut up. They didn't know what the strange American would do if antagonized.

Sloane saw that his hands were covered with grime and blood, his own and the other man's. His soiled hands did not bother him now. Last week got made a blood brother with the Yards. Today with the VC. He began noticing the forest around him. The rain had stopped, and a breeze blew through the bamboo with a soft clatter. Butterflies big as saucers glided on the currents. Parrots flew among massive trees, and monkeys shrieked in the branches. The sun glowed through clouds like a pearl. It's beautiful here. I never knew it was so beautiful. I could stay here forever . . . join the monkeys.

After a timeless span, Sloane found himself tottering into the company bivouac. He was alarmed by the shock on Wells's face as it ran toward him.

"What the fuck happened to you?" the sergeant demanded.

"I got him."

"Here, lay down. Dammit, I told you not to go." Wells checked the wound and called on the radio for an urgent medevac.

"I got 'em all," Sloane said, folding to the ground. "Well . . . strikers got one of 'em. But I got all the rest. 'Specially the last one."

"How did you get hit?"

"He shot me. First he shot at me while I was running. . . . Then I came up on him, and he shot me in the nose. I got him, though. Wish we could've brought him back. He died, though. They all died."

"Just be quiet now," Wells said. "Medevac'll be here in a minute."

Sloane closed his eyes and drifted in colors. When the helicopter arrived, it flew straight and level toward their position with the rotor blades chopping the engine noise into a machine gun staccato. Sloane sat up, blinking and flailing. "Are we hit?" he yelled. "Are we getting hit?"

"It's your medevac," Wells shouted.

"Huh?"

Wells and two CIDG lifted him onto the aircraft.

He tugged Wells's sleeve. "Tell Madsen," he rasped. "Tell Madsen about it."

Wells nodded, and Sloane went under.

Madsen stormed around the commo bunker in anguish. His friend had been shot in the head. His life might be slipping from him right now, and there was nothing Madsen could do about it. The ambush and Sloane's wound increased Madsen's sense of being cut off from intense experiences he knew must always be pulsing somewhere beyond him. Words, all I've got is words over the radio. At least Sloane really did something.

John Randall went off by himself that night. He took some beer down to the demo bunker and sat on top of it drinking and staring up at the moonless sky. His tour was nearly over and he had to decide whether to extend or go back to the States. Don't want to do either, he thought, getting up and fumbling through the darkness to take a piss. "Not enough light out here to find your pecker with," he muttered.

While the used beer streamed out of him, he thought of what he would be going back to—pointless work details. Pompous officers. A tired waste of days. His wife and the net of cruddy domesticity. He remembered her immersed in hairpins and housecoats and daytime television. The bowl of soggy cornflakes she liked to eat before bed. He thought of the other two women, the bored back-dooring. Maybe it would've been different if we'd had kids.

He shook himself dry. What the hell. Might as well extend. Got a pretty fair team. Looks like Charlie's gonna start giving us a little more action. Keep life interesting. That crazy Sloane. Hope he pulls through.

Captain Langley was promoted to major and decided against extending. He told the team he would be leaving in a few days. He also announced that the LLDB had managed to catch the district chief selling medical supplies to a VC contact. His corruption was common knowledge, but until now he had never been caught in the act. The district chief would be transferred and a new one sent in.

"Can't they jail him?" Madsen asked. "For collaborating with the enemy or something?"

"No, that's the bitch of it. All they can do is pass him on to somebody else."

"The old LLDB really came through," Randall said. "We'll have to get 'em that generator they've been asking for."

Lieutenant Krenwood, Captain Langley's replacement, gathered the team together for an initial briefing. He clasped his hands behind his back and spoke in crisp tones. "All right, men, now listen up. We got a lot of work to do around this camp to get it squared away. Sergeant Randall, I want you to get a detail to cut down all that grass that's growing up around the barbed wire. And we want to put in a requisition for some paint."

The men exchanged glances and walked away.

The next several days were spent sprucing up the area. The men treated the new CO as just another bad joke, another burden they had to bear. "He looks like he got a dick up his ass and don't want nobody to know about it," Wells said.

Captain Ngoc, the new district chief, convinced the Americans to order equipment so that the villagers could build a fish pond. They would need tools, cement, a water hoist, and an initial stocking of tilapia. He had the local geomancer pick the most auspicious location for the pond and the channel that would connect it to the river. The borders were outlined on the ground with rocks. When the equipment arrived, he dug the first shovelful of dirt and then turned the work over to the village construction brigade he had organized. He also asked Payton to begin training local medical and hygiene workers and to send in a malaria spray team.

Randall was impressed. "Either the guy's got an awful slick hustle, or he really gives a damn," he told Madsen. "Wish we could trade him for Krenwood."

Sloane awoke floating in white. All he could see was swaying milkiness. At first there was silence, then a noise, a squeaking that grew louder and louder. He tried to rise, to swim through the wash. A part of the whiteness held his wobbling arms and said, "Easy there, partner, you'll be OK. Just lie back down."

A blurred face separated itself from the amorphous background. "Just lie back down," the medic repeated. "Anesthetic's got you a little dingie. You'll come out of it after a while."

Sloane tried to speak, but couldn't form the sounds into words.

Slowly, as he lay on his back, the shapes of the hospital ward emerged and came into focus. He could see a fan above him as it languidly stirred the air, squeaking with each rotation. He could feel gauze wrappings around the middle of his face and muffled pain throbbing under them.

I was dancing in the fire. He was beautiful. Threw my life into the air, dancing. Here I am . . . out on this side. He's still back there. His body.

Several days later they took off the bandages. His nose was gnarled and smashed, covered with crusted blood. "I know it looks pretty bad now," the doctor said. "But son, when you get back to the States . . . why, they'll fix it up good as new. Rebuild the whole thing. All those scars and everything. It'll be just the way it was before."

"It's fine the way it is," Sloane said, checking out the jagged profile in a mirror. "I like it. Really, it'll do fine."

He was sent across town to the B-team to recuperate. It was an old walled compound near the beach. Sloane imagined it had been the offices of a wealthy, corrupt comprador dealing in silks, opium, and slave girls. Now it quartered twenty Special Forces men who did administrative and supply work for seven A-teams in the surrounding provinces.

Sloane took walks and lay on the beach and did occasional chores for the sergeant major. He was not quite the same. A current of tension was gone. He found he was able to look at just one thing without having to dart his eyes. And now he didn't tap his foot compulsively. He felt quiet and light and cleaned out, as if he were unclogged, but the feeling was still fragile and new, like the fresh pink skin forming on his nose.

I don't know what it is, he thought. Maybe I'm just exhausted.

In the evenings he sat alone in the club, drinking brandy for his pain and planning dozens of different demo ambushes. So many ways to do it. We'll have that infiltration route choked off in no time. He wrote to Madsen telling him he hoped to be back soon and now maybe Randall would let the two of them take a patrol out together.

The sergeant major had him go to the admin center a few blocks away to pick up some office supplies. He gave the requisition to an aloof young Vietnamese woman who abruptly drew lines through the items they were out of and went to get the rest. He had seen her before, walking on the beach during the long midday breaks. While she searched for the carboned memo forms, he watched her straight black hair falling over her downcast eyes. Her face was not beautiful, but it blended triangles and ellipses into a symmetry that made Sloane forget to breathe. She was lissome as a reed, and her body flowed with each movement.

A woman, Sloane thought. Wow, she sure is a woman. Always before, when he was so close to something he wanted so badly, he knotted up inside and couldn't communicate. But now he was sufficiently drained of pressure to be able to reach out. He didn't even care if she said no. "What time do you finish work?" he asked when she handed him the last article.

"What?" she said.

"When are you through working? We could go to dinner, and you could show me Qui Nhon."

Her lips pursed full as she regarded him for the first time. "I no date GI."

"OK. It doesn't have to be a date. See, you can be the interpreter . . . so I'll know what to order in the restaurant."

"No. Too busy." She spun around, flaring the skirt of her ao dai, and walked away.

He was back the next day on manufactured business.

"Again? What you forget?"

"Well, you see we need a survey of your available supplies. Our general is very upset. He can't stand the wasted effort that goes into ordering supplies you don't have. It's inefficient all the way around. First we gotta take the time to think up the supplies to put on the list. Then you gotta take the time to tell us you don't have 'em. Waste of manpower, the general says. And you know the general. He's a stickler for efficiency."

"I no understand."

"It's easy. All you have to do is take me around to the supplies and I'll make a list of the ones you've got. Then, from now on, those are the only ones we'll ask for."

"You talk to sergeant over there," she said, pointing to an overweight E-7 sitting at a desk in the rear of the office. "He my boss."

"Nope. General says it's the person who fills these requisitions. That's who we need. She's the one who really knows what they've got on hand. It has to be you. You know the general."

"Has to be? Well . . . OK. You tell me again what we do."

They spent the next hour going from shelf to shelf with her explaining to him about the paper clips and typewriter ribbons and office forms, and with him hovering near her, inhaling her presence, devastated by the way her eyes flashed through her heavy lashes and the way her slightly buck teeth met her lower lip when she spoke. He tried to get her to talk about herself, but she was all business. He did, however, manage to extract her name—Trinh. When they were done she said, "We fini? Good. I have boocoo work."

A spec four in the office had noticed Sloane's interest. "Take my advice," he said. "Don't even bother. Every guy around here has tried to get something going with her. Zilch. I think she's Cong, myself. Won't have anything to do with us. You try to grab her, she kicks the shit out of ya. You'd save yourself a lot of trouble by just going downtown and paying for it."

"I got a different kind of 'it' in mind."

Sloane bought some civilian clothes at the PX the next day. You almost look like a real person, he told his reflection in the mirror. Crooked nose and all.

He borrowed a jeep on a pretext and was parked in front of the admin center at five-thirty. When she emerged from the building he waved to her.

"You!" she said. "What you want today? We closed."

"Good," he said. "I thought I'd give you a ride home. Maybe talk you into going to dinner with me. You might as well say yes . . . so I can stop pestering you."

"Pester? What is pester? You funny, GI."

"Yeah, I'm funny. Hop in."

Interest and skepticism played across her face. "Why you ask me?"

"I like you, Trinh."

"You no can read food in restaurant? Poor GI. Maybe you starve. Tomorrow I help you. Tonight I no can do. Now you go way. I no want GI here see we talk. Tomorrow five-thirty you come fountain. You know big fountain? I come there. We go. But only dinner."

Sloane's face smiled and his mind whooped as he drove away.

He was waiting for her when she arrived at the fountain a few blocks from the admin center. After glancing around, she got in and they drove through the narrow, noisy streets. She told him to stop in front of a pale blue stucco building with a red tile roof and dusty green plants hanging over a second story balcony. She ran inside, saying she would be a minute and he should wait. He sat in the jeep, watching the people and vehicles stream by. Several children climbed up on the hood and stared at him. Through the noise of the traffic, he heard the faint calling of a temple gong.

A half hour passed, and Sloane began to think she had ditched him. Some of his old dejection returned when he imagined that she was peeking at him from a balcony and laughing. But then he saw her coming down the stairs. She got into the jeep wearing a brocade silk ao dai and the scent of gardenias.

Sloane's hand trembled as he turned the ignition.

They had dinner in a small restaurant with ornately tiled walls and battered wooden tables. She translated the menu for him, then ordered what she wanted him to have. When the meal arrived she showed him the correct way to drink the soup and how to dip the glazed pork into the different sauces and which vegetables to mix with the rice and which to eat separately. Perhaps because of his nose, the aroma of nuoc mam did not bother him, and the taste seemed piquant.

Sloane wanted to find out all about her—what she liked to do, where she had grown up, what she had done as a girl, what her plans were for the future. But she parried his questions and asked him about his family and what he had done before the army. She looked sad when he told her he had no brothers or sisters. "When you little boy you have to play all alone? I sorry. Better to have brother, sister. I have boocoo. Two brother, three sister."

"Are they older than you?" Sloane asked.

"No. All younger. I the very old."

"Do they live here in Qui Nhon?"

"No, they live Hue city. Very far." Then she started talking about the dinner and how the sauces weren't spicy enough and how Sloane was holding his chopsticks like a monkey. She took his hand to adjust his fingers, and Sloane shivered inside.

But when he suggested a walk along the beach after dinner, she drew herself up and said with indignation, "No. I no good-time girl. I have job. Work very hard. GI treat Vietnam girl number ten."

"No . . . I," Sloane began to stammer, appalled at himself for insulting her. "I didn't mean it that way. I just . . . I'd just like to get to know you . . . to talk to you."

"You boocoo lie."

"I'm not lying. You have to give me a chance. We'll go out tomorrow night, and I won't ask you to do anything. I won't even tell you how pretty you look. We'll just go to dinner again. Maybe try a different place. With spicy sauce."

"No can do. Sorry."

"Look, we don't have time for this. I've got to go back soon. We have to see each other now."

"You go back?" she asked, startled. "You go back America?"

"No. I have to go back to my team."

"Where you go?"

"Cung Hoa. You know Cung Hoa?"

"No . . . never. Where?"

"Phu Binh province."

"Ooh . . . boocoo VC. You go back fight VC?"

"Yes."

"That how you get hurt your nose?" she asked, looking at his scar with fascination.

"Yes."

"When you go back?"

"About a week."

"Ooo . . . you go back one week."

"Maybe sooner."

They finished dinner in silence. As they were leaving the restaurant, she said without looking at him, "Night I no go beach. But maybe OK in day. Maybe you come fountain twelve-thirty. I see you."

Sloane felt like a prisoner being released. He gathered all his remaining aplomb and said, "Twelve-thirty. Right."

When they reached her house, she hopped out of the jeep and ran inside. On the stairway, she turned around and waved to him.

"The way you been running around here, Sloane, I guess you're healthy enough to start doing some work." The B-team sergeant major took another bite of French toast. "We got to break down the rice ration for the different teams. Get it ready to airlift tomorrow. You check with the supply sergeant. He'll get you a detail of slopes."

Sloane, seeing his date with Trinh threatened by military whim, groped for an excuse. "I have to see the doctor today."

"Ain't they done with you yet? They can't make you any uglier."

"They gotta . . . they said they gotta check something."

"Yeah . . . check to see if you got a dose of the clap. What time you supposed to be there?"

"Uh . . . noon."

"No sweat . . . long as you're back by 1400. We run on Mese time around here—two-hour lunch breaks. You'll just have to miss yours."

"I don't mind."

Inside the warehouse the rice was stacked in hundred-pound burlap bags. It came from "Hobart, Louisiana, the Rice Capital of America." Trays of rat poison sat on the warehouse floor. The supply sergeant told Sloane to supervise eight Vietnamese laborers while they loaded the bags onto a truck. Supervising, Sloane discovered, meant standing there watching the man work. He did this for a while, leaning against the truck and daydreaming about Trinh, but the contrast of his idleness to the workers' exertions made him feel useless, so he soon joined them in carrying the sacks. He liked the solidity of the hefting and hauling.

At noon he rinsed his tired body in a shower and walked to the fountain. It stood in front of a government building near the embarcadero. The centerpiece was a bronze statue of a Vietnamese soldier. The water had been turned off, and the dry pool around it was scattered with bird droppings and bits of paper.

Sloane saw her coming a block away. She walked with small steps and a slight, involuntary swing of the hips. She greeted him coolly, but when they got to the beach she smiled and took off her sunglasses so he could see her eyes as they talked about their morning's activities. Trinh was disappointed that Sloane had never seen the rice paddies of Louisiana.

They bought slices of pineapple on skewers and ate them in the shade, watching the white breakers furl up the sand and momentarily hide the piles of black sludge from the navy ships. Sea gulls sliced the blue sky above them. Sloane tried to tell her that the gulls' wings reminded him of the curve of her eyebrows, but she thought he was saying that she had eyes like a sea gull's. At this, she huffily put her sunglasses back on.

They walked near the water, detoured by an occasional snarl of barbed wire. He took off his boots and she her shoes, and the sand sugared their toes.

"In America, have beach like this?" she asked.

"The water is not so blue."

"Have little bird?" she asked, pointing to a flock of sandpipers scurrying out of wave-reach.

"Sure."

At a café near the water they ate bowls of noodle soup so peppery it brought tears to Sloane's eyes. "David very sad," she said with a mocking smile. "So sorry." It took a slice of watermelon and a lime-flavored Sno-cone to cool his palate.

"That must be the spicy sauce you were telling me about."

"It good for you."

"We'll go out tonight?"

"Tonight? Very soon." She hesitated. "OK. I tell girl friend I no can see."

He took her hand as they left the place, but she pulled it away. "No can do," she said. "People speak me number ten."

Before releasing his hand, however, she gave it a squeeze.

Sloane was back in the warehouse carrying rice bags that afternoon. He had gotten to know the other men a little, and they worked together at a slow, comfortable pace. One of them approached the truck with a bag of rice over his shoulder and, instead of boosting it on in, he dropped his arm to let the bag slide off and catch the corner of the tailgate. It tore and thudded to earth, spilling rice. The laborer dramatically cursed his own clumsiness while the others began scooping up the rice with buckets and shovels and dumping in into another bag. By the time they finished bustling about, a third of the rice had disappeared.

They must have it hidden around here someplace, Sloane thought. Oh, well, fuck it. Let them have it. If they try it again, I'll shake the place down.

He met their innocent shrugs with a glare, and they all continued working.

That evening Trinh decided that Sloane was in need of more familiar cuisine, so they drove to a restaurant on the outskirts of Qui Nhon that had a French-trained chef. They ate delicious coq au vin and an unfortunate crème brûlée. In the corner, scratchy French 78s played on a new SONY record player.

It was growing dark as they left, and when Sloane slipped his arm around her waist, she did not move away. The air was fresher out here, without the taint of aircraft exhaust that hung over much of the city. Driving back, they felt they were just themselves; the rest of it seemed safely remote. They smiled at each other, with no need for speech.

A spotlight and a shout splashed over them, breaking their charmed bubble. "Hey! Hold it. MPs!" Through his dazzled eyes, Sloane could see two MPs and one white-uniformed Vietnamese policeman in a jeep parked beside the road. One of them blew a whistle and shouted again. Their headlights flashed on, and they pulled out into the road, blocking it. "Stop right there!"

Sloane had neither a permit for the jeep nor a pass to leave the downtown area after eight o'clock. If they caught him, it was all over. Unauthorized use of a military vehicle, especially for squiring a young Vietnamese civilian female, would land him back in Cung Hoa on the next flight. He might never see her again. By the panic in her eyes, he could tell that capture would also mean disgrace for her. He squeezed her hand. "No sweat. Hold on. We're not gonna let those bastards do this to us."

He cranked the steering wheel, spinning the jeep around and tossing gravel back onto the MPs, who swore, ground their gears, switched on the siren, and sped in pursuit. David and Trinh skidded around a corner onto a residential side street. A few pedestrians and a dog hustled out of the way as Sloane stomped the accelerator to the floor and charged down the dirt road. In his mirror he saw the MPs careen around the corner behind them. With their more powerful engine, the MPs picked up speed rapidly and were soon closing on them.

Afraid of the siren, people were snuffing their house lights all the way down the street. Ahead Sloane saw a traffic circle, with busier avenues converging. He pulled into it and, after a quick look, veered sharply left, against the flow of traffic. The inside lane was clear, except for a taxi, which swerved out of their path, honking. He took the first left and saw the MPs slow down and go with the traffic, all the way around the circle. By the time the MPs reached the same avenue, David and Trinh were three blocks ahead.

He turned right into a narrow street closely bordered by two-story tenements. There was no room to maneuver, and he felt trapped. Three cyclo drivers sat chatting in their pedicabs, blocking the road ahead. Sloane honked and yelled, but by the time they backed their machines out of the way and Sloane drove through, the MPs had rounded the corner and were again bearing down.

Wish I had a grenade, I'd frag the damned MPs, Sloane thought as he saw their headlights enlarging. Then he remembered a smoke grenade hooked to the back of the seat. Oh, yes. It's less than they deserve, but it'll help. He reached behind him, grabbed the grenade, pulled the pin, and tossed it out. Red smoke billowed up, covering the street and filling the space between the tenements. In Trinh's eyes glittered a wild excitement. As David turned the next corner, he heard a screech of brakes, then coughing and swearing.

Zigzagging through a labyrinth of alleys and lanes, he put as much distance between them and the MPs as he could. Then he switched off the lights and slowed down, pausing at each intersection to look for their pursuers before darting across. The road became scarcely more than a path, abutted on both sides by buildings with laundry strung between them. People peered out their windows, and dogs barked as the jeep crept down dark, winding lanes.

Finally he pulled into a gateway and turned off the engine. No siren sounds reached their ears. They sat in the stillness, breathing heavily, feeling a growing sense of elation and freedom. "We did it," David whispered. She looked at him and smiled. The night hung around them, rich with odor and small sounds. It made them move closer together, reach out and grasp hands. The fragile tenderness of their touching was a wash of delight for Sloane. I'd dodge them again, he thought, just for this.

Slowly, clumsily, with a stubborn gearshift column between them, they leaned together, sought lips, and hung there. A clear note rang through Sloane, but when it came out it was something between a sigh and a sob. He squeezed her hand and held her close into his shoulder. From the chase and from their sudden intimacy, he could feel their hearts beating like machine guns.

"You be nice to me, David," she whispered.

He held her face and kissed her cheeks and her hair and her eyes. He was shining inside. He was holding her.

Envious, hungry bugs began to seek them out, buzzing and crawling and biting. David and Trinh first tried ignoring them, then tried scratching and swatting, but finally had to retreat, starting the jeep and driving slowly down the path.

She directed him through the back streets until they were close enough to the Special Forces compound for him to find his way. By this time they were reviewing their escape with laughter. Regretfully, he hailed a cyclo to take her home, and, feeling conspiratorial, they agreed to meet in front of her place at six-thirty the following evening. She kissed her finger and pressed it to his lips.

Sloane spent the day helping the detachment clerk update the personnel files. For this assistance and a ten-dollar bill, the clerk gave him a forged Class A pass. Sloane thought of it as a safe-conduct permit through enemy checkpoints.

When he was changing clothes after work, he put his foot into his civilian shoes, and his toes felt something. He jerked his foot out, thinking, Damn, a scorpion. Cautiously, holding a rolled-up copy of *Stars and Stripes* at the ready, he turned the shoe upside down and shook it. A piece of paper fell out. Unfolding it, he saw it was a MACV memo form on which was typed:

> To David It May Concern:
>
> You now under arest for grate badness. You steal jeep, try to run away. You steal Vietnam girl, tell her all kind lies. We know you. You be good, we no arest you. You be bad, we take you and Vietnam girl. Put in little boat. Send boat very far oceun. All time you and girl float on boat. No see no one. You be good!
>
> General Trinh

He sat down on the bunk and shook his head. How did she get in here? How did she know which place was mine? What an intel net she must have.

She was waiting for him in her doorway when he drove up that evening. Her delicate features and sheer, clinging ao dai looked fragile and out of place in the dirty jeep.

Sloane took her hand. His eyes traced from her small nose out to her lips and down to the point of her chin, forming a diamond. Her lips were full in the middle and tapered thin. He kissed them, and she pushed him away. "No," she said. "In Vietnam only kiss in house. On street, no. People think me bad." She squeezed his hand and blew him a kiss.

When he confronted her with the note, her smile crinkled her eyes to new moons and exposed her two small buck teeth. She denied all involvement. When he showed her the evidence, she looked at the typescript and tossed it aside, saying it wasn't hers.

They parked near the bay and walked along the crumbling esplanade. The sky and the water were a deepening blue, and the hills behind them were a blurred evening purple. They picked their way among the puddles, most of which had a film of fuel floating on the surface. The last light sheened the oily whorls to emerald and ultramarine. Using empty C-ration boxes for sleds, children were sliding down a muddy bank and laughing. In the harbor, junks and sampans with multicolored sails floated beside gray, looming destroyers.

They had dinner in a Chinese restaurant that was the same as all the Chinese restaurants he'd ever eaten in, except that the menu was in three languages. When they came out, the hills were gone and lamps were lit on the boats.

She took his hand as they left. "Tonight we go beach."

Driving over a narrow road, holding hands between shifts of gear, bouncing through chuckholes, they wound around to a beach on the far side of the bay, where the town was a pile of lights and the water was black and smooth and broke in small slapping waves. Clouds flowed over the moon in mottled patterns.

They turned off the headlights and suddenly found themselves very much alone. Sloane wondered if being caught by the VC would be worse than by the MPs. They drew together in the dark, touching in reassurance.

Then she hopped out of the jeep and raced off down the beach. Sloane chased after her, stricken to see her fleeing. She turned and stopped and waved her arm. "Shoe number ten," she said when David arrived. "No can run." They took off their shoes and skipped over the springy sand. He circled her waist and took her arm in a ballroom pose.

"What? What is this you do?"

"Sing us a song." He glided her backward in an exaggerated waltz, steering her toward the water.

When surf foamed around her ankles, she gave a little cry and hit him. "Trick," she said, darting away. He watched her run with her head thrown back and her hair coursing out behind her, watched her limber body bound through the marbly light.

He caught up with her and ran beside her. "Hello, Miss Skippy Toes."

"Go way," she said and ran faster.

He swooped her into his arms and carried her toward the water. "You throw me in water, I swim away. Never come back!" she said, gasping air.

He lifted her higher and put his lips to hers, but they were too out of breath to kiss. Slowly he knelt and lowered her onto the sand. Their bodies touched all along their panting lengths. As their breath turned to sighs and their hearts fluttered back to a pulse, they held one another and looked laughs into each other's eyes.

He smoothed her hair and stroked her supple back. So little of her. I can hold all of her in my arms. They kissed hesitantly, shy in the face of their desire. Slowly he petted her—her neck, her breasts, her hips, and then her thighs. His tongue traced the curves of her ear. With quiet sighs she clung to him, sharing his motion.

His hands sought her under her thin clothes. Then, growing impatient, he began to slip them off. She protested, but raised her hips at the same time. When he saw her slender moonlit nakedness, he began trembling uncontrollably. His eyes seared her. She rolled over to shield herself. He pressed against her body, caressing her small breasts, trying to calm her fear and his shaking limbs. Can I touch you with my hands? Can I touch you?

She turned to him and wrapped her arms around him and kissed him full and deep. His quivering faded to an occasional twitch, and he began to move smoothly against her.

The press of his fingers brought a slick wetness to her.

Small noises, shards of words, came from her lips. Her fingers skittered over the jutting bulge of his pants.

I have to take off my clothes. What if she's disgusted and runs away?

She squeezed the bulge, and David scrambled out of his clothes so fast he turned them inside out.

She touched him delicately, curiously, while he kissed her arms and breasts. He stoked up her thighs into her damp passage, caressing her swelling petals. A long moan broke from her throat. She raised her knees, and the flesh above her loins began to pulse.

They rubbed their two warmest places together in eager, tumescent introduction. Hers was small and yielded with painful slowness to the thick intruder. She bit her lip and twisted her hips around the shaft, wanting to draw it all in. He sank through levels of joy, yearning to be fully enclosed.

Then they were fused, and they looked at each other in a new communion. They moved in slow, pulsating unison. I'm here, he thought. I'm right here. But when her slender fingers reached down and cradled his balls, he was gone—coming too soon in helpless gasping spasms.

She held him while he crumbled against her, his body emptying into hers. She was disappointed with his suddenness and didn't know what to do with the quavering form that weighed down on her.

Gradually he grew still and slipped from her to lie beside her, panting and trembling. Moved by his vulnerability, she straddled his back and kneaded his twitching muscles into repose.

He pulled her down to him and kissed her. "You were wonderful."

"You so fast. Why we stop?"

Sloane was crestfallen. "I'm sorry. I couldn't help it. I . . ."

She rubbed his leg and kissed him. "I call you Toot Sweet."

"What is that?"

"You nice, but too quick. Next time you stay long time. I like."

He smiled and picked her up. "I like you. I like you very much."

"You like me, you put me down," she said, kicking at him.

He carried her into the water and she floated naked in his arms. The sea was clean out here, with no scum from the destroyers. He lifted her and blew bubbles through her mossy tangle. She squealed and slid away from him, splashing him with water. He grabbed her and they rolled in the waves, delighting in the press of their sleek nude bodies. They stood up and embraced. "Look," she said, pointing down. "Can see toes. Your toe. My toe." She stepped up onto both his feet. "Now we dance. Dance in water."

"You're moon mad," he said, gliding them along in his fantasy of what a beguine would be.

"Moon who?"

A breeze began to chill them, and they ran, holding hands, back up the beach to their clothes. Wet, shivering, sandy, and towelless, they dressed each other. Sloane used his shirt to dry her hair.

Reluctantly, they climbed into the jeep to return to town.

"You sell jeep. We live here," she said.

"I wish."

The B-team was coordinating an operation combining CIDG troops from two different camps. "We can't fiddle-fuck around this time," the sergeant major said to a sergeant from one of the teams. "We need some body count. Colonel's breathing down our necks."

"I think we'll score on this one," the sergeant said. "The boys are psyched up and hot to trot."

"Well, good. It's about time. Hey, Sloane," the sergeant major called. "Get over here. What is this shit you been signing out jeeps to go to the hospital and not bringing them back till midnight? Your doctor work the late shift or something?"

"Uh . . . uh . . ." Sloane stammered, searching his mind for a plausible lie.

"Well, you go back to your camp tomorrow. You can mend out there just as good as you can here."

He saw the army snatching Trinh away from him. "No," he said, frantically trying to think of a way to stay.

"What?" said the sergeant major, his heavy face wrinkling.

"No. I'm supposed to take my R and R. Overdue for it. I'll take all five days of it right here in Qui Nhon."

"Take your R and R in Qui Nhon? Whoever heard of that? What the fuck you want to stay here for? Oh . . . I get it. Sloane has found himself a whore."

"Now look, sergeant major," Sloane said, bristling with anger.

"OK, you're in love. You A-team guys lose all sense of reality. Sure, go ahead. Spend your R and R in Qui Nhon. But I think you got shit for brains."

"We'll see."

That night he moved in with Trinh. They made love more slowly this time, discovering new things about each other. Afterward, cuddling lush and warm, she told him she would send a message to work saying she would not be in for a few days.

"Wonderful," he said. "It'll be our time."

She curled up close to him to sleep, with one leg through his and an arm over his shoulder, but Sloane couldn't get comfortable with so much contact. He didn't know how to lie or what to do with his head. He was afraid to move because it might disturb her. Finally he rested his head on her arm. But won't she be uncomfortable? he worried. Won't it hurt her? Then one part of him told the other, Relax, if she's uncomfortable, she'll move. You can trust her. She likes you.

She woke him up with jelly doughnuts and coffee in the morning. "What is this?" he asked, still sleepy.

"Breakfast in bed. I read in book. In America, have breakfast in bed."

"Look at that. Where did you get them?"

"Girl friend I know, work army mess hall. She take."

"Fantastic."

She got back into bed with him, and they ate the soft, sticky doughnuts and licked each other's fingers. The flaking calcimined walls of her two-room apartment were covered with prints of dreamy landscapes. The furniture was low and sturdy. Sloane admired a hand-crafted trunk with inlaid wood carvings, and she told him her father had made it for her. He was a carpenter, she explained. She showed him pictures of her family in Hue and of herself as a little girl, holding a huge balloon.

They went grocery shopping at the crowded open-air stalls of the public market and taught each other the Vietnamese and English names for different foods. Sloane bought her a parasol she liked, and she bought him sandals. In the black market section, they got a can of American apple juice, which Trinh had never tasted.

They returned for a sprawling nap through the midday heat and awoke in time to prepare dinner. They shared the kitchen with an old woman who lived below Trinh. They made several trips carrying food downstairs, with much kissing and teasing. The woman peered out and gave Sloane a look to make it clear she did not approve of such goings-on.

The kitchen was in the rear, set off from the main part of the building. It had a three-burner kerosene stove, a charcoal oven, a scarred counter for slicing, dark cool cupboards, but no refrigerator, and a stone well with a plastic bucket. In a bowl Trinh mixed mashed bananas, diced pork, chopped peanuts, and grated ginger. She formed the mixture into balls, coated them with glaze, and deep-fried them in a wok. On an iron table in the disheveled courtyard, she served them in mint sauce with slices of melon and bamboo shoots and cold, sticky rice.

"Ladykins," David said, "it's delicious."

"You like? Good. Tomorrow you make dinner . . . American dinner."

"You may regret that."

For dessert he heated the apple juice and they drank through long, rolled cinnamon sticks, like straws. So they could sit closer, they moved to a bench beside the small walled garden, now gone to weeds, except for a crooked ylang-ylang tree growing in the middle, covered with fragrant chartreuse blossoms. He held his cinnamon stick up to her face and blew through it, tickling her ears and wisping her hair, then moved down along her neck and into her blouse.

"Cinnamon wind," she said with a voluptuous shiver. "You blow cinnamon wind on me."

"I'm going to blow your clothes off."

"David have lump in pants," she said, pointing at his lap. "Big lump. What you do?"

He looked down with mock chagrin. "Oh, no. It happened again. I must be allergic to you. Whenever I'm around you I get all swollen up down there."

"Oh. Too bad," she said, stroking his affliction. "Hello, lump. How are you?"

"Let's go upstairs," he whispered in her ear.

Day followed day with both of them knowing it must soon end, believing it wouldn't and pouring themselves into the moment. On a hot, languorous night they lounged on the bed near the open balcony doors. He was brushing her long hair, flowing it out over her nude back down to her waist. It reminded him of the dark waves breaking on the night beach.

"Poor David," she said. "No have hair."

"I'll wear some of yours."

She sat up and tossed it over him, curtaining them off from the outside. Their eyelashes batted each other's cheeks. He eased her down, stroking her shoulders. "Your body's so nice. It's my playground," he said as he nuzzled under her arm, rubbing her tummy and nibbling the side of her breast. When her nipple prickled and swelled to a soft thimble, he slipped it into his mouth, rolling it around his tongue and chafing it gently against his teeth. Her thighs parted for his hand as he cupped her sex and caressed it.

His lips found hers and their tongues scuffled, charged with tension and tenderness. His fingertips ran over her legs while he kissed her ear and her arched neck. She teased his chest with her long nails and whispered incomprehensible syllables. In little bites he moved down her body, paused to kiss the inside of her knee, glided his tongue over her ankle, and sucked her salty toes. She wiggled and squealed, and he reached up and pressed her belly to calm her and then stroked his fingers through her nether lips, fondling her softness. Her body stretched taut; her breath mingled with sighs.

He slid his head up between her legs and spread her with his tongue, exploring the nectary folds. Her taste and smell were of the ocean. When he found her hidden node, he held it between his lips and enflamed it with his tongue. He sucked it long and slow, until she quivered on the edge. She cried out and surrendered to her galloping inner rhythm, her body rising and bowing and breaking into a flexing crumble.

Her thrashing hands found his penis and guided it into her. Their bodies folded together. He was relaxed and able to move slowly, deliciously through her warm, wet, enveloping chamber. They kissed and looked, awed, into each other's eyes. The feel of her breasts against his chest made him ache. He hugged her tightly and pulled out almost to her threshold, then pushed back in, back into the holding warmth. Each slow thrust forced a moan from her. She opened to more openness and took all of him, his body, his total need of her.

Deep in each of her dilated pupils David saw a skull. Then he realized it was his own reflection. He fell through it and felt a crashing and wrenching inside, like a dam giving way. He came with a swelling, surging, bursting effusion and a blind scream. All the debris of his past rolled out of him, leaving him in Trinh's arms.

They rocked together sobbing, his shoulder heaving against her cheek, his face soothed by her hands. Under heavy lids, her eyes shone dark and moist. "Never," she said. "Never happen before."

"For me, either."

He stayed inside her a long time, moving in slippery luxury. Their breath and their pulses grew gentler. Finally he eased out of her, and they smiled at each other, delightedly tired, and sprawled back on the bed, letting the night air dry their bodies. She nestled against him and laid her head on his chest. He lifted her with his breathing. They fell asleep curled up in each other like kittens.

Four hours later Sloane snapped upright. "Wha . . . what?" he asked in a loud voice with his arms wrapped around himself. "No!" He fell back on the bed, wailing. "No. I shot him down. I shot him down . . . just to do it. No," he cried again, trailing it into a dry rasp.

Trinh, startled out of sleep, tried to cover him with her small arms. He wept and babbled on her breast. "I didn't mean to. . . . I guess I did. Took a gun and he was dead. Oh, no, I killed all his friends too. Blew them up. They were running, they were trying to get away . . . and I blew them up."

With rising clarity, his mind replayed his machine-gunning of the wavering gray figures in the barbed wire, his shattering of the men on the trail with thousands of pellets from the claymore, the fire-swathed body blown from its shelter by his C-4, and the young man, lovely and real, dying on the ground, his hand twitching against his killer's. He saw again the tiny perfume-bottle lamp and the packet of letters and photos. They must have resembled Trinh's family pictures. I did all that. I killed them.

He bent at the waist and gagged. "I don't deserve . . . I don't deserve you. I don't deserve to touch anybody." He rolled around on the bed, his body jerking as if from electric shocks. His tears came in a gulping, choking flood, as he tried to talk and breathe and cry at the same time. He cried and cried, and she held him to her and stroked his forehead until his tremors gradually subsided. He blew his wounded nose, and pain shot through his head. The pain brought him back, and his crying ebbed. She was humming to him and massaging the rigid muscles of his neck.

"I think it's gone now," he said finally, taking her hand. "I think I'll be all right. Thank you. Thank you, Trinh."

She folded him back in the grace of her arms, and they slept.

In the morning, Sloane's nerves felt raw and exposed, as if abruptly and for the first time seeing his deeds clearly had stripped away layers of insulation. Sunlight was glarey, traffic noise loud. His head ached, and the thought of food repelled him. He felt washed out, exhausted, empty, and stunned. His mental activity was suspended to the point where he could hardly speak; as soon as his mind formed a concept, it dissolved.

He wished he could be asleep again, and he lay with his eyes closed while Trinh sat beside the bed, reading. The scent of her powdered womanliness drifted over him and slowly rekindled his interest in life. He listened pleased to the sounds she made turning the pages of her magazine and moving in her chair. She began humming to herself, and he smiled.

"Hello, you," he said, opening his eyes.

"Oh, you wake up," she said, coming to sit beside him.

"I'm glad you're here."

"You very sad last night."

"I feel better now. You were very good to me. You . . ." He wanted to say he had spilled into her hands like a bag of guts and she had not run away in disgust, but instead had taken him and accepted him. But he did not know how.

They spent the day in bed, hugging and reading and napping. Later afternoon shadows began patching the ceiling. Softer noises rose from the street below. A breeze from the bay furled the curtain.

"David?"

"Hmm?"

"Hungry. I boocoo hungry."
"Oh. Yeah. I guess we better get up."
They tiptoed downstairs to the stone shower and lathered and splashed each other's bodies. When she saw his back, she gave a little cry. It was striped with scratches from her fingernails. "Oh, David! I no mean to hurt you. I no remember do that," she said as she gently washed and patted it dry. "So sorry."
"It didn't hurt. You get so excited. . . . I like that." He looped the towel around her back and pulled her to him. "You're very good in bed, you know."
"You very good in me. We have number one. We . . . how you say in English? We . . . make love, yes. Make love. Nice to say. Now all people have more love. We make for them. We make boocoo love."
They kissed with happy familiarity.
"Come on," she said. "We go eat. I starve." She threw her towel at him and scampered up the stairs.

Soon their pittance of days was over. The night before David had to report back to the B-team, he and Trinh fell into a strained, awkward silence. Their pidgin could not communicate what they needed to say, and each felt isolated, brooding on separate channels.
She went into the bedroom, and when she didn't emerge for half an hour he looked in on her. She was sitting on the bed ripping newspapers into long, curling strips. Seeing him, she tossed handfuls of gray shreds into the air and watched them fall back over her. They littered the bed like ashes. "Go way," she said to him. "No like. Fini."
He sat beside her in the mess and tried to hold her, but she threw bunches of paper at him and moved away. "No! You get away." A broken smile distorted her face, curving her eyes to scythes. "You no love me, David. You think me . . . you think me just shack-up girl. Get out. You get out."
The words lashed him. "Why? Why do you say that?"

"Tomorrow you go back army, go Cung Hoa. You love me, you no go back."

"But I'm putting in for a transfer . . . so I can work here in Qui Nhon . . . and we can be together. I do love you."

She stared at him out of the cave of her hair. Tears welled in her eyes. "Soon you go back America. You leave me. You love me, David, you take me with you." She threw herself on him, crying and striking her head with her fists. Her eyes were shut tight to tiny lines, tears squeezing from the corners, trickling over her cheeks and dropping onto him. He tried to rock her and hold her and stroke her hair. When her sobs quieted, she looked up at him with eyes large, liquid, and dark. "You go home. I know. We fini."

His throat tightened and he buried his face in her shoulder. They held each other for a long time, unable to speak. Finally she sat up. She wiped her tears away with a handful of newspaper confetti, leaving inky smears on her cheeks.

"Look at you," he said as he kissed her eyes and held her face in his hands. He began gathering up the shredded paper and stuffing it into a rattan wastebasket.

"No," she said. "No clean up. Too much mess. We move. Have new house. No papers. Very clean. We happy." She made a plume out of a bunch of the curled strips and held them to her head so that they fell around her face. "I pretty bird. Live in tree. You love me. We happy all time."

David took the plume and stuffed it into the basket with the rest of the newspaper.

Trinh fell asleep, and he lay on the bed beside her, watching her slightly swollen and reddened nose dribble a little onto the pillow and watching the neon flash on the ceiling from the bar across the street.

The next morning he left. They stood at the top of the stairs hugging, and each time he turned to go they fled back into each other's arms and hugged tighter, as if by showing the strength of their feeling they might win a reprieve.

"I'm going to come back . . . and be with you."

"No . . . they take you away."
"No. I'll be back."
"You go now. Go. I no can stand it." She kissed him from tiptoes and turned him around. He walked down the stairs, and when he looked back she was gone.

The sergeant major glanced up from his paperwork when Sloane came in. He took the cigar out of his mouth and said, "Well, here's our lovebird. Back from his R and R . . . spent in beautiful downtown Qui Nhon. I hope you got your dick wet enough to last you awhile. Now you gotta get on the stick and get back out to your team. The major wants you to run some more of those demo ambushes. They work damn good. You keep it up, you'll make staff sergeant before long."
"I don't want to go back."
"What? You gotta go back."
"You've got a slot for an engineer here at the B-team. I want to transfer."
"Transfer? What the fuck? Last week you couldn't wait to get back out there and tear Charlie a new asshole. It's that gal, isn't it? She fucked your head over, didn't she? She must have a whole pussyful of tricks. Goddammit, Sloane, you blew away more VC in that one ambush than all the other camps all week. We got you wrote up for the Vietnamese Silver Star. And now you want to give up and come back here!"
"Yeah."
"That gal ruined you, Sloane. I can tell by looking at you. Best part of you done run down your leg. And it's a damn shame. It's a damn shame, that's what it is."
"I'm OK, sergeant major."
"Well . . . if you wanna put in for a transfer, I can't stop you. Major probably won't approve it, though. Even if he does, you still gotta go back to your team until it's processed. There's a chopper leaving this afternoon. You get back out on patrol, you'll see that's where you belong."
Sloane collected his gear. He tore up all the ambush plans

he'd made. He left the carbine of the man he'd killed lying in the corner. The detachment clerk drove him to the airfield. They passed miles of storage depots, barracks, fuel dumps, warehouses; motor pools of giant earth-movers, tanks, tractor-trailer trucks; a battery of 155mm howitzers with names painted on them like Stud, Fly Swatter, Sorry About That, Birth Control. Sloane saw it all through the smudge that Trinh's nose had left on his glasses during their last kiss.

The helicopter took off and flew low over the bay. As they passed along the far side, Sloane saw what he thought was the beach where Trinh and he had first made love. The beating rotors textured the water the way his kisses prickled and flushed her skin. The helicopter climbed away and headed back toward the highlands.

"Hey there, Scarface. Welcome home," Wells called to Sloane as he picked him up at the chopper pad. "We heard you been shackin' up with one of Qui Nhon's finest. How was she? Does she like a dick?"

Sloane didn't answer.

"Hope you put the barracuda on her. We gotta uphold the team reputation. If she don't wanna let you gobble her, just hit her upside the head. She'll spread 'em."

Sloane winced. Not this again, he thought. "You've been on site too long, Wells."

"No shit. Even the strikers are starting to look good. That's why I'm so mean. Never get laid out here. I ain't been fucked in so long, I don't even get a hard-on anymore."

"That'll do it." Sloane went to his room thinking, Why did I have to come back here? He unpacked and lay down on his bunk with a book.

Madsen came in. "So this is where you're holed up. I heard you were back."

"Yeah . . . back on the hill."

"That's quite a trophy Charlie gave you," Madsen said, looking at Sloane's scarred and twisted nose. "He damn sure changed your face."

"Actually I think it's an improvement. Little bit of character," Sloane said with a laugh.

"Hey, tell me about this gal." Madsen sat down. "We been hearing all these rumors from the B-team."

"Ah, she's . . . she's pretty special. Best thing that's happened to me."

"Sounds great. Too bad you couldn't bring her back with you."

"I never realized how bad this place was. Sure going to be lonely."

"Lonely? Yeah, I suppose," Madsen said. "But I'm not even sure I get lonely, you know? I think maybe I just get horny. Might be good to feel lonely."

"Not if you don't know when you're going to see her again." Sloane stared glumly at the mosquito netting above his bunk.

"Oh, I got some good news. Randall said you and me could finally go out on operation together. You did such a great job last time. He wants us to set up some more of those ambushes."

"Uh . . . I don't want to go."

"What do you mean? Not even with me?" Madsen asked, puzzled and slightly offended. "It'd be a gas, the two of us. We used to talk about it. You wrote me."

"Yeah, I guess I did. I don't care about it now. The whole scene. I put in a transfer to the B-team."

"You're leaving?"

"Hope so."

"The firefight was that bad, huh?"

"The firefight was great . . . if that's all you've got."

"It must be one hell of an experience. I can't believe I've been here ten months and haven't been in one." He looked at Sloane. "Sure you won't change your mind?"

"Yeah. It just doesn't do it for me now."

Madsen left, thinking, Sloane doesn't have it anymore. Maybe Randall will go.

Captain Ngoc, the new district chief, had invited the team down for the ceremony marking the completion of the fish pond. He stood on the bare earthen embankment that bordered the bleak pond and emptied two plastic bags, each containing a gallon of water and several hundred fast-growing tilapia fry. Then he paced around, talking to the villagers in a rapid, strident voice about how much rice bran to feed the fish and how in a short time they would be able to net their first catches.

Afterward he and the Americans walked through the poor section of the village next to the pond. Most of the houses had tin roofs, thatched walls, and floors of hard-packed, well-swept dirt. Madsen felt good, seeing the tin. Children clustered around them, staring and commenting. The Americans exchanged self-conscious greetings with a group of women who were winnowing rice on large woven discs. Through the door of a house, Madsen caught a glimpse of an altar with family pictures, joss sticks, and brass candle-holders. A charcoal peddler, bent over under his load, went from house to house. Near the path, a pig, unimpressed by the strolling visitors, snorted in the dirt.

Captain Ngoc talked with Randall about other civic action projects the village needed. "If have bridge, people can take cow over other side river. Now no can do. Have plenty grass other side. Few grass here."

Randall looked across the river, rubbing his chin. "I'll check with the army engineers, see if they can bring in some pontoons. But the people will have to build it."

"Yes," Ngoc said. "People build." The district chief's body was thin, almost fleshless, and he made nervous gestures as he spoke. His prominent Adam's apple and cheekbones stretched his skin. Glasses, thick and too big, oppressed his slim nose. His magnified eyes bulged beneath them.

As the Americans drove back to camp, Randall said to Madsen, "Quite a change, huh? He's even started sending the ARVN out on patrol."

"You think the one they had before was a VC?" Madsen asked.

"Probably not. He was probably just playing it safe. Trying to get all he could out of it."

"A little less poor."

Randall grunted and said, "People are poor all over. When I was a kid, we were so poor, used to get hungry at school and eat the paste. Lots of poor people in the world. Hey, Sloane, you want to learn how to build a threshing shed?"

"Sure. Imagine me building stuff. That'll be a switch."

"You can help them lay the concrete for the floor. And they'll teach you how to thatch walls."

"This is for the rice harvest?" Sloane asked.

"Yeah. They don't grow much of it this high up, but Ngoc thinks they can expand."

"I thought all the rice in Vietnam came from Louisiana," Sloane said.

"That's why they gotta have a good harvest. That's what the damn war's all about—rice." Randall drove the jeep fast and one-handed over the rutted road. "Bet none of you knew that, did you? You been over here almost a year and didn't know it, did you?"

"Rice?" Wells said. "Hell, no, I didn't know it was about rice. Shit, if I'd have known it was about that, I'd have left a long time ago. I thought it was about something important . . . like banana cream pie or something."

"Wells, the only kind of pie you know anything about is hair pie," Randall said. "And that won't help you when the famine hits."

"What're you talkin' about?" Wells said.

"Big famine gonna hit. In the eighties. Don't you know that? Where you been?"

"I been here, dammit."

"Well, other folks've been plannin' ahead, gettin' ready . . . 'cause somebody's gonna starve. See, South Vietnam here can grow way more rice than it needs. We bring in fertilizers and tractors, this whole country be one big farm. And the extra, well, when things get bad, there'll be enough left over here to feed a hell of a lot of people. . . ." Randall braked for a dog that ambled in front of them. "Hold on. . . . But it still ain't gonna be enough. So what they're fightin' over is who gets the surplus—China or Japan. Better for us if Japan gets it."

"What about India?" Madsen asked.

"India gets left out either way," Randall said.

"I think we should just give 'em the rice," Sloane said. "Be a lot less trouble."

"Way too many people," Randall said. "We got Europe to worry about."

"Where'd you get that idea?" Wells asked.

"When you work for the Agency, you find stuff out."

"Rice, huh? OK," Wells said. "I still only got eighteen days left over here. When I get back, I'll send you some Uncle Ben's."

Randall and Madsen sat in the team house discussing the upcoming operation. "You sure you want to go?" Randall asked him. "You been on site without a break for a hell of a long time. If you want, you can go to Nha Trang instead. Get laid."

"No," Madsen said. "I want to go out. The other'll wait. I got R and R coming up."

"OK. The way I figure it is this. For the first half the operation, we do a standard search and destroy. Stir up some movement. Then you and me each take a squad and set up along the infiltration route. Do a demo number on 'em. The main body can—"

Captain Bao, the LLDB camp commander, ran into the team house, pale and frightened. His words came in panting bursts: "You come. You bring bac-si. Aiiie. VC come Cung Hoa. Take Dai-uy Ngoc." The VC, he explained falteringly, had entered the outskirts of the village pretending to be herders. When Captain Ngoc made his morning inspection rounds, they had driven some cattle across the road, blocking it. Then, at close range, they had attacked with pistols. The district chief was wounded, his driver killed, but an aide had escaped, running back to district headquarters to call the LLDB. The aide had last seen the captain slumped in the back seat of the commandeered jeep, being driven away.

Half the team and two squads from the recon platoon piled into a jeep and a deuce-and-a-half and hurtled down the hill. Rain was falling in a persistent drizzle. "Hope they didn't mine the damn road," Randall said. "They sure as hell knew we'd be coming."

They found the district chief's jeep parked beside the new fish pond. In the pond floated his body, his intestines curling whitely in the water, his severed head bobbing nearby. The water around him was dark with his blood. His glasses lay in the shallows near the bank.

Randall was choked with rage. He looked at the body and stammered, "We'll get 'em. We'll get 'em, I swear. Man, you really tried to change it, didn't you? Those bastards."

Far to the side stood a group of Vietnamese, biting their fists and crying. They told the LLDB captain that the VC had made them witness the disembowelment and beheading. The VC had announced they were carrying out the judgment of the people.

A scared Vietnamese lieutenant drove up and said the ARVN had fired on the fleeing assassination squad, wounding one man and taking him prisoner.

"We'll interrogate that son of a bitch right now," Randall said. "Get the LLDB intel sergeant down here. Vinh, the mean one—the one with the telephone. We're gonna find them this time."

Randall looked once more at the pond and its originator. "People will never use the pond now," he said quietly.

"They'll be afraid of his ghost, afraid to go near the place. The VC really want to see them hungry. A fish pond."

The interrogated prisoner said the others were going to rejoin their unit about five kilometers north. Randall and the LLDB decided on pursuit. They changed the operation plan and arranged to leave in the morning.

As the first light of the hidden sun was striking the mountains to the west, a patrol of one hundred men marched out of camp. They were in a grudge-match mood, feeling anger for the assassination and fear because the VC had dared strike so close. Their packs were heavy with extra ammunition, and they did not speak.

Near the village they passed a cart, creaking and sagging, heaped with unhulled paddy rice. The cart was being inched up a hill by a pained, splay-legged pony, its tongue lolling and its hoofs slipping. Beside the pony walked a man with a straw hat and a length of supple bamboo, which he patiently whipped across the pony's balls. On the man's back was a basket with a dead dog stuffed inside it. The dog's head stuck out stiff and alert above its gashed throat, and its neck fur was covered with thick brown icing. Madsen forced himself to look at it, trying to control his revulsion. The carcass and the pony hummed with flies.

The sun cleared the horizon and burnished the brown, tumid river. Yesterday's rain had softened the earth, and it sucked at their boots with rhythmic slurps. Soon the mud began to dry under the waxing sun, and worms that had been washed out, almost drowned and now too weak to dig back in, began to bake on the hardening ground.

The route was a slow, steady incline, and by afternoon Madsen's sides were split with cramps and his mouth felt stuffed with steel wool. His legs were logs. His pack hung on him like a dead body.

Randall also was tired and hot. His sleeves were rolled up,

and his taut, vein-striped muscles glistened with sweat. To break the monotony, he hoisted his Swedish K across his shoulders above his pack and walked with his arms hooked over it.

"Bitch of a hike," Madsen said.

"Yeah. It's hard. It's hard, but it's fair. Won't last forever," Randall replied between breaths.

The men stopped to make camp while the sun boiled to an orange death in the west. After dinner Randall and Madsen climbed to a rock slab that topped their knoll. They lay back and watched the evening spreading cool and blue across the hills. The rocks still held the day's heat. It felt good against their sore muscles. "Madsen, you're turning into a pretty fair field soldier," Randall said, cocking his camouflage hat back on his head. "I don't think you'd be worth a damn back in the States, though. If you were in my outfit, I'd probably have to keep you in jail half the time."

"Bet you're right," Madsen said. "Nothing I hate worse than that garrison-barracks bullshit. All they want you to be is a combination janitor/shoeshine boy."

"You put in a long heavy spell down in that commo bunker," Randall said. "When we get back, the two of us can go to Ban Me Thout for a week. I want to recruit some more Yards for the strike force. We'll be spending time back in the villages."

"I would love that. No shit. I would love that."

"They're all Rhadé back in there. Best people on earth."

"Maybe you could teach me some of the language before we go."

"Sure. Lo-ee would be more help than I would, though. But forget it if you think you're going to sweet-talk any of their women. You'd end up a Montagnard sacrifice."

"Thanks for warning me."

"But last time I was there they had some passable Vietnamese whores in town. They should be able to clip your horns."

"Sounds great."

"Let's get some sleep. Tomorrow's another one."

Madsen climbed into his hammock, excited about going to Ban Me Thout. As usual when he talked with Randall he had wanted to ask him about his family. But he had never been able to bring it up. Madsen looked at a palm tree silhouetted like a spectral hand against the rising moon. I'll pretend this is Burma. We're behind the Japanese lines on a raid. Have to blow a big rail bridge. War's been going on for years. Soon it'll be over. We're just about to wrap it up. We'll all be coming down the gangplank with a slight limp. Everybody smokes Camels. The women will be waiting on the dock. Kisses and tears . . . Bob Hope singing "Thanks for the Memory." It'll be 1946 forever.

My father never had any of that, though. Wonder what Randall felt like in Korea? He must've been about my age.

Next morning walking the upland forest Madsen felt linked to an ancient succession of warriors, prowling hominids hunting their own species. He was the first man, a club-wielding primate genius who had adapted his intelligence to the service of a primal savagery. We've been doing this for a million years, he thought, gripping him M-16. Search and destroy. And they think they can end it.

"Trip wire!" Randall's voice broke Madsen's reverie. The team sergeant was standing two men ahead of him, blocking the trail with his arms. The radioman was between the two Americans. Randall made him back up, then pointed to a wire running across the trail seven feet above the ground. He followed the wire to where it was attached to the straightened pin of a grenade lashed to a tree. The strikers were talking and pointing excitedly. "This is how Charlie zaps the command group," Randall said. "Radio antenna hits it and pulls out the pin, and that's all she wrote for the guy behind him—you, Madsen."

Madsen swallowed. "Thanks for catching it."

"These kind with the wire aren't that hard to spot. But

every once in a while Charlie gets ahold of some of that monofilament fishing line, the clear stuff, you know? You can kiss your ass good-bye, then."

Randall checked to see if the booby trap itself was booby-trapped, then carefully bent back the prongs of the pin and untied the grenade. He gave it to the LLDB sergeant, who seemed less than joyous about the present. Madsen wished he could have had it because it was one of the old World War II pineapple variety.

For the next couple of hours, fear tagged after Madsen like a small dog, always there but not getting in the way too much.

They dropped into a valley that was rife with bamboo thickets. As Madsen pushed through the screens of leafy switches, the bamboo reminded him of the Vietnamese themselves: thin, graceful, proliferating, passive, pliable, indestructible. Each wand was composed of interdependent segments, with strength in the joints and the rest able to give. The leaves were elongated hearts or double-edged daggers. He saw the men's boots treading the young plants and noticed they did not break, but sprang back up afterward.

Open stretches of waist-high elephant grass separated the stands of bamboo. Here there was no shade, and the sky was sun. Spears of grass reflected the light back in bright, jagged shards. The men in the column plodded along dumbly, beads on a dog-tag chain.

Puffs of smoke stood out from a distant clump of bamboo; doubled reports of incoming rifle fire jabbed past the company. Ow, here we go, Madsen thought. With excitement rising inside him, he brought his rifle up and clicked it off safety.

Randall pushed the barrel down. "What're you supposed to do, first thing we catch fire?"

"The fuckin' radio."

"Right. Get us a FAC."

"Might as well be back in the commo bunker," Madsen muttered.

Some of the CIDG were blasting away with carbines and grenade launchers. Most were lying in the tall grass. Randall knelt figuring out their map coordinates while Madsen called back to camp.

The CIDG barrage tapered off. A tense silence hung over the field. One last shot—comic, defiant—came from the VC position.

"Just a sniper," Randall said. "Trying to slow us down."

He checked with the LLDB to make sure there were no casualties and dispatched two squads to skirt around in different directions and catch the sniper in a crossfire.

Fifteen minutes later they heard the bouncing echoes of shots across the valley as the squads fired into the grove. After cautiously walking through it, they radioed back that it was empty.

The company was moving forward when the spotter plane arrived. Randall asked him to scout an area of rice paddies that lay a kilometer to the east. The paddies were supposed to be abandoned, but to Randall the sniper meant that the VC had been cultivating the area and were now trying to delay the column while they escaped. The pilot confirmed that new rice was growing in the paddies, but saw no sign of enemy movement.

As they continued ahead, the sniper again opened fire, this time from their flank. The men stopped and looked, but the haphazard shots were not worth falling on the ground for. "I'll be damned if I'll let him slow us up now," Randall said. "We can chase the bastard now that we got air cover." He ordered the men to change course and double-time toward the sniper. It was hard to get the CIDG moving, but finally they were crashing through tall, stiff sedge, their equipment clattering and the flank squad, which had now become the point, firing wildly into the bamboo that bordered the field.

The sniper had again abandoned his position, and the company pushed through the thicket into a stretch of rice paddies boxed in by more bamboo and separated by dikes.

The rectangular plots filled with nodding green stalks were fresh and inviting after the rough country they had been moving through. Each man had to remind himself that the human presence here was a hostile one. They walked more slowly in a file along the central paddy dike, looking at the new landscape. But when the sniper fired on them from the bamboo at the other end of the paddies one hundred meters to their front, they began running, spurred by Randall's eager shouts, toward his position.

We'll catch him now, Madsen thought with thrilled certainty. This is what Kobus should've had us do.

When they were halfway across the paddies, more puffs of gunfire blew out of the bamboo. A lot more. The stutter of rifles was sporadic at first, then increased rapidly like corn starting to pop. It was punctuated by the heavy hammering of a machine gun. The strikers began to scream. Madsen stood there, confused. Screeching gusts of wind whipped past him. A hole appeared on the face of the radioman next to him. The man fell in a half-turn, and Madsen had to force himself not to collapse beside him in fear. He felt as if half his internal strings had been cut.

Randall's voice arrested his panic. "The radio! Get us some jets!"

The radioman was twitching convulsively. Help him later, Madsen thought as he stripped the blood-wet Prick-25 off his back. Hope to hell it didn't get hit. Work, dammit, you've got to work. He realized his life depended on this dull metal box. His fingers were quivering so much he couldn't turn the knobs. Remembering what Randall had told him about pausing to get hold of yourself when you first come under fire, he gripped his hands, exhaled deeply, and closed his eyes for a moment. This steadied him, and he called the FAC while the radioman writhed in the paddy mud.

"Already got a flight on the way," the pilot said. "You-all hang tough down there." Streaks of machine gun tracers reached for the small plane, and it climbed away in a fast chandelle.

The gun then returned to closer targets, flailing the shallow water and young rice twenty meters to the left of the men. The gunner found his range, and the spouts leaped closer. CIDG screamed as bullets plunged among them.

The LLDB sergeant crawled to Randall. "You get helicopt," he cried shrilly. "You get helicopt. Boocoo VC. We no can do. You get helicopt. We go back Cung Hoa."

Randall shook him till he stopped trembling. "You're gonna fight," he screamed into his face. "Your men are gonna fight. Or else you're all gonna die." Randall turned around and called, "Lo-ee, get over here."

"Yes, sergeant," the interpreter said, scrambling over.

"Tell him airplanes come now . . . bomb VC. No helicopter. We're all gonna fight. And I'm gonna shoot anybody who runs away. See that dike up there? That's where we're going. We can't stay here."

The machine gun threw another volley into the company, and the whole group began wailing.

"Let's go," Randall hollered. "Chung ta di." He ran among the men huddled beside the bank, kicking them, pulling them to their feet, pushing them forward. Madsen, Lo-ee, and the LLDB followed Randall's lead and began dragging men up by the collar and forcing them ahead. One man Madsen pulled up sagged limp and heavy. Madsen released him and he splatted back into the wet paddy. The rest of the CIDG, afraid of being left behind, struggled to their feet, and the company, minus the few already dead or wounded, ran with nightmare slowness through the gripping mud twenty-five meters to the shelter of the dike. Some in front crumpled into the rice and were run over.

Madsen threw himself sobbing into the embankment, which lay perpendicular to the line of VC fire. Wads of anger and fear seemed to block his throat and choke his air intake to a wisp. His chest was drenched, and he frantically patted it, thinking he had been hit, but discovered it was only sweat. Bullets tore close overhead with loud cracks. The enemy machine gun chewed at the dike, spitting dirt into the air. Some of it fell back on Madsen's neck, and he brushed it away as if it were burning. The taste of vomit corroded his mouth; sweat and tears blurred his vision. He knew if he relaxed, his bowels would flow. His mind was clear but no longer screened its perceptions. For a moment, a small crab retreating belligerently toward its burrow, threatening with its pincers, seemed as serious an adversary as the machine gun. A battle between a cricket and a horde of red ants was as absorbing and important as his own.

Randall's corded face brought him back. "Crawl down there. Get the strikers firing. Get some fire into that tree line."

"But . . ." Madsen said, wanting to hold on to Randall and not leave.

"Just do it." Randall lunged to the top of the dike, threw his weight forward onto his elbows and fired his Swedish K in long, ripping bursts.

Madsen crawled along the line, prodding and shouting, startled by his voice. Several strikers were lying in the mud, shaking and babbling and covering their heads. He dragged them to the top of the dike and made them fire. Except for a thin haze of smoke, the tree line ahead of them looked like just another placid stand of bamboo.

He heard Randall calling for him and ran back, crouching low. "They're flanking us," Randall said, pointing to their exposed left side where the bamboo was waving. "Tell the FAC we need those planes now. Tell him if he's got any rockets to put 'em in there."

Madsen, a clawing urgency in his voice, radioed the pilot while Randall grabbed an M-79 grenade launcher from a wounded striker and began firing it into the moving thicket.

The pilot acknowledged Madsen's directions in a calming Georgia accent. "Those jets are only five minutes off, now. You're doin' a great job down there, and we're gonna give you all the help we can. Let's see how they like this." The plane made a low pass, seemed to stop in the air and pivot on its tail, and shot a small rocket into the area Madsen had indicated. A sudden dome of fire rose over the bamboo. It faded in a second, but the trees did not wave again.

"This is a bad one, Madsen. If they can get around that side, we're in the shits. And they're sure gonna try again. Another lesson, huh, for you—it don't always pay to chase a sniper. They can channel you right where they want you. You wanted to find Charlie, didn't you, Hard Charger? Well, there he is," Randall said, sweeping his arm toward the tree line.

"Won't the jets take care of him?"

"Maybe. But if he's got reinforced bunkers in there, hell, they can bomb him all day long, and all it'll do is give him a headache, piss him off."

Madsen rose above the dike to fire his M-16, but Randall pulled him down and said, "Get back on the radio. Tell him how far along the dike our position runs. We don't want to waste any time when the planes get here."

Madsen, irritated at not getting to fire, called the FAC while Randall helped the LLDB sergeant set up the 60mm mortar. Randall was worried. I'm making all the wrong decisions, he thought. Should've just ignored that fucking sniper and kept to our course. Bastards suckered me. What's wrong with me? Shouldn't have moved us up to this dike. Soon as they work around to the side, they can pick us off. It all seemed right at the time. We should've just hauled ass back the way we came. The idea repelled him. Aw, fuck it. At least we're in contact. They're hurting too, and that's what it's all about. I been in a lot tougher than this one.

Madsen was afraid, and he was afraid Randall knew it. We can't stay here. We'll die. All of us. Die here in the mud.

There's nowhere else to go. But a glow of almost ecstatic excitement broke through his swelling fear. This is action, by damn. And I can goddamn well handle it.

A dull slap of sound carried across the paddy. "Mortar!" Randall yelled and plunged off the dike into the mud. Madsen and the CIDG followed him and waited helpless, silent seconds until a screech of rending metal hurtled past them to explode thirty meters away in a fountain of brown paddy water and yellow fire. As Madsen clawed deeper into the mud, he imagined the enemy gunner deftly clicking the mortar dial for the required adjustment and dropping another round down the tube. He heard the outgoing report and hung suspended, stealing one anxious glance skyward and seeing only a placid floating cloud and then clenching his eyes and covering his head with his arms until the sickening rush came down on him, closer this time, and the concussion knocked his eyes open and he thought he was blind until he realized he had buried his face in the water. The ground bucked and heaved and Madsen tried to hold it together with his grip. The round had struck the other side of the dike.

Again he heard the pop of a mortar shell leaving the tube, and again he doubled up, feeling fragile and exposed, with nowhere to hide. Stop it, he screamed mutely. Stop it. The tense silence was broken too soon by a hurtling roar from the opposite direction. Two long-nosed delta-winged F-105s swept low over the trees, checking the target area. As they curved off to begin their runs, the mortar screamed in, erupting the paddy fifteen meters away and hurling mud, water, shrapnel, and rice stalks at the men.

Madsen surged with fear and relief, the jets seeming objects of infinite beauty and worth. He sat up to watch as one began a graceful parabolic dive on the bamboo grove. At its nadir it released a spray of cluster bombs that fell into the trees and exploded with a prolonged, ripping snarl.

Randall grabbed the radio handset. "That looked good," he said to the FAC. "Dead on the money. Have 'em put the

H.E. right at the tree line. I thing they're bunkered in along there."

"Roger, can do," the pilot replied.

The second plane released its swarm of anti-personnels, and then the first one swooped back for the high-explosive run. The large bombs tumbled end over end, slower than the rising plane, and burst into jagged white cypress trees of fire that engulfed the bamboo. Madsen winced as the concussion hit him like a slammed door and noise ice-picked his ears.

The other jet swooped down to drop its heavy ordnance, and then they both came back to shred the bamboo with their 20mm cannons. The FAC flew in calm circles off to the side. He radioed that the jets had to leave, but more air cover was on its way. On their last pass the jets rocked their wings at the troops before flying off. The CIDG, who had been whooping and cheering before, watched the planes depart with a look of stricken abandonment.

The area bulged with quiet. Smoke hung lazily in the still air. Then Madsen through his ringing ears could hear the drone of the spotter plane, the pops of burning bamboo, and the cries of wounded men. The nostalgic smell of gunpowder drifted over the paddy.

Randall and Madsen lay exhausted against the dike. "It's not turning out so bad," Randall said, as much to convince himself as Madsen. "Good old air force. I about shit when that mortar opened up."

"You too?" Madsen asked with relief. He tried to slow his breathing. Small bundles of nerve tension raced through his body.

"Damned 81s come down on you like a Mack truck," Randall said and sat up. "Get the troops firing again. We can't give Charlie a chance to regroup. And try to get me a count on the wounded."

Madsen reluctantly started to crawl down the line when Randall said, "Oh, and Madsen . . ." He turned around. "You're doin' good." Madsen smiled and kept crawling.

The strikers had regained some confidence, and most were willing to edge above the dike and go back to work. No return fire came from the tattered bamboo. Madsen was tying a compress around the wounded leg of a young Montagnard when two A1E Skyraiders flew, slow and loud, over the paddy. The old single-engine prop planes reminded him of the diving models of Flying Tigers he had hung from his childhood ceiling. They had the same blunt noses and stubby wings and slide-back canopies. Madsen dropped the leg he was bandaging and stood up, enthralled. These are much better than the jets. Realer. It's the second world war. We're there together. It'll be different this time. He had an urge to be with Randall, so he ran back toward him while the strikers, who were all lying down, stared at him and one of the fighters began a screaming dive on the bamboo grove.

Here it is, Madsen thought. Look at that baby come in.

The plane released its canisters, and an orange globe of napalm blossomed up, topped with a pompadour of black smoke.

Just like Iwo Jima. Give it to 'em. Damn. A Zero should come in now. Dogfight over the jungle.

Driven out by flames, a dozen gray figures with leaf-covered helmets rushed from the bamboo at the end of the dike, yelling and firing their AK-47s. Their bullets tore past Madsen with dopplered whines. It's them. A suicide charge! Banzai! He snatched at his chest for a grenade, but found he had none. They're after Randall. Gotta stop 'em. A Skyraider roared in low on a strafing run. Madsen swept his rifle toward the attackers.

"I'll get 'em, Dad," he screamed.

Randall jumped up and ran toward him shouting, "Get down, you damn fool. Don't you know those people are trying to kill you?"

Madsen turned to see Randall stop in midstep, shake with spasms, and fall into the brown paddy water.

His mind broke in a shriek. He ran to the team sergeant, who lay twisted in the mud, his legs still trying to move. Three holes, spaced diagonally across his chest, bubbled blood. His eyes fluttered and darted. His mouth moved as if he were trying to speak.

Madsen wiped the mud off Randall's face and talked distractedly. "I'll fix you up. You're going to be all right. You're just going to be all right." He tried to cover the wounds, but could only reach two at a time, and that pressure increased the flow of the third.

The CIDG began throwing down their packs and rifles and running back across the paddy. The LLDB sergeant yelled at them to stop but then covered their retreat by grenading the advancing VC. The planes continued blasting the bamboo. Madsen picked Randall up and ran, splashing and frantic, back the way they came. His lurching steps jerked his vision, and his tears smeared it so that the images of bamboo and running men and nodding rice stalks registered in blurry jumps, like an out-of-focus movie with many frames missing. He looked down at Randall lying limp in his arms, his cheeks stretched by his drooping jaw. For the first time Madsen realized Randall was smaller than he. He could feel Randall's blood flowing warm and steady down his body and see it staining both their uniforms ruddy brown.

They passed through the bamboo grove from which they had originally emerged and reached another beyond it before they stopped running. He laid Randall down. Gotta keep him from going into shock, he told himself. Raise his feet. Wrap him up. Madsen tried to prop Randall's boots up, but he began thrashing and convulsing, then opened his eyes and stared at Madsen with blind total fear. He clenched and unclenched his fists over Madsen's arm. His jaws ground together, his neck lifted taut, and a sucking croak, like the sound of a stopped drain suddenly cleared, broke from his throat. He drew his knees into his chest and threw up a mass of blood. His head snapped back. His eyes opened full and did not blink.

Madsen doubled over and collapsed beside him.

The strikers stood with tears rolling down their faces, uttering loud rhythmic bursts of words. Lo-ee, crying, took off his tribal bracelet and fastened it on Randall's wrist. Sound spattered from the radio on Madsen's back: "Alpha, Alpha, do you read me? What is your status? Request bomb damage assessment. Request bomb damage assessment, over." The FAC finally gave up and flew off.

Madsen slumped next to Randall for a long time, mumbling and crying. Then with trancelike slowness he attached the long antenna to the radio and called back to camp. "Randall's dead," he told Lieutenant Krenwood. "They shot him. And he died."

"Dead? Oh, Christ," the lieutenant said. "Who else is hit? Are you hit?"

"No . . . not me . . . Randall's hit. . . . Randall's dead."

"How many wounded do you have?"

"We got . . . we got a lot. Wounded."

"OK, you get hold of yourself. Keep the men together . . . and keep your security out. We'll have a medevac there right away. Give me your coordinates."

"Oh. Wait." Madsen picked up the map to find their position and remembered Randall quizzing him about map-reading on their first operation together. He broke down again, his tears puddling the map. In a choked voice he read the coordinates to Krenwood.

"Dustoff should be there in a few minutes," the lieutenant said. "Have the wounded ready to go. I'm going to try to get another chopper. Send you out some replacements. You hang on."

"I'll . . . get him ready."

The lieutenant found Sloane writing a letter to Trinh. He

told him of Randall's death and Madsen's collapse. Someone would have to go out and bring the patrol back in, and it was Sloane's turn for an operation. Choppers would be arriving in twenty minutes.

Sloane looked at the letter he was writing and considered refusing. Everything about going back on patrol was repellent to him. But he knew Madsen's need left him no choice. What a sorry waste. Randall. Jeff. Sloane read the letter and he reread his last one from Trinh, where she ended, "You hurry up come see me, come love me." He put them both away and stood up. And I've got to go back out to the nuthouse. He picked up his carbine.

Madsen felt Randall's wrist in hope that a pulse had crept back, but at the touch of the cool flesh he dropped it. Yet he was compelled to build a stretcher out of bamboo and a poncho, as if Randall were only wounded. He gently eased him onto it, and when the two dustoff choppers arrived, he and Lo-ee carried the body out and slid it aboard. Nine wounded CIDG who had managed to straggle back in were loaded and the last chopper took off at a tilt, avalanching hot wind back over the men in the clearing.

Now he'll get put in a box, Madsen thought. With a tag on it like a bill of lading. They'll ship him back to Fayetteville.

Two more helicopters chuffed in carrying Sloane, a squad from the recon platoon, and a resupply of ammunition. Sloane saw Madsen get up from where he was sitting at the edge of the bamboo and walk slowly toward him. Sloane ran to close the distance. "Are you OK?" he called.

Madsen's head leaned forward from his limp shoulders, and his eyes hardly shifted their gaze. "They killed him," he said in a small empty voice. "I just put him on a chopper."

Sloane groped for something adequate to say, but all that came out was, "I'm sorry, Jeff. He was a damn fine guy. It's . . . it's a terrible thing."

"He died right over there," Madsen said, pointing at a clump of fan palms. "But they shot him . . . they shot him way over on the other side. We had to run back here. I carried him back . . . but he died." Madsen bit his lip. He was looking about two feet past Sloane as he spoke.

"We'll get out of here," Sloane said. "All we have to do is pick up the bodies, give the air force their damage report. You don't have to come. I can leave you here with some of the strikers, if you want."

"Here? No. I want to go."

The CIDG, however, balked at the idea of returning to the rice paddy. Lo-ee's translation of Lieutenant Krenwood's instructions failed to persuade them. But the LLDB sergeant reminded them in harrowing terms that unless the bodies of their comrades were recovered and given proper burials, their spirits would become hungry ghosts and would return to torment and pursue those who had abandoned them on the battlefield. Reluctantly, a few strikers agreed to go. They, the LLDB sergeant, the fresh squad from the recon platoon, and the two Americans circled outside the bamboo brake that enclosed the paddies and approached the ambush site from the rear. They moved through the brush with unusual quiet and skill.

The thicket was still smoking when they entered it. Much of the bamboo was smashed and burnt. The oily smell of napalm mingled with the smolder. At the far side, bordering the peaceful-looking fields of rice, was a line of bunkers and trenches. Some were collapsed, and most were scorched. They found a sandal with a melted tire-tread sole, a camouflaged helmet torn by shrapnel, some charred pieces of clothing, but no bodies.

Madsen wandered around, drained and withdrawn, poking through the rubble with his boots. "They were in here waiting for us," he mumbled. "They got Randall. We bombed 'em though." When the CIDG found several blood trails where dead or wounded had been dragged off, Madsen revived a little. "We got some, huh? I bet we got a bunch of 'em. They've been bleeding all over. Look at that. They'll be dead pretty quick. Hope so. Sons of bitches." He angrily snatched a wand of bamboo and tried to break it. Although he used all his force, it only cracked and drove a splinter into his hand.

"Let's get out of here," Sloane said. "This is enough. To hell with the report." I don't have any business here, he thought. Randall's dead. Jeff's screwed up. If they booby-trapped the place, I might never get to see Trinh again. Fuck this shit.

They moved past the bunkers and trenches out to the dike the company had fought behind. Madsen began trembling. "That's where . . . that's where they killed Randall. Right out there."

Sloane nodded. It looked like all the other paddies he had seen, except that the waving, verdant surface was broken in five places by crumpled bodies, like rocks in a Japanese garden. Their comrades dragged them out, covered with blood and mud. Some had only been wounded until they were shot in the head at close range by the VC. The CIDG wrapped them in ponchos and lashed their arms and legs to thick bamboo poles, each of which was supported on the shoulders of two men.

As they were leaving, Madsen said, "Oh, his rifle . . . he dropped his rifle in the water . . . out there. His Swedish K. I should go get it. He wouldn't want it to be out there . . . all rusted. I should go get it."

Sloane put his arm on Madsen's shoulder. "Let it stay out there, Jeff. Let it alone." Madsen hesitated, then shrugged and walked on.

In a bedraggled, muddy line, the company began the march back. Sloane saw a leech on his arm and flicked it off. The slung bodies and the walking wounded slowed the pace but, because they were anxious to get as close to camp as possible, they pushed on until evening, when shadows webbed the trees.

Madsen dumbly went through the motions of putting up a hammock and heating food, but the first taste of meat repelled him, and he let the meal sit. When the fires died down and darkness closed in, he began to shiver. Over and over, in slow-motion mental replays, he saw Randall running toward him, freezing as if he had struck an invisible barrier, and collapsing into the rice paddy. Then his convulsions, the spreading stillness, the light leaving his eyes. A pressure built in Madsen's skull, as if someone were squeezing him at the temples with steel tongs. Finally the words cracked out of him: "It's all my fault. It's all my fault. If I hadn't stood up . . . if I hadn't, he'd still be here. He'd be alive and it'd all be the same. We'd have gone on and beaten them and it would've been great. We would've been together. Now he's dead. I stood up and he's dead." Madsen's face contorted and Sloane held him while he sobbed.

"We're almost out, Jeff," Sloane said. "This is the last one. It's over. We'll be out of the army in five weeks. We don't have to do it anymore."

Madsen looked up at him. Tears had washed lines in the dirt on his face. "I'm glad you're here. I'm glad it was you that came out."

After helping Madsen into his hammock, Sloane listened while his sobs turned to soft snores. Sloane decided to sleep on the ground. The men in sagging hammocks reminded him of the poncho-wrapped bodies suspended from bamboo poles.

Madsen awoke in the morning feeling quiet and small and alone. He lay still a long time, listening to himself breathe. He was glad the sky was overcast, for colors would have hurt his eyes. But his appetite had returned, and breakfast made him feel stronger. He was glad he'd have to march.

As his shock wore off, it was replaced by frustrated rancor. "Dammit," he told Sloane as they neared camp, "I didn't even get one of them. They killed the only guy I could ever look up to. They killed him, and I couldn't even get one of them. Didn't even get a chance to shoot at them. Feel like going back there and hiding and killin' me a dozen of 'em. Just to blast one of the sons of bitches, that's all I want."

"Well, you'll have to stop wanting it," Sloane said, annoyed. "Shouldn't be that hard to do. It has to stop sometime."

"It's easy for you to say. . . . You already shot a bunch of 'em," Madsen said, and chewed on his cheek.

"Yeah. OK," Sloane said. "Maybe you're right."

They walked the rest of the way in silence.

Randall's death numbed the team. They did their routine camp jobs silently, bleakly, bitterly. Wells's tour was over, and he left with no send-off party, but only grim handshakes with his teammates. Madsen sat in the commo bunker staring at the radios.

The Catholic chaplain arrived to perform a memorial service. He was friendly and wore a green beret with a cross on it. "Sergeant Randall listed himself as a no-preference on his religion. The Protestant chaplain and I take turns doing the no-preferences," he explained.

Madsen couldn't sit through the service. He slipped out of the room and went up on the bunker, where he crouched near the .50-caliber machine gun Randall had fired during the camp attack. God, how I'd like to blast them. Rotten fucking bastards. It's not going to happen, though. Nothing's going to happen. All this time. Been daydreaming about war since I was a little kid. Spent years in the army just getting ready. And after all that, I didn't even get to fire my rifle. Just lost Randall. Couldn't even get back at them.

Madsen wanted to shoot the four-deuce mortar at Harassment and Interdiction points in the free fire zone. He asked

Sloane if he would help, but Sloane replied, "No, I want to write a letter to my woman."

"What the hell," Madsen snapped. "Is that all you think about?"

Sloane didn't know what to say. "Well . . . what do you . . . beats hell out of whatever you're thinking about. You think . . . you think blasting the trees is gonna help?"

"That's not the point . . . and you know it," Madsen said.

"The point? What do you mean, the point?"

"Yeah, you know what I mean. You're putting the whole thing down. Make Randall look like . . . how do you think he'd like it? You saying, 'No, I don't want to go on operation. No, I don't want to shoot the mortar.' What do you think he'd think?"

"I don't give a damn what he'd think. It's none of his business."

"None of his . . . That's what I mean. You don't care about it anymore."

"Well, so what? You think caring about it's going to help? You think it'll bring Randall back? It's not going to make it any better. It's just going to keep you feeling that way. I'm sorry Randall got killed. Look, I'm awful sorry. I liked him a lot, you know that. He should be here with us."

"I don't know . . . I didn't mean . . . oh, hell," Madsen stammered. "I'm really glad you volunteered to come out . . . after he . . . It was good to see you out there. I didn't mean . . ."

"I'm glad I could help. I was really worried about you. But I didn't volunteer. Krenwood told me to go. It was my turn. I've had it with all that stuff. I'm just waiting to go back to the B-team."

"Yeah," Madsen said accusingly, "you didn't want to go out on the operation with me in the first place either, did you?"

"Hell, no. And I'm damn glad I didn't. What do you think? I don't want to get killed. No way does the idea of getting killed appeal to me."

"But even after . . . even after Randall got killed? You still didn't want to come?"

"Look, I came right away. But if it had been anybody else but you—*anybody*—I wouldn't have gone. I wanted to make sure you got back in OK. I was worried like hell about you. I just came out 'cause it was you, dammit . . . not 'cause I wanted to go on some hot-shot patrol."

Madsen was still hurt and stubborn, staring at the ground. "What about Randall? You didn't care about Randall?"

"Randall's dead, Jeff. He's dead. Nothing any of us can do for him. And going out and shootin' a buncha Cong isn't gonna help. He's gone. And you can't go on . . . you can't go on living in his shadow. He was just another guy."

"Yeah . . . yeah, but you quit," Madsen said, suddenly becoming very tired. He looked at Sloane and walked away, wandering near the defenses of the inner perimeter.

He felt a wave of bitterness at Sloane, but it was replaced by a growing anxiety as he thought about what Sloane had said. Randall's gone, you fool. He doesn't care one way or the other, Madsen told himself. He picked up a handful of pebbles and tossed them one at a time against a bunker. "Gone," he said, louder with each toss, feeling chaotic charges rush through his body. Finally he stopped, breath heaving. He garbled a shout and raised clenched fists above his head. "Gone! Yes! Ha! He's dead! Ha!" Jumping into a machine gun emplacement, he scattered the ammo cans and kicked over the gun. A peal of tortured laughter ripped out of him. "It's all over! He's all gone! Yes! That's it! He's done! Thank God!" And Madsen whooped with a mixture of grief and terrifying joy, a wild burst of freedom that he tried to repress as soon as it slipped out, but it was too late and he was rolling on the ground pounding the sandbag revetment, yelling and laughing, "It's over. It's over. He's gone!"

Shame gradually returned, and Madsen lay aghast and crying. His mouth started pouring saliva, and as he got to his knees he threw up, his whole body retching. Slowly the vomiting stopped, and he streamed with new energy. His thoughts were painfully clear: No more. You've lost enough. Seared, all scorched and bombed out, you're lucky you're here at all. Give it up. It's outside. It's over. He's gone, and you're through playing soldier. But Randall? He's dead, you damn fool. He's not going to . . . At least now you don't need somebody. You don't have to want somebody like that. That's gone.

Madsen stood up, cleared his throat, and spat. Nobody you have to prove yourself to. Nobody you have to measure up to. It's just you from now on. He shuddered deeply.

For the next week Madsen plodded around, silent and remote, unable to accept that his main feeling was relief. He skipped most meals and spoke only when he had to.

A message came from the commanding officer of the B-team denying Sloane's request for transfer. "Insufficient time remaining in-country to warrant change of duty station," was how it was phrased. Damn them, Sloane thought. They stole her from me. The only good thing that's happened to me in years, and they take her away. He felt that he and Trinh were grains of dust being scattered by a huge broom. Grimly furious, he called the B-team, demanding to speak to the sergeant major, but was told he was unavailable and the denial could not be appealed.

Captain Bao, the LLDB camp commander, expressed his regrets to the Americans over Randall's death. But, he said, even such misfortunes as this can have good effects. They can serve to wake people up. In the village, the killings of Captain Ngoc and Sergeant Randall had roused anticommunist sentiment. The government-sponsored Communist Denunciation Committee had gained a dozen new members in the past week. Also, the people thought that since the geomancer had picked such a disastrous location for the fish pond, he must be a Viet Cong agent. They drove him from the village.

Lieutenant Krenwood decided he had to have a talk with Madsen, whose mood was getting to be a morale problem. "I know it's been really tough on you," he told him, "but you gotta snap out of it now. Randall wouldn't want to see you moping around like this. Especially 'cause that operation was one hell of a victory."

"Victory?" Madsen said with contempt.

"You damn right. We got an intel report in today. VC lost twenty men killed or wounded. Put their whole company out of action for at least a month. And that's damn sure a victory. So you remember this: It wasn't for nothing. Randall didn't die for nothing. They had to pay a terrible price for him. That's the way he'd look at it. So you perk up."

"A victory! I don't care if it was a victory. You can keep your victory."

"Don't push me, Madsen. Randall would damn sure care. That's what it's all about. If you had any respect, you'd care, too. This at least oughta cheer you up—air force is going to defoliate all that rice. Won't be a grain of it left to feed those gooks that killed Randall."

"The rice? So what? I don't care about the rice. And I don't care about the victory. None of it."

"You better shape up, dammit. Guy with an attitude like yours can drag down a whole team. You need some hard work. That's it. Some discipline. I'll snap you out of this. Want you to square away all those empty gas drums down at the POL dump. Get 'em lined up in rows . . . all of 'em in formation. And your appearance. Your appearance is damned unmilitary. You get trimmed. And whenever you're outdoors, I want to see that beret on your head. Pride, Madsen. Discipline and pride. You ain't got enough of it. But we'll get you shaped up. Now get to work."

"OK."
"OK? OK what?"
"OK, sir."
Madsen got the camp barber to cut his hair. Then he wrestled the empty fifty-five gallon drums into neat ranks and files. I can't take much more of this bullshit, he said to himself, and then automatically responded as he had done hundreds of times since entering the army: But you got no choice. This time the thought startled him. What do you mean? I damn sure do have a choice. That jerk can't make me do anything, unless I let him. All he can do is pressure me. I'm the one who decides. But then . . . oh, shit, I'm doing it all to myself. This both depressed and elated Madsen. He saw that he had no one to blame but himself, but he was not powerless. There was no longer an inner voice telling him he had to comply, no blocks to his natural resentment of authority.
Krenwood was back the next morning. "You're living in a pigsty down here, Madsen," he said, looking around the commo bunker. "See this rust?" He pointed to the two large metal I-beams supporting the roof. "That's corrosion, Madsen. That major comes out here and sees that corrosion, we'll all be in a bind. You gotta spruce up down here. I'm not gonna have your bum attitude givin' the team a bad report. Want you to clean off all that rust."
Madsen leaned back in his chair and looked up at the beams. "You want me to clean off all that rust?"
"Yeah. You're going to take a scraper and a wire brush and get rid of it all. Use steel wool if you have to. We can't have the slopes down here doing it 'cause there's too much classified stuff."
"That rust'll be back in a week. It's wet down here."
"No, no. We got some rustproof paint. After you get it all off, you're gonna paint the beams. You should've done it without my having to tell you."

"First you want me to scrape the rust? Then you want me to paint the beams? I got work to do. I don't have time for that nonsense."

"Nonsense? Listen, I'm your commanding officer. I'm the one who decides what's sense and nonsense around here. Stand at attention, Madsen. This shit has gone far enough."

Madsen slowly got to his feet and stood straight. He looked at the lieutenant's slightly puffy face with small ears and full lips stitched tight around the edges. I'm not going to do it anymore, he realized with a rush of fear and new freedom. They can't give me orders. I'm in charge of my own damn self.

"You wouldn't pull this with Randall, and you're not going to get away with it with me," the lieutenant continued. "If he told you to clean those beams you'd do it, wouldn't you? Wouldn't you, Madsen?"

Madsen hesitated, then said, "Not now. Not now I wouldn't."

"Well . . . you got no respect at all."

"Look, Randall was a good man. I know that damn-sight better than you do. But he was nuts, too, just as screwed up as the rest. I'd tell him the same thing I'm tellin' you." Madsen met Krenwood's eyes with a determined stare. "Answer is no."

"You're insubordinate. I'm going to tell you one time: If you want to keep those stripes, you better have those beams cleaned and painted by tonight."

Madsen remained standing, but he placed one foot forward and put his hands on his hips. "I'm not going to do it."

"Get back to attention."

"I'm not gonna do that either."

"I'll give you one more chance, Madsen. You stand at attention. And use a proper form of military address."

"Look, man, I'm not gonna do it. I'm through with it."

"Madsen, I'm giving you a direct order to—"

"You don't understand," Madsen said, cutting him off. "I'm not taking any of your orders. None."

"If you don't want to go to jail, you better stop right—"

"Did you hear what I said? I said I wasn't going to do it. Regardless."

"You're disobeying a direct order?"

Madsen's last internal block dissolved, and he said with a laugh full of angry joy, "Yeah. Fuckin'-A."

"You're under arrest, troop."

"Ha! You got it backwards. I was under arrest before. Not now. It's over. I'm ending it."

"We'll see about that." The lieutenant stormed out and was back fifteen minutes later to read him his rights under the Uniform Code of Military Justice. Madsen listened to him disdainfully. Inside he felt better about himself than he had in years. He was scared, but soberly glad. Whatever happens, he thought, it's better this way.

The lieutenant, avoiding Madsen's eyes, told him he would be placed on the next aircraft to group headquarters with the recommendation that he be court-martialed.

"Suit yourself," Madsen said.

The rest of the team treated him like a pariah, or tried to rationalize his behavior as combat fatigue, except for Sloane, who congratulated him. "I just hope they don't mess you over too bad," Sloane said.

"Yeah. So do I. But I'm not going to bow down anymore. I'm through."

"But what if they jail you?"

"I don't think they will. Be too much trouble for 'em. Hell, with three weeks left . . . be easier for 'em to just get rid of me. But, fuck it. If it comes to that . . . if they want to come down hard on me, I can take their goddamn jail. I got to live with myself. And I can do that damn-sight easier by going to jail than by kissing their asses."

Next afternoon Madsen was at group headquarters in Nha Trang, confined to barracks awaiting a disciplinary hearing. The suddenness of his transition since Randall's death left him confused but recalcitrant. He wasn't sure why, but he knew there was nothing left to obey.

With Madsen gone, Sloane had no one to talk to. The team was made up of new men, and the only things Sloane knew about most of them were their names and jobs. To them, he seemed scarred and sullen, an example of how they hoped they wouldn't end up. Finally his separation orders arrived. Wearing a smile so broad it hurt his nose, he boarded the next helicopter for Qui Nhon.

"You got two days to spend with her, Sloane," the sergeant major told him as he signed in. "Unless she's shacked up with somebody else."

Sloane flushed with anger. "Thanks for your help. I could've had four weeks, you know. It's group policy, isn't it, that you can transfer back off an A-team after six months? Other people do it."

"After six months, yeah, but not after eleven months. Too much paperwork for that short a time. Be reasonable, dammit. Look, if you're that crazy about the broad, then re-up. I'll get you a job here, and you can fuck your head off every night. If she means that much to you . . ."

Torn between his yearning for Trinh and his need to be free of the military, Sloane pictured her face as he had left her. The thought of signing away more of his life to the army made his stomach knot. How much do I love her? he asked himself. Not that much, he realized, and liked himself less.

The sergeant major saw him hesitating. "You could just extend for a year. We'll promote you to staff sergeant."

Sloane shook his head. "No way. I gotta get out."

"Well, then don't get any ideas about marrying her. That takes at least six months of paperwork. And I doubt if it'd get approved anyway."

Sloane walked away. I can't do it. Not even for her.

At five-thirty he was standing across the street from her

office. Two days is better than nothing. Be great to see her face when I surprise her. His breath caught as he saw Trinh sweep out the door. But it expired in dismay when a man, a young Vietnamese, greeted her with a wave and a smile.

Standing near a tattered kiosk, they talked with lively gestures. Sloane saw her laugh, and it rent him.

He wanted to reach across the broad avenue and snatch her away from him. Trying to absorb her features, he stared hard and could almost see, as with binoculars, the swatch of hair that fell across her forehead, catching on an eyelash. He started across the street. Maybe he's just a cousin or something. In the middle he stopped and watched her walking away beside the other man. The subtle sway of her walk held Sloane's eyes and told him achingly that he was wrong. He stood on the pavement with jeeps, cyclos, and motor scooters coursing around him. A lumbering five-ton olive drab truck blocked her from view, and when it passed they were gone.

He walked back toward the compound, past the fountain of their rendezvous, where the wind was stirring papers in the dry pool, and past the corner where they had parted after escaping from the MPs. This time we didn't get away.

Out, Madsen thought, lying on his bunk in Nha Trang. I just want out. He alternated between fear of court-martial and certainty he was leaving in the best way. Part of him was already gone, and it left the rest feeling misplaced, as if he were only in the army because of some clerical oversight. His fear sent him a steady stream of warnings not to push harder.

Finally he was brought before a major who wore a businesslike scowl and told him, "Madsen, your commanding officer has filed a serious charge against you. Disobeying a direct order in time of war is a capital offense. You know that?"

Madsen shrugged.

"You had a clean record up to now, soldier. But your

insubordination is criminal. And I can tell it's a lot more than skin-deep. We've given you every chance to come around . . . but you're still rebelling." The major waited for a reply, and when none came he continued. "We could have you on a plane to Leavenworth tomorrow morning. And those guards there have ways of making you follow orders. Is that what you want?"

"No."

"Well, if the army wanted to, we could send you back there. They'd rehabilitate you. They're experts at bringing people back into line. And it'd be the best thing for you. You wouldn't be that tough a nut a crack. I can see that by looking at you."

Madsen stood silently.

"But Madsen, I don't think you're worth the effort of rehabilitating. You're not worth the correctional personnel's time. So we're just gonna chuck you out, Madsen. Chuck you out of the service like we'd get rid of a bad apple. We'll let the civilian authorities handle you. Because I can tell, Madsen. I can tell you're gonna end up behind bars before long. But I just can't see crowding a military jail with the likes of you."

It took all of Madsen's willpower to prevent the wild, rousing joy—the swarm of birds and bells he felt inside—from making him break out into a grin.

"We're gonna bust you down to private and boot you out. You can forget about going on R and R. And you can forget about getting discharged on time. It's gonna take longer to process you. Until then you're confined to quarters. I don't want you infecting anybody else. Get rid of those stripes. And turn in your beret." He gave Madsen a lockjawed glare. "You're dismissed, private."

Madsen was so jubilant he forgot his pledge to himself not to show deference. He saluted the major before leaving.

When he was gone, the officer made a note on Madsen's personnel file that his discharge papers should carry the SPN code number 36C, indicating to prospective future employers that he was insubordinate and acutely maladjusted.

Madsen went back to the barracks and cut off his sergeant stripes. He liked the idea of leaving the army the same rank he started. For a moment he almost wished the major had sent him to jail. He might then have felt cleaner about his whole involvement. But I've wasted too much time as it is. To hell with jail. I'm getting out. Ha!

"Jeff! Hey, Jeff!"

Madsen heard a voice calling, went to the window, and saw Sloane outside at the far end of the barracks. "David! Hey, over here."

Through the screened barracks window, the two friends grinned at each other, Madsen's chipped tooth showing.

"Clerk told me this is where they put you," Sloane said. "They got you locked in?"

"No, door's open. But I think they'd like nothing better than for me to leave . . . so they could really hang me."

"You getting discharged?"

"You bet. They're holding up my orders a couple of days . . . just to toy with me. But hell . . ."

"It's over. Damn."

"When you leaving?" Madsen asked.

"Be in Saigon tomorrow, San Francisco the next day. Stone free. Incredible."

"What about your woman?"

Sloane's face dropped. "Lost her. She . . . I guess I'll . . . I'll have to find someone else."

"Well . . . that shouldn't be too hard. A whole world. Did you decide what you're gonna do?"

"Yeah, sort of. I'm going to get a big map, then pick out a place near some water where I've never been. Someplace where the only thing I know about it is that I like the name. And just go there . . . and start."

"OK," Madsen laughed.

"How about you?"

"I gotta get back to Wyoming. Really learn how to climb those mountains. You oughta stop by. I'll show you some country."

"They got any women there?"

"Antelope."

"Oh, well. Look, I'd really like to see it. Maybe when I get de-pressured I'll give you a call."

"Good. Hope so."

"We owe each other a celebration."

"Yeah. We been socked away a long time. Twenty-seven months."

"We'll catch up."

"It doesn't come to much, does it?" Madsen said. "I can't figure it out. I don't know if I regret everything . . . or don't regret any of it. I feel OK, though."

A sergeant from headquarters company shouted to Sloane, "Hey! That's disciplinary barracks. You wanna end up inside?"

Sloane looked in at Madsen. "Look, uh . . . I'll see you back in the world."

"Right." They pressed hands through the screen. Then Sloane waved, and Madsen watched him walk away in his gangling amble.

Several days later Madsen's separation orders arrived. Knowing he could now break restriction, he took off immediately. He hitched a ride to town, but it was too noisy after so long in the highlands. Madsen felt lightheaded. He wanted to skip through the air, to run off in different directions. The falling rain only stimulated him.

He hailed a taxi and told the driver to go to the coast. They drove from the downtown area, through the residential section, past the military compounds, past the refugee hovels, out to a plain of rice paddies and bamboo that ran down to the open, rolling ocean. Madsen tensed when he first saw the groves, but then told himself, It's all right. It's over. He relaxed and enjoyed the glistening, rippling green. They came to a small river, and Madsen told the driver to let him out.

He walked along the bank. In the tawny stream, women were washing clothes, and half a dozen naked children splashed and crawled over a patient water buffalo. Above them, a farmer inspected his dikes while his son hunted the crabs that burrowed the sides. A girl waded in the paddy, ochre water up to her thighs, transplanting again the new spring rice.

He passed them and was alone. The rain beat down reeds along the shore and nippled the surface of the water. The river sloshed against its muddy banks, a shoulder constantly shrugging. Where the river opened to the sea, it was shielded by a breakwater. The sea burst against the rocks in loud, white, spraying eruptions like shellfire. Each geyser swept over Madsen, colder than the rain. On the other side of the rocks, a fisherman knelt cleaning his catch. As he squeezed the large, dying fish to open its vent for the knife, one slippery baby after another jetted out and fell swimming into the water.

Madsen looked up. The sky was dancing, and the sun flared through dark clouds. He ran onto the beach, kicking off his boots and fatigues as he went. Leaping into the water, he splashed and danced and yelled through the surf. He sucked in the sharp, ion-laden air and felt it charge his body. A wave battered him down, spun him in its tumult, and tossed him back onto the beach like a mass of kelp. More waves broke over him, pounding him with crashing moans, and with each sob he told himself, Let it go, let it go. The surf kept dumping down, and the outgoing water coursed sand along the length of his body. Finally he struggled to his feet, exultant and exhausted.

The rain eased. The reeds rose. Madsen walked along the

beach with quiet growing inside him. He looked out over the fluxing Pacific. Here I am, he thought as he knelt. He closed his eyes, feeling the firm yield of the sand, hearing the washing void of the sea. He rested awhile, cupped in the hollowness. Then, opening his eyes to the sun's portal of light, he took an enormous yawning breath and stood up.

Tan San Nhut Airport in Saigon was more crowded than it had been a year before. Swarms of bewildered, apprehensive new arrivals streamed by Madsen as he waited for his flight. In addition to the Americans, groups of Australian rangers, Philippino technicians, and Korean infantrymen poured through incoming gates. The loudspeaker crackled in several languages, all of them garbled.

Madsen's group lined up and walked out to the chartered jetliner. He climbed the ramp, giddy and light, and turned at the top for one last look at a few low, ordinary buildings sinking into late afternoon shadows.

The planeful of cheering GIs hurtled down the runway, gained the air, and climbed rapidly away. Sun fell at a long angle across the land, silvering the paddy water. The sky was clear blue with one long white cloud hanging like a breaker frozen in mid-crash. Madsen thought of the man who was chasing the sun west across the ocean to take his place.